THE TRAILER PARK MURDER

THE TRAILER PARK MURDER

THE WOODHEAD & BECKER MYSTERIES
BOOK III

PAUL AUSTIN ARDOIN

THE TRAILER PARK MURDER

Copyright © 2023 by Paul Austin Ardoin

Published by Pax Ardsen Books

All rights reserved. No part of this book may be used or reproduced in any manner whatsoever without written permission from the publisher, except in the case of brief quotations embodied in critical articles or reviews.

This book is a work of fiction. Names, characters, businesses, organizations, places, events and incidents either are the product of the author's imagination or are used fictitiously. Any resemblance to actual persons, living or dead, events, or locales is entirely coincidental.

ISBN 978-1-949082-50-0

For information please visit:

www.paulaustinardoin.com

Cover design by Ziad Ezzat of Feral Creative Colony: feralcreativecolony.com

Edited by Max Christian Hansen

In memory of Marci, who brought the story to me
and
In memory of Mike, who still deserves justice

Chapter One

Bernadette Becker stared straight ahead. The silhouette of a torso on the standard QIT-99 target, twenty-five yards from the white line at her feet.

She drew the gun from her holster, raised it, and squeezed the trigger four times. Dropped to one knee, took aim, and fired four more rounds.

She got to her feet and clicked the switch on the separator next to her. The QIT-99 target zipped toward her. As the paper target got closer, Bernadette smiled: two rounds close to the middle of the silhouette's forehead, and five others on the left side of the shadow's chest. One in the left shoulder, though. Still, a passing grade if she were taking the test to become a field agent again. She pulled off her ear protectors, unclipped the target from its frame and studied it closely.

"Not half bad," said a voice behind her.

Bernadette turned. A blonde woman, a couple of inches taller than Bernadette's five foot six, her hair pulled back into a low ponytail, in black trousers and a light blue blouse matching her eyes, the black shooting earmuffs looking too large on her head—Bernadette figured hers looked equally unwieldy.

"Hi, Joanna." Bernadette gave the other woman a warm smile. Under other circumstances, they might have had a friendly embrace.

"Thanks for meeting on short notice." Joanna Quimby glanced up and down the shooting booths. She and Bernadette were the only ones there.

"I'm the one who said it was urgent. Besides, I'm usually working out on my lunch hour on Mondays, so no one was the wiser."

Joanna pulled off one of her earmuffs. "I know I said I'd have the files analyzed in a few days."

"This isn't about the files on that SD card." Bernadette's pulse sped up. "I don't want to press you too much, but this morning was the first hit anyone has had on Marguerite Kerovic in more than two years."

Joanna stepped into the booth next to Bernadette, put her bag on the floor, and clicked a button on the wall, her QIT-99 target sliding away from her to twenty-five yards. "I don't know if you heard, but we've been a little busy."

Bernadette holstered her Sig Sauer and brushed a piece of lint from her gray trousers. "Busy with what? Should I know something?"

"Two FBI agents were ambushed this morning." Joanna put her earmuffs on.

Bernadette hurriedly put her earmuffs on just before Joanna faced the target, pulled her gun out, fired four times.

"Are they okay?" Bernadette said, a little loudly.

Just as Bernadette had, Joanna dropped to one knee and fired four more shots.

The reports from Joanna's gun deadened against the

sound baffling in the large room, and Joanna stood and pulled off her ear protectors again. "One dead, one in critical condition."

Bernadette took off her earmuffs as well.

Joanna clicked the switch on the divider and the target swooped toward her. "This is an all-hands-on-deck situation. I've got a list of top priorities as long as my arm."

Bernadette was silent. All morning long, she'd been nervously awaiting news. Marguerite Kerovic's debit card, expired six months previously, declined at a RoadTrip gas station off the County Road J exit just northeast of Sun Prairie, Wisconsin. It had been six hours since she'd received the alert—sent within fifteen minutes of the declined transaction—and five hours and thirty minutes since she first called Joanna.

"You know I wouldn't ask unless—"

Joanna nodded as she holstered her gun. "I know. The gas station's only an hour away from Taycheedah, and if it's a genuine lead, you want to act quickly."

Bernadette took a black case out of her bag and put the ear protectors in. "We might already be too late."

Joanna reached up and unclipped the target from its plastic hanger. "I assume you would get notified if Annika got any visitors at Taycheedah."

Bernadette straightened up. "I'd like to think so, but you know we think Marguerite is in hiding. I'm not sure she'd walk into a correctional facility during visiting hours and just politely sign in to see her sister." Bernadette took a step toward Joanna and looked at the target. Two shots dead center between the eyes of the silhouette, the other six over the heart.

"Wow." Bernadette motioned to Joanna's holster. "I'd hate to be on the business end of that."

Joanna sighed as she put her earmuffs into the bag at her feet. "I loved my old Smith & Wesson. Something about the .40 just felt right in my hand. These new Glock 19s the FBI issued us are soulless."

"Doesn't seem like it's affecting your performance."

"I guess not. Just my enjoyment." Joanna folded the target in half, then half again. "I know the timing sucks, Bernadette, but I have my hands full. I hate to say it, but you may need to pop your head out of the groundhog hole and start making contact yourself."

"We can't reopen the case without solid evidence," Bernadette said, "and I can't risk—"

"Then get your boss to stick her neck out for once," Joanna said.

Even though the gun range was otherwise empty, Bernadette leaned forward so her mouth was close to Joanna's ear. "You didn't ask me here just to tell me you didn't have time to decrypt the SD card files."

"But I *don't* have time," Joanna said.

"Do you know what I had to go through to *get* that SD card?"

"You told me. A cross-country trip. You found it in a—a lute or a banjo or something."

Bernadette pursed her lips. It was a *gusle,* not a banjo, but she wouldn't argue semantics. "The point is, I had to work my ass off to get this SD card to you."

Joanna set her mouth in a line and looked Bernadette in the eyes. Then her gaze softened. "It looks like the encryption is AES-1024, which means they knew what they were doing. I've got some time reserved next week on a wicked-fast machine that might crack it if they took a shortcut or two. But only if we figure out who ambushed our agents."

"Next week?"

"A long time to wait. Still, nothing I can do."

"Maybe you can give me the SD card back," Bernadette said, her mind racing. "I can get someone else to look at it."

"You know the SD card is FBI property now. I can't give it back even if I wanted to."

"I thought I'd at least ask," Bernadette said carefully. "This is the first hint Marguerite might be alive since I started this case."

"I know. I'm sorry I can't do more." Joanna handed the folded target to Bernadette.

Bernadette took it—and immediately felt a tiny item shift inside the folded paper. About the right size and weight for an SD card.

Twenty feet away, the door to the hallway opened, and two men entered, discussing the Washington Nationals' chances this season. Joanna stepped out of the booth, then hurried toward the door as it was closing.

Bernadette turned the target in her hand so the folded edge was along the bottom, feeling the SD card fall against the edge, and hurried to catch up with Joanna. "Margaritas are on me next time, all right?"

Joanna caught the door with her foot just before it shut. "You're on. Hopefully, we'll get to the bottom of everything by next week. Then you and I can go get hammered."

They signed out at the registration desk and Joanna took a sharp right toward the FBI building. Bernadette looked to her left; the walk sign was on to cross the street to get to the Metro. She gave Joanna one last glance and hurried to catch the light.

On the other side of the street, Bernadette held the folded target and tilted it; the SD card slid right into her hand, and she surreptitiously placed it in her bag. Bernadette was lucky Joanna had taken the time to give her the SD card back. She walked toward the entrance of the Metro, putting the target in a paper recycling bin. She glanced around but didn't see anyone following her.

Joanna couldn't get her any information about the debit card or about Marguerite, but at least Bernadette had the SD card back. She stepped into the Metro station and got on the down escalator.

An expired debit card and a declined transaction—a hit on the debit card was almost nothing to go on. Magnetic stripes on credit cards got skimmed all the time; card information got faked. Even if Marguerite's actual debit card had been present at the gas station, it might have been stolen two thousand miles away.

The eastbound Metro was just pulling up as Bernadette reached the bottom of the escalator, and she quickened her pace to get into it before the doors closed. At one thirty, the subway car wasn't full, and she took a seat on the side. Had anyone followed her into the car? She didn't think so. She stared at the Metro map across from her seat and her eyes unfocused.

Even if the expired debit card wasn't much to go on, the short distance between the gas station where the card was declined and Annika Nakrivo's prison cell meant Bernadette couldn't afford to ignore it.

She'd hoped to have more concrete information before bringing her discovery to her boss. If she had confirmed the physical presence of the debit card, or if she had video footage from the gas station confirming Marguerite was there, Bernadette would know if the declined transaction was just false hope—or if it was a real lead.

Two stops later, she stood, exited the car, and made a beeline for the stairs leading to the Sycamore Street exit and the humid air of the June afternoon. Four blocks later, she found herself at the Controlled Substance Analysis Bureau building. Her ID got her past the guard and the gate and into the elevator, where she pushed the "3" button, and the doors began to slide shut.

"Hold it, please!" A familiar voice.

Bernadette stuck her hand out and the elevator doors opened again.

Lesley Gill got in, holding two large coffee cups with the Old Dominion Roasting Company logo. "Thanks—oh, hi, Bernadette."

Bernadette put her hand in her purse.

"Yeah, rough morning. We needed an afternoon coffee run." Lesley leaned toward Bernadette conspiratorially. "And the coffee here is disgusting."

Bernadette grinned, her hand finding the SD card. "Or it's possible—"

"That I'm a coffee snob. Yes, I'm aware. How was your workout?"

"Productive."

"Productive?"

"Yep. Here, let me help you out." Bernadette took a coffee from Lesley and slipped the SD card into her newly free hand.

"Is this—" Lesley began.

Bernadette nodded.

The doors opened on the third floor. The beige and olive green paint scheme greeted them, the black plastic CSAB logo looking cheap on the wall. They stepped into the hall-way, then opened the door to the CSAB office.

"Want me to get started on the files?" Lesley asked quietly.

"Please."

They walked to Lesley's desk in the cubicle farm and

Bernadette set the coffee down next to a figurine of a science fiction character Bernadette didn't recognize.

"Oh," Lesley said, "that one's for Maura."

Bernadette picked the coffee back up. "I was just on my way to see her."

"Thanks."

Bernadette walked past the other cubicles and turned left, approaching a set of interior offices. She stopped at the third oak door, with a silver nameplate next to the door frame in elegant, embossed letters reading *Lt. Maura Stevenson.*

Like the entry, this hallway was beige and olive, again with black plastic nameplates adorning the wall next to the other doors. Maura's was the only silver one. The year before, Maura had easily pried the black plastic nameplate off the wall and affixed the silver one. Neither of them had ever commented on it—Bernadette was surprised management had allowed Maura to keep the distinctive nameplate.

She raised her hand, hesitated, then knocked three times.

"Come in," Maura said on the other side of the door.

Bernadette opened the door. In stark contrast to the rest of the floor, Maura's office was homey and warm. A large ficus plant next to the door, an overstuffed armchair in the corner in a jewel-toned floral pattern, a fluffy rug running from under the warm, gray-washed wooden desk to the front edge of the armchair, and framed posters of jazz concerts on all four light blue walls: Melba Liston, Vi Redd, Joyce Moreno, Sarah Vaughan. Maura had banished the beige and olive green completely.

Behind the desk, Maura looked up from her laptop. "Good afternoon, Bernadette."

Bernadette held the coffee out to Maura. "Ran into Lesley on my way back from lunch."

"Oh, great, thanks." Maura took the coffee and held it to

her lips carefully, taking a sip. She set it down on her desk and looked at the cup approvingly before glancing up at Bernadette. "Did the lab get back to you on the Shreveport case?"

Bernadette shook her head. "Results in the morning."

Maura tilted her head. "So what's up?"

Bernadette turned and closed the door.

"Marguerite Kerovic?"

Bernadette nodded. "Maybe a lead."

Maura raised her eyebrows.

"I was hoping I'd have more intel to go on, but..."

"Have a seat." Maura motioned to the overstuffed chair.

Bernadette glanced at the chair for a moment. It looked comfortable. She breathed in—and the subtle scents of roses and cardamom filled her senses.

A stab of envy. Maura could coil for the hunt like the best agents she'd worked with, but then could take things down a few notches—making this office a haven from the usual madness of her job. They'd become fast friends years ago, and now Bernadette never knew when to treat Maura like a friend or like her boss.

"Go on, sit."

Bernadette sat in the overstuffed armchair. The chair was more for chatting and conversation than it was for informing one's manager of serious news. Bernadette was sure Maura had used the comfy chair to her advantage many times: de-escalating tense situations; getting her visitors to let their guards down. Even Bernadette found it difficult to keep her guard up.

"How was Sophie's softball game?"

Bernadette blinked. "What?"

"I didn't have a chance to ask you yet."

"Oh—fine." Bernadette paused. "They won."

"That's great." Maura smiled widely. "How'd Sophie do?"

"Five innings of shutout ball. And she hit a double to drive in a run."

Maura leaned forward. "You've got more restraint than me. I'd be crowing about that, strutting around the office, making sure everyone knew how great my daughter was."

Bernadette forced a smile and a nod. She and Sophie had argued that morning: first about not letting Sophie sleep over at her friend's house, then about Bernadette leaving for a work trip to Shreveport later in the week. Even so, she *should* have been bragging about Sophie's heroics in the game. "I don't want to be one of *those* moms, Maura. Bragging about my kid's trophies as if I'd won them myself. But I get what you're saying." Bernadette sat up in the comfy chair and cleared her throat. "Hey, maybe you could come to the next game."

"When?"

"Saturday. Sophie hasn't seen her Aunt Maura at a game this season."

Maura's face turned wistful. Maybe she missed the friendship just as much as Bernadette did—but it was tough after Maura had become Bernadette's boss. "I'd love to go. Maybe I can make it work—we'll see how Shreveport goes. Now—you said you wanted to discuss Marguerite Kerovic?"

"We got a hit on her debit card. Swiped and declined about five or six hours ago."

Maura's eyes widened. "Have you contacted—"

"My friend in the FBI? Yeah, I just met with Joanna."

"Intel?"

"She was too busy."

Maura furrowed her brow.

"A couple of FBI agents were ambushed this morning. She couldn't work on this at all."

"But she had time to meet with you?"

"Just now." Bernadette jerked her thumb over her shoulder. "Returned Marguerite's SD card. I just gave it to Lesley."

Maura sat back in her chair. "Do we have any better idea if Marguerite is a victim or a criminal?"

Bernadette shrugged. "Could be both."

Maura nodded. "Is that all?"

"My FBI contact also suggested," Bernadette said, casting her eyes down, "that it's time for us to move the investigation forward."

"Easy for her to say." Maura pressed her lips together.

"Can't we explain that someone hired Annika Nakrivo to commit murder? Wouldn't they rather have—"

Maura shook her head. "*We* might be sure that someone at Parr Medical hired Annika for the hit on the medical researcher—"

And Curtis almost popped out of Bernadette's mouth, but she bit her tongue. She didn't need to bring up Curtis's death and the emotional turmoil it might trigger in Maura.

"—but right now we keep our heads down until we have enough evidence to reopen the investigation." Maura looked up at Bernadette. "Unless you've changed your theory of the case."

No question in Bernadette's mind: someone at Parr Medical was behind the murders Annika had committed. She shook her head.

"Then this stays off the radar as long as we can. The FBI makes inquiries like this, it won't raise any flags. But if CSAB does?"

"We get questions from the director."

"*I* get questions from the director."

"We already know that Parr Medical hired Annika to destroy the ibogaine research project at Kilbourn Tech. We proved Annika committed one murder, and circumstances tie her to at least one more." Bernadette shifted her weight. "You know Parr Medical didn't hire Annika as a one-time thing."

Maura nodded. "Yes, we're well aware of the carjacking in Florida, too."

"And that's only what we know about—and that's just with Annika. I'd wager Parr Medical has plans to keep *all* competitive medications off the market. Who knows how many hit men Parr Medical has hired?" Bernadette paused. "And who knows how many patients have died because Parr Medical kept those other medications off the market? This goes way beyond Annika—and way beyond Marguerite."

"You're preaching to the choir."

"Then you also agree with me that if we find her sister is safe, Annika will open up. I'm sure of it."

Maura crinkled her nose but stayed silent.

"And if Annika cooperates, we can identify who at Parr Medical is behind these murders. Marguerite is the only leverage that Parr Medical has over Annika. We've got to find her first."

Maura shook her head. "What your gut is telling you and what we can prove are two different things."

Bernadette leaned forward even though the comfortable chair was drawing her back. "Which is exactly why I can't ignore—*we* can't ignore—the debit card that was swiped and declined."

"Might not mean much. Cards get stolen—"

"Someone used the card at a gas station an hour southwest of Taycheedah Correctional."

Maura straightened in her chair. "Where Annika Nakrivo is—"

"Yes."

Maura rested her chin in her palm, thinking. "Marguerite's last known location was in Florida, correct?"

Bernadette nodded.

"But now, an hour away from Taycheedah—where's that gas station? Somewhere in western Wisconsin or northern Illinois?"

"Sun Prairie. Outside Madison."

"What's Marguerite's debit card doing an hour away from her sister's prison?"

"Like you said, it might be nothing. A card number bought on the dark web. But I don't think I can ignore this."

Maura nodded. "True."

"I don't want us to get into trouble—"

"No," Maura said firmly. "You've convinced me. There's a dividing line for follow-up, and this is clearly above it. My superiors would *want* us to investigate this. Easily falls into due diligence."

Bernadette stood. "I can book a flight—"

Maura held up her hand. "Due diligence, Bernadette, not full investigation mode. Contact the debit card company. Call the gas station and see if their cameras recorded who made the transaction. Perhaps they can provide some footage." She looked down at her laptop. "Sun Prairie, you said?"

"Right."

"When?"

"This morning at about five fifteen Central Time. I got the alert about ten minutes later."

Maura typed, then narrowed her eyes at the screen. "Five fifteen is pretty early," she mumbled.

Bernadette nodded.

Maura turned her laptop so Bernadette could see the screen, which showed an online map of Sun Prairie. Maura tapped a building on the top left. "There's a cheap motel right next to the gas station. And it doesn't look like there are any other hotels for a few miles in each direction. Whoever used that card might have spent the night there, filled up the next morning, and—well, I don't know what they plan to do next." Maura tapped her chin, turned her laptop back, then continued typing.

"What are you looking for?"

"The prison schedule," Maura said. "And today's what, Wednesday? Visiting hours don't start until 2:30."

"Doesn't make a lot of sense for someone to leave at five fifteen in the morning if they'll get to Taycheedah eight hours too early." Bernadette sat back down on the overstuffed chair, this time sitting back. "Look, this isn't a smoking gun."

"No, but like you said, we can't ignore it." Maura drummed her fingers on the desk. "Look into what you can— the hotel, the gas station, maybe Sun Prairie has red-light cameras." She looked up from her laptop screen. "In the meantime, I'll call the warden at Taycheedah, put the two of you in contact. Plus, we should get more guards on Annika Nakrivo. I don't trust her, and if her sister is in the area..." She trailed off, lost in thought.

This might have been the most they'd talked about the Nakrivo case in months. Bernadette was hopeful as she stood up from the comfy chair. "Still want me to head to Shreveport tomorrow?"

Maura furrowed her brow. "Uh—give me a few minutes. I might be able to work something out."

Chapter Two

THE PHONE RANG TWICE BEFORE SOMEONE PICKED UP ON the other end. "Marcie Fisk."

"Warden, it's Bernadette Becker with CSAB." Bernadette shut the door of the conference room as her voice slipped into a fake feel-good tone, almost like she was selling a used car.

"Sure, your boss told me you'd be calling," Fisk said. "What can I do for you?"

"I've come across some information leading me to believe Annika Nakrivo requires additional supervision."

"Your lieutenant said that, too." The warden chuckled. "Why does Miss Nakrivo need to have extra personnel on her *this* time?"

Bernadette paused. "What do you mean?"

"She's a charming one, is Annika. We used to have problems with a couple of the stronger prisoners. Now they're both wrapped around her little finger. She walks around here like she's a queen. Got a guard eating out of her hand, too—we had to fire him."

"I see." Bernadette scratched the back of her head.

"Shouldn't surprise me. It's how she got her victims to trust her, too."

"Didn't fool you, though."

"For a while, yeah, she fooled me, too."

Warden Marcie Fisk chuckled again. "I heard you're the one who brought her in."

Bernadette shifted her feet. "I can't take all the credit. Dr. Woodhead was part of the investigation, too. I couldn't have done it without him."

"Woodhead, huh? He's not just a grumpy old TV star who's in it for the headlines?"

Kep wasn't always the easiest to get along with, but Bernadette kept her tone positive. "He's *definitely* not in it for the headlines. It's not just his super sense of smell, it's how he can identify them and break down what those smells mean. His insight is invaluable."

"He might be the star, but don't sell yourself short. I heard you commandeered a plane in order to take her into custody."

"Yeah."

A brief pause. "I wish you hadn't. Nakrivo's been a colossal pain in my ass."

Bernadette paced around the conference table clockwise, the cord of the telephone stretching to accommodate her. "Better than—"

"Sorry," Fisk said quickly. "Prison humor. Of course, I'm glad you caught her."

Ah. Maura wouldn't have made that mistake—she'd have probably made a joke of her own. Instead, Bernadette had come off like a humorless scold. "It's all good." She cleared her throat. "The reason I wanted to get in touch—"

"Right, right. Your lieutenant said something about Nakrivo's sister."

Bernadette stopped pacing and traced her foot in a figure eight on the carpet. "Her sister's been missing for years, then this morning we got a hit on a debit card of hers, used at a gas station just an hour away from Taycheedah."

There was silence on the other end of the line.

"Warden Fisk? Are you still there?"

"Is that all you have?"

"Of course, it's not definitive." Bernadette started pacing again, this time counterclockwise around the room. "A hit on a debit card in Wisconsin sounds pretty thin. But she was last seen in Florida, and she was missing for three years. Now this."

"I get it," Warden Fisk said. "Due diligence."

The same phrase Maura had used. Maybe Fisk was repeating something from her conversation with the lieutenant. "The last thing Annika said to me," Bernadette said, "was someone was holding her sister against her will. Her sister might have used the debit card, but it's also possible someone who harmed Marguerite has the card—and wants to hurt Annika, too." She paused. "Or it could be nothing. Just a stolen card."

Warden Fisk was silent for a moment, then spoke carefully. "I want to do the right thing here, but dealing with Miss Nakrivo isn't on the top of my wish list."

"What's the matter?"

"She's a handful. Even in here. She started a fight with another inmate at dinner last night."

"So she can't charm everyone?"

"Not this one. Got slashed across the face with the business end of a sharpened toothbrush. Nakrivo's in the infirmary—probably for another day or two—and then right to solitary for a week. Even if her sister shows up, she won't be able to see her. Law enforcement visitors only."

Like me, Bernadette thought. Was the fight tied to Marguerite's debit card? Did someone steal the debit card, then contact someone on the inside? "How—how's the security in the infirmary?"

"She's handcuffed to the bed, and there's an officer for every three patients. A better ratio than in the general population."

"But if someone wanted to harm her—"

"Then I'd be looking to see if anyone had paid off the inmate with the toothbrush," the warden said. "It's a much easier way to erase someone in jail."

"I'd like to come interview her again," Bernadette said.

Silence on the other end of the line.

"Warden Fisk? Are you still—"

"Do you think they were deliberately careless with the debit card?" the warden asked in a low voice.

Bernadette came to a dead stop from her pacing. "What do you mean?"

"I mean—maybe somebody's trying to draw you here. To Taycheedah."

Bernadette blinked. "Who even knows I'm looking for Annika's sister?"

"Miss Nakrivo, for one," Fisk said.

"She *told* me 'they' had her sister as she left the interview room. I never responded—"

"Your lieutenant informed me about what she said," Fisk interrupted. "Have you ever considered the possibility Miss Nakrivo had her outburst intentionally?"

Bernadette flinched. "What?"

"Just like researching her victims, Miss Nakrivo might have done her research into *you*."

"What do you mean?"

Fisk sighed. "I see a lot of master manipulators. Certain

prisoners? Every visitor who comes in bends over backward to do what they want. I'm suggesting Miss Nakrivo might have found something in your past to push your buttons."

"What could she have possibly found?"

But as soon as the words were out of Bernadette's mouth, she knew.

Wichita.

In Bernadette's first investigation as Dr. Woodhead's case analyst, they had discovered that Parr Medical had brought a woman, Anja Kerovic, from Florida to their headquarters, and she had gotten plastic surgery to alter her looks. She'd also received a new identity—Annika Nakrivo—and the ability to pass a university background check. She received enough information about the university's medical research staff to win an internship at the university's medical research center—and get the murder victim to fall in love with her. If Parr Medical had gotten that much information on the university's staff, the pharmaceutical company could have easily researched both Bernadette Becker and Dr. Kep Woodhead once CSAB assigned them to the case—and given their background information to Annika.

Including the death of Bernadette's partner in Wichita.

She rubbed her temples. If Annika had been talented and devious enough to make the murder victim fall in love with her, she'd be able to trigger Bernadette. That kind of emotional manipulation would have been in Annika's skill set.

"You've thought of something Miss Nakrivo could use against you," Fisk stated flatly.

Bernadette closed her eyes. Months ago, in the Taycheedah interview room, Annika's eyes had a pained, desperate look. Bernadette had seen Annika act, and she had seen Annika lie. She closed her eyes and Annika's last words to her flashed through her head. *They have my sister. It's too late for me, but I won't talk. Not until my sister is safe.*

Had that been genuine, or had Annika been playing a game?

Bernadette opened her eyes. "I still can't ignore the debit card." The hairs on the back of her neck stood up. "And emotional manipulation or not, I wouldn't be doing my job if I didn't come see her."

"I understand," Fisk said. "When?"

"I'm not sure yet. I'm supposed to go to Shreveport in a couple of days. Maybe when I get back."

"If you don't want to call attention to the visit," Fisk said, "it'd be easiest to do it when she's still in the infirmary."

"You mean—by tomorrow?"

"I could hold off putting her in solitary for another day or two, but tomorrow would be ideal. We're short-staffed, so a regular interview would be more resource-intensive."

"I'm not sure I can rearrange my schedule."

"Your lieutenant had some ideas," Fisk said. "The wheels may already be in motion, Agent Becker."

The warden hung up before Bernadette could correct her about the "agent" designation—besides, "case analyst" didn't have the same ring to it. Reaching over the conference table to hang up the receiver, Bernadette sat down heavily in a conference chair. Not as comfortable as Maura's overstuffed chair, but a lot better than the one in her cubicle.

A knock on the door. Bernadette sighed, got up, then walked around the table to the door and pulled it open.

Lesley stood there, holding her open laptop.

"Hey."

"I got the make and model of the pickup truck."

Bernadette blinked.

Lesley lowered her voice. "The one in the gas station at the same time Marguerite's debit card got swiped."

"Oh." Bernadette stepped aside and Lesley came in, setting her laptop on the conference table while Bernadette shut the door behind her.

"It's a 2018 or 2019 Toyota Tacoma." Lesley tapped the screen in front of her. "Wisconsin plates don't match a Tacoma, though. They match a 2014 Chevy Malibu, so we think the plates were stolen. We contacted the owner of the Malibu—she's in Atlanta visiting her mother. She parked her car in a long-term lot at the Madison airport on Friday afternoon."

"And the pickup itself?" Bernadette bent down behind Lesley's chair to look at the monitor.

"We think someone stole the truck, too. It matches the description of a few different Tacomas reported stolen in the last week across the country." Lesley bent over the table, tapped the trackpad on her laptop, and watched as a Missouri car registration form appeared on-screen. "Only one in the Midwest, though. The closest Tacoma theft was in Kansas City on Saturday morning. I'd bet we're looking at this truck."

Bernadette nodded. "If someone were driving a long distance to get to Taycheedah, stealing a truck in Kansas City would fit. Especially if they switched plates in Wisconsin." She squinted at the screen. "Anything else?"

"If you're casting your net, I think you should look for someone who has a lot of experience stealing cars and swapping license plates," Lesley said, pulling the nearest chair out and sitting.

"There must be hundreds of chop shops." Bernadette took the chair next to Lesley. "If we look at Kansas City as on their route, they could be anywhere from the Midwest to L.A."

Lesley shook her head. "Chop shops are mostly local operations. You steal a car for a chop shop, you're not driving it three states away."

Bernadette nodded. "Okay, that makes sense."

"If you work on stealing license plates as part of your repertoire, then we're talking"—Lesley counted off on her fingers—"drug shipments, human trafficking, or money laundering. Or something similar, anyway. And you'll have drivers who know how to avoid the forfeiture corridors."

Bernadette felt a smile creep onto her face. "Come on, Lesley, those corridors don't officially exist."

Lesley frowned, and she turned back to the laptop. "Whether or not they exist, the organized operations work hard to avoid them."

Bernadette cocked her head. "How do you know this?"

Lesley rocked back in her desk chair. "In my time with the Milwaukee P.D., I learned about a couple of trafficking operations working out of Chicago. I still have a contact in organized crime there—I can see if he's compiled a list of drivers."

Bernadette furrowed her brow. "The drivers? Not the lieutenants or the people organizing the operation?"

"Yeah, I know the drivers are low level in these organizations. But that's how he got most of his information. A lot of the drivers get into the business thinking they're going to move up, but it's dangerous work, it can land them in jail, and they don't get paid very well. Half of 'em could make more working in fast food. And when their dreams of moving up in the organization fall apart, sometimes they'll turn informant."

"I've worked in CSAB for a long time—the low-level dealers never know very much."

"Not so with the drivers. They might not know who's paying them, but they know locations, times, dates. They're more observant than most people give them credit for. And the lieutenants sometimes get sloppy."

Bernadette stared at the laptop screen for a moment. "It's worth a shot, for sure."

"First things first," Lesley said. "I'm getting a warrant for the footage from the long-term lot in Madison, but it's privately owned, off-airport. They might not have cameras."

Bernadette straightened up. "Do we have any idea who's driving the car now?"

"We were lucky to get footage from the gas station." Lesley tapped a different part of the screen, and a browser search window appeared. "We got a plate, make, and model—that's how we found out about the stolen plates—but we didn't get a good look at the driver."

"What about the cheap motel in Sun Prairie?"

"The motel clerk asked me to call back when the overnight shift was back on—she didn't seem to know anything about who checked in last night. Four rooms had guests who arrived daytime yesterday, and one of them paid in cash, including the deposit. It was two hundred fifty."

"Any description?"

"Tall, white, skinny, clean-shaven, wearing a hooded sweatshirt. She thinks it was blue or purple."

Bernadette nodded. "If I were about to do something illegal at Taycheedah, I'd pay in cash, too."

"Not many hotels take cash anymore."

"So whoever it is must have done their homework ahead of time." Bernadette folded her arms. "I know the facts are sketchy, but the more I find, the more I think something's going down at Taycheedah."

"You and—" Lesley paused.

"What is it?"

"You and Maura need to be careful."

"Careful of what?"

"I don't know." Lesley stood and paced around the table. "I've seen the two of you trying to keep your Annika investigation on the down-low. You're not being as sneaky as you think."

Bernadette crossed her arms. "How do you—"

"Your trip to Miami to talk to Monica Jiménez—"

"You found out?"

Lesley shrugged. "Credit card charges. A hotel room and rental car under your name. And knowing about Annika Nakrivo's background, it wasn't too hard to search for her previous addresses. Monica's name is on a lease from a couple of years ago, and her last known address is a motel, where you probably talked to her."

Bernadette was quiet.

"All I'm saying is, be careful. The Nakrivo case is closed, and you'll need to dot your i's and cross your t's if you want to get it reopened. If you want to pursue this, you need to cover your tracks better."

Bernadette cleared her throat. "I'm asking you for help—I don't want too many searches showing up in the CSAB system. Do *you* have a better explanation for why someone used Marguerite's debit card at a gas station an hour away from her sister's prison?"

"Not yet." Lesley tapped the keyboard. "The cameras at the gas station didn't cover the pump where her card was swiped. But there are a few more avenues we can investigate. If you think Marguerite is still alive—"

"If Annika was telling the truth and someone kidnapped her sister."

"Maybe Marguerite just wanted to get away from her

parents or run away with her boyfriend," Lesley said. "People have gone off grid before. Or someone might have stolen her wallet."

Bernadette closed her eyes. "Probably just as likely as Marguerite still being alive, wanting to go see her sister, and forgetfully using her expired debit card at a gas station."

"By the way," Lesley said, "I started my analysis of the SD card."

"Already?"

"Don't get your hopes up. It's strange—I thought the whole 'Marguerite' folder would be encrypted. It's not. But inside that folder are about thirty files that *are* encrypted— and I can't get into them."

"Yet." Bernadette smiled. "Maybe Joanna broke the first layer of encryption before she copied the files over."

"I've never heard of that, but I suppose it's a possibility."

"And Joanna said the files look like they're encrypted with AES-1024. She told me not to get my hopes up."

A vertical line formed between Lesley's eyebrows. "I don't see how she'd know. It's not like the files are walking around with a big nametag saying 'Hello, my encryption is AES-1024.'"

"She could have done a process-of-elimination thing."

"Or maybe she used some sort of tech we don't have. They *do* have all the bleeding-edge advanced technology over there."

Bernadette barked a laugh. "Not to hear Joanna tell it."

Lesley grinned. "I'll see what I can do."

Another knock. Bernadette stood and opened the door.

Maura stood at the threshold. "Everything okay in here?"

"The encrypted files on Marguerite's SD card," Bernadette said. "Lesley's giving me an update."

"She'll email the files to you." Maura held up a manila

folder. "Forget about Shreveport. I got you an assignment closer to Taycheedah. So you can keep an eye on things there."

"The warden was right," Bernadette muttered.

"What?"

"She said the wheels were already in motion, and she was right." Bernadette smoothed the lapels of her blazer. "So where am I headed? Green Bay? Madison? Milwaukee?"

Maura shook her head. "A little town about thirty miles south of Lost Dish."

"Lost *what?*"

"Lost Dish." A smile touched the corners of Maura's mouth. "County seat of Porcupine County. Right on Lake Superior."

"Doesn't sound like Wisconsin."

"Upper Peninsula of Michigan," Maura said.

"The Yoopers," Lesley muttered.

"There's a little town," Maura continued, "on the edge of the Ottawa National Forest called Banner Crossing."

"A murder?"

"A suspicious death." Maura tapped the folder. "Evan McMichael, sixty-eight years old. Body discovered in his trailer about a week ago. Trailer riddled with bullets."

"Bullets?" Lesley interjected, then frowned. "But, uh, we're the Controlled Substance Analysis Bureau. Unless I missed a memo, we do drug and poison deaths, right? Not gunshots."

"Not killed by bullets," Maura said. "The body had been there for at least a week. Significant trauma to the face and neck."

"At least a week? So time of death—"

"Is broad. Measured in days, not hours."

"If bullets didn't cause the damage to his face and neck,"

Bernadette said, "what kind of trauma are we talking about? Decomp?"

Maura gave Bernadette a tight smile. "Not according to the M.E." Maura opened the folder. "Dr. Imogen Goadbury. She says it's acid."

Bernadette cocked her head. "Closer to a controlled substance. Hardware store stuff, or something else?"

Maura flipped a page. "They're still doing the chemical analysis. Dr. Goadbury has ruled out hydrochloric acid, but based on the location of the injuries, she believes our victim ingested the acid."

Bernadette scratched her head. "And this is a homicide? People drink poison to end their life—it's, what, the third most common—"

"Yes, yes." Maura leafed through a few papers in the folder.

"I just read last year's NIH report on poisoning," Lesley offered. "In rural areas—like Banner Crossing, I guess—self-inflicted poisoning is the second most common cause of suicide." She glanced up at Maura. "Mostly pesticide ingestion. Was this a pesticide?"

Maura took a paper out and scanned it. "It doesn't seem like law enforcement found any pesticides near the body." She turned toward Bernadette. "That's one possibility you can investigate."

"We don't investigate suicides."

Maura raised her eyebrows. "Do you want to go to Taycheedah or not?"

Bernadette inhaled quickly. "Yes."

"Banner Crossing, Michigan," Maura said, closing the folder and handing it to Bernadette. "Possible homicide. Unknown poison."

Bernadette frowned. "If we don't know what the poison was—"

"That's why we're bringing Dr. Woodhead in."

Bernadette pressed her lips together, opened the folder, and flipped through the papers until she found the map. She stared at it for a moment.

"What is it?" Maura asked.

"Banner Crossing is a five-hour drive from Taycheedah."

"Four."

"Still, I'll need to be available to interview Annika more than once."

"You can't get it all with a single interview?" Maura asked.

"You know how this works, Maura. What if she gives us a little information, we act on it, then need more? What if we find out what happened to Marguerite *after* tomorrow's interview? There are a million reasons I'll have to see her again."

Maura crossed her arms, and a smile touched her lips. "Lost Dish is thirteen hours closer than Shreveport."

Bernadette stared at the table for a moment, then closed the file.

Maura looked at Bernadette out of the corner of her eye. "Unfortunately, I couldn't book you on a flight to any of the airports in a hundred-mile radius of Banner Crossing without going over budget," Maura said. "The travel department got you on a flight into Milwaukee tomorrow morning and booked you a car." She winked almost imperceptibly. "You arrive at nine. Sorry for the inconvenience."

Bernadette nodded. "Will I, uh, be meeting Dr. Wood-head in Milwaukee?"

"He's arriving on a puddle-jumper into the Houghton County Airport—about forty miles east of Lost Dish." Maura turned and grabbed the door handle. "You'll pick him up tomorrow evening, five fifteen."

Bernadette calculated the travel time. She'd have about three hours to meet with Annika. Bringing in Dr. Woodhead was a wildcard—on balance, Bernadette would have preferred not to have him there. He could be a pain in the ass. But his presence would lend respectability and believability to the whole affair. If she could keep her visits to Taycheedah from him.

Bernadette raised her head to Maura. "You're coming too, right?"

Maura frowned. "You and Dr. Woodhead don't need me there to get—"

"Dr. Woodhead doesn't drive."

"I realize that."

"So what happens when I need to follow up with Annika after our initial conversation?" Bernadette tilted her head. "Are you planning on authorizing thousands of dollars in Uber and taxi fees so *he* can investigate the death when I take an all-day round-trip drive to Taycheedah?"

"It's possible he could investigate on his own."

"As the case analyst and the official employee of CSAB, I'm supposed to accompany *any* consultant."

"That hasn't worked out on the first two cases."

"It's because he ditched me, not because I ditched him." Bernadette turned to Lesley. "What do you think, Lesley? If I disappear for nine hours for a second interview with Annika, do you suppose it would pass an audit?"

Lesley raised her hands, palms out, off her laptop. "Don't get me involved, Bernadette. I haven't been here long enough to know protocol, and I don't get paid enough to have opinions on this."

"I get your point," Maura said. "Fine." She pulled her phone out and tapped the screen. "I can get there on

Wednesday afternoon. Then, if you need to go back to Taycheedah on Thursday or Friday, I can spell you."

"Thank you."

Maura nodded, opened the door, and walked down the hallway toward her office.

"Got what you wanted," Lesley said.

"I guess I better call the warden back before I head home to pack."

"Sure. Talk to you later." Lesley left the conference room.

Bernadette lifted her phone. She hesitated for a moment, then opened her phone app and hit *Favorites*.

Bernadette listened as her call went to Barlow's voicemail. She ended the call and tapped another name on the *Favorites* screen.

"Hey, Mom."

"Hi, Sophie. You with your dad?" Bernadette shut the conference room door.

"Yeah." Sophie paused. "Did you get called out of town again? I thought you weren't leaving until Thursday. All my softball stuff is at your house."

"My schedule just changed—I'm leaving tomorrow instead. I'm so sorry."

"Maybe you can drop my gear off? Dad and Lisa have a date night."

A pang of—not jealousy, exactly, but bile rose in Bernadette's throat. "I'll be home this evening. You can get your stuff tonight."

Sophie was quiet.

"I know I promised to take you to the movies tomorrow, but we can go when I get back."

"It's not that."

"Then what?"

"Dad had me last week."

Oof. Bernadette felt that in her gut. Her daughter missed her. "Maybe we can work out something where you stay with me a little longer next time."

"Okay." A pause. "Where are you going this time?"

"Um—the Midwest."

"You going to see your boyfriend?"

Bernadette hesitated. "I might see him for a bit. I'm not hanging out where he is."

"So not Milwaukee."

The girl had done her sleuthing. Perhaps the apple didn't fall far from the tree.

"Uh—no, not Milwaukee." Bernadette cleared her throat. "Is your dad there?"

"Yeah, he's just in line."

"In line?"

"Getting me a new glove. Coach wants to try me out at first base."

"Ah." Bernadette paused. "You okay with that? I thought you enjoyed pitching."

"I can't pitch *every* inning. Hang on." Murmuring, footsteps on a concrete floor. "Here's Dad."

The sound of hands brushing against the phone, background noise.

"Bernadette?"

"Hey, Barlow. Listen—"

"I'm still dropping Sophie off at five, right? Because—"

"Yes. But my work plans changed."

The background noise ebbed; they probably had walked out of the sporting goods store. "What a surprise. When are you leaving?"

"Tomorrow."

No response. Cars passed in the parking lot.

"You still there, Barlow?"

A sigh. "We may have to talk about custody, Bernadette."

"Custody?" Bernadette scoffed. "I'm leaving two days early."

"Two days *this* week. You went to Miami with your boy toy—"

"He's thirty-six."

"I still had to change my plans," Barlow said.

At least I'm not screwing up date night with Lisa was on the tip of her tongue. But she said, "I appreciate your flexibility."

"We can look at the custody arrangement when you get back," Barlow said. "I love having Sophie with me, and I know we left the custody loose to allow for your travel schedule, but this has gotten out of control. We're going to need to hammer out an actual plan, where you are responsible without assuming I'm always going to be your backup."

Bernadette bristled. "Now, look, Barlow, you knew this was my job when you divorced me, and you knew—"

"I'll pick her up before work tomorrow," Barlow said. "And I'll take her to softball. But you and I are discussing the custody later. And the financial arrangements, too."

Bernadette's stomach dropped, but she kept the edge in her voice. "A pleasure, as always." She tapped *End call.*

She sat down heavily in one of the conference room chairs.

Maybe the Annika Nakrivo investigation wasn't worth it.

But then she remembered. Parr Medical had hired Annika to kill Kymer Thompson. And she'd killed one of CSAB's own. And who knows how many others had died?

Bernadette shook her head. They weren't getting away with murder.

Chapter Three

Bernadette walked briskly into the General Mitchell Airport's main terminal, the Summerfest store on her left, the dimly lit Starbucks just beyond that. A line of people snaked out of the coffee shop—not surprising for nine in the morning.

She looked around and wiped a bead of sweat from her temple. The sun had been beating through the plate-glass windows as she'd walked from the gate past security, and Bernadette welcomed the chill of the air conditioning in this part of the airport. Three months had made a vast difference from the snowy, chilly March days of her first investigation here—when she'd first met Lamar Chesapeake, the Milwaukee police officer with kind eyes, a great sense of humor, and a fondness for salsa dancing.

Back in April—had that really been two months ago?—she'd returned to Milwaukee for a weekend. When Bernadette had walked into the main terminal, Lamar had been waiting at the top of the escalator leading down to baggage claim, a mixed bouquet in his hand, and an offer to take her overnight case. And just two weeks ago, she'd met

Lamar in Miami for a week's vacation, touring the town in a convertible with Angelina Zaragoza's first album blasting from the speakers.

Since then, they'd texted and had a couple of video calls, but they'd been busy with work. They'd been officially dating for three months, but because of the distance, they were still trying to get to know each other.

And a bead of sweat dripping down the side of her face didn't mesh with the image she wanted to present Lamar.

Bernadette took a few steps to the side of the terminal—in front of a Spanx store, she noticed—propped her roll-aboard up, and dug for her phone in her purse. There was a text from Lamar.

Meet you outside door 2

She grabbed the handle of her roll-aboard, strode to the escalator, past the spot where Lamar had been standing only two months before, then down to baggage claim. The conveyor belt was already moving—and there was her small hard-sided case on the carousel.

She grabbed it and was soon out Door 2.

The day was muggy and warm, not much different from D.C., but the heat surprised her. The snow and cold had seemed so oppressive during her first visit to the city.

She scanned the line of cars for Lamar's black sedan. A brief tap of a horn behind her and Bernadette spun around; Lamar waved at her through the back window, waiting in the outside lane. Butterflies swooped in Bernadette's stomach.

She hurried over, the trunk popping open, and put her case and her roll-aboard in. After shutting the trunk, she walked to the passenger's side and took a deep breath.

She thought of Maura's office, the comfortable chair,

Maura's ability to separate herself from her job. To not always be wound so tight. Yes, Lamar was cool and collected at all times, and Bernadette was a bit of a mess, but if she channeled Maura enough, she could do this.

She opened the door. "Hey, Lamar." A purr in her voice as she slid into the car.

"Good to see you, babe," he said, leaning over and kissing her softly on the lips. Bernadette reached for him, her hand finding the side of his face, the kiss lingering. A car honked behind them, and Bernadette broke from the kiss, feeling the color rise to her cheeks.

"Sorry it's only for a couple of hours," she said. "But since I was flying in, I'm glad I get to see you."

He sat back in his seat and put the car into gear. "Any time I get to see you is good," he said, smiling widely. "You hungry?"

"Starving. A granola bar at National didn't do much this morning."

"Good, because I made reservations."

Reservations? At nine in the morning on a Tuesday?

Lamar looked over his shoulder and pulled out into the through lane, then got on the on-ramp to the freeway.

Bernadette cocked her head. "I thought you said on the phone we'd go somewhere close for breakfast. I've got to pick my car up by noon."

"This place is just a couple of freeway exits. Besides, I don't think you have anything like this in D.C.," Lamar said cryptically.

"Any towering Bloody Marys like I've seen on TV?"

He grinned. "Not at this place."

"Probably for the best. I've got a long drive ahead of me." As good as a Bloody Mary sounded.

Bernadette turned and looked out the window. The story

of the long drive wasn't really a lie. Yes, she'd told Lamar earlier she was driving to Lost Dish, conveniently leaving out her planned stop at Taycheedah. But the prison near Fond du Lac was still a forty-five minute drive. After Bernadette had called Warden Fisk back, they'd agreed to an hour meeting with Nakrivo. After which she *would* drive all the way to Lost Dish.

"You'll see." Lamar took the exit onto Lapham Street, and a few minutes later, he parked on the street next to a building with a neon GE Appliances & Television sign.

"We're here."

"Where—where are we?"

Lamar glanced over at Bernadette, playfulness dancing in his eyes. "Only the best television repair shop in the Greater Milwaukee area."

Bernadette knitted her brow. "Repair shop?"

"You'll see." Lamar opened the door and got out.

Bernadette glanced out the passenger's side window at the neon sign, then opened the door. If the upcoming drive to Taycheedah weren't weighing on her, this would be right up her alley. Taking her to breakfast at a repair shop—it had all the intrigue of the best parts of her job but with none of the danger. She took a deep breath. She liked Lamar. He was sweet and kind—and good-looking, especially his eyes—and he made her feel beautiful in a way that Barlow hadn't for years. "I'm not sure what you're getting me into," she said, getting out of the car, "but I'm intrigued."

"Then come on."

"First, I need to get in the trunk."

Lamar pushed a button on the key fob and the trunk popped open. Bernadette pulled her luggage keys out and lifted the lid of the trunk. She unlocked the hard case, pulled out her shoulder holster, then looked around. No one was around, so in a series of short, fluid motions, she took off her blazer, put on her shoulder holster, then put her blazer back on. She reached into the hard case and pulled out her Sig Sauer nine-millimeter and a magazine, then shut the case and closed the trunk.

She popped the magazine in.

Lamar watched her with a crooked smile on his face. "I don't know what you've heard about Milwaukee, but you don't have to arm yourself in this neighborhood."

"You know I can't leave my gun in the car. Against regulations."

"I know—just giving you a hard time." His smile broadened. "Impressive. What—five seconds?"

"I've done it a few times before."

"They wouldn't let you take it on the plane?"

"It's not like I was doing prisoner transport. You don't *need* a gun on a plane, you don't *take* a gun on the plane." Bernadette smiled flirtatiously, even though her shoulders were tight. "Now, did you want to talk about the arcane FAA rules we investigators have to follow, or did you have a TV you needed to get fixed?"

Lamar reached for her hand and took it. Her palm was sweaty, but she squeezed his hand lightly. They crossed the sidewalk and Lamar pulled the thin wooden door open for her. Bernadette stepped in.

The small space looked like a TV repair shop, with small old CRT televisions in the corner, most with dials to change the channel. One of the tiny screens showed a movie from what looked like the 1980s. An old soda vending machine—at least sixty years old—was in the far corner next to a wooden counter holding an old cash register.

The wall to Bernadette's left had green-and-white wallpaper with the 7Up logo plastered dozens of times all over it.

A pinball machine stood in the corner opposite the vending machine.

Bernadette looked quizzically at Lamar, but his smile just widened. Bernadette couldn't help but smile back.

A large white man with a bushy red beard and a *Don's TV & Repair* trucker hat eyed them from behind the counter. "Can I help you?"

"I'd like an ice-cold 7Up," Lamar said.

Bernadette's brow furrowed. He'd like a *what?*

"Name?" the man asked.

"Chesapeake for two."

The man checked a screen on the counter and nodded. "Right this way." He stepped to his right, in front of the old vending machine, then pulled on a handle marked *7Up*. To Bernadette's surprise, the vending machine swung forward—a door opened in the wall, revealing a dimly lit room with disco music playing.

"What—" Bernadette started, but Lamar stepped ahead of her, pulling her along through the doorway, leaving the TV repair shop behind.

It was a large, dark restaurant space. Rows of booths lined each side, with a large-screen television playing a music video from the early 1980s. CRT televisions and VHS tapes were stacked all around the booths.

"It's a diner," Lamar said. "Supposed to be like a speakeasy. They've got great burgers. Milkshakes with booze, too. But their brunch menu is the best."

Bernadette looked around, her eyes growing wide. It was a surprise, all right. A little different from the kind of breakfast she was expecting, a well-lit booth she and Lamar could order eggs and toast and flirt with each other before she had to concentrate on the case. But this was—well, if she could get her mind wrapped around it, it'd be delightful.

Almost all the booths and tables were full—at nine thirty on a Tuesday morning. No wonder Lamar needed to make a reservation.

"It's too bad we're both working later," Lamar said. "The 'Game Boy' shake has pineapple rum in it."

They sat in a booth, two paper menus placed in the center of the table.

"Never been to a speakeasy before." Bernadette grabbed a menu and stared at the cartoon worker at the top, holding a small CRT television in one hand and a bottle of 7Up in the other, then pointed at the first item in the left column. "Fruity Pebble Pancakes?"

"7Up is actually in the batter, see?"

She read the description. "Wow. This menu is amazing. A little weird, but amazing."

"If you need a recommendation, the Breakfast Melt is awesome."

Bernadette found it in the middle of the all-day breakfast list: a sausage, egg, and cheese sandwich on brioche French toast with a side of maple syrup. She looked up at Lamar. "That sounds crazy."

"So delicious." Lamar's eyes sparkled. "It's to die for."

"After my arteries harden, it will *definitely* be to die for."

Lamar snorted. "I set you up for that one."

Bernadette grinned and looked down at the menu. When she glanced up, he was looking at her with admiration. Not that good of a joke, but she'd take it.

"I wanted to take you to a cool place," Lamar continued. "You're in Milwaukee for all of two hours, so we didn't have time for the art museum or the Domes."

"The Domes?"

"Oh—the Mitchell Park Domes." He held up three fingers. "Three geodesic domes, each with a unique ecosystem. One of the best things about this city. Next time."

Bernadette's shoulders relaxed. "Yes, next time for sure." She flipped the menu over—lunch and dinner—then back. Bernadette raised her head and looked at Lamar coquettishly. "You're right—I haven't been to any place like this before."

The server appeared. "I'm Lynn, and I'll be your TV repairman this morning."

"Good morning, Lynn," Lamar said with a wide smile.

"You been to Don's before?"

"I have, but my lovely companion has not."

"I'm starting to think my TV won't get fixed," Bernadette said.

Lynn chuckled—ah, she'd heard that one too often, but she was still playing along. "You ready to order?"

Bernadette ordered coffee and the Breakfast Melt. Lamar seemed delighted that Bernadette had taken his advice.

After the server took the menus, Bernadette folded her arms and leaned forward. "So, how have you been? It seems like forever since we were both in the same room."

"Taking a lot of shifts."

"Really? Any reason?"

"I was hoping to take some time off later this month, maybe." He twirled a fork on the tabletop. "What do you think about coming here for Summerfest? You get my email with the list of the bands?"

"There were hundreds. I didn't get through them all." She smiled wistfully. "Maybe Sophie would know more of those artists than I do."

"There's something for everyone." He picked up his fork. "Maybe you should bring her."

Bernadette's eyes widened.

"I didn't mean—" Lamar's face fell. "I mean, I know how

important she is to you, and since it would be her summer vacation, I thought she'd like to tell her friends she went to the biggest music festival on the planet."

Bernadette opened her mouth, but nothing came out.

"Sorry," he blurted. "It's too soon for me to meet your daughter, I know that—I just thought she'd like the music festival. Be a good bonding activity."

"It's not—" Bernadette cleared her throat and found her voice. "It's a lovely gesture. I'm—I'm glad you're in a place where you think you could, you know, be more—be a part of all the stuff I—I do."

Lamar winced. "There's a 'but' coming."

"I mean, my divorce isn't even final yet. I don't think meeting Sophie is right. Not yet."

"No, I know. And we haven't been dating that long. Forget I said anything."

Bernadette leaned back in her chair. Dammit, why did he have to invite Sophie to Summerfest? Was he getting serious this quickly? Did he want her to meet his family, too? Was the music festival even appropriate for an eighth-grader?

Maybe he suggested it because he knew Barlow was already living with Lisa, and they hadn't been together for that long before he'd introduced his new girlfriend.

She took a deep breath. Who was she kidding? Barlow and Lisa had probably been seeing each other for longer than Bernadette realized.

But this wasn't about her trying to get even with Barlow. It was about what was right for her. What was right for Sophie. Bernadette looked up, reached across the table, and put on her most sympathetic face as she grabbed Lamar's hand. "Barlow was so quick to move in with—with Lisa..." Bernadette had to take another breath. "That's one reason to keep things low-key. Sophie's had enough disruption. Her grades slipped. I don't want her to think even more things are getting upended."

"It's not like I'm asking you to move to Milwaukee."

"Well, that's not gonna—" The words were out of her mouth before Bernadette could stop them.

Lamar's kind eyes glazed over a moment and his hand lost its grip on Bernadette's.

"I like you," Bernadette said, grabbing his hand back. "And I was married for fifteen years to a guy who dumped me for one of my co-workers. I'm still a little raw. And I want to do what's best for my daughter."

Lamar pulled his hand out from under Bernadette's, then leaned back in the booth. "Sure," he said, "you're right."

"I'm sorry," Bernadette said quickly.

"I don't mean to push you so hard."

She closed her eyes. "You're not—"

"No, I am. You're gearing up for a case, you've got a long drive ahead of you, and here I am talking about planning for a music festival when you're in the middle of a divorce and you're trying to make sure your kid is okay."

Bernadette looked in Lamar's eyes. He meant what he said, but he was hurt.

Unbidden, her thoughts turned to her meeting in two hours. Annika Nakrivo had hurt people, but had she really done all those things because her sister had been in danger? And she was in prison with nowhere to go. Did Annika know, the last time she saw Marguerite, she'd never see her again? Does anyone ever realize when it's the last time you see someone?

A meme she'd seen on social media: one day you will pick up your child, and it's the last time you will ever pick up your child.

For Bernadette, the last time she picked up Sophie was

years ago, now, and she didn't remember it. She hadn't recognized it at the time, but it had happened, and the moment was gone, lost forever.

"Hey," Lamar said, "I didn't mean to bring you down."

"I'm fine." Bernadette took a deep breath, her lungs shuddering.

"Don't worry about it," Lamar said. "We're in a great restaurant in one of the coolest cities in the world. We've got the whole summer ahead of us. And I like you too. Why do you think I'm pushing to spend time with you?"

"Thanks." Bernadette smiled up at Lamar just as the server appeared and set down their food. She looked down at her plate: the Breakfast Melt was enormous, and the brioche French toast slices were thick.

"I'm not sure I can even fit that in my mouth," Bernadette said, then glanced at Lamar's plate: four large pancakes with rainbow crispies all over the top. She arched an eyebrow at him.

"What can I say?" Lamar picked up his fork. "I'm a kid at heart."

❦

Lamar drove Bernadette back to the airport. Bernadette laughed at his jokes and pointed to the radio when "La Luna de Martes" began playing quietly.

"Angelina Zaragosa?" Bernadette asked.

"You got it."

"I've never heard her on the radio."

"She's playing Summerfest," he said. "This station plays a lot of Summerfest artists."

She raised her eyebrows. "I'll check my calendar."

"You can make it work. I believe in you." Lamar, grinning, elbowed her gently.

They got off the exit for Route 119, and a moment later, Lamar pulled his sedan up at the curb next to the parking garage.

Bernadette looked up. "Oh—we're already here."

"Yep," Lamar said. "In plenty of time to make your drive." He leaned over and kissed her lightly on the lips. Her internal clock was pushing her to hurry, but she turned her body, put her hand on the back of Lamar's head, and gave him a proper kiss. A bit of passion for him to remember her until they could see each other again.

They broke from the kiss. Lamar smacked his lips together. "Maple syrup," he breathed.

"Don't say I never gave you any sugar." Bernadette turned and opened the door.

"Have a safe trip," Lamar said. "Don't forget your suitcase in the trunk."

"Thanks for breakfast. And the TV repair."

"Call me when you get there," Lamar said. "Just so I know you made it safely."

"Bye."

She got out and walked behind the car. The mechanism of the trunk clicked, and Bernadette pulled out her bag and her gun case.

Bernadette stood in line at the rental car counter and gritted her teeth. Introducing Lamar to Sophie: too early, right? Three months, true; but it was all long-distance, mostly texts and video calls. They'd only seen each other a handful of times, and while they got along well and made each other laugh, she had to think about creating as stable a situation as possible for Sophie. Barlow had left the marriage, not Bernadette; Barlow was the one who moved in with his girlfriend before the ink was dry on the separation papers. And, as usual, it was Bernadette who was stuck trying to smooth things out after Barlow was the agent of chaos. A pang of anger: he didn't understand how important her job was, and now he was trying to weaponize her job—the job she'd had when they'd gotten married—to drive her and Sophie apart. She clenched and unclenched her fists, then took a deep breath. In for ten. Out for ten. Her pulse slowed to a normal pace again.

Bernadette got to the front of the line, filled in her paperwork, declined the extra insurance, and grabbed the key from the clerk. As she walked out into the rental car garage, she stepped to the side and pulled her phone out.

"Mmmf?"

"Hi, sweetie. Did I wake you?"

"What time is it?"

An hour later in Virginia. "Uh—probably about twelve thirty. You're not up yet?"

"I was online with my friend till late. I went back to bed after Dad picked me up."

"You ready for softball?"

"I will be." Sophie paused. "Is everything okay?"

"I just missed you, I guess. I'm about to start a new case, and you know how I get sometimes. Thought I'd talk with you before I got where I'm going."

"You just saw me yesterday."

"I know." She drew a figure eight on the pavement of the garage with her right foot. "You've taken those CSAB alerts off your phone, right?"

Bernadette could almost hear her daughter roll her eyes. "Yes, mom."

"I just don't want you to worry. The media doesn't know what goes on in these investigations."

"Didn't you get really sick from that mold last time?"

"I know this job isn't as safe as working in an office all day, but I'm fine, sweetie." She paused. "Have you *really* taken those alerts off your phone?"

"Yes." A pause. "Yes, I swear."

"Okay." Now it was Bernadette's turn to pause. "Listen, um—do you like to go to music festivals?"

"Festivals? I don't know. I've only been to a couple of concerts."

That's right. With Barlow over the last three or four months.

"Why?"

"There's a big music festival in Milwaukee. Thought it might be fun for us to go."

"Could I bring Jenna?"

"I don't know. That's halfway across—" Bernadette stopped and considered. "It's in a couple of weeks, so the timing probably won't work. Especially with softball. Maybe we'll find something closer to home."

"There's the All Things Go festival in September. Laney the Rich is playing."

"Yes," Bernadette said, though she had no idea what All Things Go was—though she'd heard way too much Laney the Rich in the car with Sophie dancing crazily in the passenger seat. "I'll look into it."

"Okay."

"I've got to get my car. I'll talk to you later."

"When are you going to call again?"

"When I can. Maybe tomorrow night."

"Okay." Sophie paused. "Be careful, Mom."

"I promise I'll be careful. Love you."

They said their goodbyes and Bernadette ended the call.

This year, maybe it would just be her, and she and Lamar

could hang out and watch a ton of bands. Maybe she'd want Sophie to meet Lamar next year. Maybe next year she could come with Sophie. But she didn't want to do anything to disrupt Sophie's world even more than Barlow had disrupted it already.

She strode across the parking lot, key fob in hand.

Sometimes she hated being the responsible one.

Bernadette strode to the window on the far left in the prison lobby, paperwork folder in one hand, and her identification card in her other. The clerk behind the window looked up from his computer screen through half-lidded eyes.

"May I help you?"

"Bernadette Becker with the Controlled Substance Analysis Bureau." She placed the ID on the counter. "I'm here to see a prisoner—Annika Nakrivo. I understand she's in the infirmary."

Without acknowledging her, the clerk went back to his computer, knitted his brow, and began to type. Bernadette stood for a moment, then shifted her weight from foot to foot. She looked around the waiting room of the prison with the cheap plastic chairs and the depressing cement-block walls. She was the only one in there. Not surprising; visiting hours didn't start for another two hours.

Bernadette turned back to the window. "Did I catch Warden Fisk on her lunch break?"

"One moment," the clerk murmured. "This might take some time. Have a seat."

Bernadette didn't move. "I have the paperwork—"

The clerk glanced up. "You can have a seat." His voice was firm.

Bernadette turned to the row of blue plastic chairs about six feet away from the bank of windows and slowly walked to them. She debated for a moment—she'd been sitting a lot and had another three hours in the car. She stole a glance at the clerk and remained standing.

It was just past twelve thirty, and she needed to pick up Dr. Woodhead at the airport in the late afternoon. She'd called him from National Airport before her flight to confirm, and he'd expressed surprise he was being called in on a case that seemed so clearly to point to suicide.

Bernadette wished she'd brought her laptop into the waiting room so she could review the file. She thought they'd usher her in quickly. But the situation in prisons could change in the blink of an eye. Maybe there was a fight, or perhaps an outbreak of the flu?

There might still be time to get the laptop from her car. She walked back to the clerk's desk. "Hey—if it's going to be a while, I'll go out and get something from my car."

The clerk's head snapped up. "I just spoke to the warden. We'd like you and Dr. Woodhead to go back to the infirmary now." He lifted his head and scanned the empty waiting room. "If Dr. Woodhead is waiting in the car, you can go retrieve him."

Bernadette narrowed her eyes. "Woodhead? This meeting doesn't involve him."

The clerk frowned. "Hold on, please." He turned to the computer and picked up the phone on his left. "You can take your seat. I'll be with you in a moment."

Bernadette walked uneasily to the blue plastic chairs. She tapped the tips of her fingers to her thumbs, back and forth. Pins and needles. She sat down and closed her eyes.

That night in Wichita.

Six months of planning. An embedded CSAB agent. The

night vision goggles tight around her head. Declan had crouched next to her on the side of the county road ten miles outside the Wichita city limits.

The night had been perfect: no moon, cloud cover, no security to announce their arrival. They'd trekked to the sprawling ranch-style house, five hundred yards from the road, miles from US 400. Only their target and the embedded agent inside. Declan and Bernadette would storm the front, two more agents would take away the rear exit, and two others would come in through a side window. In four minutes, assuming everything went according to plan, the leader of the Camorra cartel would be under arrest. Or maybe dead, depending on how it played out.

But Bernadette's stomach had been in knots, the tips of her fingers awash with pins and needles. Trying to tell herself she didn't have any evidence their cover had been blown. "Nerves," Declan had whispered as they approached from the county road. It hadn't been Bernadette's first rodeo, but Declan knew her well. Bernadette had nodded, swallowed hard, and kept going.

They counted down from five, and a second after Declan said "one," he jumped out of his crouch toward the front door. Bernadette willed her feet to move. But they wouldn't.

And a split second later, the door flew open, and the flash from the shotgun blast overwhelmed her night vision.

Declan crumpled to the ground.

Bernadette sprang and fired two shots—both hitting the shooter in the head. She ran forward.

Not the cartel leader. One of his bodyguards.

She ran to Declan, but it was already too late, his sightless eyes unfocused.

Inside, there had been no cartel leader, just the corpse of the CSAB agent.

With a gasp, Bernadette came back to the present. The same sense of pins and needles on the tips of her fingers—and getting worse. Her stomach flipped.

The waiting room was empty, but only one way out: the door she'd come in. Six blue plastic chairs, perfectly lined up: four next to the wall across from the clerk's desk, and two against the side wall. No plants. No magazines.

The clerk was away from the desk. When she'd been here before, there'd been three clerks at the desk. Had she seen the man previously?

She pulled her phone out of her purse—no service.

The pins and needles grew even stronger.

She reached under her blazer—shit. No guns allowed through the security checkpoint; her Sig Sauer was in the locked case in the trunk.

"Nope," she muttered out loud, hoisting her purse up on her shoulder and hurrying out of the waiting room.

Her breaths came short and hot as she turned left through a corridor. She followed the bright red *Exit* sign, then arrived at a large gray metal door. She pushed it open, and the outside air hit her face—but she was still within the gates of the prison. A concrete walkway. Grass and weeds. A crack in the red brick wall on her left.

Three bars on her phone.

She tapped Dr. Woodhead's number. Straight to voicemail. He was probably on his flight to Michigan.

She called Maura.

"Stevenson."

"Maura, it's Bernadette."

A pause. "Aren't you at Taycheedah?"

"I am. They're expecting both me *and* Dr. Woodhead. Did you tell Warden Fisk we'd both be coming?"

"Of course not." Maura hesitated. "I told her your travel

plans changed, and you'd be on a case in the area. Maybe it sounded like you'd both be showing up."

"Okay."

Another pause. "You don't sound convinced."

"Something's off."

"Off?"

"Off—" She took a deep breath. "Off like losing Declan."

Silence on the other end of the line. "Surely this isn't the same thing."

"I don't know what it is," Bernadette said. "They don't seem to want to let me in without Kep."

"Ridiculous," Maura said. "Why would they want Dr. Woodhead to be there?"

A chill ran down Bernadette's spine.

Warden Fisk had said another inmate had attacked Annika. That's why she was in the infirmary. What if Annika knew too much? Or worse—what if Annika was part of the plot to trap Bernadette and Kep?

Did they—whoever *they* were—know Bernadette couldn't bring her gun in? How deep did this go?

"I'm not staying here," Bernadette said.

"After all the strings I pulled?"

"I think I got played." Bernadette kept hurrying down the long concrete walkway, concentrating on putting one foot in front of the other. "I think maybe we both got played."

"But no one knew you were interviewing Annika today."

"Warden Fisk knew. She could have told others." Bernadette set her jaw as she quickened her pace. The guard station was in front of her.

She walked through the gate, into the guard station, and made a beeline for the sign-out sheet.

"Bernadette?"

"I'm in the guard station."

A guard stood to his full height. "Turn your phone off, ma'am."

"Gotta go." Bernadette clicked *End*, then picked up the pen and scrawled her signature next to the one where she'd signed in. Tossing her visitor's badge on the counter, she walked out of the guard station into the parking lot.

Her rental car, parked in the last row, was in view—only a few people were in the parking lot. An older Latino couple, grim-faced, holding hands, strode purposefully toward the entrance. A tall, white man in a royal-blue Kansas State hoodie walked from the edge of the lot, about thirty feet from Bernadette's rental, toward the parking lot exit onto the main road. And a young Black woman, with cropped hair and a nose ring, crossed her arms, staring down at the ground, as she passed Bernadette to enter the guard station.

No one knows you were meeting Annika today.

Not true. Warden Fisk knew. Lesley and Maura knew, too. Maybe one of them told someone they shouldn't have.

Annika knew, too.

Bernadette's head swam, but she made it to her car, hurriedly got in, and closed her eyes. A flash: Declan's dead body, his face unrecognizable—

She opened her eyes. "I don't care if I get fired. I'm not going back in there."

She started the engine, then drove out of the parking lot onto County Road K.

The Michigan state line was only three-and-a-half hours away.

Chapter Four

By the time Bernadette got to the causeway over Lake Butte des Morts just before Oshkosh, she'd calmed down enough to think straight. As she turned onto U.S. Highway 45, she picked up her phone from the center console and called Maura, putting it on speaker.

"Bernadette?"

"Hey, Maura."

"Glad you called. Just got off with the Wisconsin Department of Corrections. There's been an incident at Taycheedah."

"What kind of incident?"

"Prison's on lockdown. No one in or out."

Bernadette gasped. "I got out just in time."

"I can't get ahold of Warden Fisk, and the DOC rep said he doesn't have any info. Keeping it out of the media for now."

Bernadette stiffened as she gripped the steering wheel .

"Tell me what happened," Maura said softly.

Bernadette gave Maura the details: the clerk making her wait for a few minutes, then telling her she could go in with

Dr. Woodhead. Then, after hearing Woodhead wasn't there, the clerk left the desk.

"What made you think you were in danger?" Maura asked.

"Asking for Kep," Bernadette answered. "My fingers started with the pins and needles, like what happened in Wichita. You know how before an earthquake, all the animals go quiet?"

"Something was off."

"Yeah."

The tapping of a pen on a pad. Maura was taking notes.

"Why would they insist on Kep joining me? Even if they thought we'd be traveling together?" Bernadette looked over her shoulder and got into the left lane to pass the minivan in front of her. "Kep only interviewed Annika once, maybe twice, and never after the investigation was over."

"True."

"And Annika never mentioned Kep in any of her meetings with me. I don't even know if Annika remembers who Kep *is*."

"Who did you tell that you were going to Taycheedah?"

Bernadette scratched her forehead, keeping her eyes on the road. "You. Lesley. Uh... that might be it." She knew she hadn't mentioned it to Lamar.

"Your friend in the FBI?"

"Joanna? Maybe." Bernadette squinted and tried to think. "She knew I wanted to interview Annika again, and she knew about the debit card."

"What about your daughter? Or Barlow?"

"Absolutely not." Bernadette turned the air conditioner fan to a higher setting. "They know I'm going to the Midwest. I didn't breathe a word about Taycheedah to either of them."

"Dr. Woodhead?"

"No—he doesn't know I've interviewed Annika at all."

Maura cleared her throat. "Then it's possible the incident had nothing to do with you or Annika. Could be an escaped prisoner, a fight in the prison yard."

"But why would Kep—"

"Did you mention you were going on this assignment with Kep to anyone?"

"I listed him under *Other Personnel* on the travel request form."

Maura was silent. "Anyone at CSAB could have seen that form."

"Could Warden Fisk have seen it?"

"I suppose. Maybe the warden is a fan of *Cases That Won't Die?*"

Bernadette thought for a moment. "Warden Fisk did call Dr. Woodhead a TV star. And maybe the incident—whatever it is—has no connection to my visit to Annika. But I don't think so."

"It *is* unusual," Maura said. "Okay, we believe Annika took her orders from someone at Parr Medical. She got plastic surgery to alter her looks. Parr Medical paid for it. So someone—whether it's an employee at Parr Medical or not—thinks Annika, you, and Dr. Woodhead know something, or have information."

Bernadette grimaced. "Sounds ridiculous. Like a conspiracy theory."

"Or," Maura said thoughtfully, "Annika could be coordinating this from the inside. Maybe she had an escape plan requiring both you and Dr. Woodhead to be there. She may still be working for Parr Medical, even from her prison cell."

"Even more far-fetched."

"I don't have any better explanations. An SD card with encrypted files hidden in a musical instrument? A debit card transaction from a missing woman fifty miles away from her sister's prison? And now an 'incident' the day you arrive for an interview. Believe me, if I could see a logical explanation, I'd jump on it."

Bernadette drove past the Winneconne exit, a big white pickup truck passing her on the right. "It was just such a weird feeling, Maura. Like I was in the crosshairs." She looked over her right shoulder, then changed lanes.

"Your visit might get flagged," Maura said. "Someone might review the information and wonder why a CSAB investigator was at the prison during the incident."

Bernadette was quiet.

"The investigation in Banner Crossing might give us enough cover," Maura said. "And like I said before, an interview with Annika is due diligence with Marguerite's debit card getting declined. But this might not go well for us."

"I'll take the hit," Bernadette said.

"Don't be a martyr," Maura said.

Bernadette was silent.

"Still getting the sense you're in danger?"

Her brain shouted a *yes* at her, but it didn't make it to her lips. "My fingers aren't doing the pins-and-needles thing anymore, if that's what you mean."

"It's not."

Bernadette scratched her chin, then ran a hand through her hair. "Something's still off. Maybe not immediate danger, though."

"Trust your gut," Maura said. "I'll be there tomorrow night. If anything is suspicious before then, call me. Be careful. Vary your schedule—make sure it's hard to know where you'll be."

"What about the hotel?"

"What do you mean?"

"CSAB registered Kep and me under our own names."

"There are laws in place to protect your privacy. Besides, CSAB made the reservation. Unless we have a leak within CSAB itself, I don't think you and Dr. Woodhead will have anything to worry about."

Alarm bells went off in Bernadette's head. *A leak within CSAB itself.* Bernadette kept her demeanor calm and exhaled, long and slow. "Okay. I guess we can trust our own people."

"It's only me and Lesley who know where you and Woodhead are staying. And we vetted her thoroughly."

"Right."

After they hung up, Bernadette drove in silence.

And tried to get that night in Wichita out of her mind.

She passed a one-story house on the far side of a field: the look of confidence on Declan's face.

The road curved to the left: the night vision goggles tight on her head.

A sign for *Deer Xing* went by: the sound of a shotgun blast.

Trying to calm down, she flicked the radio on. Static. She hit *Scan*, and heavy metal blasted through the speakers. Ugh. Next, talk radio and how corrupt the current governor was. One more scan tuned to a station playing a treacly pop ballad. She turned the radio off, then wiped her sweaty hands on her trousers.

US-45 merged with US-10, but few signs of civilization adorned the intersection. Only a mile or two later, US-45 exited on the right, and she changed lanes to take the turnoff.

The road narrowed to one lane in each direction here, and the terrain became flat, with sparse trees and low bushes on either side of the highway. Every so often a house—or sometimes a cluster of houses—appeared, set back from the road.

She passed three small towns that all looked the same,

American flags flying from the front of businesses and two-story houses appearing behind groves of trees.

She glanced in her rear-view mirror. Nothing. No one was following her.

Bernadette reached for the radio button again—

Hang on. Maybe someone had placed a GPS tracker on the car.

The tall man in the purple Kansas State sweatshirt in the Taycheedah parking lot. He'd been fairly near the rental car when she came out of the guard station. Kansas State wasn't far from Kansas City, where the Toyota Tacoma had been stolen. Had that man put a tracker on Bernadette's car?

She passed a Ford dealer on her left as the posted speed limit dropped to 35. Bernadette glanced at the gas gauge: still three-quarters of a tank. But she'd stop anyway.

A gas station loomed on her right at the corner of County Road I, and she pulled in and parked next to an open pump.

She took her phone from the center console and grabbed a credit card from her purse, then thought better of it and pulled out a twenty-dollar bill.

As she opened the car door, the warm, humid air pushed its way into the rental. She walked past the gas pumps and pushed open the fading white wooden door to the convenience store. Bells on the door accompanied her entry. The place was empty except for the clerk leaning on his elbows behind the cash register.

She tossed the bill onto the counter in front of the clerk. "Twenty on pump number three."

The clerk stood up slowly, and Bernadette turned and walked from the store before he could say anything. She strode to the pump, popping open the tiny door over the gas cap, and waited for the display on the pump to change.

When the nozzle had clicked on and the gas started flowing, Bernadette turned on the flashlight on her phone, squat-ted, and shined the light into the wheel well, craning her neck. She swore under her breath; she hadn't brought a bug detector with her.

Bernadette had almost finished with the second wheel well when the gas nozzle clicked off.

There. A small rectangular case under the edge of the wheel well.

She immediately stood up and glanced around. Where was the tall white man she'd seen in the parking lot of Taycheedah? Had he followed her here?

But there was no one—a few empty parked cars, all with Wisconsin plates. She squinted and looked further down the road. Nothing from the south side.

An Acura SUV with Iowa plates pulled into the gas station from the north and stopped on the other side of Bernadette's pump. Three of the doors opened, and a mother and two kids scrambled out, the younger child shrieking for a soda.

Bernadette knelt down and pulled on the tracker—the magnet was fairly strong, but with a determined yank, she got it off. She turned it over in her hand; matte black plastic, rectangular, about a quarter of the size of a deck of cards, but just as thick. Clean, new-looking. Granted, the car's odometer only showed about ten thousand miles, but the tracker didn't have ten thousand miles of undercarriage guck.

Now what to do?

Her heart was pounding. But wait: some car rental compa-nies put GPS trackers on their vehicles. "Probably all it is," Bernadette mumbled to herself.

The driver's door of the Acura SUV opened and a man in blue jeans and a baseball cap got out. He stepped to the pump, ran his hand over his face, then swiped his credit card and put the nozzle into his gas tank.

Bernadette opened the passenger door, opened the glove compartment, and pulled out the rental agreement. She called the customer service number, hit 'o' when the hold music came on, and, after pacing around her car for a few minutes, a woman's voice answered.

"Hi," Bernadette said. "I've rented one of your cars at the Milwaukee airport, and I'm getting—uh, some interference with the—the radio." She inwardly swore at herself; she'd had time to think of a better story. "Maybe the GPS tracker will do that?"

Bernadette could hear a keyboard clicking on the other end. "License plate number?"

Bernadette told her.

More clicking. "Your vehicle doesn't have a GPS tracker installed. If you'd like to return the vehicle and exchange it for one—"

"No, no," Bernadette said, a bead of sweat dripped down her temple. "Not a big deal. Thanks for your time."

And she'd known in the recesses of her brain: rental car companies put GPS trackers *inside* the car, so they don't fall off or get stolen.

She tapped *End*. Tingling in her fingers again. The face of the tall man in the Kansas State sweatshirt in her head.

Maybe she should call Maura. Bring in a technician who could take the tracker and analyze it, see where it had come from. Perhaps they'd get lucky and be able to track where the tracker came from or who had made the purchase.

But that would take hours—or even days. And right now, Bernadette's gut was telling her she was in danger.

The Acura SUV driver removed the nozzle from the gas

tank, then sighed heavily and went into the convenience store.

Would she be putting the family in danger if she slipped the tracker onto their vehicle instead? Bernadette didn't think so. Whoever had placed the tracker on her car obviously knew what kind of car she drove—they wouldn't target an SUV.

But she stared at the Iowa plates. The SUV had come from the north, so it was probably going the opposite direction from Bernadette, maybe even back to Iowa. If she *was* being tracked, her stalker would notice a U-turn. It might warn her pursuer that Bernadette had found the GPS tracker. She wanted to buy more time, not force the issue.

She gripped the GPS tracker tightly in her hand and walked into the convenience store. The man was nowhere to be seen—in the bathroom, probably—and the kids were bouncing around the aisles, one screaming for candy, the other for pop. She took a breath and strode to the cash register.

"Pump three."

The clerk tapped on the register and handed her the change—a dollar and two dimes.

"Is there a hotel around here?"

The clerk nodded and pointed north. "Turn left on Madison. There's a Cartwheel Suites on your right."

"Great, thanks."

She walked back to her car, trying her best not to hurry—she hadn't seen anyone, but that didn't mean they weren't watching her.

The engine started up, and she drove off with a full tank. She looked in the rearview mirror. No one pulled out behind her.

Less than a mile later, she turned left onto Madison, noticing she was still following the signs for Highway 45. A couple of minutes later, the Cartwheel Suites sign, bright and bold, rose into her view on the right. She turned into the parking lot, then around the back of the hotel. No one pulled off the highway.

She drove to the back of the lot, next to a dumpster, and stopped the car. She got out and stuck the tracker to the side of the dumpster.

To the uninformed, it might appear as if she had stopped for the night. Unless people were physically following her—or had other ways to track her—this might buy her a reprieve until tomorrow morning.

But if they had known enough to stick a tracker on her car at Taycheedah, they probably knew she was going to Lost Dish and investigating a murder in Banner Crossing.

Maura. She'd told Bernadette to call if anything was suspicious. And the GPS tracker was suspicious. She picked up her phone—

Wait. If they were tracking her car, were they tracking her phone, too? Location information, who she called, who called her—and *their* location information, too? Could she even call Maura safely? Yes, the phone was government-issued, with a ton of annoying data protection and anti-malware software on the device, but her fear was running in overdrive. Maybe her pursuers had bribed or compromised someone in the CSAB IT department.

She got back in the rental car, shut the door, and closed her eyes. Getting rid of the tracker might have given her half a day or so to get herself somewhere Parr Medical wouldn't expect. The investigation could be quick and dirty. The dead man could have self-administered the poison; Maura had intimated as much. Kep might scoff at the ease of the assignment, but—

Bernadette opened her eyes. Kep.

If Warden Fisk had thought Kep was with her, he might be in danger, too. She shook her head—was her imagination running away with her? There was nothing Annika had said to make her think people would be after her. And Kep hadn't even come into the prison on any of the interviews with Annika.

How many trackers were there? Had anyone at CSAB given information to Parr Medical?

Bernadette smacked the steering wheel. She didn't have enough information. She was jumping to conclusions. And she was scared.

Worse, she didn't know who to trust.

She put the car into gear and drove out the back lot, turning onto a back road, and a few minutes later joined Highway 45 a couple of miles north of the motel.

She glanced at the clock; still plenty of time to pick up Kep.

Hang on.

She *did* know who to trust. She could trust Kep. He might be in danger, too. She was pretty sure she could trust Maura, but Kep didn't know enough about Annika—or really anything Bernadette had found—for him to be setting her up.

Maybe Kep would call her paranoid or make overly intellectual jokes at her expense. That would have bothered her at one time—maybe even a couple of months ago. But she could deal with Kep calling her names—it was better than getting killed on the side of the road or in a staged riot at Taycheedah.

She set her jaw and pushed the accelerator down. The Michigan state line was still eighty miles away.

She had someone else she could trust, too. Maybe not with her heart, but certainly with her life.

Barlow might have been a cheating husband who turned her world upside down six months ago, but he'd help her out —he might not be happy about putting a car rental and lodging on his credit card, but Bernadette would pay him back as soon as she got back. And he could get some free airline miles out of it.

She picked up her phone. Barlow could find her a decent short-term house rental near Banner Crossing.

Chapter Five

WHEN BERNADETTE PULLED UP TO THE CURB IN FRONT OF the Houghton County Airport, Dr. Woodhead was sitting on a concrete bench in front of the baggage claim area, his arms folded, his eyes staring straight ahead, his glasses slipped down his nose, his bearded chin resting on his upper chest. He leaned forward slightly as Bernadette's car stopped, then slapped his knees and stood.

She popped the trunk, got out of the car, and ran around the rear to grab his suitcase out of his hand.

"I'm perfectly capable—" he began, both their hands on his suitcase.

Bernadette leaned forward, her mouth next to his ear. "Listen to me," she hissed. "I've been investigating the disappearance of Annika Nakrivo's sister, and I think we've been targeted."

Kep took a step back and blinked. "You've been—what?"

"Get in the car." Bernadette hoisted the suitcase into the trunk of the rental car.

Kep didn't move.

"We've *both* been targeted, Kep," Bernadette whispered. "Get in the car."

Kep opened his mouth, closed it again, then finally spoke. "I apologize if I've misunderstood—did you say, 'we'? As in, 'you and I'? I am unaware of anything I might have done to gain visibility from those who may have wished harm on Annika's sister."

"Keep your voice down," Bernadette said, closing the trunk. "I just came from Taycheedah."

He sighed, clearly intending to convey his irritation to her. "Am I to understand you were interviewing Annika again?"

She stepped closer to him. "Get in the fucking car, Kep." She walked to the driver's side door, opened it, and got in. A moment later, the passenger's side door opened and Kep got in, too.

"I'm afraid I don't understand what you're talking about."

"Ever since my first visit to see Annika in prison," Bernadette said, trying to keep her nerves calm, "I've been trying to find out what happened to her sister. I've found out Annika's real name, and I've found out her sister—Marguerite Kerovic—disappeared a few years ago. A couple of months ago, I tracked down something of Annika's and found an SD card with some encrypted files in a folder called *Marguerite*. And now"—she took a deep breath—"maybe the people behind Marguerite's disappearance have targeted us, too."

"Why would they target me?" Kep asked. "I am simply an investigator with a highly developed sense of smell. I have not even *seen* Miss Nakrivo since her arrest."

"Yeah, it's baffling, but I don't have any other explanation. So we have some things to figure out."

He folded his arms. "*Smother'd in errors, feeble, shallow, weak, the folded meaning of your words' deceit.*"

"Oh, settle down with your Shakespearian deceit quotes, Kep. Parr Medical hired Annika, and if we can figure out what they were up to—and prove it—the world will be a lot better off."

"The end justifies the means."

"That's Sophocles, not Shakespeare, you heretic." Bernadette's shoulders were still tight, but she managed a smile.

"True enough." He narrowed his eyes. "Yet you still have been deceiving me these last few months."

Bernadette hesitated. "I had to keep this under wraps. The Nakrivo investigation was officially closed, but we haven't caught the people who paid for Kymer Thompson's murder."

"You are justifying your lie of omission."

"It's called plausible deniability, Kep, and don't think for a moment of getting high and mighty on me. I didn't want you to know so you wouldn't have to lie for me."

Kep grunted, but said nothing more.

Bernadette glanced around; it didn't appear that anyone was paying attention to them in the pickup zone in front of baggage claim. "When I got to Taycheedah, the clerk thought you were with me, and I think the warden did, too. But I got a bad feeling."

"What do you mean by 'a bad feeling'?"

Bernadette shook her head. "I can't explain it, but I knew I was in danger. I turned around and got out of there. Fifteen minutes later, I'm talking to Maura and she said there was some sort of incident at Taycheedah."

"What kind of incident? Such as a prisoner escaping, or some kind of health hazard?"

"I don't know," Bernadette said, putting the car in gear. "Maura's still getting details. Look, you know the death in

Michigan isn't up to your usual level of mysterious circumstances."

"It is simply an excuse for you to continue your investigation of Miss Nakrivo's sister without drawing undue attention from CSAB management."

"Right. Sorry we dragged you all the way out here."

Kep nodded. "Perhaps you should inform me of everything you've been keeping from me."

Bernadette took a deep breath. It would be a long story: the Taycheedah clerk asking Bernadette to go get Kep, the man in the Kansas State sweatshirt in the parking lot, the GPS tracker she found on her car...

Oh, wait: Kep didn't know about Annika's roommate in Miami, the SD card found in the gusle—ugh. It would be an even longer story.

"This could take a while," Bernadette said.

Kep blinked. "Do I detect the scent of maple syrup?"

❧

Bernadette pulled into the parking lot of the Up North Motel on River Street. Lost Dish was smaller than Bernadette expected. A three-block stretch of River Street served as its downtown. A hardware store on one side of the street, a diner on the other side, and the Up North Motel—which had a grand total of twelve rooms.

The parking lot held only two cars: on the far side of the lot, away from the buildings, sat a small ten-year-old faded red Mazda sedan, with rust showing on the bottom of the fenders behind the wheels, and a newer black Lexus, parked diagonally across two spaces right in front of the hotel's office entrance.

Bernadette pulled into a space about ten yards from the

Lexus in front of the second building and turned off the engine. "Leave your bags in the trunk." Bernadette got out of the car, and Kep followed her around the Lexus into the motel office.

At the counter stood a tall man in a black pinstripe suit with a pale face, a shock of silver hair, and red cheeks. He wore a pair of burgundy-and-black cowboy boots that looked both expensive and ridiculous with his suit. His brows were furrowed.

"I just can't imagine how I made that kind of mistake. I thought I reserved these rooms yesterday."

Bernadette stood a few feet behind the man in the suit.

"Our system says Windfall 29 Mine company only reserved six rooms, Mr. Zorba," the clerk said, a note of sympathy in her voice. "I'm afraid we simply don't have two more rooms."

"Probably our fault," the man named Zorba said, placing a hand on the counter. "Of course, I'm willing to pay extra if you have extra suites, or if you can accommodate a rollaway in two rooms."

The clerk nodded, clicked the mouse for the computer in front of her. "Let me see what I can do."

Zorba glanced behind him, spying Bernadette. "My apologies," he said. "I hope this doesn't take too long."

The clerk clicked the mouse and tapped the keyboard. "We have one extra rollaway for an additional thirty a night."

"That will be excellent," Zorba said, giving the clerk a winning smile. "Perhaps one of your larger suites is available? We could swap for one of the two-queens rooms?"

"The suites are both taken, I'm sorry to say."

Zorba sighed. "Okay. We'll figure something out. I appreciate you accommodating one of our workers."

"Of course." The clerk tapped her chin. "Do you mind

your workers commuting from Houghton County? The airport hotel there might have availability."

"It's not ideal, but that might be our only option."

"Or you could try one of the vacation rental companies."

Zorba nodded, a touch enthusiastically. "That's a good idea. Even if they drive from Banner Crossing or Old Victoria, that's better than going all the way to the airport."

"I'm sorry I can't accommodate you, Mr. Zorba."

"Again, our own fault." He smiled again, tapping the counter. "We'll make sure we get the number of rooms right next time."

He turned on the heel of his burgundy-and-black cowboy boot and flashed Bernadette a smile. "All yours."

"Sorry for the delay," the clerk said as the door closed behind Zorba. "Give me just a moment." She disappeared through a door behind the desk.

In the parking lot, a car started up, probably the Lexus right in front of the office. The sound of tires on asphalt as the engine sounds faded.

"What do you think?" Bernadette asked Kep.

"What do I think about what?"

"We're not planning on staying at this hotel, so if we cancel our reservations now, he'll be able to accommodate his workers. Barlow booked a cabin in Banner Crossing under his name, so the people following us might not find us."

"On one hand, I'm sure he would appreciate that," Kep said.

Bernadette raised her eyebrows.

"On the other hand," Kep said, "if the people you believe are following us—"

"*We* believe are following us," Bernadette said.

"Of course, yes, *we*—if they see we canceled our reservations without checking in, they'll look in alternate locations. It could place us in greater danger."

"Good point," Bernadette said.

The hotel clerk returned to her place behind the desk, a folder in her hand. "Good afternoon, and welcome to the Up North Hotel. How can I help you?"

Bernadette stepped up to the counter. "Checking in."

"Give me just a second," the young woman behind the counter said. She had a smattering of freckles across her small nose and high cheeks. Her nametag read *Darcy Moncrief, Lost Dish, Michigan.*

Bernadette blinked; where had she seen the name *Moncrief?* She turned and looked at the door. "Who was that?"

Darcy raised her head. "Victor Zorba. He works for Windfall 29."

"Windfall what?"

"Windfall 29. The copper mine."

"Oh, I see." Bernadette cocked her head. "Booked quite a few rooms, huh?"

Darcy rolled her eyes, then lowered her voice a register to imitate Zorba's voice. "'We'll make sure we get the right number of rooms next time.'" She shrugged. "Please."

Bernadette was silent, hoping she'd continue.

"Not the first time he's messed up his reservation. He comes in here with his sweet-as-pie attitude and expects us to accommodate him."

"Really?" Bernadette stared at the door to the hotel, as if she expected Zorba to materialize.

Darcy Moncrief sighed. "Maybe I'm too hard on him. He *is* a nice man. And he gives a lot of business to the hotel. To be honest, I'd probably be out of a job if he didn't have his workers stay here."

"High maintenance customer?"

"You said it, not me." Darcy smiled. "Name on the reservation?"

"Woodhead and Becker." Bernadette took out her credit card and placed it on the desk.

Darcy Moncrief typed on her computer keyboard. "Two rooms, five nights?"

"Right." Bernadette tilted her head. "Does everyone bend over backward for Windfall 29?"

"In Lost Dish?" Darcy shrugged. "People need copper. And jobs. The mine was doing fine until a few years ago."

"Did something happen then?"

"The CEO had a stroke in the middle of a board meeting. He left the company to his son, and the company started going downhill."

"Three cheers for nepotism," Bernadette said.

Darcy turned to her workstation and entered Bernadette's information. "There's hardly any copper left in those mines, so Windfall 29 has tried other stuff. Every couple months, they're advertising new businesses. New opportunities for jobs." She motioned to the rack of brochures next to the counter. "I get to see them all firsthand."

Bernadette stepped next to the rack. "These all Windfall 29 businesses?"

"About a third of those. A boat rental company at the marina. Cross-country skiing tours in the winter. A resort—well, it's really just a little group of cabins out by Porcupine Lake. But those retail positions pay minimum wage. Compared to a mineworker's salary?" Then Darcy shook her head. "I didn't even mention the craziest one."

"What?"

"The underground amusement park."

Bernadette furrowed her brow.

"Windfall 29's making an amusement park out of the copper mine. High-speed rides through the old tunnels."

Bernadette blinked. "Sounds crazy."

Darcy stepped to her right, leaned over the counter, and tapped on a brochure in the top row.

Bernadette bent to look. *Windfall Adventures: The World's First Underground Amusement Park.*

"He says it'll employ hundreds of people." Darcy rolled her eyes and turned back to the computer. "I appreciate his optimism, I guess." She stopped typing for a moment.

"Something wrong?"

"You're from CSAB."

"I am."

"My—" Darcy hesitated. "My mom is the one who found the body."

Of course; she'd seen the name *Moncrief* in the report. Bernadette sneaked a look at Kep, whose expression hadn't changed. "Is—is that a problem?"

"She just—she's been acting weird since then. I ask her what's wrong, she says it's work, and I bet it's something to do with finding the body down in Banner Crossing."

The gears started turning in Bernadette's head. "Did she say anything else?"

"She says she can't talk about the open case, so no. I hope I don't get her in trouble—maybe she wasn't supposed to tell me CSAB was taking over the case." Darcy leaned forward. "But I think something's up. I read the news story online a couple weeks ago—'apparent suicide'—but I bet my mom doesn't think so."

Bernadette shifted her weight from foot to foot. This might not be the open-and-shut case she was hoping for. "Your mom is one of the first people we plan on talking to tomorrow."

Darcy nodded, typed in a few more keystrokes, then picked up four keycards and ran them through a machine connected to the computer. "Okay," she said, handing the cards to Bernadette, "rooms five and six on the first floor, out the front door of the building on your right. Have a pleasant stay."

"Nice to meet you, Darcy. Sorry to take so much of your time."

"Don't be sorry—you have no clue how bored I am here. Read me your grocery list, and I'll applaud."

Bernadette gave Darcy a smile as she and Kep walked out the door, back to Bernadette's sedan.

"Good," Kep said. "Now the clerk will remember us if asked."

"Yep. Now we need to get another rental vehicle."

"I didn't see a car rental location in the vicinity."

"I called Barlow to take care of it," Bernadette said.

Kep blinked. "And he wasn't suspicious?"

"I used to go under fake names all the time before my demotion." Bernadette gritted her teeth on the last word. "He was suspicious, yeah, and he reminded me we weren't married anymore, but he still did it without too many questions."

Kep nodded. "The 'need-to-know' basis?"

"Yep." Bernadette only wished that Sophie hadn't been at softball practice. She wanted more than to leave a message on her voicemail, then changed the subject. "The only place to rent a vehicle in this town is the U-Move-It on State Highway 64." She pointed back the way they came. "Back down Rockland Road, then across the Lost Dish River Bridge, and about half a mile. Barlow said it was next to the boat rental place."

Kep took off his glasses and rubbed his eyes. "Am I to understand you are considering walking?"

"I found a GPS tracker on the car, Kep." Bernadette looked down at the ground. "Someone is following us, and they know what car I'm driving. I suspect they'll come looking for us, and our names are on the reservation at this motel. So once they get here—could be five minutes or two days—they'll see my rental car in the parking lot. See whether we've checked in. But hopefully by then we'll have taken the U-Move-It pickup to the cabin in Banner Crossing."

"It does have the added advantage of placing our home base closer to the location of the death."

"You don't have to come if you don't want to. I'll drive back and pick you up."

"No," Kep said. "I—I'd rather come with you."

Bernadette raised her eyebrows. "You feeling gallant all of a sudden? Think I shouldn't walk alone by myself? It won't get dark for another couple of hours."

"No. I find your assessment of the level of danger in our situation to be compelling."

Bernadette tried not to let her jaw drop open. "You believe me?"

Kep shuffled his feet as they got to the car. "I'm saying the likelihood of us being in danger suffices to persuade me to take the same preventative measures as you."

Bernadette nodded and popped the trunk.

Kep held up his hand. "What are you doing?"

"If we're being followed, I don't want to come back here. So we should take our suitcases with us."

Kep shook his head. "As you said, we don't know if those following us will come in five minutes or two days, but if they come in the next half hour, certainly they would see the two of us rolling our suitcases for two kilometers down the main street of Lost Dish."

Bernadette paused. "Maybe we shouldn't walk at all, then. Think this town has a taxi?"

Kep turned and went back toward the hotel lobby. Bernadette followed. As he opened the door, he smiled at Darcy Moncrief and turned to his left, stopping at an ATM.

"They could track our financial transactions," Bernadette hissed under her breath.

"Precisely," Kep replied in a low voice, inserting his card. "But we have reservations and proof we've checked in at this motel. An ATM transaction at the same motel won't provide any additional clues to our location. And—as you just said—if they can track our financial transactions, it behooves us to have as much cash available to us as possible."

Bernadette nodded. Her mortgage payment had just gone through, so taking a few hundred dollars would make things tight for the rest of the month—but she'd worry about it later.

She took a few steps to the counter, where she looked at the rack of brochures. Below the Windfall 29 businesses, a few smaller brochures and business cards: Mathers & Evans Tax and Accounting services. Upper Peninsula Tree Removal —Free Quotes!

Ah—there it was: a business card for Lost Dish Taxi Service. The rideshare companies had apparently not killed off all the taxis that took cash in this small town.

The machine hummed, then spat out a large stack of twenty-dollar bills. Kep took the cash and his card, then stepped back. "Five hundred is the daily limit on this machine."

Bernadette took out her ATM card.

When Bernadette's wallet was five hundred dollars fatter, they walked out of the lobby. In the late afternoon, the sun was bright, and the pavement was hot. "We need to get to U-

Move-It in the next hour," Bernadette said. "Maybe we should call the taxi service from the hotel."

"If we make one additional stop before summoning a taxicab," Kep said, pointing across Rockland Road to a convenience store, "we can kill the proverbial two birds with a single stone." There was no traffic—not even at this time of day—and they hurried across the road.

Ten minutes later, they owned two new but inexpensive prepaid smartphones. While Kep completed his purchase, Bernadette activated her smartphone and called the taxi service. After a few minutes, a green-and-white Chevy pulled up at the café next to the motel, where Kep and Bernadette were waiting with their suitcases.

As the taxi came to a stop in front of the U-Move-It, Bernadette gave the cab driver an extra twenty. "If anyone asks, you dropped us at the marina," she said. "We asked you about boat rentals."

"Sure, boat rentals. The marina. I didn't get a good look at either of you, anyway." The cab driver took the cash. "Tell Eddie that Giorgio says hi."

After getting their cases, they entered the small shop, an obnoxious electronic beep announcing their arrival. Bernadette looked around. This was an old building with brick masonry for walls. Flat cardboard boxes in varying sizes, all bearing the bright orange U-Move-It logo, were stacked against two of the walls. A counter topped with scratched beige Formica and an electronic tablet mounted on a stand stood near the back wall near the rear door. After a moment, the rear door swung open, revealing a skinny white man, possibly in his early fifties, with deeply reddened skin and light brown hair. His beard was short but unkempt, with a hint of red at the corners. His blue denim work shirt, with a sewn-in white name badge reading *Ed*, had three buttons at the top undone, showcasing a chest just as skinny and reddened as the rest of him.

Ed blinked at the two of them. "Yeah, can I help you?"

"We're renting a pickup," Bernadette said. "My—my husband called earlier with the reservation. It's under the name Barlow Finnegan."

"Yep, I remember." Ed stepped to the tablet and tapped. "You're the wife?"

"That's me."

Ed lifted his face to look at Kep. "This Mr. Finnegan?"

"No," Kep said.

"Oh—then you can't drive the pickup. Only Mr. Finnegan's spouse."

"Won't be a problem," Bernadette said.

Ed leered conspiratorially. Bernadette had to fight not to recoil; two of Ed's teeth were missing, and the other visible ones didn't look in good shape. "Yeah, good. Just need a copy of your driver's license, then we'll walk around the pickup and make sure there's no damage."

Kep adjusted his glasses slightly, placing them down a little farther on his nose. "Perhaps I'll wait outside."

Bernadette nodded; she'd caught it too: a whiff of burnt plastic, a slight tang of ammonia. The rotted teeth, the smell —Ed had all the signs of meth use. The smell had been faint in the taxi, too.

Aha—Giorgio assumed Bernadette and Kep were buying meth from the U-Move-It owner. She suppressed a grin, then breathed through her mouth and dug in her purse for her license as Kep left the office, letting the front door close behind him.

As Bernadette drove the tiny white-and-orange pickup across the Lost Dish River Bridge and turned right onto U.S. 45, heading south toward Banner Crossing, a chuckle came from the passenger seat. She glanced over; Kep had his glasses off, pinching the bridge of his nose, and his shoulders quivered.

She narrowed her eyes. "Are you laughing at our tiny creamsicle pickup truck?"

He kept giggling.

"Are you laughing at *me*?"

Kep caught his breath. "*And this, our life, exempt from public haunt, finds tongues in trees, books in the running brooks, sermons in stones, and good in everything.*"

Bernadette gritted her teeth; she hadn't liked Shakespeare in high school, and Kep's constant quotes hadn't endeared the Bard to her any further. "What's that supposed to mean?"

"Though the perils are great, they remain distant, and the resulting situation we find ourselves in is ridiculous."

"I thought you were taking me seriously." She blinked a few times as the road narrowed to two lanes. Even if he was making fun of her, at least he was going along with it.

"Finding the humor in our circumstances does *not* mean I am failing to take this seriously." Kep clicked his tongue. "I caught myself thinking I'm a character in an espionage film." He held his hand out, palm up, as if he were holding Yorick's skull during a *Hamlet* soliloquy. "'Quick, Bernadette, our cover is surely blown. We must hide deep in the woods until we figure out what nefarious scheme the terrorists have cooked up for us!' At least I cannot complain of dullness when I find myself on these adventures with you." He dropped his hand, then sat back in his seat.

Bernadette glanced over at Kep. He grinned through his beard, but his eyes were turned down at the outer corners, with worry in the creases of his forehead. Ah—humor as a defense mechanism. Bernadette turned back to the road. Rare for Kep, but not unheard of.

"Whether we're hiding in a cabin in the forest or not," Bernadette said evenly, "we still have a case to solve. You read the file. Any ideas?"

He exhaled—a more relaxed breath than he'd taken in a few minutes. "Our victim is Evan McMichael, who was sixty-eight years old, never married, and lived alone. He worked as a lab technician at Washburn Medical Center in Minneapolis until he retired three years ago. Statistically speaking, it's likely he died by his own hand. I printed out the file and pored over it on the plane; usually CSAB chooses not to call for my services on such mundane cases."

"True."

"I thought I might be missing a critical piece of evidence I would need to unearth with a great deal of effort." He tapped his fingers on the armrest. "Now that I've discovered our investigation is merely a ruse for you to further your work on the disappearance of Annika Nakrivo's sister, I'm more convinced than ever our investigation will conclude that Mr. McMichael took his own life."

"Even though the cop who found his body doesn't think so?"

Kep crinkled his nose. "Statistics show no homicides in this county for three years. Any law enforcement representative looking for excitement in an otherwise dull job might see foul play where none exists."

Bernadette gripped the steering wheel tightly. Kep was right—this looked like a suicide to her, too. With the two of them potentially facing danger, he'd probably be eager to wrap this up and get back home—just like her. Bernadette wouldn't have time to continue trying to find out about

Marguerite's expired debit card, but getting out of immediate danger was her priority.

"What about McMichael's trailer getting shot up?" she asked.

"The bullets match the semi-automatic rifle found in a neighboring trailer."

"Belonging to Gabriel Constantine," Bernadette added.

"Mr. Constantine has been in and out of both jail and mental health facilities in the last five years," Kep continued. "The likeliest explanation is he experienced a paranoid episode and fired—what was it?—fifteen rounds into Mr. McMichael's trailer."

"After a near-death experience," Bernadette said, "do you think Evan McMichael would be more likely to poison himself?"

Kep smoothed his beard with the fingers of his left hand. "I am uncomfortable postulating about Mr. McMichael's state of mind."

"If we could study the crime scene, we might get a better idea of what our victim was like. We might find something the locals missed."

Kep nodded. "While I have my doubts the sheriff's office overlooked a suicide note, other signs might exist. I'm in favor of meeting local law enforcement first thing tomorrow."

Bernadette cleared her throat.

"What is it?"

"We both want to finish this up as soon as possible, right?"

"Not at the expense of shoddy investigative work, but you are correct."

"I was thinking we should stop at the crime scene before we go to the cabin."

Kep cocked his head. "We have yet to check in with the local sheriff."

Bernadette shrugged. "I have my badge. It's a thirty-minute drive to Lost Dish. Our cabin is just a couple of miles away from the site." She tapped the clock on the dashboard. "We've got about two hours of daylight left. If we go back to Lost Dish now, it'll be dark once we get the paperwork sorted out and get back here. It'll potentially save us a couple of hours tomorrow."

"You wouldn't be following protocol."

Bernadette cackled softly as the truck crested a hill and a sign reading *Banner Crossing 8 Miles* appeared on the side of the road next to the aspens growing twenty feet from the shoulder. "There are two things we need to do here, Kep." She held up her index finger, keeping her left hand on the wheel. "One: we need to appear to the outside world as if everything's proceeding as planned." She held up a second finger. "Two: we need to minimize anyone—and I mean *anyone*—being able to track us down or find us."

Kep scoffed. "And to you, that means entering the crime scene without informing the Porcupine County Sheriff's Office."

Bernadette nodded. "Tell the sheriff we'll meet tomorrow morning at the office and show up thirty minutes late. Arrange an interview with a suspect and not show up."

"The victim's sister is still in town," Kep ventured. "We could make an appointment for her to come to the sheriff's office, but then go to her hotel room an hour beforehand instead."

"You're getting the idea."

"So you're suggesting that we investigate the crime scene tonight, arrange a viewing with the sheriff for tomorrow morning, but arrive late?"

"Exactly."

Kep folded his arms. "I know it's important to you to regain the previous level of employ you attained at CSAB. Doesn't your conduct with local law enforcement factor into any decisions about potential promotions?"

Bernadette nodded. "But I've got a daughter I want to see grow up, Kep." She bit her lip. She'd never considered it—but now that she'd said it, maybe getting back to being an agent *wasn't* as important as she thought. Her job had a certain amount of danger, but CSAB had been the driving force of her career, and—well, if her mother were still alive, she might have suggested Bernadette's singular focus on her career drove Barlow into another woman's arms.

Bernadette turned right at the corner onto Highway 28, passing Saucy's Co-Op, with its neon *Open 24 Hours* sign featuring a burned-out H.

"Are we close to arrival?" Kep asked.

They passed a pub on the right with a faded *St. Matthew's Pub* sign. "The trailer park is just past St. Matthew Road—if the pub is any indication, we're close."

Bernadette was correct: after less than a quarter-mile, Sugar Maple Estates was on the right just past the intersection of St. Matthew Road; the paved driveway stood a few feet past the wooden sign with the hand-carved letters. After about a hundred feet, the asphalt gave way to hard-packed gravel.

"Not a big park," Bernadette murmured. Three mobile homes were on each side of the wide gravel road. The rectangular structures, four of them with covered carports, were tidy if old. Three of the trailers had well-kept gardens in front.

A three-foot-high chain-link fence encircled the last trailer on the left, with police tape wound through the frame.

Neither a covered carport nor a garden were on the lot. Wild clover and low bushes filled the front yard. The beige aluminum siding of the trailer had about a dozen pieces of duct tape stuck in random places, and a large piece of cardboard covered one of the window openings.

"We're obviously in the right place," Bernadette said as she slowed the pickup to a stop and shifted into *Park*.

Kep placed each of his hands on his knees, closed his eyes, and sucked in air through his teeth. Then he slapped his knees and opened the door. "All right," he said, "let's embark on this course of action."

They walked toward the trailer and Kep opened the gate in the chain-link fence and Bernadette entered first.

"The gate wasn't secured," said Bernadette.

"Perhaps the sheriff assumed the police tape would sufficiently dissuade anyone from entering."

"Speaking of tape," Bernadette said, stepping next to the trailer. She examined one piece of duct tape stuck to the siding, lifting a side of it carefully with her fingernail. "Yep—bullet hole."

"I assume every piece of duct tape I see covers a bullet hole," Kep said.

"Our victim made a few band-aid repairs on the trailer."

"One challenge springs to mind," Kep said, following a few paces behind Bernadette.

"What?"

"I believe the sheriff's office possesses the key to the trailer. As we haven't coordinated with them, we don't have the means to enter the domicile."

"True." Bernadette scanned the side of the trailer, following the pieces of duct tape with her eyes. The shots, evenly spaced, were about five feet above the bottom of the trailer. And with the bottom of the trailer's front door about two feet off the ground—

There it was—a piece of duct tape over the deadbolt lock in the front door.

Kep saw it at the same time as Bernadette. "It appears Mr. Constantine solved the problem for us."

Bernadette climbed up the steps to the front door of the trailer. While the deadbolt had been shattered, the knob below the duct tape was scratched but otherwise untouched.

She turned the doorknob, and the hinges creaked as the door swung in.

Chapter Six

As they entered the trailer, Bernadette took out her phone, tapped a few times, then scanned the screen. "After the shooting, they arrested Gabriel Constantine."

"Which trailer is his?" Kep asked.

Bernadette scrolled to the next screen. "He lives in the trailer on the other side of the driveway."

"Where is Mr. Constantine currently?"

"He was out on bail after the shooting," Bernadette said. "But when the police found McMichael's body, they revoked Constantine's bail. He's now in the county jail in Lost Dish."

Kep took a step forward, then paused. "Oh—gloves."

Bernadette rummaged around in her purse and pulled out two pairs of latex gloves, handing a pair to Kep. "These might be a little small for you, but better than nothing."

The trailer was cozy, with a small kitchen across from the front door. Next to the kitchen, the bathroom door was slightly ajar. In the living room sat a narrow sofa and a tiny coffee table. A television was mounted above a horizontal bookcase. Beyond the living room was the bedroom door.

Past the kitchen was a small dining area with two windows above it—one window covered with cardboard.

Though outdated, the interior was clean and tidy. Bernadette had seen her share of trailers, and this was the cleanest of them all. A faint sour smell—probably left over from the dead body and the cleaning products—remained.

Kep pushed up his glasses to the bridge of his nose, closed his eyes, and inhaled deeply.

"It's been over a week," Bernadette whispered. "You won't smell anyth—"

"Shh," Kep said. He shook out his arms to the tips of his fingers, then inhaled again. He turned ninety degrees and repeated the process, then twice more, until he'd made a complete circle. Then he opened his eyes. "If you would be so kind as to refresh my memory, what was the poison discovered in Mr. McMichael's system?"

"Unknown," Bernadette replied. "Something highly acidic, but the toxicology report hasn't come back yet. The medical examiner has ruled out hydrochloric acid. Maura, Lesley, and I thought it might be some kind of pesticide."

"I have not identified the scent of any type of toxic pesticide in the trailer," Kep said. "If Mr. McMichael purchased some, he didn't store it here. Is there a shed or outbuilding?"

"A utility shed."

"We must gain access before we leave." Kep turned toward the bedroom at the back of the trailer, then stopped. "They found the body in the kitchen, correct?"

Bernadette took her phone out as she pointed to the small kitchen table. "Next to the chair, on the floor, face down."

"And if I remember correctly, the report mentioned a glass on the table next to him."

She tapped on the screen. "Yes. The police report notes there was a smell of whiskey in the glass."

"I assume they took the glass into evidence?"

Bernadette scrolled, then nodded.

"Is there a picture of the glass?"

Bernadette scrolled again, then tapped. A photo of a short, rounded-bottomed glass appeared. She showed the screen to Kep.

He lifted his glasses and squinted at the screen, then gave a curt nod and turned to the kitchen cabinet. He opened the first door, then glanced up and down. "For a small living space, this is exceptionally well-organized."

"Mm-hmm."

He closed the first door, then opened the one next to it. "Aha," he said. "Two of those glasses are here." He pulled out a taller round-bottomed glass. "I see four of the larger glasses, but only two of the smaller ones. If the CSI team took one glass into evidence, there's one glass missing."

"McMichael might have broken one. He lived on his own —not a big reason to replace a glass."

"A reasonable explanation." He closed the cabinet, then opened the next door, then took a small step back.

"What is it?"

"I have discovered the fourth short glass."

"So he put it back in the wrong place."

Kep looked back and forth the length of the trailer. "I see nothing out of place in this room. Mr. McMichael appears to prefer a state of order and cleanliness. I doubt he would put a glass back in the wrong cabinet."

"You think someone else was here?"

Kep pointed into the open cabinet. "Do you believe the crime scene team would have dusted that glass for fingerprints?"

Bernadette folded her arms and shook her head. "Hard to know for sure, but if they didn't think there was foul play, they probably didn't go through all the drawers and cabinets, randomly fingerprinting stuff."

Kep leaned his face into the cabinet.

"What are you doing?"

"I believe this glass should be taken into evidence. Fortunately, I can detect the scents in the glass without touching it."

"And what do you smell?"

"Whiskey," Kep said. "Notes of oak, cherry, vanilla, and macadamia nut."

Bernadette had seen Kep's overactive olfactory senses before, but it never failed to amaze her. An empty glass, not used in at least a week, and he could not only identify whiskey, but the subtle flavors as if he were swishing it around in his mouth at a distillery tasting. "Wasn't the glass washed?"

"Hastily," Kep said. He opened the door under the sink. "A grocery store-brand dishwashing liquid. And while the scents of the soap have overpowered the whiskey, I am still quite able to identify the unique flavor profile."

"You're saying—you know what *kind* of whiskey it is?"

"Widewaters Reserve Bourbon. On the expensive side, but not outrageous. I believe it has a retail price of two hundred dollars a bottle."

"Not outrageous?"

Kep shrugged. "Some whiskeys are more than two thousand a bottle." He opened the cabinets underneath the counters.

"What are you looking for?"

"The location where Mr. McMichael stored his liquor."

Bernadette slumped her shoulders. "I take it you're revising your opinion on whether the victim died by suicide?"

"I simply follow where my nose leads." Kep stepped to the refrigerator and opened the door. "Inexpensive American lagers," he said. "Mr. McMichael doesn't seem the type to drink a two-hundred-dollar bottle of artisan whiskey."

"Try the small cabinet above the fridge," Bernadette said.

Kep reached up and opened the door. An off-brand fifth of vodka, a liter of cheap scotch in a plastic bottle, and an equally cheap bottle of rum. Kep glanced at Bernadette quizzically.

"It's where I kept my alcohol in my first apartment in college." Bernadette walked into the living room and bent down in front of the bookcase. "He may be neat, but he's still a bachelor."

The books were mostly non-fiction. On the bottom shelf, a few books about hiking trails in the Upper Peninsula were next to books about Keynesian economics, woodworking, strip mining, rainforest preservation, birdwatching, and global warming.

"Seems like McMichael was an environmentalist," Bernadette said. She touched the books on the top shelf, several with a decidedly small-press look: *Organic Pest Control for Beginners, Sustainable Energy for the Twenty-First Century, Nocturnal Birds of the Great Lakes,* and *Market Dynamics of Underground Economics* were four of the books whose spines had cracked, revealing heavy use. "Not exactly light reading."

"*The clamorous owl that nightly hoots and wonders at our quaint spirits,*" Kep said, pointing at a book titled *Owls of the Upper Midwest.* "I believe Mr. McMichael graduated from the University of the Upper Peninsula with a degree in biology. It follows that wildlife and the environment hold particular interest to him."

Next to the wildlife books sat several books on carpentry: *Joinery and Fine Woodworking, Mastering the Basics of the*

Craftsman, and *Woodworking with Natural Timbers*. Bernadette stood.

"Woodworking, environmental books—you think he and Constantine had some sort of disagreement? Maybe about McMichael hammering too early in the morning, or maybe he was mad about something Constantine did? Like dumping motor oil on the ground?"

"Pure conjecture," Kep said. "Does Constantine's police report make any mention of a motive?"

"I'll look." Bernadette woke up her phone and tapped the screen.

"Interesting," Kep said.

"What?"

"There are fifteen cardboard coasters from St. Matthew's Pub."

"Aha—he wasn't spending his money on bottles of expensive whiskey—he was spending it at the local bar," Bernadette said. "So he was a regular."

"If I understand your tone," Kep said, "you wish to gather more information about Mr. McMichael through a visit to the public house."

"Right. Was McMichael there in the week before he died? Did he act strange? Did he seem scared or out of sorts?"

"Perhaps he spoke of the ordeal of Constantine shooting at his domicile."

"We should be so lucky."

Kep coughed lightly. "It's possible local law enforcement has already covered this territory."

"We'll find out soon enough."

The two of them looked through the small trailer. The tidiness continued into the bedroom, and Bernadette turned to the closet. It was tiny, with a thin, accordion-style door, but the polos and flannel shirts were neatly hung and evenly spaced, as were the khaki trousers and jeans. Three pairs of shoes—brown work boots, black athletic shoes, and black dress shoes with a thin layer of dust—were at the bottom of the closet.

Bernadette pulled out the drawer of the large nightstand next to the double bed—neatly made, although the duvet cover was threadbare. The drawer took some effort to pull, but only a bottle of aspirin and a cell phone charger was in the shallow drawer. She knelt on the floor.

"Kep?"

"Anything of note?" Kep asked as he smelled each of the shirts in the closet.

"This is weird," she said. "The drawer is heavy, but hardly anything is in it. And the drawer is much shallower than the front of the drawer would suggest." She tapped on the bottom of the drawer. "I think the woodgrain of the bottom of the drawer is different than the sides." Bernadette took out the aspirin and charging cable and ran her hands along the inside edges of the drawer. Her fingertip dipped into a half-moon cutout near the back. She pulled up slightly and the bottom of the drawer lifted.

"Did you find something?" asked Kep.

"Yeah—it's a false bottom."

Under the thin piece of veneered pressboard lay five notebooks. Bernadette took them out one by one, stacking them in reverse order to how she removed them. Once she removed all five, she grabbed the one on top and started flipping through it. "A lot of times and dates and tables," Bernadette said. "I think it's something about birdwatching."

"I'm sorry—did you say 'birdwatching'?"

"Right." Bernadette hooked her thumb over her shoulder toward the living room. "Our victim might have not just liked reading about wildlife. Maybe he liked watching it, too." She looked through the top four in the stack, then grabbed the last notebook and opened it. "Huh—this one looks a little different."

"How so?"

"These tables and drawings. They're organized differently. While the others are full of notes and lots of drawings, McMichael made these tables with a little more care." She turned the first few pages. "The tables are labeled one through, let me see, eleven. And there's a row labeled A, one J, and one E, each with one digit. Then the bottom-most row is labeled 'LL,' with six numbers—two groups of three separated by a slash."

Kep stepped over and looked over Bernadette's shoulder. The first table read:

A: 3
J: 7
E: 0
LL: 46 43 6.2 / 89 13 55.5

Below, a drawing of a tree, with an unusually detailed branch system, and an X nestled about two-thirds of the way toward the top.

"It's gotta be birdwatching," Bernadette said, tapping the tree drawing. "A drawing of the tree with the nest in it."

"Perhaps the table is information about the nest."

Bernadette's eyes darted between the rows. "Maybe the 'A' stands for *adults*, and the 'E' stands for *eggs*. What would 'J' stand for? Aren't baby birds called 'chicks' or 'hatchlings' or something?"

"Usually 'chicks,'" Kep said.

"Then I don't know what the 'J' stands for." Bernadette

flipped through the pages with the tables: they were all simi-lar, with the same rows and numbers, then a drawing of a tree with an X. "You know, if it weren't for the drawings of these trees, I'd think this was a ledger or something."

"Code for something else?"

"Yes." She looked back in the drawer. "This is the last notebook. He must have written this down recently."

After ten more minutes of Kep searching the room and Bernadette reading the notebooks, the sunlight through the bedroom window faded.

"I'd prefer to look through the utility shed while we still have sunlight," Kep said. "If we can find an open container of toxic pesticide, we could be a step closer to determining the cause of death."

"Yeah," Bernadette said, placing the five notebooks back below the false bottom of the drawer. "I don't see anything suggesting why McMichael would have taken his own life. A motive for murder isn't jumping out at me, either."

Kep rubbed his bearded chin in thought. "Given the glass in the wrong cabinet, as well as the remnants of a whiskey we cannot locate, I believe it would be prudent to treat this case as a homicide."

"Or at the very least, someone came in and disturbed the scene," Bernadette said, putting the aspirin and the phone charger back in the drawer. "So much for getting in and out of this investigation quickly."

"I would like to get many of these items back to the lab," Kep said. "I am particularly interested in the misplaced glass."

"Yeah, me too. We'll take it when we come back tomorrow morning."

"You don't wish to antagonize local law enforcement?"

Bernadette shook her head. "The whiskey glass requires chain of custody. Assuming we could even get it established with the trailer being unlocked. Tomorrow, we'll come back with the sheriff and ask for the glass to be bagged and fingerprinted."

They stepped out of the bedroom into the living room. Law enforcement had missed more than the misplaced glass on their sweep—Bernadette was sure of it.

Chapter Seven

"I PREFER TO CONCENTRATE ON THE PHYSICAL EVIDENCE." Kep pointed across to the small table in the trailer's kitchen. "Although the evidence is not conclusive, the glass and the missing whiskey suggest a second person was sharing a drink with Mr. McMichael at the kitchen table. When McMichael was unconscious, the other person hastily washed the glass, put it in the cabinet, and took the whiskey with them."

"After McMichael was unconscious?"

"That is what the evidence suggests."

Bernadette sucked in air through her teeth. "Great. Now we'll have to contact Maura to update her."

"Is that a problem?"

"I'm worried about being tracked, remember? How are we going to call Maura without giving away our location? We're not supposed to be in Banner Crossing tonight."

"Will there be a problem contacting her with our prepaid smartphones?"

"If the people after us are monitoring Maura's phone, yes. They could get our burner numbers."

Kep shifted from foot to foot. "Technically, a burner

phone refers to a device which can only receive calls and text messages. We have cameras and web access—"

"The point, Kep, is that they could get our numbers. And then they could track our—our prepaid smartphones. And we don't want that."

Kep thought for a moment. "We'll contact the lieutenant tomorrow on our regular phones when we approach the sheriff's office. Our pursuers will expect a check-in call."

They walked out of the front door of the trailer. Bernadette stood next to the small pickup truck and stood next to the driver's side door for a moment, looking around; no one was there. She went around the back of the trailer to find Kep.

A wooden shed, about six feet high, eight feet wide, and perhaps five feet deep, abutted the rear of the trailer. Double doors with ironwork for hinges and the latch adorned the front.

"No padlock," Bernadette observed.

"Which unfortunately means we have no way of telling if the contents of the shed have been compromised since Mr. McMichael's death."

"Right." Bernadette sighed as she reached out and unhooked the latch. The hinges groaned slightly as the door swung out.

A push mower sat inside, along with a canvas grass-catcher. Two bottles of Neem oil were in plastic jugs on a metal baker's rack, next to a large bag of diatomaceous earth. On the top rack stood five clear plastic spray bottles, the contents in an assortment of muted colors.

"Could any of these be our culprit?" Bernadette asked.

"All non-toxic to humans," Kep said. He leaned forward and sniffed, moving his head left and right as he did so. "Garlic spray." He turned his head to the next bottle. "Chili powder and liquid soap. These would give our victim, at worst, mild diarrhea. No, we're looking for something toxic. I smell nothing like that here."

Bernadette pointed to a small drawer organizer that sat on a small table opposite the baker's rack. "Screws and nails?"

In the drawers, however, were tiny rings, less than a half-inch in diameter. Some were even smaller. Each drawer held a different color, in every color of the rainbow, and mostly in bright colors. At first, Bernadette thought they were plastic, but as she ran her finger over the top of them, the metallic smoothness of aluminum was cool to the touch.

"What are these?" Bernadette asked, then snapped her fingers. "Birdwatching. I bet these are bird bands. So he can track what birds he's seen."

"Banding birds requires a bit of hands-on effort."

"He was a biology major, wasn't he? Maybe he trained for that kind of thing."

Another ten minutes of searching revealed nothing else of interest. Bernadette closed the shed, and they trudged back to the orange-and-white truck.

"Waddaya say, Kep, can I buy you a drink at the local bar?" Bernadette asked as they got into the tiny pickup. "Meet some new friends, have some friendly conversation?"

Kep smiled. "In addition to our fact-finding goals, I'm sure I could use a libation."

"Long day."

"It would have been a long day simply with the flights and the drive out to Banner Crossing. Now that you have informed me our lives might be in danger, I fear I'll need some artificial alteration of my brain chemistry to fall asleep."

"And a drink would do it, huh?"

"Perhaps more than one."

It was less than five minutes from the driveway of Sugar

Maple Estates to the parking lot of St. Matthew's Pub. Bernadette parked at the end of the row; there were six or seven other vehicles in the lot, mostly pickups, though a black Lexus sedan had parked diagonally across two spaces on the far side of the lot, away from the bar, and a burnt orange Kia Soul parked next to the side of the building.

The sun dipped behind the hills as Bernadette and Kep made their way to the front door of the pub. Kep pushed the heavy wooden door open, and Bernadette stepped around him to enter. She blinked as her eyes adjusted to the low light. A long bar stretched from the front door down the left-hand side of the narrow room, a large flat-screen TV above the bar showing a baseball game. On the right, four high-top tables were in front of a dartboard on the back wall. A sign for the bathroom, with an arrow at a ninety-degree angle, hung to the left of the dartboard. Three people sat at the bar, and at a table on the right sat a couple: a tall man in his early fifties with long white hair and a blonde woman ten years his junior with the biggest blue eyes Bernadette had ever seen. The couple stared at Bernadette and Kep as they walked toward the bar.

At the right-hand side of the bar, a silver-haired man in a pinstriped suit stood with his back to Kep and Bernadette. He was talking to the bartender, a white woman in her forties with curly brown hair and a strong jawline. The man leaned forward, almost dipping his red tie into the glass of whiskey on the bar, and the bartender stepped back, crossing her arms. Over the conversations and the noise of the baseball game, Bernadette couldn't make out what they were saying, but the man's mannerisms struck a chord in Bernadette. Ah, yes: the burgundy-and-black cowboy boots.

"Victor Zorba?"

"Who?" Kep asked.

"The man at the bar in the suit with the cowboy boots. Isn't he the same guy who was trying to get the desk clerk at our hotel to get two more rooms for his workers?"

Kep pushed his glasses up on his nose. "I cannot be entirely certain from this angle, but it looks like him." He paused. "Especially his footwear. Shall we attempt to get a closer look?"

They walked across the room and stood at the bar. Kep turned toward Bernadette and she looked over his shoulder at the man in the suit.

"Yep, it's Victor Zorba, all right. I wonder what he's doing here?"

Kep shrugged. "A town the size of Lost Dish has only a few establishments such as this."

"Maybe this is the closest to his house—" Bernadette began, but she stopped talking as the bartender raised her voice.

"Even if the bar *was* for sale, Mr. Zorba, I'm not sure your offer has taken into account the assets of the equipment—"

Zorba replied, but Bernadette couldn't make out the words. He stood, relaxed and smiling, talking with gentle movements of his hands. After a moment, the bartender dropped her hands to her sides.

"Look," the bartender said, "I guess that is a pretty generous offer, but it's a big change. I have to think about it."

Zorba nodded and took a step back, straightening his suit jacket. "I'm not trying to lowball you, even though I know you're in a tough spot. Perhaps you can appreciate that I'm coming from a position of concern."

"I do appreciate that."

"If you kept the equipment, you'd be able to continue your business in another location."

"I've already got a successful business in this location. Moving takes time and effort."

"Think about my offer and see if it's worth your while, then." Zorba took his whiskey, then turned away from the bartender. Bernadette caught his eye and nodded.

Zorba sauntered over to Kep and Bernadette. "Hello again—you two were checking into the hotel in Lost Dish, weren't you?"

Kep smiled beatifically. "We reserved two rooms. I suppose you could have used them for your workers."

Zorba grinned back, though the smile didn't reach his eyes. "My own fault. I underestimated the number of experts the new equipment would require for install. Fortunately, I found lodging for them." He stuck out his hand. "Victor Zorba. I work for the mining company just west of Lost Dish."

"Windfall 29, correct?" Kep said, shaking Zorba's hand.

"Hey, that's right."

"We heard about the amusement park," Bernadette said. "Interesting way to repurpose your assets."

Zorba took a drink from his glass, then swallowed. "I don't want to brag, but I think it's one of the coolest concepts out there." He pointed back and forth between Kep and Bernadette using the hand holding his glass. "A little bird told me you two are federal investigators."

"That's correct," Kep said. "CSAB."

"The controlled substance agency, isn't it?" Zorba took another sip, then lowered his drink. "My cousin's son got caught up in meth. Such a shame." He sighed. "I can't imagine the meth problem is any worse here than in other parts of the nation."

"We're not on the drug enforcement side," Bernadette said.

Zorba cocked his head. "No? Well, then—" He stopped talking, stared at the bar for a moment, then knocked back the rest of his drink and set it next to Bernadette. "You in town for long?"

"Depends on how long our case takes," Bernadette said carefully.

Zorba took out a business card from his suit jacket pocket and held it out to Kep. "My company has resources local law enforcement doesn't. You need anything, you contact me, okay?"

"How very kind of you," Kep said, taking the card, inclining his head slightly.

Zorba nodded back. "Lovely to meet you. Maybe I'll see you again while you're in town."

"Have a good night," Bernadette said.

The bartender watched Victor Zorba leave, then walked over to Kep and Bernadette. "What can I get you?" Her hazel eyes, set far apart, were serious—the interaction with Zorba had clearly put her in a bad mood.

Kep smiled at her. "Do you have Widewaters Reserve Bourbon?"

"Not the Reserve—we don't get much call for the pricey shit in here. I've got a Widewaters Number Five."

Kep nodded. "That will suffice. Neat, water back, if you don't mind."

The bartender nodded at Bernadette, who took the stool at the bar next to where Kep stood.

"What can I get for you, hon?"

Bernadette tapped her fingers on the bar. "I don't know."

"I've got top-shelf tequila on special. *Traición de Ideales*—both the añejo and silver."

Bernadette shuddered. "I had an awful experience with tequila shots in college."

The bartender grinned. "Not time to get back up on the horse?"

"Not yet." Bernadette looked at the bottles behind the bar; they all ran together. "I guess I'll have a rum and coke."

"You want to see a menu?"

Right. In all the stress of trying to coordinate the vacation rental and laying a false trail for her pursuers, she'd neglected to eat. Her stomach rumbled.

The bartender brought menus, then stepped away and busied herself making the drinks as she nodded to a customer at the bar who got up and left.

"I believe our mixologist friend, who also appears to be the owner of this establishment, may be our best bet to obtain information about Mr. McMichael," Kep whispered to Bernadette as he sat on a stool.

Bernadette gave a curt nod in reply as the bartender returned with their drinks. Kep didn't get his water back.

The bartender set the drinks down on cardboard coasters —the same ones Kep found in Evan McMichael's kitchen drawer. "You decided?"

They ordered their meals. The bartender put in their orders, then brought Kep a short glass of water with a straw.

"Here's your water back," she said.

Kep raised his whiskey in thanks.

Bernadette nodded her head at where Zorba had been standing. "We ran into that guy in the suit at our hotel. What did he want?"

"Zorba?" The bartender laughed and shook her head. "He's trying to single-handedly keep Lost Dish from becoming a ghost town."

"Windfall 29, right?"

The bartender nodded. "Wants to buy this place, but it's not even for sale."

"Why does he want to buy it?"

"Says he wants to help me out."

What do you need help with? Bernadette bit the question back into her mouth before she could say it. That kind of question would put her on the defensive, and they needed information.

Bernadette took a sip of her drink. Whoa. The bartender had a heavy hand with the rum, but it was pretty good. "You own this place?"

"Yep. About twelve years now." She pushed her chin at the rum and Coke in Bernadette's hand. "How's the drink?"

"Not bad at all." Bernadette put her elbows on the bar. "I have a couple more questions—"

"Investigating Evan's death, am I right?" the woman said. "State troopers?"

Bernadette hesitated. "Federal, actually."

The bartender's eyes widened. "Oh—I didn't realize the FBI would be interested."

"CSAB," Kep corrected.

"The drug agency?" The bartender clicked her tongue. "You've got the wrong idea. Evan wasn't mixed up in any drugs. I know the reputation of this county, especially for meth, but Evan wouldn't get near anything like that."

"We don't just investigate cases involving illegal drugs," Bernadette added quickly. "All controlled substances. Which means"—she paused, closed her eyes for a moment, debating with herself, then soldiered on—"substances that can be used as poisons, too."

The bartender leaned forward and lowered her voice. "I know people think Evan killed himself, but I don't believe it. He was excited about something."

Bernadette cocked her head. "Something big?" she asked, as encouragingly as she could.

The bartender hesitated.

Bernadette smiled widely and held out her hand. "Bernadette Becker. I'm a case analyst with CSAB." Oh, how her tongue longed to have the word *agent* dance across it again. "This is my colleague, Dr. Kep Woodhead."

The bartender shook Bernadette's hand. "Bonnie Farmington."

"So you knew Evan?"

"He's been coming in here pretty much since he moved to town. Must be three or four years now."

"What sort of plans was he making?"

"Something to do with the university," Farmington said.

"Which university?"

"U-Yoop."

"I'm sorry?"

"Sorry—University of the Upper Peninsula. He was working with a grad student there. He was talking about a discovery he'd made. Said he couldn't talk about it yet, but he thought U-Yoop would be interested."

"What kind of discovery?"

Farmington straightened, then shrugged. "He said it was too nerdy for anyone else to be interested in. But *he* was excited about it, I'm sure of it."

"Did he interact with anyone here at the bar?"

"You mean, did he have any friends?"

Bernadette nodded as she took another sip of her rum and Coke.

"Not really. He joined in with a couple other people on trivia night. Mostly kept to himself, although I talked to him a lot."

"Would you consider him a friend?"

Bonnie shrugged. "At first, he was just one of the few regulars who didn't hit on me constantly or talk directly to my tits, you know what I mean? But then, yeah, we became friends. Not super close, but we talked."

Bernadette gave Farmington a sad, knowing smile. "You don't know about the grad program he was working with, do you?"

A spark flashed in Farmington's eye. "Yes—uh, give me a minute. He mentioned her name in conversation once."

"Her?"

"The grad student he was working with. She had an unusual name. Some sort of city or country or something."

"Like London?" Bernadette ventured. "Paris? Brooklyn?" Kep took out his phone and tapped the screen.

Bonnie scratched her scalp. "I think it was a European city—not Brooklyn, for sure. And not London or Paris, either."

"Berlin? Stockholm?"

"It'll come to me. He was talking about meeting her and sharing his research. I wish I could remember her name."

Kep tapped Bernadette's shoulder and showed her his phone screen. It was the website for the University of the Upper Peninsula's graduate program in ornithology. Halfway down the screen was the T.A.'s name for Biology 205.

Barcelona Lute.

Chapter Eight

Bernadette opened the front door to the cabin with the four-digit code Barlow had texted her. When Barlow had messaged that he'd rented her and Kep a cabin, she'd expected something made from logs, not a royal-blue bungalow-style house with vinyl siding and a small covered porch. She supposed the word "cabin" was all about marketing—the ad had also said, importantly, that the house included wi-fi.

The inside of the house was "cozy" as advertised—which meant small: the entry opened right into the kitchen, with a small round table and four chairs across from the stove and refrigerator. The living room had just enough space for a loveseat, a coffee table, and a wall-mounted TV. But a small place was all right with Bernadette; it was just the two of them, and the two-bedroom, two-bath house afforded them both proximity to the crime scene and many of the deceased's acquaintances, but also a level of privacy Bernadette appreciated. There were no Windfall 29 Mine workers coming and going, and the house was at least a quarter mile from its nearest neighbor. Bernadette made a mental note to put the small pickup truck in the attached two-car garage, but she was too tired.

Kep, however, seemed to have gotten a second wind. As soon as the door shut behind him, he set his suitcase down next to the door and pushed his glasses up on his nose. "I believe it would be prudent to make a strategic plan."

"A—what?"

"We must carefully coordinate our time," Kep continued. "Too close to our established schedule and we risk being found by the people who are following us. Yet if we stray too far—"

"Kep, I've been driving all day, trying to avoid some unnamed bad guys following me, and I'm dead tired. Can we pick this up in the morning?"

"The morning may be too late to implement an effective strategy," Kep said, taking out his laptop and setting it on the kitchen table.

"Kep, don't connect to—"

Kep waved her off as he sat down and opened the computer. "I have a VPN. If anyone sees my connection, it will look like I'm in Philadelphia."

"Oh, good."

"It's the same VPN software on your machine. We should be safe enough."

"I'm debating whether I should wait till tomorrow to give Maura an update. She must be expecting one by now—she might have left me several messages on my phone."

"I'm concerned we have already stoked the lieutenant's wrath by not contacting her yet."

"Not wrath," Bernadette said. "She knows we're in danger. I don't want her worried too much, but I don't want to contact her unless it's necessary."

Kep was quiet, his eyes focused on the laptop on the table.

"What?" Bernadette asked.

"You don't trust Lieutenant Stevenson?"

"Of course I trust her. She's my—my best friend." *Or at least she used to be, before she became my boss.*

"I was under the impression that we were obfuscating the truth from her simply because we had no way of knowing who might intercept our communications."

"That's part of it."

"Then is there something I'm missing?"

Bernadette hesitated.

Kep nodded. "Ah. The new member of the team."

"I just don't know Lesley that well yet. We've only worked together a couple of months."

"And you think Lieutenant Stevenson is sharing information with Lesley?"

Bernadette's shoulders slumped, and she leaned against the kitchen counter for support. "Maura is one of the few people who knew I was going to Taycheedah. I trust Maura, but I know Lesley is in the loop—hell, she was in the room when Maura and I were discussing it."

"Once the lieutenant arrives, you plan on informing her of our location, correct?"

"Yes."

Kep thought for a moment. "She coordinated your visit with the warden, did she not? Anyone the warden discussed your visit with—"

"I know, I know, and my visit wasn't top secret." Bernadette was quiet for a moment. "But it doesn't feel like Warden Fisk put this all in motion."

Kep blinked, looking at Bernadette over the top of his glasses.

"I know she makes the most sense," Bernadette said. "But it doesn't sit right with me. This has deeper roots—ones that go all the way to Parr Medical. We've gotten close to something. Something Parr Medical doesn't want to go public."

"Then I cannot understand why Annika Nakrivo is still alive. Surely she knows enough information to have a target on her back."

Bernadette rubbed her forehead. "All I can think of is Annika is too valuable to kill."

"Too valuable?" Kep's brow crinkled.

"She's got the talent to transform into a different person and persuade people to do what she wants. She can gain access to places no one else can—she pretty much single-handedly destroyed Kilbourn Tech's cancer research so Parr Medical could sell their less effective medication, remember? We might have solved that murder, but we didn't save all the cancer patients who'll die. Parr Medical probably thinks they need her."

"How much can Annika help them from the inside of a prison cell? Would she trade her information for a lighter sentence?" Kep ran a hand through his salt-and-pepper hair. "Or do you believe Annika to still be taking orders from Parr Medical?"

"All possibilities," Bernadette said.

"Perhaps Parr Medical will attempt to murder Miss Nakrivo." He looked. "Or try to break her out."

Bernadette shrugged. "If they kept her alive, maybe it's because they want to use her again—whether or not she's taking orders from them right now."

Kep stroked his beard. "Whatever their plan is," Kep said carefully, "the 'incident' might have been part of their execution strategy."

Bernadette leaned against the counter. "Of course."

"Then let's piece together what we know." Kep scratched the side of his face, just above his beard. "Didn't you tell me the warden said Annika Nakrivo was in the infirmary?"

"Yes—she'd gotten attacked with a knife." Bernadette paused. "Hang on, no, not a knife. A sharpened toothbrush."

"Was she injured?"

"Slashed across the face, Warden Fisk said."

Kep folded his arms. "But you didn't see her?"

"Like I told you, I bolted out of there when I got the feeling something wasn't right."

"Perhaps Lieutenant Stevenson would have more information about the incident in question." Kep drummed his fingers on the table. "Neither you nor I have spoken to—"

"This would be a great time to fire up your VPN and get your email."

"You should do the same."

Bernadette nodded. She took her suitcase and bag into the bedroom—the larger of the two bedrooms, but Kep had the one with the en suite bathroom—and lifted the case onto the bed. She pulled out her laptop from the bag and walked back to the kitchen. Kep was sitting back down at the table, a manila folder open in front of him with the McMichael case file printouts inside. Bernadette put her laptop down opposite him.

Kep pointed into the kitchen. "The wi-fi password is on a card affixed to the front of the refrigerator with a magnet."

"Gotcha."

Two minutes later, she was online, connected to CSAB's email server through her VPN, and the emails started downloading.

She started a new email—and drew a blank. "What should I say to Maura?"

"As close to the truth as possible without providing exact

details about our location, I suppose." Kep tapped the trackpad. "I received an email from Lesley that we are to meet the sheriff at the Lost Dish office at eight o'clock tomorrow."

"So we'll need to be out of here by seven fifteen."

"We don't want to meet the sheriff in the U-Move-It pickup, do we? Won't it take us another fifteen minutes to swap cars at the hotel?"

"If we were planning to be on time, yes."

"Ah, yes. Our strategy of planned tardiness."

Bernadette started a new email, but an incoming message from Maura caught her eye and she clicked on her email client. "Hang on, Kep—message from Maura." Her eyes went to the header. "Sent about an hour after you landed at Houghton County Airport."

To: Bernadette Becker

From: Maura Stevenson

Date: June 17 18:28:22

I haven't heard from Dr. Woodhead, so I assume you picked him up. Your cellphone is going straight to voicemail. Please update me ASAP.

Given the incident at Taycheedah, I agree you may be in danger. Wrap this investigation up quickly. You don't need to wait to inform local LEOs. All signs are pointing to suicide. I want you out of danger and back in D.C.

I can't reach our mutual contact, and I'm not getting updates on the incident at her workplace. Left a voicemail asking why she thought Dr. Woodhead would be there.

I'm still coming tomorrow. 5:35 PM flight into Houghton County. Meet me at the hotel at 7.

—M

She read the email out loud to Kep, then locked eyes with him.

"I will answer in the affirmative to your unasked question," he said. "I feel better about our entering the trailer with this directive from the lieutenant."

Bernadette nodded.

"Who is 'our mutual contact'?" Kep asked.

"The warden at Taycheedah. I told you Maura said there was an incident there. She's being vague because the Nakrivo project is outside of CSAB official channels."

"Ah, of course." Kep tilted his head. "Are you wondering if I have any advice for your response?"

"I guess."

"I'm afraid I don't want to take the chance it would be safe to call her. Respond via email. Report you're unharmed."

"You've gotten a lot more distrustful in the last couple of hours."

"Every new piece of information we receive about the Annika Nakrivo situation erodes my optimism."

"All right, here goes nothing." Bernadette cracked her knuckles, then began typing.

To: Maura Stevenson

From: Bernadette Becker

Date: June 17, 20:54:34

Maura—I'm safe. Trying to minimize contact in case I'm being tracked. Dr. Woodhead and I have conducted an interview and did a walkthrough of the victim's trailer.

She hit the backspace key and retyped the last sentence.

Dr. Woodhead and I have conducted an interview and started the investigation. Might not be suicide. Contacting Lost Dish sheriff tomorrow. See you at 7.

   —BB

"Good?" Bernadette asked.

"I have no suggestions for improvement," Kep said. "Send it off."

Bernadette clicked, and the email disappeared from the page. "There. She can rest easy tonight."

Oof—rest easy.

She hadn't talked to Sophie since she arrived in Michigan. Would her daughter think something was wrong? She always called Sophie on business trips.

Bernadette considered taking out her phone and calling Sophie—but she couldn't risk it. If they'd put a GPS on her car, surely they'd be tracking phone calls. And she couldn't risk her pursuer getting her burner phone number. She could safely call Kep's new phone on her prepaid phone, but not Sophie. Maybe she could call Sophie from the sheriff's office or the hotel—from a phone she was expected to use.

Crinkling her nose, Bernadette sighed. She couldn't risk it tonight—and as much as she didn't want Sophie to worry, the truth of the matter was Bernadette *was* in danger.

❧

Bernadette sat bolt upright, breathing hard.

She was falling, falling—

No, she was in bed.

Where was she? Where was Sophie?

Oh—Bernadette wasn't in her own bed at home.

She wasn't at Lamar's, either.

It was quiet—much quieter than her house in the Northern Virginia suburbs, much calmer than Lamar's house in the Harambee neighborhood of Milwaukee.

She blinked, but nothing got brighter. There was no light in the room.

Oh, right. The vacation rental in Banner Crossing.

She took a deep, shuddering breath and closed her eyes. Her nightmare came back to her: she had found the GPS tracker on her rental car and held it in her hand—then suddenly, the tracker turned into a bomb. One of those old Hollywood-style bombs, with sticks of dynamite and an old-school alarm clock with red and black wires curling from the alarm pin to the wrapping of the dynamite. The visual might have been worthy of an old Road Runner cartoon, but the terror had been real. Had she woken up when the bomb had gone off in her dream?

She looked at the digital alarm clock on the bedside table. The red LED numbers read 1:46. She'd been asleep for three hours. Was she worried about everything they had to do? Her alarm would go off at six, and they'd get on the road at seven.

She fluffed the pillow and turned it over, kicking off the covers. Then she lay back down. She turned on her side and tried to go back to sleep.

Then she opened her eyes. They had nothing for breakfast. Not even coffee.

She lay on her back. Nothing to worry about. They could pick something up on the way in.

But suddenly Bernadette's brain went into overdrive. Would the people who had put the GPS tracker on her car have figured out she'd removed it? Would they be looking for financial information? Would they have discovered Bernadette's ex-husband had booked this cabin in Banner

Crossing and the U-Move-It pickup? Would stopping for breakfast put them in danger?

Bernadette was wide awake, doomsday scenarios spinning in front of her eyes, each more unlikely than the next.

The neon sign with the burned-out H popped into her mind. *Open 24 Hours.*

"Screw it," she said out loud, throwing on a sweatshirt over her pajamas, sticking her feet into her flats, and grabbing her purse with the pickup's key in it.

Chapter Nine

There were two other cars in the lot when Bernadette pulled the pickup into a parking spot in front of the entrance. The heat of the day had softened this late at night, and a breeze from the north was almost chilly. When she pushed the door of Saucy's Co-Op, an electronic beep almost made her jump out of her skin.

Bernadette looked around. There were only five aisles of groceries in the store, as well as an espresso bar to the right side of the entrance. It was dark behind the counter—a hand-written chalkboard sign said *Coffee Bar Hours: 6 AM–9 PM*—and the small bistro tables looked lonely with their tiny metal chairs pushed in. To her left, a single bored cashier in a green apron stood behind one of the three cash registers. Bernadette bent over and grabbed a plastic handbasket from a stack on the floor—just large enough for cereal, milk, instant coffee, maybe even some fruit or pre-wrapped pastries if anything struck her fancy. Then maybe her brain would shut up and she could get back to sleep.

She wandered the aisles for a few minutes before finding the cereal. She didn't know what kind of cereal Kep ate. He struck her as an oatmeal person, and there was a three-pack of instant oatmeal next to the corn flakes. She grabbed the oatmeal and a small box of Lucky Charms—they used to be Sophie's favorite a couple of years ago—then walked to the back of the store to the dairy case.

A woman came around the corner and almost ran into her.

"Oh," the woman said, jumping back slightly.

"Sorry," Bernadette said reflexively. "You okay?"

The woman looked shocked at first. About five foot five, she wore no makeup and her face looked puffy, almost haggard. She wore a green-and-gold sweatshirt with "UUP Herons" on the front and a pair of blue jeans with white sneakers. Bernadette looked at her—she seemed familiar. Then the woman's face crumpled.

"No, no," Bernadette said hurriedly. "You're okay. *I'm* okay. I didn't drop anything—"

"It's not—" the woman choked out. She was obviously trying to hold herself together and failing.

Oh, she'd seen the woman in the Evan McMichael file. This was his sister.

"Laura Donaghy?" Bernadette said.

Laura stopped mid-sob and took a step back. "Do I—do I know you?"

"Sorry," Bernadette quickly said. "I shouldn't have—uh, look, I'm one of the investigators sent here to investigate your—your brother's death. I recognized you from your photo in the file."

"Oh—oh." Laura took another step back and reached out to the shelving unit to steady herself. "I didn't expect to run into anyone from the investigation."

"Me neither." Bernadette reached out a hand and took Laura's elbow. "I didn't mean to startle you." With her other hand, she reached into her purse and pulled out her badge to show it to Laura.

Laura closed her eyes, breathed in deeply, then out. She let go of the shelving unit and opened her eyes. "What are you doing here?"

"I couldn't sleep." Bernadette looked down at the floor. "Had a nightmare, actually."

"Join the club."

Bernadette raised the basket slightly. "Figured I'd make myself useful and get some breakfast for tomorrow morning."

"Same with me. I'm staying at a rental house down the road, but I feel like a stranger being here. I suppose I *am* a stranger here." Laura looked around at the modest grocery store. "Not much, but at least it's open." She pulled on the hem of her sweatshirt. "I didn't expect this chill at night—I had to buy this from the co-op last week."

"I understand."

Laura took off her glasses and rubbed her eyes. "I got a message from the sheriff to be available for an interview."

"We haven't set anything up yet."

"That's why I've been hanging around this town, you know." Laura put her glasses back on. "I'd like to go back to Tucson, but I don't think Evan—Evan..."

"You think the police haven't figured it out yet," Bernadette said gently.

Laura shuffled her feet. "Or aren't telling me."

Bernadette looked at Laura's plastic basket—nothing frozen or refrigerated—then turned and squinted at the espresso bar. The lights were off above the section, but there wasn't any sign saying they couldn't sit there. "Do you— maybe want to talk to me now?"

"Now?"

Bernadette shrugged. "I don't have anything better to do. Do you?"

Laura smiled sadly. "No, I guess I don't."

The two of them walked down the aisle to the espresso bar area, and Bernadette pulled two chairs out from a table, then motioned to the chair facing in toward the coffee machines.

Laura sat.

Bernadette walked around the table and took the chair facing Laura, looking out over the rest of the grocery store. She'd have to play this carefully—she didn't want to scare Laura away.

"So—you're the federal investigator assigned to Evan's—to Evan's death?" Laura placed her hands flat on the small, round metal table. "What do you want to know?"

"Tell me about Evan." Bernadette sat back in her seat. "He moved to the Upper Peninsula after he retired, right?"

"Yes. He moved here over Thanksgiving weekend—four years this November."

"Why Banner Crossing?"

Laura smiled. "We grew up in the Chicago suburbs, but Evan always loved the outdoors. He was in heaven at UUP. He's a catch-and-release fisherman. He used to love mountain biking, but he had a fall the first spring he was up here, and I think he gave it up."

"Did you talk to him frequently?"

Laura's face fell. "Not—not as much as I should have."

"When was the last time you spoke with him?"

"May tenth."

Bernadette raised her eyebrows. "Pretty exact."

"I gave him a call on his birthday. He turned sixty-eight."

"I see." Bernadette leaned forward and put her elbows on the table. "How did he seem?"

"What do you mean?"

"Did he seem worried? Skittish?"

"Not at all. He was the same old Evan. He was about to go out banding with some grad student from UUP, so he was excited. Sounded a little distracted. Some eagle or hawk or something, maybe not from the area."

"I remember—" Bernadette started, but then clamped her mouth shut. Telling Laura she'd been in Evan's house looking at a shelf full of nonfiction books was not information she should share. She straightened in her chair. She wanted to talk to Laura, thinking she'd be less likely to be guarded when she was running without sleep in the middle of the night. But Bernadette had to be careful she didn't talk out of turn. She'd already mentioned her nightmare. That was too personal, even if it had helped make Laura comfortable enough to agree to talk.

"He and I were on the phone for about ten minutes," Laura said. "Evan was talking about his plans for the summer. He'd just planted some deer-resistant plants. He'd bought some tools, too—I think he was talking about putting together a workshop behind his house."

"You mentioned he was going banding with a grad student. Did he give you the grad student's name?"

"Uh—not her last name. I think it was a woman. She had an unusual name. I remember I first thought Evan stuttered saying 'Barbara,' but no, it was 'Barcelona.'"

"Barcelona Lute."

"Maybe. Like I said, he didn't give me her last name. But how many Barcelonas could there be?"

"Did he talk to you about his mobile home getting shot up?"

"No. That happened two weeks later." Laura tightened her jaw. "I didn't even hear about the shooting until *after* they'd found his body." The tendons in her neck strained. "Nothing will change until we get those drug dealers in jail."

"I'm sorry?"

"The meth problem. Especially in rural areas like this. No one has any prospects for decent paying jobs. Companies shipping their jobs to China or Mexico so the CEO can buy their fifth helicopter or a mega-yacht."

Bernadette blinked.

Laura crossed her arms. "So people lose hope, and they turn to meth. The neighbor who shot up the house? Gabe something?"

"Yeah?"

"I found out they arrested him three times for possession." She cocked her head at Bernadette. "Isn't that why you're here? From CSAB? Trying to see how Gabe's suppliers or dealers or whatever were involved in Evan's death?"

"To be perfectly honest, we're here because Mr. McMichael's cause of death was from an as-yet unknown substance."

"An unknown substance. That's rich." Laura's mouth curled into a scowl. "I've only been here for a week, and even I can see the meth problem here. But what can you do? The sheriff's office is a half hour away." Laura pushed the sleeves of her sweatshirt up her forearms, her rant gaining momentum. "They're already overworked, there's no money for additional staff—and even when they make an arrest, it's usually a user, not a dealer. So nothing happens."

"The cause of death wasn't methamphetamines, Ms. Donaghy."

Laura unfolded her arms and intertwined her hands, then stared at the tabletop for a moment, her shoulders relaxing slightly. "I'll tell you, I can't wait to get out of here." She lifted her head. "I'm glad you came to talk to me—hopefully I can leave in the next day or two."

Bernadette was quiet.

"Anyway," Laura said, spreading her hands flat on the table again, "The sheriff's department said on the twenty-fifth of May, right around four in the morning, this meth-head neighbor got high and shot twelve bullets into Evan's house."

"Had Evan and his neighbor had confrontations before?"

"Not that I know of." She pursed her lips. "I talked to Evan's other neighbors in the trailer park, and they said this meth-head—Gabe—lost his job a few months ago and just went off the deep end." She tapped the table. "He was pointing those pen-light lasers at the other mobile homes. He told one neighbor Evan was an Interpol agent out to get him." She sniffed. "Cars always drove up to the house late at night, too. He was either cooking meth or selling it, or both."

"This neighbor went to jail immediately after shooting up Evan's house, though, right?"

"That's what I heard. Spent a few nights in jail, then got bailed out. I guess he'd sobered up while locked away, and they didn't think he'd be a danger—I don't know. But Evan had gotten a restraining order against Gabe, and when Gabe tried to come back to his trailer, there was a sheriff's deputy who wouldn't let him into the park." Laura shrugged. "Fat lot of good it did. Evan was found dead a week later. They think he died the night after Gabe got out of jail."

"I see." Bernadette paused. "Where's Gabe now?"

"Been in the Lost Dish jail ever since they found Evan's body."

"Why? Doesn't the sheriff think Evan—uh, died by suicide?"

"I haven't seen the final report." Laura looked down at the table. "I know they revoked Gabe's bail."

Bernadette paused. Why would the county revoke bail if they'd determined that Evan McMichael died by suicide? Shooting up a mobile home and poisoning someone—two very different ways to commit murder. It screamed different people. Of course, maybe no one actually thought Gabe was responsible—but since the guy who had shot up Evan's house was free on bail when Evan died, maybe law enforcement weighed this as their best option. Bernadette didn't like to think that local sheriffs played fast and loose with the rules, but sometimes they did. "What else can you tell me about Gabe?"

Laura shook her head. "Nothing. I did a little internet research—his arrests are a matter of public record—but the sheriff didn't tell me anything else. I can't even get a copy of the police report." She scoffed. "The funeral home is telling me they can't keep Evan there much longer, and they want me to pay them twenty-five hundred dollars." She sighed. "I haven't even been able to go through the house yet. There's police tape all around it."

Bernadette reached out and patted Laura's arm. "I'll do everything I can to get this moving as quickly as possible."

Laura put her hand on top of Bernadette's and patted it as well, then dropped her hands into her lap.

Bernadette let the silence settle between them for a moment, then asked in a quiet voice, "Was there anyone else who might have wanted to hurt your brother?"

"Not that I know of." Laura smiled. "It's funny—Evan was such a manly man in a lot of ways. He could fix anything you gave to him. Not scared of wild animals—well, nothing stupid, he wouldn't confront a bear or a mountain lion—but those birds, he had a way with them. It was almost like they *let* him band them." She sighed, a faraway look in her eyes.

"Any other problems? Any disagreements at the bar he went to?"

Laura shook her head. "Evan got along with just about everyone. Sometimes he could talk too much about the migration patterns of coalhawks, but not enough for—" Then she stopped speaking.

"Is something wrong?"

"It's probably nothing, but Evan told me about an angry phone call he got from the president of one of the local bird-watching groups."

Bernadette paused. "How angry was this birdwatcher?"

"Evan said the man didn't like him banding the birds—particularly the hawks. Something about him harming the birds. But Evan's fully licensed by the Fish and Wildlife Association, and when I talked to him on his birthday, I know he was excited about discovering—oh, let me think—some sort of coalhawk thought to be extinct in the 1930s, after all the copper mining." Laura's eyes flashed. "I can't remember the name of the species." She snapped her fingers. "Keweenaw. I remember—he had to spell it for me. He said he'd found a new kettle near Old—uh, one of the British names. Old Philippa or something."

"Old Victoria?"

"Of course, yes, like Queen Victoria." Laura chuckled. "Evan wanted me to keep the hawk sighting hush-hush. I guess it's pretty common for people to say they've found a new species and it turns out to be a hoax, so he wanted to make sure before he said anything." Her smile ran away from her face. "Now I guess it doesn't matter."

Bernadette's brow furrowed. So that was the discovery Bonnie Farmington said Evan was excited about—and maybe the notebooks in Evan's nightstand showed this discovery. "If I remember the map right, Old Victoria is about halfway between Banner Crossing and Lost Dish." She cocked her head. "You said a kettle? Is that some sort of hot spring?"

Laura laughed. "Oh, no, a group of hawks is called a kettle—well, it's called a lot of things, but Evan called it a 'kettle of hawks.'"

Bernadette nodded. "Oh, of course. Like a murder of crows."

"Exactly." Then Laura's face darkened.

Bernadette ran her hand over her face. It was late, and she was sleep-deprived, but it was no excuse to put her foot in her mouth—she could have used anything but *murder*—a pride of lions, a gaggle of geese. Why did she have to pick *murder*?

The answer was obvious: because as sure as the sheriff was that Evan McMichael took his own life, Bernadette was sure it was murder. And she was almost equally sure Evan's neighbor sitting in the Lost Dish county jail wasn't the culprit, either.

"You don't know the name of the president of the bird-watching group, do you?"

Laura shook her head, then she looked at Bernadette full in the face. "I don't believe my brother would have—would have done this to himself," she whispered.

"I promise—" Bernadette said, then stopped herself from saying something she couldn't deliver. "I promise I will do everything I can to find out what happened." She paused. "And I'm so sorry for your loss."

A glimmer of hope shone in Laura Donaghy's eyes. Bernadette gritted her teeth—she had her work cut out for her.

Chapter Ten

THE NEXT MORNING, BERNADETTE SAT AT THE KITCHEN table in the same sweatshirt and pajama bottoms she'd worn to Saucy's Co-Op the night before, spooning Lucky Charms into her mouth, a mug of instant coffee next to her cereal bowl.

"Good morning," Kep said, appearing from his bedroom, sportscoat over a crisp white Oxford shirt, his hair neatly combed. "You haven't showered yet?"

If the sweatshirt and pajama bottoms weren't a giveaway, Kep's nose probably did the rest. Bernadette picked up her phone. "I've got time."

Kep looked uncomfortable.

Bernadette glanced up at him. "Remember, we need to vary our schedule to make us harder to track. We agreed we'd show up late."

"I would rather show up fifteen minutes early."

"Showing up late won't kill you, Kep." Another spoonful of cereal went in Bernadette's mouth.

Kep tilted his head. "Did you not sleep well?"

Bernadette shook her head, then chewed and swallowed. "Aren't you wondering where we got the cereal and milk?"

Kep pulled out the chair on his side of the table and sat down. "I suppose I am a bit curious."

"I couldn't sleep, so I went to the twenty-four-hour market down at the intersection of Highway 45. And you'll never guess who I ran into."

"Bonnie Farmington?"

"What, the bartender from St. Matthew's Pub? No, not her. Our victim's sister, Laura Donaghy."

"Ah."

"And I interviewed her."

"You—" Kep's eyes bored into Bernadette. "You're telling me you interviewed a person of interest without informing the sheriff's office?"

"It was two in the morning, Kep. And she was willing to talk. I got a few leads out of it, too." She stood up, then drained the last of her coffee, then grabbed her empty cereal bowl and walked to the kitchen counter. "And I wouldn't call her a person of interest. She's the next of kin." Bernadette put her dishes in the sink, clattering the spoon against the bowl, and turned on the water to rinse it out. "I don't know what to tell you, Kep. I ran into the sister at the Co-Op. She couldn't sleep either, and she was ready to talk. What would you have done?"

"I'm a consultant. I am not required to follow the guidelines as strictly as an agent does."

Case analyst, Bernadette thought as she turned off the water. "If you're done criticizing me, are you interested at all in what I found out?"

Kep looked down at the floor. "Yes."

"So first, Laura mentioned two people Bonnie the bartender talked about: Barcelona Lute and Gabriel Constantine. We'll need to put them both at the top of our interview list."

"Which shouldn't be a surprise."

"No. But I found out our victim, who we suspected was a bird-banding hobbyist, ran afoul—no pun intended—of a local ornithological society."

Kep cocked his head and his glasses slipped down his nose. "A birdwatching kerfuffle doesn't seem to be a strong motive for poisoning someone."

"Doesn't have to make sense to you, Kep—just to our killer." Bernadette held up her index finger. "First, let's work off your theory that there was a second person in the trailer who poisoned Evan McMichael. Someone who put away a whiskey glass in the wrong cabinet."

"I believe that's a reasonable conclusion," Kep said. "But I haven't established a timeline."

"Gabe Constantine was out on bail, but when he approached his house, a sheriff's deputy turned him away, referring to the restraining order."

"According to Bonnie Farmington."

"We can check her story." Bernadette held up a second finger. "It's unlikely Gabriel Constantine was McMichael's guest for the whiskey drinking. Restraining order, not a neighbor on good terms—besides which, Mr. Constantine can't exactly afford a two-hundred-dollar bottle of whiskey."

"All excellent points."

"So we need to broaden the scope of who would've been the guest. The president of a local birdwatching group would be a good candidate." Bernadette held up a third finger. "Shows up with a pricey bottle of booze, apologizes for over-reacting, let bygones be bygones. McMichael sees the expensive whiskey and thinks the president is serious. Then the birdwatching president distracts McMichael with a photo of a Striped Warbling Nuthatch or whatever, puts the poison into Evan's drink, cleans up after himself, and leaves. We could go to his house, and you can use your nose to see if he's got top-shelf whiskey and some kind of poison lying around."

"There is no evidence to support your assertion." The corners of Kep's mouth turned down. "Bonnie Farmington is an equally good if not superior candidate, if we are giving in to flights of fancy." Kep looked up. "No pun intended."

"Okay, Mister Supershnozz, what's your hypothesis with the bartender?"

"Bonnie Farmington could have done exactly what you're accusing this unnamed birdwatching president of doing."

"But why would she kill him? And how would she have gained access to the trailer?"

"Mr. McMichael would have opened the door for a friend of his. As you've noted, an expensive bottle of quality spirits can lower the guard of many people. At the risk of appearing insensitive, I might suggest Mr. McMichael, being nearly seventy years old and single, and Bonnie Farmington, being significantly younger and quite attractive—"

"Right, right, I got it," Bernadette said tersely. "Still no motive, though."

"We have yet to find one, it's true."

She paused. "What about Victor Zorba?"

Kep narrowed his eyes. "We have had few interactions with the man," he said. "No hint he even knew who our murder victim was. He has power in this county, yes..." Kep's voice lilted on the last word.

"Laura Donaghy said McMichael was excited about the discovery of an endangered hawk."

Kep's eyes widened. "Of course. That could delay construction on Windfall 29's amusement park plans."

"Might even stop the project altogether."

"But Zorba would have to know about the discovery of the hawk."

"True, but you just said he has power in this county. Not a stretch to think he might have known."

"I do not wish to speculate further." Kep raised his eyebrows.

"Something to ask about next time we see him."

"I agree," Kep said. "We should also interview the president of the ornithological society. But currently, we have enough evidence to suggest Mr. McMichael did not die by suicide. We have the names—and sometimes not even those —of the people with whom he may have had conflicts during his last days."

Bernadette stepped away from the sink. "I've gotta hurry and clean myself up. Grab some oatmeal or one of those muffins if you want something to eat."

As Bernadette drove through the small downtown of Lost Dish in the rental car, searching for the sheriff's office, she was amused by the names of the streets crossing Rockland Road: Gold Street, Silver Street, Copper Street. The road ended in a T, a large sign announcing the end of U.S. Highway 45, the shimmering water of Lake Superior in front of them. She turned right on River Road, then in two blocks, on the corner of Superior Avenue, stood the Porcupine County Sheriff's Office.

The building was wide, with a solid wall of cream-colored brick on the right half with polished steel lettering announcing the building's function. The left half was glass, with five vertical supports equally spaced between the edge of the building and the halfway mark. Just past the sheriff's office, in front of the County Records Building, ten parking spaces were diagonally arranged on the street itself.

"Bigger than I thought it would be," Bernadette murmured to Kep, parking the car in one of the diagonal spaces next to a black Lexus.

She and Kep got out of the car; the June morning was hot and humid. Bernadette stopped and stared at the Lexus. "Kep, is this the same Lexus we saw at the hotel yesterday morning?"

Kep raised his head and looked closely. "And at the bar yesterday evening."

"Victor Zorba, right?"

"Correct."

"What do you think he's doing here?"

Kep shrugged.

They turned and walked in the front entrance, a glass door going all the way to the ceiling. Bernadette briefly wondered about security with so much glass in the building's façade, but Lost Dish had low crime except for the meth problem. Breaking into the sheriff's office probably wasn't an issue, although Laura Donaghy's warnings about the drug dealers bounced around in her head.

As clean and bright as the front of the building was, the interior of the waiting room was sterile and intimidating, but fortunately air conditioned. Cheap, harsh fluorescents shone from the ceiling despite the early morning sunlight coming in through the windows. A high reception desk in a buttery natural oak stood near the back wall with a closed door next to it. Bernadette suspected the entry had looked modern when completed, but two or three decades had passed since it was new.

A white woman with curly brown hair, round glasses, and a plastered-on smile sat behind the oak desk. "Good morning, good morning!" she chirped. "How can I help you?"

Bernadette was glad she'd had a cup of coffee—otherwise, she couldn't deal with so much enthusiasm this early. She pulled out her badge. "I'm Bernadette Becker, a case analyst with the Controlled Substance Analysis Bureau, and this"—she indicated Kep, who was standing a couple of paces behind her—"is Dr. Kep Woodhead, my colleague."

"Sheriff Koskinen is expecting you," the woman said. "He'll be right with you."

Bernadette put her phone back in her purse and tapped the screen of her phone—8:23 a.m. They were late.

They both stepped back from the oak desk and stood in the sunlight coming through the windows. Bernadette started to sweat under her blazer, so she stepped out of the sun.

The door in the back wall to the right of the desk opened, and a gaunt man with thinning gray hair stuck his head out. "You the folks from CSAB?"

"Right," Bernadette said. "I'm Berna—"

"Yeah, come on back," the man said, then turned and walked away, the door swinging slowly behind him.

Bernadette rushed over and caught the door before it closed, Kep following on her heels, and stepped over the threshold into the back of the sheriff's office.

Though the front of the office was modern, if fading from its former glory, the back room was significantly older. Four metal desks took up the space, with a short, worried-looking woman with short black hair wearing a uniform shirt halfway between olive green and brown with tan trousers. The other desks were empty, though a large mug with rising steam sat next to a computer at the desk at the back of the room.

"I was hoping you'd get here a little earlier," the man said, then turned around and stuck his hand out to Dr. Woodhead.

"Sheriff Aatos Koskinen," he said. "We should get to work—already lost quite a bit of time."

"Please forgive our tardiness," Kep said. "I'm afraid I was a rather poor navigator. I had Agent Becker here turn the wrong way out of the hotel parking lot, and we were halfway to Banner Crossing before I realized it."

Bernadette blinked in disbelief at Kep. The "strategy of planned tardiness," as Kep put it, had been her idea. And yet, here Kep was, falling on the sword.

Koskinen's face softened. "Hell, that's all right. Tourists get turned around in our little township all the time." Bernadette noted Koskinen's accent—his *th* sounds were either *d* or hard *t* sounds. His name was old-country Finnish, but with the way he spoke, he must have been born and raised in this part of the Upper Peninsula—maybe his parents were first-generation.

"Like I told your lieutenant on the phone," Koskinen continued, "I'm pretty sure our M.E. will tell you the guy down in Banner Crossing killed himself. Moved here a few years ago, lonely, his neighbor shoots up his place, doesn't have the money or the insurance to get it fixed? I've seen this kind of depression before. It's hard on the family—I know the sister doesn't believe his death could be suicide—but believe me, with the dark, cold winters we get here in Porcupine County, I'm not surprised. Like I said, I've seen this type of tragedy before."

Bernadette cocked her head. "But—it's the middle of June, not the middle of winter."

Koskinen paused. "I just mean that suicides aren't uncommon here."

"And yet," Kep said, "the bail bond for Gabriel Constantine was revoked and he's back in jail."

Koskinen nodded. "Yeah. Unfortunately for Mr. Constantine, that's the way bail revocation works in this county. I personally might think McMichael's death was suicide, but until the M.E. signs off on the cause of death, we revoke the bail of *anyone* who assaults someone who turns up dead." He rubbed his chin. "I mean, what would you have me do? Constantine shot up the guy's house, he's got a restraining order against him, and then a couple of days after he's released on bail, the attempted murder victim ends up dead?"

"But there is no proximate—" Kep began.

"Look, I don't have to justify my decision to the feds on the bail revocation. I can't have Gabe Constantine running around the community. Hell, it's not safe for *him*. You think that sister of our victim won't think Constantine killed him? No matter if there is or isn't proximate cause, or whether or not he was at the murder scene?" Koskinen shook his head adamantly. "I've only got myself and four deputies to cover four thousand square miles. Someone wants to play judge, jury, and executioner—well, Gabe's a lot safer in the county jail than he is on his own." He shook his head. "Besides, with the restraining order against him, he can't even stay in his house right now."

Bernadette tilted her head. "Doesn't the restraining order go away with Evan McMichael's death?"

"For sure, a judge would dismiss it," Koskinen said. "But Constantine would have to get in front of a judge first."

"Sort of a chicken-and-the-egg problem," Bernadette said.

"We do what we can with the resources we have."

"I understand," Kep said quickly.

"We'd still like to interview Mr. Constantine," Bernadette added.

Koskinen nodded. "I understand, Miss, uh—"

"Becker. Bernadette Becker."

"Right. Miss Becker. He's still going through withdrawal, though. Maybe you can wait a few days?"

"A few days? But he could point us toward a viable suspect *now*."

"I've seen him." Koskinen paused, tapped his thumb and forefinger together a few times, then continued. "He's not well, poor bastard. You might get a few grunts and dry heaves. I guarantee you'll be wasting your time—and he'll be combative."

"That surprises me," Bernadette said. "The symptoms of the meth 'crash' fade in over half of all patients within forty-eight hours, and the physical withdrawal symptoms fade in over ninety-five percent of patients in a week to ten days—even *without* with the right medication. Whatever he's experiencing should be significantly milder than when he was first brought in."

"I agree with you," Koskinen said. "Except Constantine is in that five percent of patients who are still going through those severe withdrawal symptoms. Look, I get it. You want to solve the case quickly. I'll contact you as soon as he's coherent enough to be helpful, yeah?"

Bernadette opened her mouth to say something, but Kep cut her off. "We appreciate that, Sheriff."

"Certainly, Dr. Woodhead."

Bernadette gritted her teeth.

"I have one more item of discussion, Sheriff. We understand one of your deputies found Mr. McMichael's body."

Koskinen nodded. "Mr. McMichael didn't show up for a birdwatcher's meeting two weeks ago, and he was supposed to meet with a graduate student at U-Yoop later that day. We had one of our deputies assigned to enforcing Mr. McMichael's restraining order against Mr. Constantine, so I had her stop by and do a welfare check. She found him then."

"That was me," the woman at the desk in the middle of the room said. She stood, standing tall despite her short frame—perhaps five-foot-two.

Bernadette turned to the woman. "You're Deputy Carla Moncrief."

"Yes," the deputy said. "I found him at"—she grabbed a small notebook from a pile of papers on her desk—"hold on a second." She flipped pages in the notebook. "June fourteenth. Nine forty-three in the morning."

Bernadette nodded. "Your daughter works at our hotel."

"Oh—Darcy? You must be staying at the Up North."

"Did you find any signs of foul play?"

"It's all in the report," Koskinen said.

"Did you notice anything in the house not on the report?"

"Everything's in the report," the sheriff said, a note of haughtiness in his voice.

"I see." Bernadette fought to keep her face neutral, but she was sure her disapproval registered. "The preliminary report says Mr. McMichael died from poisoning. I assume, based on the photos we received, the poison was in his glass on the table in front of him."

The sheriff shifted his weight. "We haven't gotten the tests back from the M.E.'s office, but yeah."

"I didn't see anything on the table or the counters in the photos," Bernadette continued, as if she and Kep hadn't already been through the trailer. "Did you find any evidence of poison—or, for that matter, the liquid in the glass?"

"I'm not sure I follow."

"You've stated that suicide is a likely cause of death. If Mr. McMichael prepared a poisoned cocktail, surely he didn't pour rat poison directly into the glass and drink it straight. He must have combined the poison with something to make it more palatable. So where is the bottle—or container—of poison, and where is the liquid he used in his drink to choke it down?"

The sheriff frowned. "We didn't find anything like that. But that means nothing."

"Why wouldn't it mean anything? You're saying the bottle of poison and whatever he used to cut it just disappeared?" Bernadette folded her arms. "Maybe we should go back to the trailer and see what Dr. Woodhead and I can find."

Almost imperceptibly behind her, Kep's sharp intake of breath.

"*Back* to the trailer?" the sheriff asked.

"Yes," Bernadette said, thinking quickly. "You've already been there, haven't you? Then you'll go back there, and you'll take us with you."

"Without interviewing Gabriel Constantine, however," Kep added, "our investigation won't be complete. He was the one to attack Mr. McMichael's domicile and I don't believe his motive was in the police report either."

"It's pretty clear to me," Koskinen said. "He's a junkie, he was on meth, and he was paranoid. Give him access to a firearm and he's just lucky he didn't kill McMichael." The sheriff cleared his throat. "Not with the gun, anyway." He took a few steps toward the desk in the back of the office. "I have a few things I need to finish up before I take you down to Banner Crossing. I'll meet you out front in, say, fifteen minutes?"

"We can meet you at the crime scene," Bernadette said. "We could take Deputy Moncrief."

Koskinen looked over at Carla Moncrief, who hesitated, then nodded.

"Suit yourself," the sheriff said.

Bernadette turned, then snapped her fingers. "One more thing before we go, Sheriff."

Koskinen pursed his lips, probably trying not to appear too annoyed. "What is it?"

"Constantine was charged with assault with a deadly weapon, if I remember right."

"Yeah."

"That kind of offense usually carries a pretty hefty bail amount."

"Maybe back in D.C. you'd see seventy-five grand," Koskinen said. "Here, cost-of-living being what it is, the wages being lower, it was twenty-five."

"Still, it's a lot of money. And Constantine doesn't seem the type to have even ten percent lying around for a bail bond. Who bailed him out?"

"Oh—his sister."

"Ah. She's got money?"

"She owns St. Matthew's Pub down in Banner Crossing. Does all right for herself, I guess. Bonnie Farmington's her name."

☙✲❧

As they drove on a straightaway on Highway 45, Bernadette turned to Deputy Moncrief in the passenger seat. "What kind of crimes do you usually see out here?"

"Drugs, mostly. Probably ninety percent meth."

"Yeah, not surprising."

"We're seeing some firearms, too. This is the first homicide I've ever worked on, though."

"Firearms, huh?"

"A lot of unlicensed gun sales here—they filter down to Chicago. We started a program to get those before they leave the state, though."

Bernadette nodded. Illinois had strict gun control laws,

but neighboring states were far more lax. It was a hundred times easier to get a gun in Wisconsin, Indiana, or Michigan and simply drive it down to Chicago than it was to buy a gun there. "Has it worked?"

"We confiscated twenty Rossi .38s last year."

"Wow. Don't hear about those very often."

"Only holds five bullets, and they weren't a very popular brand, but they're fairly small and cheap." Deputy Moncrief shook her head. "We've still got a long way to go. The FBI confiscated over two hundred in Chicago last year."

Bernadette's jaw dropped. "Two hundred guns?"

"Two hundred Rossi .38s. It was quite a haul, let me tell you."

"I don't suppose the woman who owns the bar down the street from the crime scene is involved with any unlicensed gun sales."

"Not to my knowledge," Moncrief said.

"She was not only friends with the victim—" Bernadette began.

"According to her," Kep added from the backseat.

"—but she's the sister of the guy who shot up our victim's house."

Moncrief looked out the window. "I don't know what to tell you. Lost Dish doesn't even have a population of two thousand. Heck, the whole county's got less than five thousand people. Everyone knows everyone."

"Even though Banner Crossing is a half-hour drive from Lost Dish?"

"Out here, might as well be next door," Moncrief said, still staring out the window. "Gets a little tough to visit your friends and family in the winter when there's a snowstorm, but the plows do a good job on the main road, and you don't get more of a main road than U.S. 45."

"So you know Bonnie Farmington."

"My kid sister went to high school with her. Of course, back then, she was Bonnie Constantine. Kept her married name after the divorce—I mean, who can blame her, with Gabe in and out of jail and rehab?"

"I see," Bernadette said. Why hadn't Bonnie said anything about being the sister of the guy who'd shot up the victim's house—her *friend's* house?

They turned at Saucy's Co-Op toward St. Matthew Road, and they passed the pub just before the turn into Sugar Maple Estates. Bernadette slowed; the sedan rode roughly on the gravel driveway. Bernadette parked and the three of them got out. Excitement in the pit of her stomach. Evidence was waiting inside: the misplaced glass in the cabinet, the bird-watching notebooks, the lack of poison anywhere in the trailer or the outside shed. She kept her pace slow and her breathing even so Moncrief wouldn't think they'd been in the trailer before.

"Stop!" Kep called sharply.

Bernadette looked up.

The front door to the mobile home was wide open.

Chapter Eleven

After Moncrief radioed to Sheriff Koskinen to report the break-in, the three of them stepped inside the trailer. Whereas everything had been in its place when Bernadette and Kep were there the night before, now everything was everywhere. The cabinets were open, broken glass littering the kitchen floor.

Bernadette surveyed the wreckage, hands on her hips.

"This isn't how we left it." Moncrief raised her hands to her face in disbelief. "I know a lot of these trailers can be messy, especially when there's a single man who lives alone, but this place was spotless when I found the body. Nothing out of place except the glass on the kitchen table, and now—"

"Someone broke the lock?" Bernadette asked.

Moncrief scowled. "Constantine hit the deadbolt when he shot up the trailer a few weeks ago. Before he died, Evan put some duct tape on the door handle, but it doesn't lock." She folded her arms. "I told the sheriff we needed to get the locksmith out here, but he didn't want the expense. Thought the police tape would be enough to keep people out."

"I can't believe this," Bernadette muttered, stepping over

a torn couch cushion, its stuffing strewn across the room. The wildlife books were in a pile, some books open with their pages creased. One paperback had been ripped in half. Bernadette took out her phone and began taking pictures.

"I'm going to see if there's any more damage to the outside of the trailer," Moncrief said, exiting back through the front door.

Kep carefully made his way into the living room, toward the bookshelf. "Despite my discomfort with our presence here yesterday," he said in a low voice, "it seems your decision to enter ahead of time was prescient."

Bernadette dug in her purse and pulled out two pairs of latex gloves. "Do you think they just wanted to trash the place, or do you think they were looking for something?"

"An excellent question." Kep took a pair of gloves from Bernadette and snapped them on.

"I vote for the first one," Bernadette said. "The glass put away in the wrong cupboard? We wanted to take it for evidence, maybe fingerprint it, maybe even if we were lucky get some DNA out of a saliva sample. Now? It's in a hundred pieces on the floor. Even if we *could* separate those pieces from the others, we have no way to fingerprint anything."

"I cannot argue with that logic." He straightened up and took a long look at the inside of the trailer, from the bedroom door to the front window. "A thorough job of obfuscating evidence."

"Yeah. It seems like they were looking for something, got frustrated and started tearing open sofa cushions and dumping the contents of drawers and cabinets when they got frustrated." Bernadette followed Kep's sightline toward the front window, then squinted. "I'd estimate they were here for maybe an hour, hour-and-a-half. Perhaps one of the neighbors saw something while the place was being ransacked."

"A good place to start."

Bernadette turned her head to look at Kep. "Hey—why aren't you doing your whole supersmelling thing? Get a good whiff of this place—maybe whoever did this wore cologne or some special moisturizing cleanser."

Kep pointed to the bottles of vodka, scotch, and rum smashed in the middle of the floor. "My nose can detect many things, but that olfactory atrocity has permeated everything. Most colognes contain a high level of alcohol, and I'm afraid someone simply wearing cologne and walking through the house upending everything is going to be challenging to differentiate from the spirits spilled in high quantities."

"I've never known you to shy away from a challenge, Kep. Didn't you detect the brand of whiskey over dish soap—"

Kep narrowed his eyes at Bernadette.

Bernadette kicked herself for saying they were there the night before—in a voice loud enough to carry. She looked at the front door; Moncrief didn't seem to be in hearing range. "Sorry."

"At any rate," Kep said, "the inside of a whiskey glass provides a limited palette for my senses. The entire interior of a mobile home does not."

"Okay," Bernadette said. "We'll have to do this without following your nose. I get it." She turned back to the pile of books.

Kep stood still for a moment, then took off his glasses, closed his eyes and breathed in deeply. Despite his protestations, he was still trying.

Bernadette bent down to pick up the book with the broken spine, watching Kep out of the corner of her eye. She leafed through the ruined book—all about predatory birds of the Great Lakes.

Kep grunted, frowning, and stepped over the mess into

the kitchen, where he spread his arms and inhaled deeply again.

She put the half of the book onto the top of the book-shelf and knelt to go through the other books on the floor. *Woodworking Basics: Chairs.* She looked around—no hand-made chairs that she could see. *Native Plants of Ottawa National Forest.* That looked to be from a small press—and yes, on the first page, University of the Upper Peninsula Press. *Nocturnal Birds of the Great Lakes.* An old microbiology textbook. The old standby: *The Inconvenience of Climate Change.*

At least Evan McMichael had been relatively consistent. Environment, woodworking, nature, sustainability.

The bottom row of books sat untouched. A few spy thrillers with worn covers and spines. Three histories of the Franco-Prussian War, and a biography of John Adams, the second U.S. president. One on sources of protein in a vegan diet. Another about building your own website at least a decade old.

Bernadette scooted a foot to her left and looked at the pile of discarded books on the floor. No, it wasn't Evan McMichael who was consistent: it was whoever had ransacked the bookcase.

"Kep?"

Dr. Woodhead turned from his spot in front of the bath-room door. "As I suspected, I sense too many conflicting smells—"

"Not that." Bernadette gestured around at the books on the floor. "These books are all from the top two shelves. The bottom row wasn't touched."

"I see." Kep put his glasses back on.

"Whoever trashed this place was looking for something and found it. Maybe in one of these books."

Kep stepped carefully over the pile, then pointed. "The book on top. *Market Dynamics of Underground Economics.*"

"Right. He was interested in a bunch of nonfiction. That biology textbook looks like it's from the 1800s."

"Do you recall when the book became a bestseller?"

"The biology textbook?"

"No, no, *Market Dynamics of Underground Economics.*" Kep pushed his glasses up onto the bridge of his nose. "Dr. Sabrina Waller made the rounds on the late-night talk shows two or three years ago. Her research spanned centuries, going back to the opium trade of the 1700s—specifically, the business forces driving the illegal opium export from China to Great Britain. It's quite fascinating how much work she put into it."

Bernadette raised her eyebrows.

"But the later chapters focus on the twenty-first century," Kep continued. "This was published soon after the American politicians gave lip service to fighting the scourge of white-collar drugs."

"Sounds like a good way for the cartels to put you on their hit list."

"Or the pharmaceutical companies," Kep replied drily. "However, I'm specifically thinking of—" He grunted and leaned over Bernadette to pick up the book, then he stood, flipping through the last quarter of the book. "Aha. Here it is. 'Chapter Thirty-Five: The Elasticity of Demand for Methamphetamines in Rural America.'" He held the book up. "The page is dog-eared."

"What does elasticity have to do with—"

"Waller provided evidence that the influx of methamphetamines in many rural towns across the United States exploded because many city and county governments accepted bribes from a loosely connected distribution framework. The cartels owned the cities, but the rural areas were often up for grabs. People would cook methamphetamines, but when the police caught them, representatives of this distribution framework would pay city and county officials to perform services where they would purport to clean the houses and apartments where the meth was being cooked."

"Right, because it can be highly toxic."

"These representatives did a passible job of removing the toxic residues and making the homes livable," Kep said, "but their real motive was taking the equipment and ingredients for themselves, along with the incarcerated person's customer base. They'd move the manufacturing somewhere out in the middle of nowhere where they weren't on law enforcement's radar, and the bribes kept the police at a distance."

"You're saying the cops were on the take?"

"In some cases, yes, but according to Waller, the methamphetamine distributors primarily bribed the county supervisors, the town's mayors, even school board members. They controlled the budget, and they controlled zoning laws. They could schedule audits and inspections, so they made sure no one ever surveyed their manufacturing facilities."

Bernadette stood, stretching her arms above her head. "Sounds like a great book, and I get why Dr. Waller was on the talk show circuit. But what does that have to do with our victim's death?"

Kep paused. "I am unsure if I should comment, as I fear this is primarily speculation."

Bernadette raised her eyebrows.

"That book being on top of the pile suggests it was one of the last books—if not *the* last book pulled from the bookcase, correct?"

"Not definitive proof," Bernadette said, "but yes, it would suggest that."

"And the chapter is dog-eared, which suggests that McMichael referred to this section on multiple occasions."

"Yeah, I guess," Bernadette said slowly.

"Gabriel Constantine has been involved, as both a user and a dealer, in the methamphetamine trade for over a decade. His arrest record proves the assertion."

"Okay."

"Suppose Mr. McMichael suspected bribery of a county official who suppressed law enforcement's ability to remove the drugs from the county."

Bernadette tilted her head. "Maybe not a crazy supposition."

"This book is on top of the pile. This chapter is dog-eared. What if Mr. McMichael had proof of this bribery? Where might he have put the proof?"

"In a safe."

"Do you see a safe in this domicile?"

"No, I don't." Bernadette scratched her forehead. "You're suggesting our victim had this proof folded between the pages of that book?"

Kep pressed his lips together. "As I said, pure conjecture. And yet strongly suggested by the placement of the book and the pages. Whoever was looking for something stopped when they got to this book."

"Or at least they didn't go through anything else in the bookcase."

"Mr. Constantine doesn't have a clear motive for going after McMichael. But if our victim discovered proof of bribery for methamphetamine dealers like Mr. Constantine, that *is* a motive." Kep scratched his nose. "However, I do not wish to act on that theory without further evidence. We do not even possess definitive proof this was a murder."

"But we have a lot of strong hints."

Kep nodded. "Perhaps this unsavory business with our unknown pursuers has led me to make conspiracy-like connections where there are none, but it's possible Mr. Constantine was not acting of his own accord."

"Hired? Coerced?"

The corners of Kep's mouth turned down. "I suppose either is a possibility, especially when you consider he was involved in the local drug trade."

Bernadette took her phone out and took a picture of *Market Dynamics of Underground Economics,* resting on top of the pile of discarded books. "It's an interesting theory, Kep."

"Your interest has no effect upon its veracity. I raise it as a possibility."

Bernadette bent down to dig through more of the books, then stopped. "Hey, Kep? Another possibility just occurred to me."

"Equally based on conjecture?"

"Maybe." She glanced out the open door. No sign of the deputy, but she lowered her voice anyway. "You know those notebooks we found under the drawer's false bottom?"

"Yes."

"What if those tables weren't birdwatching times and dates at all, but a coded ledger for the distribution of meth?"

Kep scoffed. "I would call that theory far-fetched, but certainly could make an entertaining subplot in an action film."

"I don't know—my theory would explain an awful lot. His disagreement with Constantine, for example."

Kep stood. "Shall we go see if the notebooks are still under the false bottom of the drawer?"

"Wouldn't necessarily prove me wrong if they were still there. The false bottom might have fooled whoever was trashing the place."

"True."

They walked into the bedroom. The mattress was pulled off the base. The clothes, hung so neatly in the closet the day before, were on the floor. But the bedroom was not nearly as pulled apart as the rest of the house.

Bernadette made a beeline for the nightstand. She pulled it open and almost yanked it out of the cabinet.

"Are you all right?" Kep asked.

"The drawer's a lot lighter—" She looked down. The false bottom had been pulled out of the drawer; it lay on the floor partially underneath the bed.

Nothing in the drawer.

She turned to Kep. "No notebooks."

Kep looked around the room. "I don't see any notebooks torn up the way the books were in the front room."

"So I think the likelihood of my theory just increased."

"We could reasonably conclude the ransackers were looking for the notebooks and stopped when they found them—even though the notebooks' absence is not conclusive proof of your methamphetamine-centric theory."

"Right." Bernadette stepped closer to Kep and lowered her voice. "Here's a question for you, then. Someone trashed this place between sundown last night and nine o'clock this morning. Why didn't they trash it before now?"

Kep blinked. "It's within the realm of reason that someone thought federal investigators would uncover a piece of evidence local law enforcement missed."

Bernadette tapped her nose with a gloved finger. "Right. Let's suppose whoever trashed the place assumed the sheriff's office wouldn't find the notebooks—or some of the evidence. But they hear the feds are coming—now they have to take action."

"The misplaced glass in the cupboard," Kep said. "We

wanted to take it in for evidence today, and now it's damaged so thoroughly as to be useless to our case."

"So," Bernadette said, "two days ago, we decided to come here. Maura coordinated our visit with the sheriff's office, so I'll assume everyone in Sheriff Koskinen's office knew we were coming."

"Bonnie Farmington knew we were in town," Kep said.

"And we just found out she's Constantine's sister. Maybe she tried to destroy the evidence pointing to him." Bernadette furrowed her brow. "But everyone who was in the bar last night knew we were federal investigators. We didn't even get anyone else's names."

"We cast the net wide."

"Sure. Not exactly a state secret, either. I mean, whoever is following me—us—from Taycheedah probably knows CSAB assigned us to this case."

Kep crossed his arms. "Are you thinking the person pursuing us took the notebooks and destroyed this evidence to prevent us from closing the case quickly?"

"I don't know. Maybe."

"And, further, to force us to stay in Porcupine County for several more days?"

Bernadette winced. "That seems way too complicated."

Kep stroked his beard for a moment. "Yes, I suppose that level of planning would be unrealistic."

Bernadette's head spun. Trying to navigate these two investigations—the McMichael death and the Nakrivo case—was overwhelming. How many roadblocks would they face?

Kep walked around the bedroom, inhaling the scents. As Bernadette walked back into the living room, the deputy walked into the trailer through the open front door. "It's a total loss," Deputy Moncrief said, sticking her head in the doorway. "Everything was out of the shed, bags of fertilizer spread all over the yard, broken tools—I found half of the shovel handle a hundred yards away at the edge of the woods."

Bernadette snorted in frustration.

"I'm taking pictures of everything," Moncrief continued. "Maybe you and Dr. Woodhead should leave the trailer."

"Give us a few minutes. We're still looking at some things."

Moncrief glanced around the inside of the trailer. "What do you mean? This place is a complete wreck."

"We're trying to figure out if whoever did this was destroying something or looking for something." Bernadette adjusted her gloves, deciding whether she could trust Moncrief with the information about the missing notebooks. She almost explained everything—their visit last night, the misplaced glass, the false bottom in the drawer—but changed course. "Hey, do you know the players in the local meth trade?"

"You mean besides Gabriel Constantine?"

"Right. He was both a user and a dealer, right? He must have reported to someone."

"We haven't arrested anyone."

"But you have your suspicions, right?"

Moncrief hesitated. "I don't want to speak out of turn, but the owner of the U-Move-It over across the Lost Dish River Bridge from the township—his name is Ed Eskola."

Bernadette blinked. The unbuttoned denim shirt with the sewn-in "Ed" name patch; the taxi driver's familiarity with "Eddie." It was likely the same Ed—she'd rented the small creamsicle pickup from him the day before—and he'd had telltale signs of meth use. That's why Kep waited outside while she finished the transaction. Strange that someone who had so many symptoms of meth use was the first person

Moncrief had pointed to as a higher-level dealer. Though Ed Eskola wouldn't be the first dealer to get high on the drugs he should be selling.

But if anyone from the sheriff's office were to talk to Ed Eskola, they'd soon find out Bernadette had not only rented a pickup from Ed, but had done so under her soon-to-be-ex-husband's name. That would erode trust with the locals faster than anything.

Kep came back in from the bedroom. "The smell of alcohol isn't as prominent in the bedroom, but the intruder did an equal amount of damage in there, if not more so." He stopped when he saw Deputy Moncrief.

"I asked the deputy who Gabe Constantine might have gotten his meth from," Bernadette said quickly. "There's a guy who owns a U-Move-It across the bridge from Lost Dish. His name is Ed Eskola."

Realization dawned in Kep's eyes, but he quickly relaxed his face; hopefully Deputy Moncrief didn't notice.

"I recognize the scent of coffee in the bedroom," Kep continued. "It was quite strong by the nightstand, as if the intruder had sat on the bed for several minutes."

"Why would the intruder drink coffee in the bedroom?" Moncrief asked.

"No," Kep said, "he had coffee before he entered the mobile home."

"You—you can smell his coffee breath? From hours ago?"

"I can't smell everything," Kep said. "But that? Yes, I can smell it."

"Coffee breath fits if the intruder were looking through papers, trying to find information," Bernadette said, glancing at Kep.

The notebooks. She wished she'd taken them last night, chain of custody be damned.

Chapter Twelve

MONCRIEF WALKED ALL THE WAY INSIDE THE TRAILER AND stood in the kitchen, hands on her hips. "Okay, you two—out. I need to take pictures and get this evidence bagged up when the sheriff gets here."

"We're leading this investigation—"

"If it's true, I'll let the sheriff tell me. I don't report to you, I report to him."

Bernadette looked at Kep; she tried to convey *I told you so* to him telepathically, but Kep just blinked back at her, seemingly unaware. She halfway expected him to push back on Moncrief as he had the first day Bernadette met him. A couple of positive experiences where they worked together had made Kep less mean, maybe even less egocentric. But she could have used more of a spine from him right now.

If you want something done right, Bernadette thought, *do it yourself.*

"No, Deputy Moncrief—that's not the way this works. We're the lead investigators now, and we have been since we arrived in Michigan."

"But I don't—"

"We're given the guidance to work alongside local law enforcement, make it a partnership. No one wants to fight over jurisdiction. But you won't kick us out of our own crime scene—"

"Bernadette!" Kep said sharply.

She turned and glared at him. He'd never taken that tone with her—but at least he hadn't called her *Bernie.*

"In the interest of interagency cooperation, I suggest you and I *step* outside. Nothing in here will sprout legs and escape into the woods. I agree you and I are lead investigators, but Deputy Moncrief is simply looking out for herself and her county's best interests. We can wait for twenty minutes until the sheriff's arrival."

Bernadette stared at Kep; her jaw had dropped open. Kep wouldn't be the asshole to Moncrief he'd been to Bernadette during their first meeting—and worse, he was even taking the deputy's side.

Her hands were balled up into fists. She relaxed and flexed the fingers of each hand. "Certainly," she said.

Moncrief gave a curt nod. "Appreciate it."

Bernadette took a deep breath and exhaled slowly as she stepped over a couple of piles toward the front door. Kep navigated his way from the threshold of the bedroom door to the front, staying a few yards behind Bernadette.

They both walked down the two steps of the mobile home until the gravel driveway crunched under their feet. Bernadette kicked at a rock among the gravel, sending it skittering toward the woods. "What the hell?" she hissed.

Kep motioned with his head, and she followed him down the gravel driveway until they stood a few feet from the Sugar Maple Estates sign. "I know I was rather abrupt—"

"I'll say."

Kep set his mouth in a line and glared at Bernadette. "Will you allow me to complete my explanation?"

Bernadette closed her eyes briefly, rolled her shoulders, and exhaled loudly. "Go ahead."

"If we insist on staying in the mobile home, what are the actions Deputy Moncrief will likely undertake?"

"Calling the sheriff and tattling on us."

Kep shook his head. "The sheriff is already on his way, and that option would be both repetitive and impractical."

Bernadette folded her arms. "She'd probably stand in there and stare at us until we left."

"Perhaps," Kep said. "But she saw the mess of the interior and immediately went outside to check the shed. She knew the shed had potential evidence in it, and instead of standing in the trailer gawking at the mess, she took action. I took notice of her proactivity."

"Okay, so Porcupine County made a decent hire. What of it?"

Kep took off his glasses and rubbed his eyes. "If faced with federal investigators who won't leave a crime scene, what might a proactive deputy do if someone's home had been ransacked the night before?"

It came in a flash to Bernadette. "Go knocking on doors. Five other mobile homes here—well, four, since Gabe Constantine is still locked up."

"I agree, a likely scenario. Now, if Deputy Moncrief—"

"One of the neighbors might remember an orange-and-white pickup truck parked in front of the police tape last night," Bernadette said. "If Moncrief hears that, she'll go to the U-Move-It place for sure, and then we'll get outed."

"Precisely," Kep said. "I propose, therefore, that we canvass these domiciles before the deputy seizes upon the opportunity."

"And that's why you wanted us to get out of there. That was a good idea. Sorry."

Kep nodded.

"We should split up so we can cover the other four mobile homes before the sheriff arrives."

Kep pointed to a mobile home with white vinyl siding. "I shall take those on the far side of the driveway."

Bernadette turned to a light blue double-wide trailer and walked up the gravel walkway, then up three steps leading to the black front door. She pulled her badge out of her purse, held it out, and knocked.

Rustling inside, then silence. She knocked again.

"Federal investigator!" she called.

More rustling from inside. Finally, the door opened a crack and a woman's eye appeared, the rest of her face in shadow.

"He's not here," she said, her voice hoarse with either sleep or crying. Maybe both.

"I'm not—" Bernadette paused. "Are you okay?"

"I told the sheriff I don't want to press charges. If you think—"

"I'm not here about that," Bernadette said hurriedly, raising her badge. "It's about your neighbor, the one who lives at the end of this row."

"Didn't he kill himself?" The crack in the door opened a little wider, the light falling on her right cheek, where heavy makeup hadn't completely covered the bruise.

"Well, that's just it," Bernadette said, trying to keep her tone light and conversational, but willing the woman to open the door a little more. "We came to catalog some items in the trailer, and someone ransacked it last night. I wanted to know if you heard or saw anything."

"No, sorry," the woman said, clearly not giving it any thought.

"Any strange noises?"

"No."

"Were you at home all evening?"

The woman hesitated. "I better not answer any more questions." She began to shut the door.

"Wait!" Bernadette said. "Take my card. If you think of something else."

"I don't think that's a good idea." The woman closed the door, not impolitely, but firmly.

Bernadette sighed. All the signs of an abusive, controlling partner. She'd have to mention it to Moncrief. Maybe the deputy already knew. But the woman either didn't see anything or wouldn't say anything.

Maybe it was a good thing she hadn't taken Bernadette's card—her phone was off, after all.

The second mobile home had similar siding in an eggshell color. The door was a tan color with a glass storm door in front of it, with a concrete slab about six feet square with a brown welcome mat. The storm door was locked, but Bernadette pushed the doorbell on the right: electronic Westminster chimes.

A tall Black man with close-cropped black hair, a mustache, and goatee answered. He wore a light blue oxford dress shirt, untucked, with a pair of loose-fitting sweat shorts and flip-flops. His eyes had bags under them, but his face was handsome.

"Yes?"

"Bernadette Becker from the Controlled Substance Analysis Bureau—"

"Hey, hey," the man said, holding his hands up in front of him. "I don't know what my ex told you, but I haven't—"

"I'm investigating," Bernadette interrupted, "the death of the man who lived in the end trailer."

"Evan," the man said. He stepped out onto the top step in front of his door. "Yeah. Nice guy. Let me borrow his snow shovel when I first moved in. Didn't think to ask for mine in the divorce."

"Can I get your name?"

"You're not from Interpol, are you?" The man smiled.

Bernadette blinked. Had she heard that before? Oh, yes, from Evan's sister. Gabe Constantine had told a neighbor that Evan was an Interpol agent.

The man looked down at the porch. "Sorry, that was an, uh, inside joke."

"Believe it or not, I got it."

He looked up at Bernadette's face in mild surprise, then said, "I'm Alvin Davies."

"Thanks, Mr. Davies." Bernadette returned her badge to her purse. "Did you hear or see anything unusual last night?"

"At his place?" The man ran his hand over his face. "I don't think so. I think Gabe had a visitor."

"What makes you say that?"

"Ever since I moved in a few months ago, a guy comes every couple of days to visit Gabe. I don't know if it's his brother or a friend of his or what. Sometimes he's in a beat-up Honda Civic, sometimes he's in a U-Move-It car or pickup."

Bernadette winced inwardly. This might be trouble for her.

"And you think he visited last night?"

"I work from home." Alvin gestured to his outfit. "Business casual on camera, dreaming of a Cancun vacation on the bottom. Anyway, I looked up from my conference call yesterday about six-thirty, and through the window I saw a U-Move-It pickup drive out."

"A U-Move-It pickup?"

"That terrible shade of orange and white? I'd know it anywhere."

"You're sure it was six-thirty? Pretty late for a conference call."

"Meeting with a rep in our San Francisco office from six to seven. They're two hours behind. It was during the call, and it seemed to be about halfway through, but I didn't notice the exact time."

"What about later?" Bernadette pressed.

Alvin shrugged. "I finished work about seven-thirty, and, uh, I walked to the bar."

"St. Matthew's Pub?"

"The only one within walking distance. I had one of those days." Then he scoffed. "Who am I kidding? I've been having one of those *years*. I went to the bar, had a burger and fries and four or five beers. Then I got a ride back home and fell asleep on the sofa."

"What time?"

"Don't know. I was a little drunk when I left. I don't really pay attention to the time. Work, pay my bills, try not to fight with my ex when she calls, lather-rinse-repeat, you know?"

Bernadette nodded. When Barlow had first left, those first few weeks were rough. On trash day, maybe three weeks after he'd officially moved out, she was putting out the recycling and counted several empty wine bottles in there. She'd gone back into the house, looked at her face in the mirror, and gasped with horror. Puffy eyes, red cheeks—she looked like a hollowed-out, bedraggled mess. She wondered if Sophie saw her the same way. "Pitiful," she'd said to the mirror, then spat at her reflection.

What would have happened if Sophie hadn't been there? She pulled herself together because she was embarrassed about what her daughter would think of her. But if there had been no Sophie, would she have continued to spiral down? Would she be like Alvin, going through the motions every day with nothing but the hope of getting drunk at a bar after work?

She shook her head to clear the cobwebs.

"Now hang on a second," Alvin said, stroking his goatee. "The Tigers game was on the TV. They were up by a run in the bottom of the eighth. Costa came in and struck out the side, and some businessman who was a huge Detroit fan bought me a beer and we finished watching the game. I drank the new beer—well, I guess he bought me a couple more after that, too." He looked at Bernadette. "If you can figure out when the game ended, then I left about a half hour later."

A spark ignited in Bernadette's head. "You said someone gave you a ride home?"

"Oh—yeah. The guy who bought me the beer. Said I was looking a little wobbly and I probably shouldn't drive. I told him I was walking home, but when I hopped off my stool, I had kind of a hard time keeping my balance. Usually—especially lately—I can handle three or four beers without much of an issue. But I don't know, I've been under a lot of stress lately. Or maybe I had more than I thought I had."

"So this person drove you home?"

"Yeah. Nice car, too, one of those luxury cars."

Bernadette rubbed her chin. "Was it a Lexus?"

"Maybe. Don't see a lot of those in Yooper country."

"You're not from around here, are you?"

"My wife—my *ex*-wife was. I work for a company down in Minneapolis. She wanted to move out here, close to her family. I convinced my company to let me go remote, then it turns out she thinks she's the main character in a damn Hall-mark romance movie and she starts seeing a guy she went to high school with who's an *actual lumberjack* over in Escanaba." He grinned and straightened up. "The role of the uptight city-slicker will be played by Alvin Davies." He gave a slight bow.

Bernadette tipped her chin in acknowledgment and decided not to tell him the main character never cheats in a Hallmark romance movie.

"So," Davies said, "is it obvious I'm not from here?"

"You just said *Yooper* with a kind of inflection I don't usually get from the locals."

Alvin laughed. "I was kind of kidding. I think I might be the only Black person in the whole county."

"Did you get a name?"

His brow furrowed.

"The guy who drove you home?"

"Oh—uh, he might have introduced himself, but I didn't really pay attention."

"Was he wearing a suit?"

"Yeah." Alvin snapped his fingers. "And these fancy cowboy boots. I was about to make fun of him when he offered to buy me a drink. Don't bite the hand that feeds you, right?"

"Or the foot." She paused. "Have you heard of Victor Zorba?"

"Oh—of course. You saying he's the guy who drove me home?"

"It's pretty likely."

"If so, he's a nice guy. When the game was over, I was in terrible shape. He had to help me into my own house." He chuckled. "My mom would be mad at me for getting a ride from a stranger."

"But proud of you for not drinking and driving, I bet." Bernadette cleared her throat. "And you heard nothing after you arrived home?"

"Man, I didn't even make it to my bed. Passed out on the sofa, woke up with a terrible crick in my neck. I'm glad I don't have to clock in—I got a late start this morning for sure."

Bernadette pulled a card out of her purse. "You think of anything else, you let me know, okay?" She glanced at the number on the card. "Leave a message if I don't answer—I don't have great coverage here."

He took the card from her. "Sure. And thanks."

"Thanks?"

"My ex has been reporting me for a lot of stuff I didn't do. I think this is the first interaction with law enforcement I've had in the last year where I haven't feared for my safety."

"Oh. I'm sorry you've had to go through that."

Bernadette turned to go, and Alvin started closing the door.

"Hang on," Bernadette said, "one more thing."

Alvin turned.

"How much interaction have you had with Gabe?"

"Gabe? Uh—not much. I try to stay away from him." Alvin scratched his nose. "You heard he's into meth, right?"

"Right."

"I don't touch the stuff. I used to smoke pot every now and then, but since my ex is reporting me to the cops if I look at her wrong, I don't even do that."

"But—marijuana is legal in Michigan, isn't it?"

"There's still a federal law against it. And it's against the morality clauses of a bunch of workplaces. She reported me to HR at my company about a week after I moved out. Fortunately, they didn't test me, but I haven't done it since."

"All right. Thanks a lot."

"Have a good day," Alvin said, sounding sincere.

Bernadette stepped off the concrete landing just as Kep walked to meet her across the gravel driveway.

"There was no answer at the home occupying Space One," Kep said. "Carol Blakely, the sole resident of Space Two, reported a small orange-and-white pickup parked in front of Mr. McMichael's home at about six o'clock. She further told me she thought nothing of it because a driver in a similar pickup truck regularly visits Mr. Constantine."

"The man in Space Four saw an orange-and-white pickup drive by about six-thirty." Bernadette paused. "So thanks for suggesting we canvass the trailers. We'll have to figure out what to say to the sheriff, so he doesn't find out it was us."

"I shall leave explanations to you," Kep said. "I have more information, however."

"Go for it."

"Mrs. Blakely also saw a black Lexus parked in front of Space Five."

"What time?"

"A quarter after ten o'clock. She saw it as she was getting ready for bed and doesn't know when the vehicle arrived or left. She had several unsubstantiated allegations about the driver and their motives for being here, most of which had to do with criminal activity."

"The guy in Number Five—Alvin Davies—got drunk at the bar last night and a businessman driving a luxury car, wearing a suit and ugly cowboy boots, drove him home."

"That sounds like our friend Victor Zorba."

"Yep. I'll have to check the time the baseball game ended —Alvin says he left thirty minutes later. Ten fifteen sounds reasonable."

Kep nodded. "Anything else?"

"Alvin has a terrible ex-wife."

"How about Space Three?"

"Yeah, uh, a woman answered the door but wouldn't open it all the way. Sounds to me like an abusive partner."

Kep frowned. "Did she have anything to say about comings or goings last evening?"

"I think she saw something, but she clearly didn't want to talk. She was scared. And I should mention it to Deputy Moncrief."

The sound of an engine made them both turn: a green-and-white SUV with *Porcupine County Sheriff* painted on the side pulled into the gravel driveway, coming to a stop in front of Space Six.

"Sheriff Koskinen might even be angrier about the break-in than Deputy Moncrief," Kep said.

Bernadette patted Kep's shoulder. "We'll figure out a way to soothe the savage beast."

Chapter Thirteen

Sheriff Koskinen crossed his arms and surveyed the devastation of the living room and kitchen. He sucked in air through his teeth.

"Yeah, this isn't helpful," he grumbled. He took off his hat and smacked it against his thigh.

"It appears Mr. McMichael's death is more complicated than a simple open-and-shut suicide," Kep said from behind Koskinen.

Koskinen turned and glared at Kep. "What makes you say that?"

"Someone ransacked the house yesterday evening," Kep said.

"We don't know that. It could have been any time in the last week."

Kep shook his head. "No, because we—"

Bernadette shot a look at Kep, and he clamped his mouth shut.

"Because we came in when we arrived with Deputy Moncrief," Bernadette said, turning to Koskinen. "Dr. Woodhead, as our lieutenant probably told you, has an extremely keen sense of smell."

"I used to watch *Cases That Won't Die*," Moncrief piped up from the kitchen.

"Right." Bernadette glanced at Kep again.

Kep pointed at the floor, where the liquor bottles lay smashed. "Alcohol evaporates," he said. "It's clear these spirits have been lying on the floor for less than twelve hours."

"You can tell from just the smell of the alcohol?"

Kep nodded. "I can. So we're looking for a perpetrator who was here after nine o'clock last evening. *The jaws of darkness do devour it up.*"

Koskinen looked sideways at Kep. "*A Midsummer Night's Dream?*"

Kep smiled. "It is. Lysander to Hermia, Act I."

"I played Lysander in a high school production."

Bernadette rolled her eyes. *Great—another one.*

"The girl who played Hermia was the prom queen." Koskinen chuckled. "Got to kiss her in Act IV. Made the hours I spent memorizing lines worth it." He cleared his throat. "Can you put a cap on the other end of it?"

"What do you mean?"

"I mean, ten to twelve hours? Six to twelve hours? Could the perpetrator have left just as you and Carla pulled up?"

"I'm unsure of how warm the trailer was last night," Kep said. "The electricity doesn't appear to be off, and if the air conditioner was running—"

"Okay, we can check," the sheriff said. "Carla, see if you can find the thermostat and figure out if it's programmed, or what it's set to. It's on now."

"Sure, boss," Moncrief said, stepping over a few couch cushions on the floor toward a plastic box mounted on the wall.

"Do you want to hear the residents' statements?" Kep asked.

Koskinen rubbed his eyes. "I suppose."

"I should mention," Bernadette said, "the woman in Space Three might be the victim of an abuser."

"Yeah, Emma Mortensen," the sheriff said. "Travis is a good guy, a little rough around the edges, and yeah, he can drink too much." He shrugged. "I can't do anything if she doesn't want to press charges, though."

Bernadette sneaked a glance at Deputy Moncrief; her face looked pinched, a vertical crease between her eyebrows.

Kep and Bernadette related their interviews with Alvin Davies, Carol Blakely, and Emma Mortensen, although they purposely only mentioned what the witnesses had seen after seven o'clock. The deputy took copious notes and asked good questions while the sheriff harrumphed and skulked around the edges of the room like a mountain lion in a cage.

After the last question, the sheriff tapped his foot and looked at his watch. "Carla, can you call the county CSI team and get them on cleanup? I've got a meeting in an hour."

"Uh—sure," Deputy Moncrief said. "But I don't have a ride back to the station."

"We can give you a ride back," Bernadette said.

"Don't be silly. You've done plenty already. One of the CSI folks can drive Carla back." Sheriff Koskinen touched his hat, then stepped behind Bernadette and Kep and left the mobile home. A moment later, an SUV door opened and slammed shut and the engine turned over.

Bernadette arched an eyebrow at Deputy Moncrief as the sound of the SUV faded. "Something about Emma Mortensen you aren't telling us?"

Moncrief shook her head. "Aatos and Travis go way back. They were best friends in high school."

"So—he's protecting Travis?" She paused. "Is Emma in danger?"

The deputy bit her lip. "I think I better get to the thermostat."

Bernadette glanced at Kep's face, which betrayed no emotion. "Right," she said. "I guess we'll see you back at the sheriff's office in a few hours."

The deputy turned and stepped toward the small plastic box mounted on the wall. Bernadette and Kep walked out.

"I didn't like that at all." Bernadette closed the driver's side door and turned on the engine. "They're keeping stuff from us."

"And we from them," Kep said, putting on his seatbelt.

"Our lies of omission are because we're being followed, and we could be in danger. But the sheriff is looking the other way while his friend abuses his wife."

"You'll still have an equally difficult time justifying our falsehoods to your superiors."

The bile rose in Bernadette's throat as she backed out onto the gravel driveway, swung the car around, and turned onto the road to head back to Lost Dish.

"So we're in the rental," Bernadette said, "and if anyone is tracking us, they'll expect us to be somewhere in the area. Do you think we'll be safer if we turn our phones on and make a call?"

Kep furrowed his brow. "Why would we be safer if they can track us?"

"It would tell them they have nothing to worry about. If we keep our phones off, they'll maybe think we're onto them."

"If we *don't* have our phones off, these mysterious stalkers of ours could find us and potentially do us injury. As unsure as we are of their existence, we're even less confident in their goals and motives."

Bernadette was quiet for a moment as she turned north toward Lake Superior. "True. But we also need to deal with Maura—and, you know, our day jobs."

"Our day jobs won't matter much if our rotting corpses are found in a ditch next week."

"But we're on official business," Bernadette said. "We're around other law enforcement officers. We have to check in with them multiple times a day. Do you think our stalkers will risk targeting us when the police are expecting us?"

Kep scratched his forehead in thought.

"I could see them attacking me when I was on my way to Lost Dish," Bernadette continued. "No one expected me to show up at the Porcupine County Sheriff's Office until this morning. They'd have almost a full day to get away. But now, they don't know if they have ten minutes or three hours."

Kep shrugged. "I have no experience being stalked and in danger. I—I suppose I will have to trust you."

"That's the spirit." Bernadette grabbed her phone from the center console and turned it on. The welcome screen flashed, then loaded, then the window full of applications appeared. She glanced at the screen, tapped the speaker-phone icon, then scrolled to *Lesley Gill*. Then she hesitated.

"What is it?" Kep asked.

"I don't know. CSAB vetted Lesley, but there's something in me that's worried about calling her."

"But we're *supposed* to be here," Kep pointed out. "Even if our communications—or Miss Gill herself—have been compromised, you have discussed laying the trail for us being where we are supposed to be."

"True." Bernadette tapped Lesley's name on the phone screen.

Lesley answered the phone on the first ring. "Bernadette

—I'm glad to hear from you!" She lowered her voice. "Lieutenant Stevenson is worried. She just left for the airport."

"She got my email this morning, though, right?"

"That's right. Doesn't mean she isn't worried."

"She'll be at the hotel soon enough." Bernadette ran a hand through her hair; she had a few tangles in it. Could she trust Lesley? Maura was keeping her in the loop anyway.

She had to trust somebody. Call it a leap of faith. "You're on speaker, by the way. Dr. Woodhead is here in the car."

"Hi, Dr. Woodhead," Lesley said.

Kep leaned forward slightly in his seat. "Good morning, Miss Gill."

"I mentioned this in my email to Maura," Bernadette said. "Evan McMichael's death might be a murder, not a suicide."

"The lieutenant told me," Lesley said. "What evidence is there?"

"A whiskey glass in the wrong place."

Lesley paused. "Anything else? Did the glass have fingerprints? Any DNA evidence?"

Bernadette paused, weighing her options, then decided to open up to Lesley. "The glass was destroyed last night."

"Destroyed?"

Bernadette hesitated. "You know Maura told me to hurry up and close this case. Not to wait for the local sheriff, right?"

"Going rogue. Your favorite."

"Dr. Woodhead and I visited the crime scene in the early evening yesterday without the sheriff's department in tow."

Lesley started to say something.

"Yes," Bernadette interrupted, "I know Maura set up an initial walkthrough of the crime scene with the sheriff's office this morning. But we needed to get started early."

"Okay. So how did you find the glass?"

"The victim was meticulous—everything in its place, the kitchen spotless."

"Except," Dr. Woodhead cut in, "I discovered a drinking glass, the same style as the one found next to Mr. McMichael's body, in the wrong cabinet. The glass smelled of a brand of whiskey we were not able to find in Mr. McMichael's domicile."

"But you're saying the glass was destroyed?" Lesley asked.

"Right," Bernadette said. "When we went back this morning with the deputy, the place had been ransacked. Glass was smashed all over the kitchen floor—I assume the whiskey glass was in there, too. The cabinets were empty."

"You think the killer did that?" Lesley asked.

"Probably a safe assumption," Bernadette said. "But why last night?"

"The perpetrator had over a week to obfuscate evidence," Kep said. "Why did they choose yesterday—between the time we left, around seven at night, and when we arrived at the trailer this morning at nine o'clock?"

Bernadette broke in before Lesley could answer. "We believe it's someone who knew federal investigators would be there today. We didn't exactly keep it a secret. Kep and I interviewed the owner of the bar where the victim was a regular, introduced ourselves as federal investigators—and there were about a dozen people in the bar, any of whom could have gone to anyone else in town and told them."

"Hang on," Lesley said. "Isn't the guy who shot up the trailer in custody right now?"

"Right—Gabriel Constantine." Bernadette looked at Kep. "And I'm not sure I believe Gabriel poisoned Mr. McMichael —even if he *was* out on bail."

"Why not?" Lesley asked. "If shooting didn't work, wouldn't he try something else?"

Kep rubbed his hands together. "The presence of the glass in the wrong cabinet—and the expensive whiskey in the glass—suggests someone came to McMichael's home, poured both of them a drink, then cleaned up one glass and one glass only, and placed it in the incorrect cupboard."

"Because McMichael was already dead or unconscious," Bernadette added.

"Perhaps the person who brought the whiskey was someone McMichael wanted to impress, or didn't want to insult by being too—uh—"

"Persnickety?" Bernadette suggested.

"I would have chosen a word like *obvious*," Kep said. "Perhaps the visitor was someone McMichael had a romantic interest in, or perhaps a potential employer."

"Or a birding expert," Bernadette added. "McMichael had dozens of books on wildlife and birds of prey. He was a biology major, so maybe hawks were his biggest hobby. He could have had a birding expert over to his house."

"Are you suggesting Barcelona Lute?" Kep asked.

"I'm sorry," Lesley said, "what kind of lute?"

"A grad student at the University of the Upper Peninsula," Bernadette replied. "Barcelona, like the city in Spain, and Lute, like the stringed instrument from the Renaissance."

"Ms. Lute is high on our list of potential interviewees," Kep said, "but we would appreciate some background information."

"And given the shooting of the trailer and the poisoning of Mr. McMichael," Bernadette continued, "We might be looking at multiple suspects, or maybe even some puppet-master who's pulling all the strings."

"I'll look into this Barcelona Lute person," Lesley said. "Any other names?"

"Bonnie Farmington," Bernadette responded. "We interviewed her, then later discovered she's the sister of Gabriel Constantine."

"A pertinent piece of information she failed to disclose," Kep said. "And, as the proprietor of the local watering hole, it's possible she had access to the expensive bottle of whiskey."

"Right," Bernadette said. "McMichael also appears to have had a run-in with a local birdwatching group."

"Ornithological society," Kep said.

"I know birdwatching is pretty big up here," Bernadette continued, ignoring Kep's correction, "so there might be multiple groups. The president of the group was the one with his feathers in a ruffle, and the victim's sister referred to the president as a 'he.' Maybe that'll help narrow it down."

Lesley's voice perked up. "Financials, criminal records, big transactions, employers, relatives?"

"The works," Bernadette said.

"Anyone else?"

"Well, I..." Kep trailed off.

"What is it?" Bernadette asked.

"The employees at the sheriff's office all knew we were coming," Kep said. "I don't enjoy making unfounded accusations, especially for law enforcement officials, but we would be remiss if we discounted them."

The clattering of fingers on a keyboard. "Old Victoria Ornithological Association," Lesley said. "Jasper Fortescue, President. The other groups in the county are national or state organizations with regional leaders. This is the only group with a head who's called a 'president.'"

"The victim's sister called the guy the president of the society," Bernadette said. "She might have just meant head of the local group. I don't know if 'president' was the official honorific."

"However, it seems a reasonable place to begin our queries," Kep said.

Bernadette shrugged. "Sure."

"Anyone else?" Lesley asked.

"I'm sure we'll uncover additional suspects in the course of our investigation," Kep said.

"Be careful," Lesley said. "And remember, Maura's planning to meet you at seven o'clock tonight at the Up North hotel."

"We're counting down the seconds," Bernadette said.

"All right, weirdo. Hanging up now."

The line clicked off, the phone going back to the home screen, and Kep looked out of the window. Bernadette turned her phone off.

They traveled in silence for another few miles.

Bernadette watched the scenery fly by in her peripheral vision. A sign on her right: *Hiking Trail*, with a blue, square P sign. Then a smaller, wooden sign, hand-lettered: *Peanut Butter Falls*. She tapped her fingers on the steering wheel as they passed the trailhead. "We need to talk to Gabriel Constantine."

"Perhaps we do." Kep took his glasses off and rubbed his eyes. "However, I fail to see how I can add value to that endeavor."

"What do you mean?"

"He's been in a jail cell for several days, likely not in the clothes he was in when he came in. I suspect there will be little olfactory evidence to go on."

"Oh, right." Bernadette looked at Kep out of the corner of her eye. "What do you propose, then? We split up, like sorority sisters in a slasher film?"

Kep frowned. "I certainly wouldn't use such a banal—if vivid—comparison. I believe you can be more effective at convincing the sheriff to let you interview Mr. Constantine in his cell if I am elsewhere."

"Not sure I should let you out of my sight." Bernadette felt a smile tug at the corner of her mouth.

Kep turned his head and looked at her skeptically. "What do you mean?"

"You've disappeared for hours in both the cases we've been on."

Kep pushed his glasses up his nose. "I had perfectly valid reasons for that."

Bernadette nodded. "And you might this time, too. And I'm the one who'll get chewed out." She glanced over at him. "We didn't have strangers following us in the last two cases, either."

Kep folded his arms and sank down into the passenger seat. "Point taken."

She reached over to the center console and turned the radio on. Static greeted her, and she tapped the *Seek* button. A classic rock station, but it went to commercial almost immediately. Then it faded out. She tapped *Scan* again: a country-music station, then a preacher talking about original sin, then another country station, then a commercial for a car wash, then static.

Bernadette turned the radio off. "I guess I didn't tell you this earlier, Kep, but I appreciate you backing me up on this whole is-someone-out-to-get-me thing."

Kep dropped his arms and turned to look at her. "You are not someone who brings up issues for the sake of being dramatic."

"Yeah, I guess." Bernadette blinked and stared through the windshield. "But, you know, there's a lack of evidence."

"Lack of evidence? What do you call the GPS tracker you pulled out of your wheel well?"

Bernadette paused. "Shit. The GPS tracker."

"What?"

Bernadette smacked the steering wheel. "If I'd been smarter, I would have kept the GPS tracker—maybe we could have traced it to its original owner."

"And risked your life with someone much more able to follow you?"

Bernadette hesitated. "If someone's following me in a car, I can lose them pretty quickly. If I'm in a confrontation situation, I know ways to de-escalate it, and I know how to win if I have to."

The corners of Kep's mouth turned up slightly. "As demonstrated admirably by your interaction on the airplane with Annika Nakrivo."

Bernadette ignored the implied compliment. "But when it goes from being followed to being electronically surveilled, I'm not as confident in losing my tail."

"I'm surprised this wasn't a course rigorously taught at whatever training facility you had to attend in order to become an agent."

"Twelve years ago. Technology marches on. And my last refresher course was three years ago."

Kep sat back and tapped his bearded chin. "What did you do with the GPS tracker when you removed it?"

"Attached it to a dumpster in a hotel parking lot near Oskhosh."

"I see. You attempted to deceive your pursuer into believing you had stopped for the evening."

"Thought I could buy some time. Maybe they'd even think the GPS device got stolen or fell off the car in the parking lot."

"But you're fairly certain they know CSAB assigned you to this case in Lost Dish."

Bernadette shrugged. "I have to operate as if they know it. And even if they don't know it, once they find the GPS tracker on the dumpster, all they have to do is drive on U.S. 45 all the way north until it ends at Lake Superior and they'll find this car parked in front of the Up North Motel."

"You could report the GPS tracker to Lieutenant Stevenson and she could have a Wisconsin-based CSAB employee retrieve the device."

"True. It's probably been long enough where they've figured out the tracker isn't on my car anymore."

They drove in silence for a few moments, Kep resting his bearded chin in his palm, when he suddenly shifted in his seat and grunted.

"What is it?" Bernadette asked.

"I'm going over our interviews in my mind, and I find it curious that we spoke with our bartender last night, and someone broke into McMichael's trailer several hours later."

"Yeah. A big coincidence. Whoever it was tried to keep something from us—and that's why the place wasn't trashed until after we arrived."

Kep scratched his head. "Perhaps they, whoever *they* might be, made an assumption we would simply accept the suicide—or Constantine's involvement—as gospel. It's possible when they realized we would do more than simply sign off on the original assessment, they took action." He steepled his hands.

"I'd like to see if we can talk to Bonnie Farmington again."

"For what purpose?"

"To ask her why she didn't tell us she was Gabriel Constantine's sister. And then we can ask her where she went after she got off work. *Someone* ransacked McMichael's trailer, and like you pointed out, she ticks a lot of the boxes for our suspect—for the ransacking *and* for McMichael's murder."

"An excellent point. Shall we go to the local watering hole?"

"At ten in the morning?"

"It's almost certainly open. Perhaps this is when Ms. Farmington does her accounting for the week. Or perhaps the retired regulars who wake early could provide some additional information."

"Yeah, okay."

The drive to St. Matthew's Pub was short, and Kep was right: the establishment was open. But a different bartender, a white man in his early twenties, was behind the counter, chatting with two men sitting on stools, each with a half-full light-colored beer in front of them.

"Can I help you?" the bartender asked.

Bernadette pulled out her CSAB badge and showed it to the bartender. "We just have a couple of questions for Ms. Farmington."

The bartender blinked. "She'll be in around four."

"Where is she now?"

"At—" The bartender cocked his head, then glanced at the two men sitting at the bar; they were studiously not making eye contact. He clicked his tongue, then hesitated before talking again. "Visiting hours at New Sunset House go until lunchtime. She's usually there at this time of day."

One man at the bar shook his head, then took another sip of his beer.

"You have different information?" Bernadette said, taking a step forward.

The man glanced up at Bernadette's face. "I—uh, no. I just wouldn't want the feds to bug me when I'm visiting my mom." He glared at the bartender. "And I wouldn't want to give the feds information about my boss, either."

"We'll be sensitive to her situation."

The man scoffed, then rubbed his hand over his face.

Bernadette turned to the bartender; he looked stricken.

"Thank you for your assistance," Kep said, pulling a twenty-dollar bill out of his wallet. "Next round is on us."

"Keep your money," the man at the bar said.

Kep's hand froze; he blinked, then he set the bill down on the bar and walked out. Bernadette followed.

They were both lost in thought on the half-hour drive back to Lost Dish. Kep stared out the window most of the time. Bernadette tried not to let her negative thoughts spin out of control—driving was a welcome distraction.

They pulled into the parking lot of the assisted living facility on River Street.

"I don't believe it," she said.

A black Lexus sedan had parked over three parking spaces, and there were no open spaces in the lot.

Chapter Fourteen

"IF I DIDN'T KNOW BETTER," KEP SAID TO BERNADETTE with a wry smile, "I'd say we were following Mr. Zorba."

They parked on the street.

"Do you see any cars from the parking lot at St. Matthew's last night?"

"Besides the Lexus?" Bernadette shook her head. "A bunch of pickups all looked the same. It was dark, and I wasn't paying close enough attention."

Kep pointed at a burnt orange Kia Soul parked in the third space in the row next to the sidewalk. "That car was in the bar's parking lot last night."

Bernadette raised her eyebrows. "Are you sure it's the same car?"

"I would imagine few Kia Soul S-trim models in Mars Orange are in the Upper Peninsula."

"Mars Orange?"

"The name of the color."

"How do you know?"

Kep cocked his head. "I am a federal investigator. I don't simply walk into crime scenes, inhale, and walk away."

"But—paint colors?"

"My knowledge only extends to the top two hundred makes and models each year."

"Only the top two hundred? Slacker." Bernadette grinned.

They walked in through the front door, closing it behind them.

The waiting room was about ten feet by ten feet, with four chairs next to the door they walked in. Motivational posters featuring dogs and cats covered one of the side walls; the opposite wall featured maps: one a Mercator projection of the world, one an artist's depiction of Lost Dish, with cartoon representations of businesses and streets.

Zorba, this time in a tan suit and brown patent leather dress shoes, was at the counter, in discussion with a woman behind the desk in scrubs. She had a clipboard clenched in her hand.

"Mr. Zorba," she said, "we appreciate your donation, but we simply cannot give out that information."

"I understand," Zorba said. "Can't get it if I don't try, right?"

The woman smiled back warmly. "It'll be about ten minutes."

"Thank you so much."

The front door opened, and an older clean-shaven man in a sportscoat and Oxford shirt, with golden brown skin, lines deeply etched into a frown, glared at the counter. "Mr. Zorba," he said, trying to be calm, but with a note of frustration in his voice. "I told you twenty minutes ago you are illegally parked."

Zorba's eyes widened. "Oh—I'm so sorry. I thought I'd just be a moment, but this took longer than I expected. You must think I'm horrible."

"We have a patient who needs—"

"Say no more," Zorba said. "I'll move my car right now."

Bernadette stepped over to the wall and pretended to be engaged in the cartoon map of Lost Dish as Zorba hurried out the door.

Once the door closed behind him, Bernadette stepped up to the counter with her badge. "Hi, there, we're from the Controlled Substance Analysis Bureau. We'd like to speak with Bonnie Farmington."

"Take a number." The nurse narrowed her eyes. "She's not a patient here."

"We were informed she was visiting her mother here. We'd like a word."

"Do you have a warrant?"

Bernadette pressed her lips together. "I can get one, if you like."

"If you'll be walking through our medical facility where our patients are based, I'm afraid I'll have to insist."

"I see."

"You can wait for Ms. Farmington in the parking lot. Our waiting room is for visitors and patients only."

She didn't want to scare Bonnie off, so perhaps a note would soften the appearance of the investigators at her mother's assisted living facility. "Can I leave a note for her?"

The nurse pursed her lips, placing her clipboard on top of the counter, and grabbing a notepad. "I suppose."

Bernadette put her purse on the counter—and the clipboard clattered to the floor at Bernadette's feet.

"Oh—sorry—" Bernadette said.

"I'll come around and get—" the nurse began.

But Bernadette had already reached down and grabbed the clipboard. *Incident Report: Theft of Medication*, the top page read, and a long name beginning with a C.

Constantine?

But she didn't see the rest of the name—though she caught a couple of other words—like *axadabutin*.

Bernadette almost gasped.

No wonder the facility was filling out an incident report. She'd dealt with a Medicare fraud case a few years before, and she'd found out how expensive blood thinners like axadabutin were. A month's supply cost more than her car. There was also a list of side effects and interactions as long as her arm, so patients had to jump through hoops to get it prescribed. Was the mother of Bonnie Farmington—née Constantine— the theft victim?

Bernadette put the clipboard face-down on the counter and nodded to the nurse. "Sorry—I can be a real klutz some- times. We'll just wait in the parking lot."

Bernadette motioned with her head to Kep, and they walked out to the parking lot. The black Lexus was making a right turn out of the lot onto River Street. Bernadette hung back for a moment, then when the Lexus turned, walked toward the parked rental car.

"I thought we were waiting for Ms. Farmington," Kep said.

"We were. But I don't want Zorba seeing us here."

"Surely he saw us in the waiting room."

"I don't think he did—he was distracted. I don't want him *thinking* we're following him."

Kep shook his head. "I believe he *did* see us. His hackles will surely be raised if we're gone when he returns."

"What do you suggest?"

"I propose staying here. We have questions we can ask Mr. Zorba."

"Such as?"

"Such as where he was last night." Kep pushed his glasses

up on his nose. "As we have a witness who puts him in the trailer park."

"Two witnesses saw a black Lexus."

"And one of them identified Mr. Zorba's boots."

Bernadette motioned with her head toward the assisted living facility building. "What about Bonnie Farmington?"

"If she's seeing a relative, we can interview her when she exits."

Bernadette wished she had a pair of sunglasses with her. She stepped back toward the building and stood in the shade of an alder tree. Kep followed a few steps behind.

After a few moments, Victor Zorba hurried up the sidewalk. He stared at Bernadette and Kep as he walked across the parking lot.

When he was about thirty feet away, Bernadette spoke. "Good morning, Mr. Zorba."

"Fancy meeting the two of you again," he said brightly, but with a cautious tone in his voice. "And you'll have to forgive me, but I'm afraid I don't remember your names."

Bernadette pulled out her badge. "We're federal investigators, Mr. Zorba."

Zorba cocked his head and stopped in his tracks. "Listen, we had auditors in last month, and Windfall 29 passed all the appropriate state and federal—"

"No, no," Bernadette said. "We're investigating the death of Evan McMichael. I'm Case Analyst Bernadette Becker, and this is my colleague, Dr. Kep Woodhead."

"Oh, goodness," Zorba said. "So tragic what happened to him."

"True." Bernadette took a step toward him. "So—did you know Mr. McMichael?"

"I don't believe I ever met him," Zorba said. "I saw the

news—and of course, a small town like this, a suicide is all some people talk about."

"Suicide?" Bernadette pressed. "Where did you hear that?"

Zorba cleared his throat. "It's the rumor going around. Probably from the workers."

"Any other rumors we should be aware of?"

Zorba looked from Bernadette's face to Kep, then back. "Some people think there's a cover-up."

"And what," Bernadette asked, "are they covering up?"

Zorba looked from Kep to Bernadette. "The man who shot up Evan's trailer. Many people believe he's got something to do with it."

Bernadette nodded. Okay—a confirmation the rumors had reached the upper echelons of the Lost Dish social scene.

Zorba shifted his weight from foot to foot. "Listen, I have to get back in—"

"Just a couple of questions, if you don't mind," Kep said, holding up his hand. "Multiple witnesses saw a vehicle matching yours in the same trailer park where Mr. McMichael lived."

"When?"

"Last night."

"Oh." A serene smile slid over Zorba's face. "I was in St. Matthew's Pub last night."

"We saw you there," Kep said.

"Of *course*, that's where I've seen you," Zorba said.

"But," Kep continued, "we saw you leave the pub long before our witnesses spotted a black Lexus at Sugar Maple Estates."

"Well—anyway, I came back."

"You were talking to the owner of the pub."

"I was." Zorba widened his smile. "I suppose if you saw

me speak to Ms. Farmington, you probably know I'm trying to buy the pub from her."

Bernadette pressed her lips together. Why did Zorba want to buy the pub in the first place? But she needed to confirm the evidence. "You stayed until the end of the Tigers' game."

"Uh—yes. I'm a Tigers fan, and when the game came on, I got some dinner and stayed there."

"When did you leave?"

"When the game was over, of course."

"What time?"

"I didn't really pay attention." He snapped his fingers. "But one of the other patrons there had a bit too much to drink."

Bernadette nodded. "I understand you bought him several beers."

"I could tell he was having a rough week. He and I started talking about our ex-wives. We were sitting next to each other at the bar. I paid his tab. He looked like he could use a small kindness."

"Then you drove him home?"

"He wasn't far away—I think he might have walked to the pub, but he was in no condition to walk home. He lived in the trailer park just down the road."

"All right, so you drove him back to the trailer park. Did you stick around?"

Zorba frowned. "You mean, did he invite me in?" He chuckled. "Oh, I see what you're getting at. I go back to the bar, I buy him several drinks, I drive him home? No, I hate to disappoint you, but I don't swing that way. Nothing wrong with it, of course—"

"I meant," Bernadette interrupted, "did you hang around the parking lot?"

His brow furrowed. "Well—I plugged in my phone and got directions back to the highway. Then I started one of my driving playlists—it's a good half hour back to my house."

"But you didn't park at the trailer park."

"I pulled into a space, but just to be sure he made it inside." His smile was back. "I suppose I dithered a bit selecting my playlist. Five minutes, maybe."

"Did you get out of the car?"

Zorba blinked. "I had some trash to throw away. Uh—I suppose, strictly speaking, it's not legal to dump your trash into someone else's trash can, so shall we just say I stretched my legs?"

"Did you go by Evan McMichael's trailer?"

His smile grew taut across his features. "I'm afraid I don't know which one it is."

"The one with all the police tape around it."

"Ah." Zorba cocked his head. "Well, I saw there was an empty trash can sitting in front of the house. Barely sitting inside the police tape. I thought—well, if there was police tape surrounding the trailer, I figured it was unoccupied."

"So you threw your trash in the garbage."

Zorba folded his arms. "Surely it's better than littering."

"No, no, you're fine." Bernadette thought for a moment. "Why buy the pub?"

Zorba smiled, the lines in his face showing sympathy. "We're diversifying. We've already expanded into resorts. St. Matthew's is popular—and well known throughout the county, we'd be able to use the St. Matthew's Pub brand throughout our properties. With the soft real estate market right now, it makes some sense."

"So *you're* not trying to buy the bar? You're representing Windfall 29."

"Companies make investments in their future," he said

with a twinkle in his eye. "Now, if you don't mind, I have a situation to deal with."

"Just one more question," Bernadette said. "How would your amusement park plans change if an endangered species were discovered on the property?"

Zorba took a step back. "Did something change about the environmental impact study?"

Bernadette paused. "Uh—I'm not sure."

"When we had the study done, we showed that our construction plans had little impact on existing wildlife. The changes are occurring on existing property."

"So you're not buying the pub to expand the land for the amusement park?"

Zorba stifled a laugh. "My apologies—I don't mean to be derisive, but we've got a copper mine that's half a mile deep and covers almost a thousand acres. It's *plenty* of room for any plans we have. If we get even *half* the plan completed, it'll still be the largest amusement park in the Midwest."

"And what if an endangered species were found—"

"Look," Zorba said, "the environmental impact study's been done. If there are changes, I guess we'll deal with it then. Now, I really must get inside."

Bernadette nodded. "Thanks for your time, Mr. Zorba." She stepped to the side.

Zorba opened the door—just as Bonnie Farmington was walking out.

"Good morning, Bonnie. I was hoping to run into you."

Farmington jumped slightly. "Oh—Victor. Hello."

"Hope your mother is doing well."

"Uh—yes. Today looks like a good day so far."

"Have you given my offer any more thought?"

Bonnie let Zorba go around her and step inside. "Still weighing my options."

"Take your time."

The door swung shut behind Zorba. Bonnie turned toward the parking lot and saw Kep and Bernadette. "Oh, come on," she said, rolling her eyes. "Not the two of you again."

"Usually people are so much more welcoming when we're investigating a murder," Bernadette said. "Especially when they've bailed out the guy who shot up our murder victim's home."

Bonnie closed her eyes, and her shoulders drooped. "Okay—yes, you're right. I didn't mention Gabe is my brother."

"And why not?"

"Because—"

The door opened behind her, and a middle-aged woman walked out, stepped in between Bonnie and Bernadette, and walked to her car.

Bonnie looked around, then walked to the side of the parking lot. Kep and Bernadette followed her. Bonnie turned to face them and lowered her voice. "Because I'm embarrassed. Gabe screws up everything he touches. And I know I shouldn't keep giving him chance after chance after chance, but—I mean, listen, he was a lot younger than me during the divorce, and it really messed him up."

"Twenty-five thousand dollars bail," Bernadette said. "A lot of money."

"I took out a loan and put the bar down as collateral."

"And—since his bail got revoked?"

"I didn't get the money back, if that's what you're asking."

"Did they charge him with another crime?"

"I don't think so, but they didn't explain themselves to me. First I heard about it was when Gabe was already in jail again."

"So what happens to your bar?"

Bonnie barked a laugh, but Bernadette could see the pain in her eyes. "I'll make it work. It's just like a second mortgage, I guess."

"Or take an offer from Victor Zorba," Kep said.

"Yeah, well," Bonnie said, "He didn't come in twice yesterday for the drink specials."

"We heard he came back after we left," Bernadette said.

Bonnie nodded. "I was slammed, though. At least he had the good sense not to talk about buying the pub when I was rushing around like crazy."

"He bought another guest a few beers, then drove him home?"

"After the Detroit game was over? Yeah, I think he paid Alvin's entire tab. I'm not really in the position to refuse his money. I probably have the credit card receipt if you want it."

Bernadette took a small step closer. "And what did you do after you closed up the bar last night?"

"Me? Why?"

"We're trying to narrow down possibilities," Bernadette said.

Bonnie clenched her jaw. "It was probably one o'clock when I got out of there. Went home. I watched some TV, then I went to bed."

"Anyone see you?"

Bonnie shrugged. "I don't know if you noticed, but we live out in the boonies. My nearest neighbor is about a quarter mile away."

"You live alone?"

"Yes."

"What did you watch?"

"On TV? I'm, uh, bingewatching a new vampire series on Flixtune. But I was exhausted—I think I only watched for maybe thirty minutes. I think I was in bed by about two-thirty."

So not a regular TV program where Bernadette could check the time—although Flixtune had user records. But, of course, the trailer could have been broken into any time after Bonnie said she went to bed.

"Anything else?" Bonnie asked. "I need to get back to the bar."

"We appreciate your time," Bernadette said.

Bernadette and Kep walked back to the rental car. "Let's drop the car off at the hotel and walk over to the sheriff's office."

"I assume you still want to obfuscate our movements?"

"Can't be too careful." Bernadette opened the driver's side door. "You can go to the evidence room to smell the glass found next to McMichael, and I'll go to the jail to talk to Constantine."

Chapter Fifteen

Koskinen wasn't back from Banner Crossing yet. The receptionist offered to walk Kep over to the evidence room, and he accepted. After the interior door closed behind them, leaving Bernadette alone in the waiting area, she turned and walked out the front. She followed the brick-and-glass building around the corner to the sign for Porcupine County Jail, which shared the building.

She'd taken out her badge and was about ten feet from the front door. A siren: quiet at first, then getting louder as it approached.

The ambulance was on its way to the jail.

Should she enter the jail building and try to see Gabriel Constantine before the ambulance arrived?

Her feet didn't move.

Thirty seconds later, the ambulance pulled up in the loading zone, its lights flashing but its siren off, and two EMTs hurried out of the back of the ambulance, efficiently pushed out a gurney, pulled the wheels down, and rushed into the jail.

She stepped back to the corner of the building, hesitated,

then paced on the sidewalk. She knew better than to go in there during an emergency, and her stomach flipped with anxiety.

It felt like an hour, but was only a little over ten minutes later when the door opened again. The EMTs rushed out, a body underneath a blanket, a face mask over the head sticking out of the top, back into the ambulance. A large, balding white man in a deputy's uniform, hand on his forehead, staggered out after them, but the ambulance was already pulling out of the loading zone.

Bernadette slowly walked up to the deputy, her badge in hand. "Bernadette Becker with CSAB," she said.

The man turned his head to Bernadette. The metal nametag on his breast pocket said *Mueller.* "Uh—how can I help you?"

"I assume you were working in the jail today?"

"Yep. I'm here until seven."

She tilted her head toward the jail door. "I wanted to interview Gabriel Constantine."

He shook his head. "He just got loaded into the ambulance."

"Can you tell me what happened, Deputy—Mueller, is it?"

The man nodded. "Jens Mueller, yeah." He hesitated. "We don't have a doctor on staff here."

"Small rural jail like this? I'm not surprised. Haven't been to many of these with a doctor on full-time."

"The guy was an addict—I mean, he's been in and out of jail a few times before, yeah? But he's been here over a week, and I figured he'd been through the worst of it."

"The worst of it?"

"Withdrawal."

"Right. The sheriff said he was still struggling."

Mueller hesitated. "I don't think I'd call it struggling. His medication—modafinil—seemed to help. In fact, he seemed fine the last couple of days. Then this morning, right after he took his medication, he was complaining he felt cold. He had a fever, so we gave him some Tylenol, but he—uh, he soiled himself. I cleaned it up, but then he started shaking all over. That's when I called the ambulance."

Bernadette took out her phone, but it was off; Kep's was probably off too. She didn't want to dig her prepaid phone out, either. "Do me a favor and go get Dr. Kep Woodhead. He should be in the evidence room."

Mueller turned to leave.

"Hang on." Bernadette reached her arm out awkwardly as if to stop the deputy. "We'll need access to Constantine's cell."

❦

Bernadette stood at the entrance to the jail cell, Deputy Mueller standing a few steps behind her. There were two other cells, both along the same wall, neither occupied. The smell of pine-scented cleaner was strong enough to sting her nasal passages. Still, she guessed she'd likely choose the strong pine scent over what it had cleaned up, assuming the deputy was telling the truth about Constantine soiling himself. She blinked hard and tried not to let her discomfort show. "So Gabriel Constantine was the only guest of the county yesterday evening?"

"The only one in this section," Mueller said. "Drunk tank had a couple people in it. The women's side is holding two people for transfer later in the week."

"How long has he been in this cell?"

"Since the day after he was picked up on suspicion of violating his parole."

"Has the county charged him with McMichael's murder?"

The deputy shrugged. "I don't think so, but I just hear rumors, yeah? I don't follow the legal proceedings of these guys."

"But even attempted murder is a big deal. Why hasn't he been transferred to a state prison?"

"You'd have to ask the sheriff, but my guess is Baraga and Ojibway are both full right now."

"Those aren't the only places—"

"I don't know, Agent Becker."

Bernadette flinched slightly at the misnomer.

The deputy sighed. "I saw a form a couple days ago—I think we've put in paperwork to have him transferred elsewhere in the state. But I don't know if it was accepted. Hell, I don't even know if we submitted it. Like I said, you'd have to ask the sheriff."

"So he's supposed to stay in the county jail for now?"

The deputy sighed, folded his arms, and leaned on the concrete wall across from the bars of the jail cell. "Gabe's been in and out a bunch. He's a user and a low-level dealer. Nothing violent before."

The door at the end of the hallway opened and Kep strode in, a short woman in a business suit, black hair piled on top of her head, at his heels.

"You asked for—" Kep stopped talking and crinkled his nose, then took a handkerchief from the inside pocket of his sportscoat and held it over his face as his eyes darted to Bernadette. "If you had wanted to harm me, I can think of nothing so effective as pine cleaner and human feces."

"Sorry, Dr. Woodhead," Bernadette said, "but Gabriel Constantine had some kind of seizure—"

"And I called for the ambulance immediately," Mueller interrupted.

Bernadette held a hand straight out and indicated the cell. "Whatever happened here, Constantine left the jail with two EMTs."

"An EMT and a paramedic," Mueller said.

Bernadette blinked. "Okay, right. Anyway, Dr. Woodhead, I thought maybe you could detect something."

"Detect what?" Mueller asked.

"Dr. Woodhead has a keen olfactory sense," a woman with a heavy English accent behind Kep interjected. "He's able to determine a variety of smells and compounds, even in very low quantities. He's rather well known in some circles."

"You're like a forensic smeller, yeah?" Mueller said.

"Forensic toxicologist, yes," Kep said.

The deputy nodded, then his face fell. "Constantine shat himself pretty bad earlier today. I—I had to use a lot of pine cleaner. I put him back in here—and that's when he had the seizure—or whatever."

Kep took a small step forward. "I can differentiate scents underneath large amounts of a wide range of disinfectants, including alcohol-based solutions, chlorine and chlorine compounds, formaldehyde, hydrogen peroxide, iodophors—"

Bernadette held up her hand. "We get it, Kep."

"My scent differentiation is less exact with quaternary ammonium compounds."

She raised her eyebrows.

Kep took a step toward the cell and lifted his nose. After a moment, he spoke. "This is a broad-spectrum disinfectant with pine essential oil. I'll be fine." He turned to the woman behind him. "Bernadette Becker, meet Dr. Imogen Goadbury. Dr. Goadbury is the medical examiner for Porcupine County."

"I'm on staff at St. Joseph," she ventured. The short "A" of "staff" revealed an English accent, maybe from the north.

Mueller piped up. "That's where they took Constantine. County isn't big enough to have a full-time M.E., but Dr. Goadbury does a good job, yeah?"

"Many thanks, Deputy." She raised her eyes to Dr. Woodhead. "I was dropping off my report on Mr. McMichael when I saw the ambulance."

Bernadette shot a quizzical look at Kep.

"Dr. Goadbury made a final determination on the cause of death," Kep continued, catching Bernadette's eye, "Her professional opinion is that Mr. McMichael was poisoned by sulfuric acid."

Bernadette scratched her nose. "Sulfuric acid?"

"Mr. McMichael's esophagus and stomach lining were burned," Dr. Goadbury said, "though much of the damage appears to be postmortem."

"Did someone pour the acid down his throat after he was dead?" Mueller asked.

"A whiskey glass was on the table when his body was found." The medical examiner smiled patiently. "It appears the acid was mixed with the whiskey."

"And it did that much damage?" Mueller's eyes went wide.

"Sulfuric acid doesn't stop damaging tissue once the victim is deceased." She took a step forward. "The lab results came back this morning, and the findings support the theory that the victim drank the whiskey mixed with the acid."

"So it *is* suicide," Mueller said.

Bernadette furrowed her brow. "What?"

"Sulfur smells like rotten eggs, yeah? And the whiskey wouldn't hide the smell. He'd have noticed it for sure."

"I'm afraid," said Kep, "that you have confused sulfuric acid with *hydrosulfuric* acid, more commonly referred to as hydrogen sulfide. Hydrogen sulfide has the famed noxious odor of spoiled eggs. Sulfuric acid is colorless, and most people cannot detect its odor."

Mueller pressed his lips together and gave a faint nod.

"As far as the evidence is concerned," Kep said, "Dr. Goadbury made the glass from our victim's kitchen table available to me."

"And did you smell it?" Bernadette asked.

Kep's face fell. "Such a pedestrian way to describe a crucial part of my process."

"He did," Dr. Goadbury said.

"And?" Bernadette pressed.

"Present were notes of oak, cherry, vanilla, and macadamia nut," Kep said.

Delight and wonder crossed Dr. Goadbury's face.

"That would suggest the same—" Kep paused for a moment and stole a quick glance at Bernadette. "The same, uh, flavor profile as found in a top-shelf bourbon-style American whiskey called Widewaters Reserve."

"I believe Widewaters is a local distillery," Dr. Goadbury said.

"Over in Alger County," Deputy Mueller said. "Employed a bunch of people when the mines laid off practically everyone a couple years ago."

Bernadette nodded, then tilted her head and looked at Mueller. "We've spoken with Victor Zorba. He seems to think his company is, uh—"

"Going to save the county from sliding into recession," Mueller finished. "But when their copper mine goes from employing almost half the county to having thirty people run a skeleton crew, you lose your credibility pretty fast. Mark my words, unless they do something drastic, the company's going to be dead in the next year."

"I was under the impression," Kep said mildly, "the

mining company had some sort of amusement park venture."

Mueller nodded. "Zorba's a nice guy. And I guess we'll know more details after today's board of supervisors meeting, yeah?"

"Fair enough." Kep nodded. "Now I need to analyze the cell."

He stepped forward into the cell, stopping less than a foot from the metal bunk bed frame holding two mattresses. Pushing his glasses up, he took a long whiff and kept sniffing. Bernadette thought she could see his eyes water.

The first time she'd seen Kep in action, he'd turned to the local law enforcement detective and complained about her perfume. Now, he opened his eyes and turned to Dr. Goadbury.

"Dr. Goadbury, did you use Sapphire Creek B-Vitamin Face Moisturizer this morning?"

The medical examiner reddened. "Erm—yes, I'm afraid I did."

"Would you mind stepping out past the outer door for just a moment?"

Bernadette shook her head. "The scent of a moisturizer can't be stronger than the pine cleaner, Kep."

"Nor the undertone of human feces," Kep said. "However, as I'm attempting to identify scents under the most dominant ones in this cell, the fewer conflicting scents, the better."

"Want me to leave, too?" Bernadette asked.

Kep turned his head to Bernadette and sniffed. Wow—he was actually taking her question seriously. Bernadette wondered why she was surprised.

"No," Kep said after a moment of consideration. "I appreciate you used no perfume and washed your hair with unscented shampoo and conditioner this morning."

"Anything for you, Kep," Bernadette said.

"I'll just pop off to the other room, Dr. Woodhead," the medical examiner said, although her tone suggested she wasn't happy with this turn of events. She turned and walked down the hall and through the door at the end.

"However," Kep said, turning to Deputy Mueller, "you have some Spencer & Kelly Wild Mountain aftershave, affecting my ability—"

"You've gotta be kidding me, yeah?" Mueller asked.

"I'm afraid he isn't," Bernadette said.

"Federal agents or not," Mueller said, "I can't let you stay in here without a representative of county law enforcement—either me or Dr. Goadbury need to be in here. I'd get fired otherwise."

"Then I must insist you stand over on that side," Kep said, pointing to the door Dr. Goadbury had just walked through.

Mueller harrumphed, but walked over to where Kep indicated, then folded his arms.

"We appreciate it," Bernadette said.

Kep looked around the cell. A small shelf next to the bunk held a book—a dog-eared spy thriller popular twenty years before, and a metal cup.

Kep bent over the shelf, closed his eyes, and took a long sniff.

"Deputy Mueller," Kep said, his eyes still closed, "did you supply Mr. Constantine with the cup this morning?"

"I gave him some Tylenol to help get his fever down. Some water to wash it down with."

"This metal cup here?"

Mueller was silent for a moment. Then he spoke, a note of snark in his voice. "You okay if I come over so I can see what you're talking about?"

"Certainly." An icy edge crept into Kep's voice.

Mueller walked over—taking his sweet time, Bernadette thought—and looked at the metal cup Kep pointed to. He frowned. "Well, that's one of ours, for sure, but I remember taking the water cup back right after he used it." He ran his hands through his short hair. "Hang on a second. He asked for more water after I took the cup. I brought him more and then left to take care of some paperwork. Maybe I didn't go get the cup afterward."

Kep nodded.

"You smell anything?" Bernadette asked.

"Very faint," Kep said.

Bernadette took a step forward. "Faint, as in there was something in the cup?"

Kep frowned. "I wouldn't make that assertion. It's possible the scent was transferred from Mr. Constantine's mouth to the cup."

"Sulfuric acid?" Bernadette asked.

Kep shook his head. "No. Slight notes of chalk and turmeric."

"Modafinil?"

"No—modafinil has a hint of cloves and black pepper. I believe this is a different medication, though it isn't something I recognize. I might be better able to tell if I obtained a comparison sample."

Bernadette turned her head toward Mueller. "I thought you said he'd taken modafinil."

"He had!" Mueller insisted. "You—you're saying he took something else?"

"Certainly in the last forty-eight hours, although I suspect Mr. Constantine received the substance much more recently."

"Like last night?" Mueller said.

"I believe this morning is more probable." Kep stepped to

the concrete wall and continued to sniff. "Can you ask Dr. Goadbury to come back in?"

"Uh, sure." Mueller walked to the door and opened it.

"Everything okay?" Dr. Goadbury's voice carried from the hallway.

"The smeller guy wants you back in."

Dr. Goadbury walked in carrying a clipboard, a calm expression on her face, although Bernadette suspected she was upset at being left out.

"Thanks for your understanding," Bernadette said. "You doing okay?"

"Tickety-boo." Dr. Goadbury raised the clipboard. "I found Mr. Constantine's medical file in the front office. Did you need my opinion on something you found?"

"Mr. Constantine may have consumed an additional medication in the last twelve hours. Might that explain the fever?"

"I'm sorry," Dr. Goadbury said. "Did you say he took an additional medication?" She looked down at the clipboard, flipped through the pages, then shook her head. "I quite dislike using the word 'impossible' in my line of work, but the jail monitored his intake carefully."

Bernadette turned to Mueller. "You said Constantine was taking anti-withdrawal medication—modafinil, was it?"

"Right. We made sure he got the correct dosage."

"That medication is not the smell I identified," Kep said.

Dr. Goadbury tapped the top page on the clipboard. "Nevertheless, modafinil is on Mr. Constantine's chart. No fatal drug interactions, and no indications for any interactions with paracetamol."

Mueller furrowed his brow. "Not with *what?*"

"Paracetamol?" Dr. Goadbury startled. "My apologies. You Yanks call it 'acetaminophen'—the active ingredient in your

Tylenol." She held up a finger. "If there was an additional medication Mr. Constantine somehow slipped by our security protocols, however, there's no telling what the interactions could have been."

Bernadette turned to the deputy. "Would you go get Mr. Constantine's medication?"

"Uh, sure." Mueller hesitated a moment, looking at Dr. Goadbury, then exited into the hallway.

"With the symptoms described by Deputy Mueller," Kep said to the medical examiner, "do you have any theories as to what might have occurred?"

"I would have to run a tox screen."

"I see."

The three of them stood in uncomfortable silence for a moment, then the sound of a distant door opening and closing, and Mueller came hurrying back in, holding two bottles in his hand and a binder.

"Modafinil," he said, slightly out of breath.

"An off-label use, but not an uncommon one for a long-term addict," Kep said. "A stimulant with dopaminergic effects."

"It is what the county recommends in their rehabilitation programs," Dr. Goadbury said.

Bernadette nodded. Most CSAB employees had run across modafinil in their line of work—with the spike in meth use in the last twenty years, doctors commonly prescribed modafinil. Experts considered it good for withdrawal symptoms as well as recovery from long-term addiction. Its positive effects on memory and attention were anecdotal, but the medication had an excellent reputation.

"Worked great for Gabe," Mueller said. "Until the last couple of nights. Sweats, nausea—it was bad yesterday and obviously worsened this morning." He put his hands on his hips. "But Gabe's been using for so long, I just figured he'd built up a tolerance to the withdrawal medication or something."

"Or it just didn't work for him." Dr. Goadbury tilted her head. "I saw no indications in his medical file that Mr. Constantine suffered from narcolepsy or another type of sleep disorder. Deputy, did he make you aware of any conditions he had?"

Bernadette looked over at Kep, who was visibly holding back from speaking.

"No, ma'am," Mueller answered.

Bernadette looked at Goadbury quizzically.

"Narcolepsy is an on-label use for modafinil," Kep said.

"Exactly right," Goadbury said. "It may not have worked for withdrawal on Mr. Constantine if he had taken it for a sleep disorder previously."

"You said there were no lethal drug interactions," Bernadette said. "And none with Tylenol. What are the worst interactions with?"

"Opioid painkillers and alcohol," Goadbury said. "But you're correct—the contraindications are not usually severe enough to result in such a severe adverse reaction."

"I found something else, yeah?" Mueller said. "I don't know if it matters, but I figured I'd let you know—you're the investigators."

"What is it?"

"No modafinil pills left in the bottle," he said, "and I know there were a couple of pills left in there when I put it back. Even if we needed it for another prisoner, no one here would've put an empty bottle back in the cabinet. Doesn't follow protocol."

"So—you're saying someone took the modafinil?"

"That would explain why I smelled no modafinil near

Constantine's water glass," Kep said under his breath.

"I can't think of another explanation," Mueller said. "Either accidentally or on purpose, I don't know, yeah?"

"You said a couple of pills were in the bottle the last time you gave it to Mr. Constantine?" Bernadette asked.

"I didn't count. Only three or four." Mueller looked at the ground. "I know I'm supposed to keep close inventory, but there was a lot going on this morning."

"What do you mean, keep close inventory?"

"I noted on the sheet yesterday morning there were eighteen pills left. But this morning there were just a couple. I didn't count because I wanted to figure out if I had accidentally put the number in the wrong place on the sheet, or if someone else had been in the cabinet."

"Hold on," Bernadette said. "So you're saying that yesterday, you had eighteen pills. This morning, there were three or four, and you gave—how many?—to Mr. Constantine."

"I gave him two pills this morning."

"And now—no pills?"

Mueller looked abashed.

"Who has access to the drug cabinet?" Bernadette asked.

"Not the prisoners," Mueller said quickly.

"I figured," Bernadette said. "I mean, who here besides you?"

"The sheriff and the deputies."

"I do too," Dr. Goadbury said.

"Anyone else at the hospital?" asked Bernadette. "Is there a pharmacist?"

"The pharmacist doesn't have access to the cabinet."

"So one other thing I noticed," Mueller said. "Again, I don't know if it means anything..."

"What is it?" Bernadette asked.

"When I found out the modafinil was missing, I checked

the other medication. And all of it was there, just like I noted it in my sheet."

"But?"

"Well, it's the Tylenol."

"How many of the Tylenol pills are missing?"

"Uh—that's the weird thing. I've got *too many* pills."

"Too many?"

"According to the sheet, I should have twenty-three pills left. I've got forty-one."

"Let me see." Bernadette stepped closer and Mueller handed the bottle over.

Bernadette shook out a pill into her hand. The pill was bright white, smooth, and slightly oblong. She lowered her face closer to the pill in her hand. "Looks like acetaminophen to me."

"To me too," Mueller said.

Bernadette turned the pill over in her hand. A small number was etched on the face. Bernadette squinted: *800*.

"Yep, it's—" Then she cocked her head.

"What is it?" Kep asked.

"Eight hundred," Bernadette said. "The number etched onto this pill."

"So?" Mueller said.

"Acetaminophen doesn't come in an eight-hundred-milligram pill."

"Prescription strength?"

Dr. Goadbury piped up. "The maximum dosage is six hundred fifty milligrams per pill, at least in the States. However, no manufacturer I know puts numbers on parac-etamol—excuse me, acetaminophen—caplets."

"So what's with the eight hundred?" Mueller asked. "Is it a different brand name or something?"

"I don't think it's Tylenol—it's not even acetaminophen,"

Bernadette said, raising her hand slightly.

"The number '800' might suggest ibuprofen," Kep said.

Dr. Goadbury nodded. "Over-the-counter extra-strength ibuprofen is eight hundred milligrams in the States. That would explain the number etched on the pill."

Kep dipped his face until it was less than an inch from the pill in Bernadette's palm. She almost flinched. He breathed deeply, then straightened. "Ibuprofen," he said confidently.

Bernadette put the pill on the desk and set down the bottle.

Dr. Goadbury crossed her arms as if nothing happened, as if Kep hadn't just bobbed his head like a drinking bird toy. "Confusing paracetamol—sorry, acetaminophen—and ibuprofen is a common mistake."

"But not for a hospital pharmacist," Bernadette said.

"Perhaps more common than you'd think."

"Maybe," Bernadette said. "Look, Gabriel Constantine is a person of interest in the murder of Evan McMichael, and he just left here on a stretcher. They prescribed him two medications. One of those medications is missing, and the other one was substituted out. Neither count of those pills matches what's on the inventory sheet." She looked around at Dr. Goadbury, then Kep. "Am I the only one who thinks we need to focus on the medication?"

Kep nodded. "I support that assessment."

Bernadette turned to Dr. Goadbury. "What's the name of the pharmacist at St. Joseph?"

Goadbury hesitated. "Trudy Fortescue."

Bernadette blinked. Where had she heard her name before?

"Is she related to a Jasper Fortescue?" Kep asked.

"Oh—yes. Jasper is her husband."

Bernadette turned to Kep. "Oh, right—he's the president

of the Old Victoria Ornithological Association."

The man who had threatened Evan McMichael.

Bernadette and Kep hurried out of the Porcupine County Jail building. "I need to get this information to Maura as soon as possible," Bernadette said. "She should be in the air now, so before we head over to see the Fortescues, let's find a wi-fi signal so I can connect my laptop."

Kep pointed toward their hotel. "We've got two rooms and five full days of wi-fi access at this local inn. We might as well use it."

"Oh—right." Bernadette hesitated. "I haven't called Sophie since I arrived. I think she might be worried."

"As much as I hesitate to reveal our location, I think the hotel is probably a good place to contact her." Kep quickened his pace. "Once we send the lieutenant our message, I believe you can call your daughter without putting us in additional danger."

A few minutes later, they opened the door to Room 5. A small, low desk with a brass-plated desk lamp and a cheap-looking desk chair was on the far side of the room.

"All right," Bernadette said, pulling her laptop out of her bag and striding over to the desk. "Let's get this party started."

She typed out in a bullet list everything they'd found out, and this time Bernadette didn't hide that she and Kep had been at the crime scene the night before.

"Someone with law enforcement access is behind this, right?" Bernadette said, staring at the laptop screen.

"We cannot discount the possibility." Kep sat on the bed a few feet behind Bernadette. "I assume our theory provides enough comfort and assurance for you to justify breaking the directive to work closely with local law enforcement."

"Our theory seems to give enough comfort and assurance to *you*," Bernadette said, trying not to crack a smile. "Did I miss anything?"

Kep leaned forward over Bernadette's shoulder and skimmed the email text Bernadette had written. "I'm afraid you neglected to mention the sulfuric acid smell in the victim's glass, but not in the glass found misplaced in the cupboard."

Bernadette looked at Kep. "I thought you said sulfuric acid was odorless."

"I believe I said that most people cannot detect its odor."

"Right, right, you're not most people." Bernadette moved the cursor up to the bulleted list and kept typing, then sat back. "Okay. I got the wildlife books, the maniacal state of cleanliness, the Old Victoria Ornithological Society, the neighbor who I think is a victim of abuse, her shitty husband, the other two neighbors, the pharmacist, the toxicology report on McMichael, and the possible foul play with Gabriel Constantine."

Kep's phone buzzed in his pocket and he took it out.

"You still have your phone on?" Bernadette turned around in her chair. "Kep, what are you—"

"I'm doing what we agreed to," Kep said. "We are at the hotel, and if there are people following us, you want to make sure they can't tell we're onto them. So the fiction of a lack of service any time we leave the downtown area of Lost Dish is in full effect. Having my phone on when we are here is just taking steps to establish that fiction as believable."

"Okay, sure," Bernadette said.

"And this message is from Dr. Goadbury." Kep looked up. "Gabriel Constantine died about fifteen minutes ago."

Chapter Sixteen

AN HOUR LATER, BERNADETTE STEPPED OUT OF THE HOTEL room. "We still haven't gone to see Barcelona Lute." She checked the door behind her to make sure it had locked.

"I believe the more prudent action would be to interview Trudy Fortescue," Kep said. "Not only is the University of the Upper Peninsula one hundred fifty kilometers away, but we have a woman with means and opportunity and her husband with a motive."

"For two different murders," Bernadette said.

"While there is no tangible evidence the two deaths are related," Kep said, "I believe it would be remiss if you and I did not attempt to make a connection."

"Hopefully, she'll be able to shine some light on her actions—or on her husband's reasons for fighting with our first murder victim."

"If our Mrs. Fortescue has made any physical contact with sulfuric acid in the last two or three days," Kep said, "or if there is any residue at her work area at the hospital, I should be able to identify—"

Then he stopped in his tracks.

Bernadette kept walking. "We agreed, right? As long as our movements get reported back to the sheriff, we take the rental—"

"No," Kep said sharply. "Stop."

Bernadette stopped walking. "Okay, Kep, you're kind of freaking me out."

"Good." He took off his glasses, closed his eyes, and inhaled, long and slow. Then he pointed to Bernadette's rental car. "C4."

Bernadette blinked. "What?"

"C4. Plastic explosive. Start walking away, now."

The synapses in Bernadette's head stopped firing for a moment, then she turned and ran as fast as she could in her flats, Kep right behind her.

They turned the corner of the hotel building and slowed to a stop.

"Okay," Kep said, catching his breath. "Ammonium nitrate is not a particularly strong explosive, so we should be safe here."

"Not particularly strong?"

"It would be strong enough to blow up the car and kill us both," Kep said, "but the damage to the hotel building would be contained to a fairly small radius."

"You smelled it?"

Kep nodded. "Tar and motor oil."

"Maybe someone changed their oil in the parking lot—"

"Let me clarify. While the smell of C4 is not dissimilar to tar and motor oil, it possesses its own signature smell."

"You're sure?"

"I am positive."

"Do you think Lost Dish even has its own bomb squad?"

"We must get the staff to evacuate the hotel."

"Right." Bernadette stood.

Kep grabbed her arm.

Bernadette looked down at Kep's hand. "What are you doing?"

"Whoever did this might be watching the hotel. Looking for signs their plan worked. Waiting for us to get in and blow ourselves up."

Bernadette scratched her head—it was not only a good point, it's something she should have thought of. "I—I suppose I'll need to check if anyone is watching the parking lot." She immediately thought of the tall man in the Kansas State sweatshirt.

Kep rubbed his forehead.

Bernadette turned the corner and looked out at the parking lot. Her rental was the only one in the front parking lot; the U-Move-It pickup truck was in the rear lot with three cars Bernadette assumed belonged to the staff. All looked empty.

She looked up and down the street; no signs of life. There were two shopfronts across the street, but blinds covered their windows and the sun shone directly into them—anyone sitting there would stare into the sun if they looked toward the hotel.

A few parked cars might be next to the curb farther down the block, but a hedge was blocking the view of the rental car —and to the entrance to her hotel room.

She turned and walked back toward Kep.

"If anyone is watching the hotel, I think they're parked far enough away where they can't see the car."

Kep frowned. "What would be the point?"

"If the bomb is set on some kind of timer or connected to the ignition, it might be enough for them to simply hear the explosion. They might not want to risk being seen— after all, if they left their car somewhere they could watch us, then the chances are pretty good we could watch them, too."

"I suppose that makes sense."

Bernadette slapped her knees. "Okay—evacuation." She turned and rushed into the office, in the other building facing the parking lot, but a good fifty yards from Bernadette's rental sedan.

Darcy looked up from the computer screen behind the front desk. "Yes, Ms. Becker, right? How can I—"

"Get everyone in the hotel out—now," Bernadette said, showing her badge, although Darcy already knew she was with CSAB. "As far away as possible from the front parking lot."

"I can't just—"

"There's an explosive device in one of the cars parked there," Bernadette continued, raising her voice and talking over Darcy. "Get them behind this building if possible."

All the color drained out of Darcy's face. "I don't—how long do we—"

"I don't know if it's on a timer or if it'll get triggered as soon as I turn the ignition," Bernadette said, "but—"

"Wait—this bomb is on *your* car?"

"Focus, Darcy," Bernadette snapped. "All those workers Victor Zorba booked rooms for?"

"They're all at their job site—I think it's just the house-keeping staff and me."

"Then immediately get yourself and the staff on the other side of this building and wait for the all clear from us."

"How will I know when?"

Bernadette looked at Darcy out of the corner of her eye. "I'll come find you if I'm still alive."

Darcy reached for her walkie-talkie on the counter, and it

slipped from her grasp and banged against the keyboard. Her breathing came hard and fast. Oof, not the right thing to say.

Bernadette reached across the counter and grabbed Darcy's hand. "Hey, hey, you can do this. Radio your co-workers and tell them to get out of the hotel and go behind this building. And you get out too."

"I've never—"

"I know. But you can freak out later. Now you've gotta get on the radio."

Darcy grabbed the walkie-talkie. "Monique, Destiny—drop what you're doing and get behind Building 2 now."

A crackle. "What? I'm in the middle of a deep clean!"

Darcy pushed the talk button again. "Now, now, now. I don't care what you're in the middle of. This is an emergency. Drop everything and get to the back of Building 2 right away."

Bernadette turned and rushed out, going behind the first building—Building 1, she supposed. Kep was in the middle of putting his phone back in his pocket.

"Your regular phone? Not the burner?"

"Technically, burner phones do not have cameras or web browsers—"

Bernadette stomped. "Not the time, Kep!"

Kep grunted. "I cannot see the difference mobile phone selection will make since our pursuers have apparently discovered our location." He straightened his sportscoat and drew himself to full height, although he was visibly shaking.

"Did you call someone?"

"9-1-1. The nearest bomb squad is over two hours away. The dispatcher said they'd put an evacuation order in place for a two-block radius."

"The whole downtown area."

"This complicates our plan to meet Lieutenant Stevenson in this parking lot," Kep said.

"Let's cross that bridge when we come to it." Bernadette pointed at the U-Move-It pickup. "You smell anything there?"

"No. The pickup truck has no scent of C4—or any explosive." He paused. "I examined the undercarriage of the vehicle as well. I—well, I wanted to completely assure myself there were no plastic explosives there."

"And you're sure about the C4 on the rental car?"

Kep raised his eyebrows. "Are you informing me you no longer trust my, uh, what did you call it? My *supershnozz?*"

"I just can't believe this is happening to us," Bernadette said.

"The clear and present danger does have the general atmosphere of a surrealist movie."

Bernadette reached into her purse and pulled her phone out. "I think we need to ditch our phones. Not just turn them off, but ditch them completely."

"Perhaps that should wait until after the bomb squad has been here and gone."

"I don't know—usually my phone can't be tracked when it's turned off. But I know there are some IMEI trackers that can do some marginal tracking. If that car blows up and our phones keep moving, they'll know we survived the car bomb. But if the C4 goes off and the phones are destroyed…"

Kep nodded. "I understand the point you're making, but I don't believe it's worth the risk to life and limb placing our phones back in our rooms."

"Not our rooms." Bernadette held her hand out. "My aim is decent. I'll toss 'em under the rental car."

Kep shook his head. "It's too unsafe."

"What's more likely? The car blowing up in the next sixty

seconds? Or whoever is after us tracking us when our phones are off?"

Kep reluctantly got his phone out of his pocket and handed it to her. "I just powered it down."

Bernadette put her purse down on the ground, grabbed her keycard and her phone—making sure it was also off—then took a deep breath. She sprinted around the building, almost slipping in her flats as she turned the corner. She stopped, then took her phone and gave it an underhand toss. It bounced on the asphalt of the parking lot in the space next to the rental car, clanged against the passenger's side door, and came to rest about two feet from the right front tire.

She tossed Kep's phone next. It banked off the right rear hubcap, and the case cracked when it bounced off the asphalt and landed about three feet away from her phone.

She sprinted back around the building.

Kep looked up. "You're alive," he said simply.

"Not perfect, but it'll do," Bernadette said, slightly out of breath. "Come on, let's get back to Banner Crossing."

"Do you think we can escape without being seen by our pursuers?"

Bernadette considered this for a moment, halfway expecting an explosion. "A hedge is blocking the sightlines to the rental car. But if they're watching, I bet they're somewhere where they could see the explosion. They're probably not watching the back of the motel."

"However, if they were watching the front, they might have just seen you toss our phones under the rental car."

"Like I said, blocked sightlines," Bernadette said. "I'm not a hundred percent sure, but the fact they didn't remotely detonate the car when I was out there gives me some hope that I'm right."

Kep scratched his beard. "I am unsure I am willing to wager my life on that supposition."

"We don't have a choice," Bernadette said. She pointed to the U-Move-It pick up. "If we drive out the back way, they might not see us."

"I don't know if I agree."

"You have a better idea?"

Kep pushed his glasses back up onto his nose. "We could approach the young woman at the front desk and ask if the hotel has cameras. We could review the footage and perhaps identify a suspicious car or person."

"Not a bad idea if we weren't twenty yards away from a C4 bomb."

Kep was silent for a moment.

"We can't stay here, Kep. We're sitting ducks. And we can't go into the hotel lobby, either. Maybe we can get the footage later."

Kep put his hands on his temples and closed his eyes. Then he dropped his hands. "I believe you have a better grasp of the situation than I do."

"So," Bernadette said, "let's get to the pickup truck and hightail it out of Lost Dish."

Kep opened his eyes and nodded.

They hurried across the back parking lot to the U-Move-It pickup, and Bernadette hopped in and turned the engine on as Kep was climbing into the cab. Bernadette threw the gearshift into reverse before Kep had even grabbed his seat-belt. Bernadette tried not to be too obvious as she went out of the back driveway onto Shoreline Street, turning away from Highway 45.

"Isn't this the wrong way?"

"It's not the most efficient way. But if anyone is waiting for us at the front of the hotel, we shouldn't drive past. I know we're not in the same car, but the two of us might be pretty recognizable."

"Excellent point."

"I'm going to head down Firesteel Road, then turn on Woodspur and catch Highway 45 about two miles south of the township limits." Bernadette slowed at a stop sign and tried to accelerate as sanely as possible.

"And what about our investigation? What about Lieutenant Stevenson?"

Bernadette shrugged. "We'll have to find Wi-Fi somewhere for the laptop." Then her eyes widened. "Oh, no. My laptop. It's still sitting on the desk in my hotel room."

"Do you—"

"Absolutely not, Kep. I'm not turning back for anything at this point. After the bomb squad—"

Boom.

The hotel was four or five blocks away, but the explosion was loud. It didn't shake the pickup, but Bernadette was so surprised she jerked the steering wheel, then immediately straightened out.

Kep turned to look at her.

"Looks like I won't have my laptop with me for the rest of the trip."

"Or our phones."

"We've still got the burners."

Kep dropped his head, his beard almost touching his chest.

"Now I *know* I'm not being paranoid." Bernadette glanced in the rear-view mirror—no one seemed to follow the pickup —and she focused on the road ahead.

A thumping noise, fast and loud. Not another explosion— a rhythmic low noise—

Oh. It was her heart beating in her ears. She was

breathing fast, too—almost as fast as Darcy had been at the front desk.

Bernadette loosened her death grip on the steering wheel and took a deep, shuddering breath. She looked over at Kep, who was frozen in his seat.

"You okay, Kep?"

He grunted but didn't move. "If I hadn't smelled the C4..."

Bernadette nodded. "We'd both be dead." She stole another glance at Kep out of the corner of her eye. "Don't tell me with all the investigations you've been on, you haven't been in danger before."

"Not like this, no." He cleared his throat. "Except for the corpse in Oregon last time."

Bernadette shifted in her seat. "We've had a couple of near misses, for sure." She made a left turn onto Firesteel Road, the asphalt turning from rough to smooth. She checked the rearview mirror but saw nothing. Looking over her left shoulder, she caught a plume of smoke rising from the downtown area. "It looks bad."

"I am hopeful no one sustained any injuries." Kep cleared his throat. "Or worse."

Bernadette scratched her scalp. "Actually, we did."

Kep blinked, then turned to Bernadette. "What? Are you all right?"

"No. I'm dead. We both are."

Kep turned to Bernadette. "I don't follow."

"Look—if someone was watching the hotel, maybe they *were* in a location where they could see the car and the front door, and maybe they know that the car explosion didn't kill us."

"So why did the car explode when it did?"

Bernadette sucked in air through her teeth. "I think our

phones were being tracked."

"So you've said."

"And if the car wasn't being watched…"

"Ah," Kep said. "Someone saw that both our phones were near the car—and activated a remote detonator."

"Makes sense to me. Since the car blew up, they're probably pretty sure the explosion killed us."

"It's certainly a possibility."

"Especially since no one knows we're in this pickup truck —including local law enforcement. If the sheriff's office can't find us—if we disappear—won't our pursuers be that much more certain that we're dead? They'll watch for the news stories online or on TV, right?"

"Possibly. However, if they don't recover our bodies—"

"Maybe we figure out how to feed information to someone who'd report our deaths."

Kep pursed his lips. "I do not care for this kind of misdirection. Won't your daughter be hysterical?"

"I—I know. But if they've tracked our work phones, I have to assume that Sophie's phone is compromised, too."

"But we have our prepaid phones."

"With an area code from the Upper Peninsula. If I call Sophie, they'll know we survived—and they'll have my burner number. If they have access to a law enforcement tracking system—"

Kep set his mouth in a line. "Then they could track the location information of your prepaid smartphone, too."

"Right." Bernadette took a deep breath. "You haven't called anyone from your burner phone, have you?"

"Fortunately, no."

"Great. Just make sure you only call my burner. I haven't figured everything out yet. But this might buy us some more time."

"And what about Lieutenant Stevenson? She's going to land in a few hours, and she'll hear about the explosion. If she thinks someone associated with the Annika Nakrivo case murdered us—"

"She'll be worried sick."

"I believe that to be a monumental understatement."

"And her judgment might get a little clouded," Bernadette admitted. "Okay, so I haven't thought this through."

Kep turned to look out the window, and the next couple of minutes passed in silence. The gears turned in Bernadette's head, and she gritted her teeth. They still needed to solve this case.

Kep swiveled his head toward the rear window. "You just missed the turn for Woodspur Road."

Bernadette nodded. "I know. Instead of going back to Banner Crossing, we're going out to the University of the Upper Peninsula. We're going to interview Barcelona Lute."

Kep started to chuckle. And then he didn't stop, his chuckles turning into a giggle that threatened to go off the rails.

"What's so funny?"

Kep held his sides and caught his breath. "You. You have just been through a traumatic experience. I am riding the ragged edge between apoplectic and catatonic, and what do you do?"

Bernadette's smile froze.

"You're still on the case!" Kep roared, collapsing into maniacal laughter again. "Not even pulling over to the side of the road to collect your thoughts. Not even calling the University to ensure Barcelona Lute's availability for an interview. Just standing on the accelerator as if the last half hour hadn't even happened."

"What do you suggest we do instead?"

"No—no, I am certainly not criticizing you." Kep shook his finger at Bernadette. "For all the invective you lob my way with my prim-and-proper ways and my 'snooty' vocabulary, you have four fingers pointing back at yourself." He chuckled again. "You can be quite the unemotional automaton when you so desire."

Bernadette stared at the road ahead of her and felt a flash of anger. What did he *want* her to do? Cry? Rock back and forth uncontrollably? Scream like a little kid?

She scratched her nose.

He was right, though.

She took in a deep breath through her nose, exhaled through her mouth.

"Some might call it—" Kep began, searching for the right words.

Bernadette clenched her teeth. What was it going to be? *Heartless? Ice queen?*

"Grace under fire," Kep finished.

She blinked. "Oh. Thank you."

A few miles ticked by in silence.

"You got your burner phone, Kep?"

"My prepaid smartphone? Yes, I do."

Bernadette ignored the semantics. "Would you see if we can interview Miss Lute in about—uh, looks like about an hour and a half?"

"I thought you directed me to only call your prepaid phone."

"No one's tracking U-Yoop's phones," Bernadette said. "You can make the call."

"Gladly," Kep said gratefully, pulling his cheap pay-as-you-go smartphone out of his pocket. "Anything to distract me from my brush with mortality."

Chapter Seventeen

KEP HAD THE SPEAKERPHONE ON WHEN TALKING TO THE administrator, and he set up an appointment with Barcelona Lute following her last discussion section. They would have to drive faster than the speed limit to get there in time and hope there were no traffic accidents, but Bernadette was oddly confident they would make it on time.

After Kep hung up, the truck was silent. Bernadette turned onto Highway 41 after twenty minutes, heading toward the university.

"What are you so keen to ask Miss Lute?" Kep said.

"Both Bonnie Farmington and Laura Donaghy said our victim was working closely with Barcelona Lute on some project—and I think it had to do with hawks. I'd like to get any information about hawks from Lute before we talk to the Fortescues—especially if Lute can shine a light as to the nature of their conflict."

Kep nodded. "I suppose I wanted to talk to the Fortescues because the couple seems too connected to Evan McMichael for it to be entirely coincidental." He cocked his head and tapped the screen of the burner smartphone. "I believe you are the one who frequently mentions your dislike of coincidences."

"True," Bernadette said. "But I also like knowing the answers to the questions we ask suspects."

Kep nodded and concentrated on his phone.

After another ten minutes of silence with the road lined with pine trees and scrub brush, Bernadette piped up again.

"You don't have the case file on that phone."

"No," Kep said.

"Then what are you doing?"

"I'm getting additional information on sulfuric acid."

Bernadette furrowed her brow. "Why—"

"I know I can detect the scent of sulfuric acid, but I am unfamiliar with many of its uses," Kep continued. "Whoever killed Evan McMichael had access to sulfuric acid."

"And Widewaters whiskey."

"The evidence suggests that, but it's not a certainty. The sulfuric acid, however, *is* a certainty."

"What have you found out?"

"Sulfuric acid is in fertilizers, but more commonly in fertilizer manufacture. It's also used for mining."

"Mining? Jeez, there are a million mines near Banner Crossing." She shot Kep a quick look. "Maybe the Windfall 29 mine?"

Kep shook his head. "Sulfuric acid is not used in the process of copper mining. Silver mining, yes, but no silver mines have been active in the Upper Peninsula for almost a hundred years."

"Any fertilizer manufacturers in the area?"

"I'm focusing on a third use case."

"Which is?"

"The cooking process for powder and rock forms of methamphetamines."

Bernadette tapped the steering wheel in thought. "Probably a few cooks in the area."

Kep put down the phone and took his glasses off, pinching the bridge of his nose.

"What is it?"

"It seems Mr. Constantine was also the victim of foul play."

"Right—and we need to figure out how the two deaths are linked."

"*If* the two deaths are linked."

Bernadette switched to the right lane as a Chevy Malibu sped past on her left. "We know someone—or more than one someone—messed with Constantine's medication. We're looking at two poisoning murders, not just one."

"But," Kep said, "the method of poisoning was completely different. Sulfuric acid in whiskey—enough to burn through the esophagus and lining, entering the bloodstream—not an instant death, but fairly quick. Quite painful, however."

"And Constantine?"

"With the bottle of Mr. Constantine's withdrawal medication missing, perhaps his medication was replaced with something poisonous."

"Why not just use sulfuric acid? Why replace the medication?"

"My thoughts exactly," Kep said. "Assuming the same murderer, it was someone who already had access to sulfuric acid—"

Bernadette interrupted. "But it's in liquid form. And if Constantine is in jail, the killer has to be cleverer. They can't just waltz in with a fifth of Widewaters and a container of sulfuric acid. They've got to trick the system so he dies while in jail—without anyone touching him."

Kep nodded. "That theory explains why the murder weapon changed."

"So you think the killer had access to both the jail's locked medications and sulfuric acid?"

"Possibly," Kep said.

"But theft of prescription medications isn't that uncommon. I mean, look at the axadabutin that just got stolen at New Sunset House. Even if it was just three or four pills, that could be four or five thousand dollars."

"People don't use axadabutin to alter their moods," Kep said. "So there is no financial motive to steal axadabutin, as there is little demand."

"That's true. Still, my point stands. Medication theft happens all the time."

"There is another possibility we haven't considered," Kep murmured.

"What?"

"Perhaps Constantine really *did* murder McMichael."

Bernadette scoffed. "How do you explain the poisoning *after* shooting up the trailer?"

Kep turned to look out the window. "I cannot explain those events as of yet."

"And how do you explain Constantine's death?"

"The missing modafinil," Kep said, "may have been replaced by something poisonous. Perhaps it was something Constantine was allergic to."

"Someone would have to sneak that in. Someone with access to either the locked medicine cabinet in the jail or to Constantine himself."

"I admit, many pieces do not fit together."

"If you think Constantine killed McMichael, don't forget that the Widewaters whiskey is *way* too expensive for Constantine's budget." Bernadette arched her back, the muscles stretching. "Besides, do you really think McMichael would have opened the door to the guy who had just shot his house up two weeks before?"

"I have yet to develop an adequate theory of the case," Kep said, a note of exasperation in his voice. "Nevertheless, we must consider the possibility that Constantine finished what he started, and someone else finished off Constantine."

"Like who? The pharmacist—Trudy Fortescue? Or Gabe's own sister, Bonnie?" Bernadette leaned back, ran a hand through her hair, and rested her other arm on top of the steering wheel. "Now that both names are out of my mouth, though, maybe we need to examine them. They both had means—or at least access to the victim or the medicine. We can look to see if they had opportunity. And I think we should talk about motive."

"We have established no motive yet—for either murder." Kep looked at his phone again. "I hesitate to go down this path, because we rest on a set of assumptions that may, firstly, be incorrect, and secondly, may get wedged in our minds so firmly we fail to see the truth when it finally presents itself."

"Hard to believe you're a forensic toxicologist instead of a philosopher."

Kep let a smile flash across his face. "This career pays considerably better."

"We *do* have some evidence, though," Bernadette said. "McMichael and Constantine died with different MOs, which suggests two killers. And while I don't believe it, the sheriff still considers McMichael's death a suicide."

Kep stared at the dashboard for a moment, then raised his head. "Have we considered whether Constantine was killed because he knew too much? If so, a third party may have hired or coerced Mr. Constantine into killing Mr. McMichael."

Bernadette's eyes widened. "Of course. Some third party hires Constantine to kill McMichael, and he shoots up the trailer, but that doesn't kill McMichael. So the third party decides to kill McMichael themselves. Maybe Constantine gets vocal—you know, 'get me out of jail or I start talking about who hired me,' so the killer has to off Constantine too."

Kep sighed. "I have previously warned you about the folly of making assumptions, Bernadette."

"You seem to have taken part in your share of *folly* during this investigation." Bernadette straightened in her seat and put both hands back on the steering wheel. "And besides, this isn't making assumptions. It's putting forth a hypothesis we should test."

"Under normal circumstances," Kep said, "we could contact Lesley and ask her to track Constantine's phone records, as well as the visitor records for the jail."

"She could also research purchase records for sulfuric acid in the last few weeks."

"But we do not currently have that luxury," Kep coughed lightly as he turned back to look out the front windshield. "Even if we can trust our compatriots at CSAB, we cannot possibly know who's tracking their phones. We may inadvertently provide our pursuers the information they need to locate us."

Bernadette squinted at the road ahead: the turnoff for U.S. Highway 141, just after a sign for Keweenaw Bay Logging, loomed ahead. She looked over her shoulder and got in the left lane to stay on U.S. 41 toward Ishpeming and the university beyond.

She stared at the Keweenaw Bay Logging sign, an itch in her brain.

The highway turned from the south to the east at nearly a ninety-degree angle, then Parent Lake passed on their right.

"I think after we go to the university," Bernadette said slowly, "we go to the Houghton County airport and meet Maura when she gets off the plane."

Kep blinked. "I apologize—did I hear you correctly?"

"Go to the airport and meet Maura. I trust her, and if we meet her, there aren't any phone calls to compromise or emails to intercept." Bernadette ran her hand along the top of the steering wheel. "I agree, using our burner phones to contact anyone at CSAB is a terrible idea. So we need to go to the airport to pick her up."

"What if our pursuers are following Lieutenant Stevenson as well?"

Bernadette shook her head. "They were targeting us, Kep. Something you and I know about Annika Nakrivo or Marguerite. So they wouldn't—" She stopped midsentence.

"What?" Kep asked.

"The SD card," Bernadette said, almost in a whisper. "It had files on it—encrypted, but Lesley was trying to break them. My friend Joanna at the FBI too. Maybe they're trying to keep the files hidden. So maybe Maura and Lesley and Joanna are all targets."

"While I appreciate your conjecture," Kep said. "I cannot believe the SD card is the catalyst for the target on our backs."

"Why is it so hard to believe?"

"Me," Kep said simply. "I had no knowledge of the SD card—I had no knowledge of your adventures in pursuit of Annika Nakrivo's sister. Clearly, however, I was in their sights before."

"Maybe they *thought* you knew."

"I suppose," Kep said, skepticism thick in his voice.

"What's your theory?"

"I am loath to admit I have yet to develop a theory supported by a convincing amount of evidence."

Bernadette grunted in agreement. "Once we figure out what we're not supposed to know, maybe we can blow this whole thing wide open."

Kep looked out the passenger window as they crossed the small bridge over the Tioga River. "I am thoroughly puzzled. Until yesterday, I was uninformed you were still making inquiries into the Annika Nakrivo case."

"So why were you targeted?"

"Perhaps our villainous pursuers concluded my olfactory sense could solve some kind of crime."

Bernadette thought for a moment. "Parr Medical hired Annika Nakrivo to wreck the ibogaine research at Kilbourn Tech."

"And she succeeded."

"But we weren't able to prove Parr Medical was behind it." Bernadette tapped the wheel. "I've assumed Parr Medical is behind the disappearance of Annika's sister. And of course I think Parr Medical wants us dead, too."

"It makes sense that a third party hired the people pursuing us."

Bernadette chose her words carefully. "What if the third party isn't Parr Medical?"

Kep blinked. "What do you mean?"

"What if someone else is coming after us?"

"I certainly do not know what other investigations would cause someone to pursue us."

Bernadette kept her tone even. "What if it wasn't *my* investigation?"

"Are you then suggesting I am the object of the pursuit?"

Kep scoffed. "I haven't been involved in any open—" But then his voice cracked, and he stopped talking.

Bernadette's breath caught. Yes, Kep *was* involved with an open investigation: the murder of his son. The investigation Kep had spent five years and thousands of dollars on, only to have his private investigator fire him as a client about a month before. But his son's death was not only an open investigation, it was an open wound.

Bernadette changed tacks. "Nothing else? Maybe one of your cases from way back? Someone who's out on parole now, or maybe someone who's still in prison but is rich and well-connected?"

Kep thought for a moment. "I have—" His voice cracked again, then he swallowed hard and continued. "I have solved many cases where the perpetrator was caught and incarcerated."

"Any who have been released lately?"

"I have not been following their progress in prison. None, however, seem to particularly stand out as desirous of revenge." He took off his glasses again and rubbed his eyes; Bernadette thought he might have wiped away a tear before replacing his spectacles. "But none of those cases involved you."

"You never know—maybe there's a connection to one of your old cases that *did* involve Annika Nakrivo or Parr Medical."

Kep was silent for a moment, drumming his fingers on the armrest. "I suppose I could do some research online."

"Sure."

He made no movement to look at his phone.

"Maybe we should talk about the questions we want to ask Barcelona Lute."

Kep exhaled. "Yes. That would likely be the most prudent course of action."

❧

U.S. Highway 41 passed by many small lakes and drove through forests with tall spruces on both sides of the highway for miles at a time. The sky had been clear and blue leaving Lost Dish, but the cloud cover increased the farther east they traveled, and as they drove on the causeway between George Lake and Ruth Lake, the skies opened up and dumped heavy rain for a few minutes, then slacked off to a drizzle.

The speed limit dropped to twenty-five miles per hour as they passed through two or three small towns, and there were even stoplights at a few intersections in Ishpeming, where the drizzle stopped. Bernadette glanced at the clock on the dashboard: they'd made good time, and if they found parking close to the building where Barcelona Lute's last class was, they'd even have a few minutes to spare. Kep found a map of the University of the Upper Peninsula online and was confident in not only the closest available visitors' parking lot but also the walkway between the lot and Lute's building that would take the shortest amount of time.

A few minutes before four o'clock, they stood in front of the Seeborn Science Hall. Despite the gray skies, the June afternoon was heating up, and a tang of ozone hung in the air.

Kep glanced at his phone. "My notes say we can find Miss Lute in Room 331. Third floor."

They took the stairs. After the first flight, Bernadette's hamstrings and quads tightened up, sore from sitting too much—first on the airplane, then on the long drives—over the last few days. They opened the door onto the landing of the third floor, the hallway stretching ahead of them.

"Three oh one," Kep read on the door to his left. "We are at the wrong end of the building."

Room 331 was all the way at the other end of the hall on the left-hand side, and as Kep and Bernadette approached, students started trickling out of the room. Kep and Bernadette squeezed their way in through the doorway. A tall Black woman in a white lab coat stood behind a counter, her back to the room, erasing a whiteboard full of chemical equations.

"Barcelona Lute?" Bernadette said.

The woman turned. Her large brown eyes were bright and curious, and her skin was clear and luminous. The woman's hair was long and full, a mass of tight black curls that framed her round face. She towered over both Bernadette and Kep—she had to tilt her head down to look at them. "You're the agents from CSAB, yeah?" Her voice was light and high-pitched, not matching her physicality at all—Bernadette almost cracked a smile at the juxtaposition.

"We're from CSAB, yes." Bernadette indicated Kep with a wave of her left arm. "Dr. Kep Woodhead is CSAB's forensic toxicologist, and I'm Bernadette Becker. We'd like to ask you a few questions about Evan McMichael."

Lute set her jaw and put down the eraser on the counter. "I found out Evan passed away only a few days ago." She leaned on the counter, and the smooth, unblemished skin on her forehead creased with worry and her bright eyes darkened —she aged a decade in a few seconds. "I liked him. He was an alumnus here, you know. B.S. in Biological Sciences, 1976."

"How did you get to know Mr. McMichael?"

"Ran into him at the library. He was researching local birds of prey—he'd just moved to the U.P. about two months before and noticed a bunch of coalhawk nests in the woods behind his house. Found a couple of nests on the ground, wanted to know how he could create any kind of environment more suited for them."

"And you—what, helped him?"

Lute shrugged. "I was doing my master's thesis on the effect of human interference in the migratory patterns of predatory birds. Seemed like a perfect way to get first-hand research into it."

"But that was—what, three years ago? And you've kept in touch?"

"I'm in my Ph.D. program now. Still focusing on ornithology. And Evan was still helping me out."

"Did you ever go out to Banner Crossing?"

"Oh, yeah. Dozens of times. Field research." Lute smiled. "Got reimbursed for the mileage, too. Not a bad way to augment the crappy stipend I get."

"Did you work with him continuously?"

"For the first year? Pretty much. He was retired, but he loved birds of prey. Categorized them meticulously."

"And after the first year?"

"I didn't see him after the summer." She pointed to the whiteboard. "Finals are next week, and despite my best efforts, I'm afraid half the students in here will fail."

Kep looked at the half-erased equations on the board. "Organic chemistry," he murmured. "Weeds out those students who aren't serious about the subject."

"Weeds out students who aren't good at rote memorization," Lute corrected. "And I've been told in no uncertain terms I must teach this class in a certain way." She sighed. "But next year, I defend my dissertation, and then maybe I get to do field research in the Galápagos and get paid for it."

Bernadette stepped to the side of the counter. "When you went to Banner Crossing, was it usually to meet up with Mr. McMichael?"

Lute nodded.

Bernadette blinked. Even though she and Kep discussed this in the car, she wasn't sure how to phrase the next question.

Lute beat her to it. "If you're wondering if we slept together, no. I'm a poor grad student, so instead of a hotel, I slept on his sofa when I went down there. But he was a perfect gentleman. Maybe I was stupid to get into a situation where I was sleeping in an old guy's house, but—I don't know, he just wasn't the type." She stole a glance at Kep. "Look, I don't care if you believe me or not, but he and I didn't have that kind of relationship. Maybe he was gay, maybe he was ace, maybe he was intimidated that I was a foot taller than him, I don't know."

"I didn't mean to imply anything. We just need to get a full picture of your relationship."

"Let me spell it out for you, then. We sat in trees and watched hawks and took a ton of notes. That's what we did every weekend I went there." She paused. "And I didn't like going into the forest at night without someone else. Evan knew what he was doing." A sad smile came over her face. "He had an extra pair of night-vision goggles he let me borrow."

Bernadette nodded. "Okay." She pictured the two of them together: Barcelona Lute, the tall, strong young woman, and Evan McMichael, the five-foot-three sexagenarian fireplug, traipsing through the dark woods with tech equipment strapped to their faces. She shifted her weight and looked at Lute's face: the tall woman seemed sincere and helpful. "Did you know of anyone who Mr. McMichael didn't get along with?"

Lute arched an eyebrow. "Yeah. The birdwatching president."

Bernadette nodded. "We've heard that he wrote a letter to Mr. McMichael."

"Oh—right. Yes, I took it."

"*You* took it? From his house."

"With his permission."

"Why?"

"Oh, well, the birdwatching group—uh, the Old Victoria Ornithological Society—they get a grant from the university every year for sharing their findings and statistics. Then the university makes their data available to their students and to the U.S. Fish and Wildlife Service. But the letter is clearly threatening. I suggested that the Biological Sciences department put a stop to the threats."

"Could we see that letter?"

Lute frowned and stared down at the counter. "I took it about a month ago and I handed it in to my advisor. I don't know if anything was ever done—and then, well, when I found out Evan was dead..." She looked up at Bernadette. "I know a lot of people are saying he died by suicide, but I—well, I don't believe it. He might not have had a lot of money, but he was content, you know?" She pushed herself away from the counter and crossed her arms. "His trailer got shot up, did you hear?"

"Yes."

"Well, you should look at the gunman."

"We have," Kep said. "And we still have quite a few questions."

"Anyone else who might have wanted to harm him—besides the president of the birdwatching group?" Bernadette asked.

"Ornithological society," Kep muttered under his breath.

Lute dropped her eyes to the floor. "Did you know," she

said softly, "Evan found a species of coalhawk that scientists thought had gone extinct in the thirties?"

Bernadette blinked. Had Laura been the one to tell her? "Yes. Was it the Kissimmee coalhawk?"

"Keweenaw," Lute said, smiling. "Kissimmee is the city next to Disney World."

"Right—Keweenaw. A new"—Bernadette scoured her brain for the right word, then found it—"kettle, right?"

"*Eleven* new kettles," Lute said. "About sixty coalhawks in total. If those are the only ones, they'd probably still be classified as critically endangered, but with the right protections in place, they could come back."

"Did you get any credit?"

"Oh, no," Lute said. "Maybe a nice feather in my cap, but even if I were the kind of person to steal someone else's thunder, there's no way I'd get away with it. He had too much documented in those notebooks."

"You know about the notebooks?" Bernadette blurted.

Lute tilted her head slightly. "Of course I do. He always had those notebooks with him on our walks."

Bernadette paused. "Did you know those notebooks were stolen?"

Chapter Eighteen

❧❧

"What do you mean, stolen?" Barcelona Lute asked.

"Maybe someone stole them so they could take credit for discovering the existence of the Keweenaw coalhawks."

Barcelona Lute blinked. "I—I don't know. I guess it's possible."

The wheels spun in Bernadette's brain, recalibrating the motives and suspects, reorganizing the information. Did the president of the ornithological society want to claim credit for discovering the Keweenaw coalhawks? Is that why hc scnt McMichael a threatening letter?

"Do you think the president of the"—Bernadette glanced at Kep—"ornithological society discussed the Keweenaw coalhawks with McMichael?"

Lute shook her head. "Maybe, but it's not what they fought about. They had a dispute about bird banding."

Bernadette frowned. "Okay—you'll have to educate me on this. Bird banding is just when scientists catch birds and put little metal tags around their ankles, right? So they can track migratory patterns?"

"You're on the right track. Tags aren't just for migration—

we study all kinds of behaviors in banded birds. Because of the banding Evan did, we know a lot more about the migration paths of all kinds of predatory birds who live in the Ottawa National Forest."

"And where the Keweenaw coalhawks are making their nests in the spring?"

"It isn't public yet," Lute said, "but yes, we know about them."

"So what's the problem?"

Lute folded her arms. "The president—I forget his name—"

"Jasper Fortescue," Bernadette said.

"That's it. Anyway, he thinks the Fish and Wildlife Service isn't strict enough in issuing bird-banding permits."

"Ah. He's a gatekeeper."

"He made a big stink at the last county board of supervisors meeting. He said banders like Evan—and, I guess, me, by association—are more likely to injure or kill a bird by mishandling them."

"But *Jasper* can do it."

"He makes a big deal out of the fact that he's a professional ornithologist."

"Is that—" Bernadette almost asked *Is that a real job?* but bit her tongue in time—Lute had mentioned getting paid for field research, after all. "Who does Mr. Fortescue work for?"

"The Michigan Department of Forestry."

"Ah."

"Used to be a big-shot CEO, but took early retirement. Now he leads tours in the summer for birders in the area—all throughout the U.P., not just Porcupine County."

"How do you know all this?"

"Oh—when I started my master's thesis, my advisor gave

a bunch of people's names to me as resources. Fortescue was pretty much at the top of the list."

Bernadette thought for a moment. "Did Evan get any credit for discovering the Keweenaw coalhawks?"

"Not yet," Lute said. "Evan wanted to keep it relatively quiet—no press, no science periodicals."

"He wanted to be sure, so no one could accuse him of a hoax, right?"

"Well, yes," Lute admitted, "but Evan wasn't interested in glory or recognition. He wanted to keep the coalhawks safe. They were safe because no one knew they were there. Besides, there'd be a lot of work involved."

Bernadette tilted her head. "What does that mean?"

"Finding a supposedly extinct species is just the first step," Lute said. "To everyone else, it may seem like a happy ending."

"Sure."

"But the discovery is just the beginning. Sure, the coalhawks that Evan discovered have the telltale blue wingtips and crest, as well as the larger hooked beak, but there are a ton of questions out there. Genetic testing needs to be done —the wingtips and crests don't mean much if the DNA reveals that it's just a differently colored subspecies of the Eastern coalhawk. And with the population so low, do you bring the hawks into captivity where you can breed them and protect them better, or do you leave them in the wild and protect the land? And, maybe most importantly, do we think we can breed the Keweenaw coalhawks back to a healthy wild population?"

Kep took a step forward. "And what would your recommendation be?"

"Mine?"

"Certainly," Kep replied. "You're getting your doctorate in

ornithology, are you not? That gives you the foundation and practical experience to possess an informed opinion on the subject."

"I agree with Evan," Lute said simply. "He thought the birds should be left in the wild. He'd found four distinct areas where the birds were nesting, but he suspected that there were more—maybe another hundred hawks out there. With the right protective measures, the Keweenaws might only take twenty or thirty years to repopulate."

"What sort of protective measures?" Kep asked.

Lute shrugged. "Nothing we haven't seen before for other endangered species. No development of their lands—either the state or federal government would buy it. It's close enough to the Ottawa National Forest, and it's all undeveloped. Hiking trails, maybe some seasonal ATV trails or cross-country skiing. I don't think there'd be too much opposition—and anyway, we're talking about a critically endangered species in a state where the governor won on an environmental platform. Would have been as close to a done deal as you can get."

"'Would have been'?" Bernadette leaned her elbows on the counter. "What do you mean, 'would have been'?"

"Evan and I shared our findings with each other," Lute said. "I might have been the only other person who knew about them. I asked the sheriff's office earlier this week if they'd found his birding notebooks, and they said they couldn't comment because I wasn't family."

"Laura," Bernadette murmured.

"What?"

"Evan's sister. She was family." Bernadette paused. "She knew about the coalhawks, too."

"I never met Laura. Evan mentioned her, wanted her to

come visit. But she lives down in Arizona, a long way away, yeah?"

"Yeah," Bernadette replied. Laura had mentioned the Keweenaw coalhawks but had mentioned no notebooks; maybe she didn't know about them. Maybe the sheriff's office didn't even know about their existence until Lute had said something.

Then a light bulb went off in Bernadette's head. "You know Evan's trailer got ransacked this morning."

Lute's eyes widened. "What?"

"If you called the sheriff's office asking about those notebooks, and they told you the contents of his home would be released to his sister and not you…"

"Wait," Lute said sharply. "You're accusing *me* of ransacking his mobile home?"

"I'm not accusing you," Bernadette said. "I just want to know where you were last night, say after seven p.m., and this morning."

Lute rocked back on her heels. "I can't believe this. Why would *I* ransack his house? I have my own notebooks."

"Exactly," Bernadette said. "Only you and Evan had notebooks, and you didn't tell anyone else about them. So if you took his notebooks, you would get all the credit."

Lute furrowed her brow. "But—but I wouldn't do that."

"You said yourself," Bernadette said, "that the discovery of a species everyone thought was extinct was a big deal. Wouldn't that look great on your résumé?"

"I told you—that would be the stupidest thing I could do. If I got found out, I could kiss my career goodbye." Lute crossed her arms. "And I'm going to have a brilliant career with everything I've done, whether or not the Keweenaw coalhawks are part of it."

Bernadette held up her hands in surrender. "Again—we're

not accusing you of anything. But we need to cover our bases. If we can't locate those notebooks, someone at the sheriff's office will tell me about your interest in his notebooks, and I want to be able to tell them your whereabouts."

Lute gritted her teeth. "Look, Banner Crossing is a two-hour drive from here."

Less if you speed, Bernadette thought to herself, but said nothing.

"All right, so, let's see. I was in the library last night until about nine."

"Okay. Anyone see you?"

"I checked out a reference book—*The History of Mining in the Upper Peninsula.*"

"Mining?"

"I'm doing my research on the impact of humans on predatory birds, remember? Mining in the early part of last century is a huge reason species like the Keweenaw coalhawks went extinct—or close to it—to begin with."

"Okay. When did you leave the library?"

"Right after I checked out the book—probably around nine o'clock. The librarian can tell you I was there—and their checkout system can, too."

"So nine o'clock. Where did you go afterward?"

"I hadn't had dinner, and I had a craving for Thai House. So I called my friend, and he met me at my apartment, and we walked down there."

"We'll need his name and number."

"Robbie Porregino. Getting his master's in chemistry. I have his number in my phone."

"So he'll say the two of you ate at Thai House?"

"Well, no, Thai House was closed—they close at 8:30 on weeknights—so we walked another few blocks to The Pizza Company. We both got a couple of slices." Lute crossed over to the desk next to the side wall, opened a drawer, and pulled out her purse. "I've got the receipt." She dug for a moment, then took out her wallet, unzipped it, and pulled out a small, creased slip of paper. "See?" She unfolded it. "9:41 P.M. And we sat in a booth for maybe twenty, thirty minutes. He got us both another beer. We left the pizza place at, I don't know, ten fifteen. I don't know what time I got back to the apartment. Maybe ten thirty."

"And did Mr. Porregino come in with you?"

Lute rolled her eyes. "No."

"I'm just asking to establish your whereabouts. No judgments."

"If I had known I'd need an alibi, I would have invited him in." She dropped her hands to her sides. "All right, well, I got back in my place at ten thirty. Then I got ready for bed, read a little of the library book, and fell asleep. I think it was right around midnight, but I'm not sure. Then my alarm went off at seven thirty and I was teaching my first class at nine fifteen."

"You live alone?"

"In a four-hundred square-foot studio? Yes. But I mean—come on. If I had done it, I'd have left at ten-thirty, gotten to Banner Crossing at, what, one-thirty, two in the morning? Then you're saying I turned around after—what, trashing a mobile home? Breaking windows, maybe?" She rolled up her sleeves. "Not a cut on me, by the way."

Bernadette glanced at Lute's arms—as she had said, there were no cuts or blemishes of any kind. Lute had suggested broken windows, of which there were none, but the high amount of broken glassware and plates in the kitchen could have made cuts as well. Glass would certainly have gotten on her shoes.

"Just so I could steal his notebooks," Lute continued, then

put her hands on her hips. "If I'd wanted to steal his notebooks, I sure wouldn't have messed his place up to do it. I wouldn't broadcast that something had been stolen. I bet no one would have even figured out that Evan had notebooks if I hadn't said anything."

Bernadette nodded.

"How long do you think it would take to trash a mobile home?" Lute frowned and shook her head. "An hour, maybe two? I guess maybe less time if you aren't looking for something and you only want to destroy the place. I bet whoever trashed the place took at least an hour."

Bernadette tilted her head. Lute wasn't wrong.

"Let's do the math, if you want to know where I was." An edge to Lute's voice had crept in during the last few minutes. "I have someone who can vouch for me until ten thirty. If you think I went right to my car and drove straight through to Banner Crossing, I'd have gotten there after midnight. At least an hour to trash the place..."

Lute stopped talking. She'd done the math in her head.

"Then another ninety minutes—or two hours—back here," Bernadette said. "You could have gotten back by two A.M., maybe three, and even gotten a few hours of sleep."

Lute began to speak, and Bernadette held up a hand. "I know," Bernadette said. "It was the middle of the night, and everyone we talk to is probably going to say they were in bed with no one to give them an alibi."

"I didn't leave my apartment," Lute said lamely.

"All right." Too bad the time of Evan's death had been so broad, or Bernadette would have asked about Lute's whereabouts then. "Is there anything else you can tell us about his notebooks?"

Lute shook her head. "We both wrote the locations of the kettles—"

"Hang on." Bernadette held up a hand. "You mean you've got the locations of the kettles written down?"

"Of course. We both did. My tables weren't as neat as his, but—"

Bernadette's jaw dropped open. "Can we see them?"

"They're in my office."

❧

Bernadette and Kep walked out of Lute's office fifteen minutes later, crossing campus and going back to the pickup truck. The afternoon had turned beautiful, the oppressive humidity turning into a gentle breeze. Bernadette scrolled through the photos she'd taken of Barcelona Lute's notebook. She'd paid particular attention to the eleven tables showing the number of adults, eggs, and juveniles—Lute had confirmed that the "J" they'd puzzled over in McMichael's notebook stood for "juvenile." More importantly, however, the "LL" stood for latitude and longitude, and was fairly exact. Kep began an enthusiastic conversation with Lute about the Polynesian practice of using frigatebirds in sea navigation before Bernadette pulled him away.

"If you have need of my opinion," Kep said, "I don't believe Barcelona Lute had anything to do with Evan McMichael's death."

"Me neither," Bernadette said. "She was so confident the timeline would exonerate her—she wouldn't have gone down that road if she'd done anything."

"Not necessarily true, but I agree your conclusion is more likely." Kep pushed his glasses up. "In addition, she would likely have not shared the tables in the notebooks with us if she were the killer."

"Probably not."

"I noticed you did not ask her for her whereabouts the night McMichael was poisoned."

Bernadette shot a glance at Kep as she opened the driver's side door of the pickup and tapped the power lock control to unlock Kep's door. "I should have."

"For what it's worth, I detected no suspicious scents on her—or in her office," Kep said.

"I sense a 'but' coming on."

"However, McMichael certainly would have welcomed her into his abode," Kep said, getting into the truck. "Additionally, more than two weeks have passed since his death. Any scent from sulfuric acid would have dissipated long ago."

"But where would she have gotten the sulfuric acid?"

"Miss Lute has access to a university science department. I would expect sulfuric acid to be available here—if not readily so, at least available to order. She may have access to storage lockers or facilities where those types of hazardous materials are contained."

Bernadette rubbed her chin. "We already know Lute could have driven to Banner Crossing and back in the middle of the night without being missed. So she had means and opportunity. What about motive?"

Kep put on his seat belt. "The discovery of the Keweenaw coalhawk, rescued from the cold hands of extinction, would be enough to make a name for herself. No matter what she says, it would assist her in obtaining the job of her choice once she gets her doctorate—and it would also contribute positively to her dissertation, as well."

"So then why blab to us that Evan discovered it?" Bernadette started the engine.

"I believe the colloquial term is 'cutting her losses.' Without those notebooks, she can't take credit for the discovery, and if she *does* take credit for it and the truth comes out, the community would brand her as dishonest, and her career prospects would be in ruins."

Bernadette backed the truck out of the parking space, then drove out of the lot and onto the street. "Then why not take the notebooks the night Evan was killed? She had access to Evan and his trailer; she might even convince him to tell her the location of the notebooks before she offed him."

"I do not have an explanation."

"One thing we need to figure out," Bernadette said, "is how the almost-extinct hawk might affect the mine's plans to open the underground amusement park."

Kep nodded. "True. Perhaps the local mining companies didn't know about the discovery—considering how secretive McMichael and Lute were about it—but if the secret were out and the Keweenaw coalhawks affected Windfall 29's plans, that could lead to a motive. Amusement parks need land, and they have construction commitments."

"Yeah."

They drove toward the highway and stopped at a red light.

"I need to tell Sophie I'm okay," Bernadette said under her breath.

"I'm sorry, what was that?"

"Sophie," Bernadette said. "I still haven't called her. I need to tell her I'm okay."

Kep blinked.

"What?" Bernadette asked.

"I know you want to call your daughter to reassure her," Kep said carefully, "but, as you have mentioned, her phone may be monitored. Therefore, I fear I agree with your earlier assessment of the situation: that would put her in danger. And could lead our pursuers to the location of your pay-as-you-go cellphone."

Bernadette said nothing.

"Think of the escalating danger we have faced," Kep continued. "At first, the GPS tracker was worrisome. As was the clerk at Taycheedah asking where I was. But the C4 explosive has confirmed positively that our enemies wish us dead."

Bernadette pressed her lips together. "I know, I know. I just want to talk with her."

"You were right to distrust our communications."

"Thank you."

"So, how are you going to communicate with your daughter?"

"I'm not going to, okay?" Bernadette snapped. "I want to. I'm telling you I *want* to. But I know I can't. I know it's better—safer—for everyone if our pursuers think we've been killed."

Kep nodded.

Bernadette tightened her grip on the steering wheel.

After they'd driven another few miles, Kep turned around in the tiny pickup's seat and stared out the back window.

"Are we being followed?" Bernadette asked.

"No. Not a vehicle in sight." He turned to face forward. "Who knows that we have this pickup truck?"

"You and me and Ed from the U-Move-It place. No one else."

"Anyone at the hotel?"

"No. The staff sheltered behind Building 2—that's on the other side from where the truck was parked." Then Bernadette shook her head. "And I told Darcy—the hotel clerk who checked us in—that I'd come find her if I were still alive."

"And you didn't."

"No."

"I see by your face that you feel a measure of guilt about that, but you shouldn't. It will help obfuscate our tracks." He furrowed his brow. "If we are not in the hotel, and if no one observed us departing in the pickup, we may have effected the convincing illusion that we are deceased."

"Especially since the explosion probably destroyed our phones."

He turned to Bernadette. "Perhaps interviewing Barcelona Lute wasn't a good idea."

"No, but Barcelona Lute is two hours away from Lost Dish. And it's not like she's in contact with anyone in Porcupine County."

Kep folded his hands in his lap. "I am not sure I share your optimism, but I am unsure we have another choice."

Bernadette glanced at the clock on the center console. "Maura's plane arrives at Houghton County airport in two hours. We have just enough time to buy her a burner if we hurry."

❧

U.S. Highway 41 turned north at the sign for Keweenaw Bay Logging, and twenty minutes later, as the highway turned into Broad Street while driving through the town of L'Anse, they stopped at a fast-food place for a quick meal. Kep turned his nose up at the food, but he said nothing as Bernadette unwrapped her burger with one hand while turning back on the highway toward Balaga.

As they left L'Anse, Highway 41 ran along the shore, and a sign a quarter mile down announced the body of water as *Keweenaw Bay*. Bernadette wondered if this shoreline was where the coalhawks bearing the Keweenaw name originally came from, or if there was a Keweenaw Forest or Keweenaw County.

Bernadette kept one eye on the shoreline as they drove alongside it, hoping to see birds, maybe ravens or gulls—were there gulls here?—or even jays. But the skies were clear.

Despite the food stop, they made good time, crossing the Portage Canal bridge into the town of Hancock, and by the time they turned onto Airpark Boulevard, they had ten minutes to spare before the scheduled landing time.

The airport was tiny, and Bernadette spied the area she'd picked up Kep the day before. She parked in the single parking lot about a hundred yards away from the entrance, just as a small Lakeshore Airways jet descended from the sky.

Bernadette pointed. "I bet that's Maura's plane."

They got out and walked across the mostly empty lot to the small terminal, taking a seat in front of the TSA area—no one waiting in line. Bernadette could see all the way to the back of the airport, where the glass door below a sign saying "Gate 1" was being pushed open by a young man in a Lakeshore Airways uniform. About five minutes later, people started filtering in.

And there was Maura.

Bernadette had never seen Maura look so disheveled. Ordinarily, Maura was a vision of elegance, always in a flattering outfit, hair perfectly in place. Professional, tasteful, stylish.

But today she wore a pair of jeans and a sweatshirt—even from this distance, Bernadette could see a coffee stain on her left shoulder. Maura's makeup was haphazard, and she looked like she hadn't slept. She had her purse over her shoulder and carried a large satchel.

Bernadette shot a glance at Kep, who raised his eyebrows for a moment.

Maura, her head down, walked through the exit of the TSA area as Bernadette and Kep made a beeline for her. The lieutenant turned toward the baggage claim sign, not seeing them.

"Maura," Bernadette called—not too loud.

Her head snapped up, and as Maura's eyes focused on Bernadette, her eyes got wide, then her face crumpled. She dropped the satchel and rushed to Bernadette, grabbing her and enveloping her in a huge embrace.

"You absolute *asshole*," she whispered in Bernadette's ear, her breath hitching into sobs. "I thought you were dead."

"It's—it's a long story."

Maura broke from the embrace and wiped her eyes with the heel of her hand. "Why the hell didn't you let me know you were alive before now?"

"Part of the long story."

"I'm pulling you off the Nakrivo case. And off the McMichael case, too. It's too dangerous."

Bernadette recoiled. "What? No!"

"Oh, yes." Maura gripped Bernadette's shoulders. "There's a little thing called protocol, Bernadette. We pull our agents out when the danger is too great." Maura looked Bernadette dead in the eye. "Case analysts, too."

"But it's perfect right now, Maura. Whoever is trying to kill us thinks we're dead. They can't track us—"

"This isn't a negotiation," Maura said, firmly but quietly. She glanced over at Kep, who was standing awkwardly a few feet away. "Hello, Dr. Woodhead. I'm relieved you're alive, too." She stepped forward, then awkwardly pulled him into a quick hug.

Kep flinched, but patted Maura on the back. "I appreciate your sentiment, Lieutenant."

Maura took a step away from Kep and turned to

Bernadette. "How did you survive the explosion? And how did you get here?"

Bernadette pulled the new prepaid phone out of her purse, handed it to Maura, then thrust her chin toward the parking lot. "Get your rental car and follow Highway 41 south to Quincy Street. There's a diner on the corner. Let's meet there and we'll get you up to speed."

❦

After finding a table in the back of the diner, Bernadette and Kep told Maura the whole story, from the GPS tracker Bernadette had discovered on the rental car to the vacation rental they were staying at in Banner Crossing. Bernadette even told Maura about going to the trailer against protocol, the stolen notebooks, finding the C4, and the interview with Barcelona Lute.

Maura ordered a large plate of pasta and chicken, and vacuumed it up like she had just returned from being marooned on a desert island. "I haven't eaten anything since I got on the plane," she said between bites.

"I'm sorry you were so worried," Bernadette said, trying to sound as sincere as possible.

Maura's head jerked up. "Oh!"

"What?"

"The incident at Taycheedah—I finally heard what happened. They're calling it a prison riot. Confined to just a single cell block."

"Were there any casualties?" Kep asked.

"Two prisoners were injured." Maura turned down her mouth. "And the warden was killed."

Bernadette's mouth dropped open. "Marcie Fisk was—was *killed?*"

"Yes."

"Did anything happen to—"

"Nothing about Annika," Maura said. "Incident didn't reach the infirmary."

"We can conclude she is still alive," Kep said. "If no prisoners were killed in the riot."

"Assuming we can trust the official report." Bernadette rubbed her hands on her trousers—they'd become sweaty. Then she looked up at Maura. "I don't think you should take us off the case."

"Which case? Nakrivo or McMichael?" Maura said with her mouth full.

"Well—McMichael for sure." Bernadette turned to Kep. "Once Kep found the misplaced glass in the cabinet, we thought it was a murder. Everyone else seemed to think it was a suicide."

"Not everyone," Kep put in. "A certain subset of law enforcement believed Gabriel Constantine was the perpetrator."

Maura nodded and swallowed. "Sheriff Koskinen says he's closing the case. Constantine killed McMichael, then died from withdrawal."

"Only that's not what happened," Bernadette said.

Maura arched an eyebrow. "Proof?"

"Constantine's medication."

Maura sat back in her seat, hands on the table.

"First, he was supposed to be given Tylenol for his fever," Bernadette continued, "but someone switched it with ibuprofen."

Maura paused for a moment. "People mistake acetaminophen for ibuprofen all the time. I think you're making a mountain out of a molehill. Let's concentrate on where the sulfuric acid might have—"

"Look at the inventory," Bernadette insisted. "The killers are *hoping* we gloss over this. Forty-one ibuprofen pills instead of twenty-three Tylenols. And, second, look at the other medication."

"The bottle for the medication that Constantine took for methamphetamine withdrawal," Kep put in, "was empty."

Bernadette nodded vigorously. "Not the six or seven pills he was supposed to have, and not even the two or three Deputy Mueller saw in there when he gave Constantine his medication that morning. The bottle was *empty*. Someone replaced that medication—and they didn't want us analyzing the leftovers."

Maura looked skeptical.

"Maybe people at home might make this mistake," Bernadette continued. "Not professionals. Not pharmacists. Not jails."

Kep shook his head. "We have no proof this medication substitution contributed to Constantine's untimely demise."

"If it didn't," Bernadette said, "then why? Why take away modafinil? Why swap acetaminophen for ibuprofen—when the acetaminophen was *already* in the locked medicine cabinet?" Bernadette looked defiantly at Kep. "It only makes sense if someone wanted to swap the pills out with no one noticing. And I can't think of a single reason someone would do that unless they wanted Gabriel Constantine dead."

"Modafinil is expensive," Maura said.

"But Tylenol isn't. And there's no black market for it. No—something is going on with the medication situation, and we need to figure out what."

Maura leaned forward, her forehead creased in thought, and took another bite.

"We could talk to the medical examiner, but she can't know we survived the car bomb," Bernadette said. "But if we can figure out what killed Constantine, we'll be closer to finding the killer."

Maura shook her head. "Your gut may tell you the two cases are related, but there's no evidence yet."

"But—"

"The sheriff's pressuring me to close the case, and with you two almost getting killed, I'm not in the mood to go on a fishing expedition—even if we don't have a good explanation for the medication situation."

Bernadette counted on her fingers. "The glass. The ransacked trailer. The missing medication. This isn't a fishing expedition, Maura."

"If the M.E. doesn't follow up on Constantine's death, there's not—"

"Then she's not doing her due diligence. And neither is the sheriff." Bernadette folded her arms and looked Maura in the eyes.

After a moment, Maura set down her fork. "The local cops we work with aren't all dirty, Bernadette."

"Look how the last case turned out," Bernadette said.

Maura kept eye contact with Bernadette, and Bernadette finally looked down at the table. "I'm not saying Koskinen is dirty. Maybe he's over his head. Or looking for a quick win. They aren't used to murders here."

"The options are 'dirty' or 'incompetent'?"

Kep leaned forward. "I respect your opinion, Lieutenant Stevenson, but I was under the impression the medical examiner *had* begun her investigation into Constantine's cause of death. Perhaps you can make a discreet inquiry yourself."

Maura shook her head. "My priorities have changed, Dr. Woodhead. I'm here to gather evidence and information on the 'murders' of two of my best investigators. I'm not here to ruffle the locals' feathers."

"We're safe as long as they think we're dead," Bernadette said.

"Which is why you shouldn't have interviewed Barcelona Lute," Maura snapped.

Bernadette stared at the table for a moment. "She's a two-hour drive away. She won't even hear about our deaths."

"Perhaps. Still a risk you shouldn't have taken." Maura softened her gaze. "But you're right. As long as the people who planted your car bomb think you're dead, you'll be safe. Did you talk to anyone else?"

Bernadette shook her head.

"What about the hotel staff?" Maura asked.

"No. I told Darcy that I'd come find her if I made it out alive. I didn't, so I'm pretty sure she assumes I'm dead." She glanced at Kep. "And so far, no one knows we're in the rental pickup. I don't think anyone saw us leave."

Maura nodded. "I can make an announcement to local law enforcement that you two died in the explosion. I bet whoever did this is monitoring the police scanner—as soon as they hear that the officials have confirmed your deaths, they'll stop looking for you. Then we can get you to safety."

"You'll keep it local, though, right?" Bernadette asked. "I don't want anyone to worry."

"I'll do what I can, but you know I can't promise that."

"It occurs to me," Kep said thoughtfully, "the people who are responsible for killing McMichael and Constantine don't know why we were attacked."

Bernadette cocked her head. "So?"

"Perhaps their killer—or killers—could believe our inquiries into Constantine's death were the catalyst of our murders. After all, they don't know about the Nakrivo investigation."

Bernadette widened her eyes. "Yes. We think there's

someone else pulling the strings. You think they're freaking out a little?"

Kep sat back in his seat. "To extend your metaphor, if the marionettes are afraid the puppeteer murdered two federal investigators, I would expect them to communicate with each other."

Maura grinned and picked up the last bite of pasta with her fork. "An excellent point, Dr. Woodhead. I'll call Lesley and have her dig into phone records." Maura took the last bite and sat back in the booth. "And she'll be relieved to hear the two of you are still alive."

Chapter Nineteen

THEY WROTE DOWN THE PHONE NUMBERS FOR THEIR burners for Maura before they left the diner, and Bernadette and Kep got back in the pickup, taking the highway to the vacation rental in Banner Crossing, leaving Maura to scramble for accommodations near Lost Dish; Bernadette assumed the explosion had caused the hotel to close. The sun was low in the sky, the June evening stretching its extended fingers of light over the Upper Peninsula sky.

"It's not even dark yet, Kep," Bernadette mused as she drove. "I wish we could go interview Jasper Fortescue while the conversation with Barcelona Lute is still fresh."

Kep looked at Bernadette out of the corner of his eye. "Lieutenant Stevenson expressed how concerned she was for our safety. She clearly does not want us to continue with this investigation."

"I know, I know," Bernadette said. "I wasn't suggesting we actually go. I just don't like to sit around waiting."

"Yet that's what our situation requires now," Kep said, his voice kind. "I understand that one of your many strengths is your tenacity to get to the truth. That strength has served our previous two investigations well. It has so far served *this* investigation well. But now, we wait."

Bernadette paused for a moment, then nodded at Kep. "Call Maura's burner."

Kep took out his prepaid phone and tapped the screen.

"Hello?" came Maura's voice from the speakerphone.

Bernadette straightened in her seat. "Is there any way *you* can interview the Fortescues?"

"What?"

"I think the Fortescues are important to the case," Bernadette said.

"We are *not*—"

"Also," Bernadette said quickly, "any investigation into our deaths would include an interview with them. Just look at our notes."

Maura was silent.

"And, coincidentally," Bernadette added, "Michigan is a one-party consent state for recording conversations."

❧

Even though it wasn't quite seven o'clock when they opened the door to the cabin, Bernadette was exhausted. She fell onto the bed and stared at the ceiling. She hadn't even taken her makeup off, but the desire to close her eyes and drift off was nearly overwhelming.

A little itch in her brain nagged at her. Finally, she crossed the room to the dresser, took her phone from her purse, and tapped the photos she'd taken of Barcelona Lute's notebook.

She sat on the bed and scrolled through the photos to the last few entries in the notebook and stared at the tables. The tables looked exactly like the tables in Evan McMichael's journal—as close as her memory would allow, anyway.

After talking with Lute, Bernadette was sure these were bird sightings, not any kind of coded drug ledger. She scratched her head. Whoever had trashed McMichael's apartment, with the discarded book about underground economics, had wanted to send them on a wild-goose chase.

Bernadette stood.

If she couldn't interview suspects, maybe she could at least get a workout in. To stay in good enough shape to be a CSAB agent, she needed to run for at least a few miles. Get some sprints in, too. She wondered if she could go for a run in the woods around the cabin. If she avoided the main road, no one could see her.

But Kep's words rang in her mind.

Maybe she could focus on weight training instead. She didn't have barbells or dumbbells, but she was sure she could find something in the cabin.

Bernadette walked to the closet and opened it. Totally empty—nothing on the floor, nothing on the top shelf. Just her blazer, two pairs of trousers, and three blouses hanging up.

She walked out to the kitchen. These vacation homes often had kitchen items that the owners didn't use anymore —a heavy stand mixer would be a good stand-in for weights. Maybe thirty pounds.

But there were no stand mixers in the pantry. No cast-iron skillets—just a single flimsy aluminum frying pan and two smaller saucepans.

She sighed and went back to her bedroom, closing the door. She lowered herself to the floor and began doing crunches. Bernadette concentrated on her breathing: deep, slow breaths in through her nose, out through her mouth.

The question was, how was the information about the

Keweenaw coalhawks relevant to McMichael's death? And why were the journals stolen?

After fifty crunches, she got up and grabbed her phone, bringing up the photo of the coalhawk table, putting it on the floor, and then doing push-ups over it. She stared at the tables, getting closer and farther away from her face with each push-up, until the writing blurred in her vision. She lost count of her push-ups around thirty-five.

How involved was Jasper Fortescue in the murder? He'd threatened McMichael after finding out about the bird banding. With Jasper's pedigree, perhaps he felt entitled to the discovery.

Then she rolled onto her back and did more sit-ups, the light in her room fading with the setting sun.

After five sets, she wished she'd purchased an electrolyte drink at Saucy's.

She stood, a little light-headed, then walked to the bathroom and drank water out of her cupped hand, slowly, as her heart rate decelerated.

A knock at the door.

Bernadette tensed, then hurried to her room and got her nine-millimeter out of its case.

Another knock, then a muffled shout outside the front door.

"It's Maura!"

Bernadette exhaled, putting the gun back in its case, then walked out to the living room. Kep was already in front of the door, unlocking the deadbolt.

"She's done already?" Bernadette asked.

"It's been two hours." Kep opened the door.

"Were you followed?" Bernadette asked.

"No." Maura handed a digital recorder to Kep. "You were right, Bernadette. The Fortescues know something. I don't know if they're the killers, or even if they're working together, but they both know more than they're telling us."

So maybe Jasper Fortescue was the key to solving the murder.

"I just got emailed a recording of Deputy Moncrief interviewing Trudy," Maura said. "I'll send that later."

"Thanks for doing this, Maura," Bernadette said.

"What are friends for?" she said. She pulled out her phone and tapped the screen. "Took photos of both Jasper and Trudy. Sending them to you now."

From the bedroom, Bernadette's phone dinged.

"I'm going." Maura took a step back. "Don't want anyone to see me."

She pointed at the digital recorder. "Listen to that and make notes. I need to get back to the hotel or the sheriff will wonder what's taking me so long."

"I will ensure the recorder's safe return to you tomorrow morning," Kep said.

"Have a good night." Maura turned and stepped back off the porch.

Kep closed the door behind Maura and turned to Bernadette, holding the recorder up. "Shall we?"

❧

The rub of fabric against the microphone of the recorder.

"Okay?" A familiar voice, not Maura's. Ah—Deputy Moncrief.

"I appreciate you meeting me here." That was Maura's voice.

"Of course." Moncrief's voice softened. "I can't even imagine."

"You understand why our organization has a top priority

on continuing the investigation," Maura said evenly, but letting her voice crack a little. "The first forty-eight hours of an investigation are the most critical, and if my team was getting too close to the truth, well..."

Moncrief cleared her throat. "Of course. Anything to help."

The crunching of feet on gravel. According to the file, the Fortescues lived in Stansky Township, a few miles north of Banner Crossing, and the map application listed directions through a few twists and turns off Michigan State Highway 26. The satellite image on Bernadette's phone showed a long gravel driveway of a large, three-story house behind a thicket of black spruces, then, closer to the house itself, the driveway changed to pavement.

After a moment, the sound changed to footsteps on concrete.

Maura cleared her throat. "Since we have to question them both, we should split the two of them up—you ask Mr. Fortescue about whatever unspoken birdwatching rules McMichael might have violated, and I'll ask Mrs. Fortescue about the pills."

"You want me to take Mr. Fortescue?" asked Moncrief.

"I know one of my agents was quite suspicious that the acetaminophen had been replaced by ibuprofen. She made several references to it in her notes." Maura let out a sigh. "I don't know why she ratholed on that, but I know Bernadette well enough—sorry, I *knew* her well enough—that I trust her gut."

"I'd feel far more comfortable with Mrs. Fortescue—"

"Jasper," Maura interrupted, "is a rule-follower, according to my dead investigator's notes. You've got the uniform. That will get better engagement with him than I can get. I believe I can get Trudy to trust me."

"I know Jasper."

"Then that's even better."

The clicking of shoes on concrete stopped, then the ring of a doorbell.

A moment later, the sound of a door opening.

"Can I help you?" A man's voice.

"Evening, Jasper." Moncrief's voice was reticent.

"What are you doing here?"

"I'm here—" Moncrief took a breath and started again. "I'm here with Lieutenant Maura Stevenson. She's from the Controlled Substance Analysis Bureau."

"Looking into the murders," Maura said, "of my two investigators who were assigned to the Evan McMichael case."

"The—the murders?" Genuine surprise in Jasper's voice.

"We believe," Maura continued, "that whoever is responsible for the deaths of Evan McMichael and Gabriel Constantine is a person of interest in the murder of these two federal investigators."

Silence. Bernadette felt the awkwardness in the recording.

"Mr. Fortescue?" Moncrief ventured.

"I—I'm sorry. You said you were with CSAB?"

"I am," Maura said.

"The two investigators for, uh, Evan's death—they're dead?"

A pause; Maura had probably nodded. "And you're Jasper Fortescue?"

A low cracking sound. Was Jasper cracking his knuckles? "I had nothing to do with Evan's death. Or your investigators' deaths."

"We just have a few questions," Moncrief said.

"And I've never heard of this Gabriel Constantine person."

"Is your wife home, Mr. Fortescue?" Maura asked.

Jasper's voice raised in pitch, ever so slightly. "I'm the one who sent that letter to Evan. My wife has nothing to do with his death."

"Maybe she doesn't," Maura said. "However, we have questions regarding prescriptions she may have filled."

Silence.

Maura broke it a moment later. "She works as a pharmacist for St. Joseph's. And for the general store by the Porcupine Lake Cabins, right?"

Jasper's voice was rough. "Perhaps I need to get my lawyer on the phone."

"Of course," Maura said. "You don't have to answer our questions now." A rustling of something—a purse, a pocket? Then the clicking of the pen, several times. "As you can see from Deputy Moncrief's presence, CSAB is coordinating these investigations with the sheriff's office up in Lost Dish. Maybe a half-hour drive from here. We can ask the sheriff to bring you in for questioning. We could do it tomorrow morning if your lawyer can meet us there."

"Bring us in?"

"Not 'us,' Mr. Fortescue, just you. We have evidence of a motive for you, so we can ask the sheriff to bring you into the station."

"I thought you said you wanted to talk to my wife."

"We do, but we wouldn't bring her into the sheriff's office."

Silence.

"We have evidence medications were switched, which would violate the Federal Anti-Tampering Act of 2003. The Act specifies a punishment of twenty years in prison and a twenty-thousand-dollar fine, but if the M.E.'s report says the medication tampering resulted in Mr. Constantine's death, the penalty is life in prison." The sound of footfalls; perhaps Maura had taken a few steps forward. "Because we're talking about a federal offense, not a state offense, things get done a little differently. We'd be picking up your wife and transporting her to the CSAB field office in Minneapolis."

"Minneapolis?" Jasper's voice was faint.

"Surely that's not necessary," Moncrief said softly, an aside to Maura.

"Well, of course, Deputy Moncrief, that's assuming the M.E. doesn't find evidence that the switched medications crossed state lines. Then we'll have to bring Mrs. Fortescue to D.C."

"Depending on what the M.E. finds?" Moncrief said, a bit of incredulity in her voice.

A tap; maybe the sound of a hand falling against the door frame. "You're not taking my wife *anywhere*."

"Not tonight, no, but by the weekend, we should know for sure. I'm not sure we'd arrest her right away—probably just a material witness warrant."

"I know you're concerned about your agents, Lieutenant —" Moncrief began.

"The whole agency is concerned, Deputy," Maura said. "We take the murder of federal investigators seriously." The shuffling of feet; Maura maybe turned from Moncrief to Jasper. "If we determine she's simply a witness, we should only have her for a few days. We'd pay for her transportation and lodging, of course, though I doubt she'll have time for sightseeing."

Silence. It stretched for a moment, into discomfort. "Hold on a moment."

The sound of the front door shutting gently.

Moncrief's voice was low. "I didn't know you were going to—"

"Use the powers of my agency to solve the murders of my dead investigators?" Maura finished. "This is hardball, Deputy. With any luck, he's doing a web search for the 2003 Anti-Tampering Act, as well as federal investigators' rights to transport material witnesses."

"I was under the assumption we were just—"

"My investigators were murdered," Maura said evenly, but with force. "I'm not planning to be nice."

Bernadette sat back in her seat at the kitchen table. Maura was selling this so well—not just that Bernadette and Kep had been killed, but that CSAB was connecting their deaths to the murders of McMichael and Constantine. If whoever had planted the bomb were to hear this, they'd think they'd gotten away with killing both Bernadette and Kep.

A moment later, the door opened again. Jasper's voice, softer this time. "Trudy wasn't involved in anything like what you're suggesting."

"I'm glad to hear it," Maura said. "So if the M.E. agrees, we will obtain a material witness warrant."

"What if she speaks to you now?" Jasper asked.

"I'll ask my questions, and if I'm satisfied, we'll be on our way."

Shuffling sounds, the squeaking of hinges, the closing of a door. Jasper must have brought Maura and Deputy Moncrief inside.

"You have a beautiful home," Moncrief said.

No response.

"My wife can speak to you in the kitchen," Jasper said.

A momentary pause. Was that a whisper? Then Moncrief's voice. "Mr. Fortescue, is there anywhere you and I could talk?"

"I'd like to be there when you talk to my wife."

"We'd like to do this as quickly as possible," Maura said. "I plan to ask your wife about information she cannot discuss in front of civilians."

"In front of *civilians*?"

"About some medications found at the county jail." Maura replied. "You aren't a member of law enforcement, so you might not be authorized to hear those answers."

"Nonsense. Trudy isn't in law enforcement—"

"It's a HIPAA violation for you to hear her answers, Mr. Fortescue." Moncrief's voice, more forceful. "I'm afraid we must insist."

Maura *had* sold the ruse well—Deputy Moncrief was on her side.

A pause. The tension was clear in the recording. Then, finally, Jasper's voice. "Twenty minutes."

"We will take as long as we need to," Maura said.

More rustling. Footsteps, tentative. "We can speak in my study," Jasper said.

Background noises, mumbling, fabric brushing against the mic.

Bernadette stood from the table, not pausing the recording, and hurried to the bedroom. She grabbed her phone and tapped the message from Maura. She walked back into the kitchen as Maura's voice came back on.

"Mrs. Fortescue?"

Bernadette sat down, putting her phone face up on the table.

The photo of a tall, slender white man, standing in what looked like the foyer of his house. His skin was pink with the sun and his hair was long and white, almost touching his shoulders. Bernadette thought he looked familiar but couldn't immediately place him.

She swiped to the next photo. A blonde woman of about forty with a round face and large blue eyes sat on a stool at the bar of a large white kitchen, her hands clasped in front of her. Bernadette narrowed her eyes. She swiped back to Jasper, then back to Trudy—then it hit her.

Jasper and Trudy had been the couple sitting at the table in St. Matthew's Pub the night Evan McMichael's trailer was ransacked.

Trudy's voice: "Jasper said you're a federal investigator?"

"Correct." Maura's voice was calm, measured. Footsteps on tile; Maura was pacing around the kitchen. "I understand you work as a pharmacist."

No response.

"You work for both St. Joseph Hospital and for the Porcupine Forest Rec Cabins?"

"Uh, yes. The Porcupine Forest has a general store. I work there on the weekends—just for a little extra cash."

"When the county jail has prescriptions for their prisoners, or when they need to stock over-the-counter medications, they come to you?"

"St. Joseph has the contract," Trudy said carefully. "When I'm there and the request comes in, yes, I'm often the one who fills it."

"When my investigators reviewed the contents of the medicine cabinet yesterday," Maura said, "they came across a bottle of acetaminophen with a label from St. Joseph."

"Acetaminophen is a pretty common request."

"But when they looked at the pills in the bottle, they weren't acetaminophen. They were ibuprofen."

A waver in Trudy's voice. "I—I don't understand."

The swish of fabric against—what, a tabletop? The counter? "A prisoner who was going through methamphetamine withdrawal had a fever yesterday morning, and we believe he was given ibuprofen—from the bottle labeled as acetaminophen—in error. A few hours later, he was dead."

A barely audible gasp from Trudy. "But—but those are just—"

Maura's voice lowered in pitch. "Over-the-counter painkillers?"

Trudy was quiet. The silence grew uncomfortable before Maura spoke again.

"Does the name 'Eric Cropp' ring a bell?"

Trudy's voice tensed. "He was a pharmacist in Ohio who made a bunch of mistakes. Ended up going to jail for a year."

"That's correct. How did you hear about him?"

"He came to speak to our pharmacy tech program. They tried to drill into us the importance of accuracy when filling prescriptions."

"Sort of a 'scared straight' program?"

"I guess so." Trudy took a deep breath. "One of his mistakes killed a two-year-old girl."

"Right," Maura said.

"He told us he was charged with involuntary manslaughter, went to jail, got his license permanently revoked, and now he spends court-ordered time telling pharma students how badly he screwed up."

"Let me ask you something," Maura said. "What if those mistakes he made had been on purpose instead of merely negligent?"

Trudy was silent.

"When your husband answered the door, I mentioned to him the Federal Anti-Tampering Act."

"I heard," Trudy said softly. "Twenty years in prison and a big fine."

"*If* the negligence doesn't kill anyone," Maura said. "My investigator had a question in her notes. Did you put the wrong medicine in the acetaminophen bottle on purpose, or by accident? Because if it was an accident, maybe you'll just be another Eric Cropp. But if you did it intentionally, you could be looking at life in prison."

Trudy spoke so softly it was almost inaudible. "I—I think I might need a lawyer."

Bernadette stiffened. That was *very* close to asking for an attorney—only saved by the *I might*. If Trudy worded her request properly, Maura would have to end the interview.

"Here's the thing, Trudy." Maura's voice was measured. She knew she had to walk a tightrope. "The man who died at the jail this morning? He shot up Evan McMichael's trailer a week before McMichael died. We know your husband wrote threatening letters to McMichael."

A scrape of a chair on the floor. "Wait—you think Jasper asked *me* to switch the medication?"

Maura continued in her even, calm voice. "Look at the events from our perspective. The suspect in McMichael's death gets killed. And my investigators uncovered that your husband was in the middle of the conflict with the victims. You can see why we have to ask."

"Jasper didn't tell me to do anything." A note of pleading in Trudy's tone. "No—you have to believe me."

"Your husband sent a letter three weeks ago to Mr. McMichael threatening physical harm if he didn't stop banding the coalhawks in the county."

A smacking sound—maybe Trudy slapped an open hand on the counter. "I should have known this whole fight was about those stupid birds."

"So the conflict *was* about the coalhawks." Maura hesitated for a half-second. "I'll tell you, with my investigator's notes, your husband looks like a prime suspect."

Trudy did too, if she was the one who purposely switched medications, but obviously Maura was trying to avoid saying anything to make Trudy ask for her lawyer.

"It's not—" Then Trudy went silent.

"Not over-the-counter painkillers? Then what else did you switch out?"

"No." Trudy's voice surged with frustration, maybe even anger. "With the drug interactions today? I'd have to be crazy."

"I understand, Trudy. I bet doctors accidentally order a bunch of common medications and get it wrong. Like those allergy pills—loratadine, cetirizine, who knows? Especially during hay fever season."

Trudy's voice was firm. "Not a chance."

"Look, Trudy, someone placed an order from the jail for acetaminophen, but the bottle wound up full of ibuprofen instead. Of everyone who had access to the medicine, you're one of the few people who could have switched the medications with no one noticing."

A tapping sound—maybe Trudy's fingers on the counter. "Did I put it in the wrong bottle?" Trudy asked herself quietly.

"Did you, Mrs. Fortescue?"

"I don't—I don't remember. I didn't think I did, but maybe I didn't replace the label properly." Her voice hardened. "They cut hours on other pharmacy workers, you know. I'm there by myself most days, and sometimes the lines are out the door. It's not fair."

"We just want to understand what happened," Maura said, still calm and measured.

"And with my luck, Gabriel Constantine was allergic to ibuprofen."

"Did you fill any other prescriptions for the county jail?"

"I don't—" Trudy took a deep breath. "I think maybe—"

Bernadette braced herself for Trudy to explicitly lawyer up. But Maura cut Trudy off.

"We'll be able to access the pharmacy records, Mrs. Fortescue," Maura said. "Will the records show you were the pharmacist on duty when both the acetaminophen and the modafinil prescriptions got filled?"

Trudy sighed. "Modafinil," she said in a whisper. "I filled a prescription for modafinil."

"And did you swap the pills—"

"That was *definitely* modafinil," Trudy snapped. "I made sure. Acetaminophen, ibuprofen—I mean, okay, I get how I might have screwed up."

Maura paused.

Bernadette didn't believe Trudy—mixing up any medication, whether a schedule one narcotic, an over-the-counter drug, or anything in between—was unprofessional at best and deadly at worst. Maybe Bernadette could check Trudy's records.

"But I wouldn't have made a mistake with modafinil," Trudy continued. "It's got a ton of interactions."

"Any with ibuprofen?"

"No!" Trudy raised her voice. "A lot with HIV medications, par for the course. But nothing over the counter like aspirin or ibuprofen. You think I would *purposely*—"

Maura interrupted, her voice even calmer than it had been before. "We need to explore all avenues. We have a man who died while in custody, and someone clearly tampered with his medications. You can see why we had to follow up with you."

"I didn't do anything wrong."

"All right," Maura said. "How well did you know Mr. Constantine?"

"I didn't know him at all."

"How about your husband?"

Trudy scoffed. "I don't think Jasper even knows who he is."

"How about Evan McMichael?"

"Well, of course, Jasper knows *him*."

"They met in person?"

"Several times. He came to some of the Society meetings."

"Where were you last night?"

Trudy was silent for a moment, then: "St. Matthew's."

"Is that a church?"

"St. Matthew's Pub. It's the only bar in town."

"Was Mr. Fortescue there, too?"

"Yes."

The rustling of papers. "My investigators were both at the pub in Banner Crossing last night. You saw them?"

"Uh—I don't know. There were quite a few people there. And I don't know what your investigators looked like."

But Bernadette knew—they were all there.

"Where did you go after you left the bar?" Maura asked.

"Home."

"You didn't make a stop at the trailer park just up the road from the pub?"

"The trailer park? Why?"

Bernadette cocked her head and listened closely. It wasn't a denial.

"Any number of reasons," Maura said.

"Well, we didn't. We came straight home."

Okay, *that* was a denial.

Bernadette rolled her tongue around in her mouth. If she'd been running the interview instead of Maura, she'd provoke Trudy to see if she'd let her guard down, maybe say something she didn't mean.

"Is there anyone," Maura said carefully, "who threatened to harm Mr. McMichael? I mean, besides your husband?"

"That'll provoke her," Bernadette mumbled to the tape recorder.

She was right: Trudy's voice had an edge of anger. "Jasper did no such thing."

"He did." The scraping sound of a chair on a tile floor. "My investigators saw the letter he wrote Mr. McMichael."

Bernadette couldn't help but smile: they hadn't seen the letter, but Maura wasn't letting that stop her.

"He may not have *intended* his threats," Maura continued, "but he wrote them down."

Trudy was silent.

"So I'll ask you again," Maura said. "Did Mr. McMichael anger anyone else? Maybe in the ornithological society? He got under your husband's skin, after all—did he bother anyone else?"

"The society is Jasper's thing, not mine." Trudy cleared her throat. "I don't want to answer any more questions without a lawyer."

A small cough from farther away from the microphone. The rustling of fabric, a scrape. Then Moncrief's voice. "I've completed my interview."

"I think we're done here, too." Maura's voice was clipped —had Trudy seen Moncrief in the doorway and mentioned the lawyer because of it? "Thank you for your time, Mrs. Fortescue."

Background noise, footsteps, the opening and closing of doors. Then the sound of rustling branches, footfalls on concrete, then gravel.

"Did Jasper say anything?"

"He wouldn't tell me the reason he wrote that letter. Kept saying it was a dumb thing to do. And he asked several times if he was under arrest."

A few more crunches of shoes on gravel, then the recording stopped.

⚜

Bernadette looked up from the recorder and tilted her head at Kep. "Remember what you said about the marionettes and the puppeteer?"

"Of course," Kep said.

"Maybe Jasper got nervous when he heard about our deaths. Maybe he'll sound the alarm to his conspirators."

"Assuming such conspirators exist."

"Did you look at the photos Maura sent?"

"Yes."

"Did you recognize them from St. Matthew's Pub last night?"

Kep's brow knotted. "Not at first. He and his spouse were sitting at a table near the bar, weren't they?"

"Yes." Bernadette turned the recording device off. "It's odd, though. Jasper threatened McMichael, and Trudy has the means and opportunity for Constantine's murder—"

"Pending the medical examiner's findings," Kep said quickly.

"—but we still don't know how the two murders are connected."

"We have made an assumption they are." Kep got up from the table, walked to the refrigerator, and opened the door, staring inside. "Perhaps our assumption is incorrect."

"It's too coincidental to be a coincidence," Bernadette said. "We need to have Maura contact Lesley. See if we can find any major transactions from the Fortescues' accounts— and see if Jasper or Trudy called anyone after Maura left."

"I shall call Lieutenant Stevenson."

⚜

An hour later, Bernadette went into her bedroom after washing up, plugged the burner phone in, turned off the light, and fell into a deep sleep.

In her dream, she walked into the waiting room of the Porcupine County Sheriff's Office. Behind the desk, instead of the peppy receptionist, sat Evan McMichael. He looked the way he looked in the photos Bernadette had seen, but his skin was pallid and his eyes were vacant.

"Evan!" Bernadette said in her dream, running up to the desk. "Tell me—who did this to you?"

He reached under the desk and pulled out a large sheet of paper, smoothing it on the desktop with jerky, pained strokes. Bernadette leaned over the desk: a map of Porcupine County —similar to the one she'd used to figure out how to get from Lost Dish to Banner Crossing a few days ago.

She looked up into Evan's face, devoid of emotion. "A map? What's important about the map?"

The dead man pointed at a section of the map west of Highway 45. "Keweenaw," he said, in a voice straight out of a campfire ghost story.

"Yes, yes, you found the Keweenaw coalhawk. We know. Did someone try to take the discovery away from you, Evan?"

He tapped the map, harder this time. "Keweenaw." He enunciated clearly, pausing between each syllable, making it sound morbid, even threatening.

"I don't know what you mean," Bernadette said.

Evan tapped the map again.

Bernadette leaned forward and looked closer. It wasn't Keweenaw Bay—it was a section just outside the Ottawa National Forest, just north of Old Victoria.

"What's there?" Bernadette asked. "Is something hidden in the forest?"

"Keweenaw," Evan said.

"The hawks? Are you talking about the hawks?" Bernadette looked up into Evan's face—

And as Bernadette watched in horrified fascination, Evan transformed. His chin lengthened, his face narrowed, his brow grew more prominent.

Bernadette's eyes widened—he was transforming into *Barlow*.

Her ex-husband had the same dead eyes and pallid skin as Evan had.

"I helped you, Bernadette," Barlow said. "And this is the thanks I get?"

Bernadette awoke with a start.

Light streamed in through the narrow opening between the curtains, spilling into the room. Her sheets were tangled up in her legs, and she tried in vain to kick them off. Finally unwinding the sheets from around her calves, she pulled her legs up and swung herself into a sitting position on the bed. She ran her hands over her face.

The dream was fading, but she unplugged her phone and tapped until she saw a photo of Barcelona Lute's notebook pages. She scrolled through several of the photos and stopped when she saw the tables.

Eleven of them.

What had Barcelona Lute said? Bernadette closed her eyes. Evan had found eleven new kettles. A match: one table for each of the kettles.

And what were the coordinates?

Bernadette flipped to the first table.

A: 3
J: 7
E: 0

LL: 46 43 6.2 / 89 13 55.5

Bernadette jumped to her feet to get her laptop—but no. She'd left it in the hotel room back in Lost Dish. Possibly blown up along with the rental car.

She opened the nightstand drawer. A cheap ballpoint pen and a small notepad. They would suffice. She scrawled the numbers down from the table, then she tapped on the screen, opening the map application, then entered the coordinates for the degrees, minutes, and seconds.

Yes, there it was. A quarter mile north of Old Victoria Township, about halfway between Banner Crossing and Lost Dish. Between a hiking trail and a small creek feeding into the Lost Dish River. She tapped on the "terrain" button, and it looked like it was a wooded area on a steep hill, if the elevation lines were to be believed. She set the phone back on the nightstand and flopped back on the bed, staring up at the ceiling.

Barcelona Lute might have been to this area with Evan McMichael. Her nightmare—was it a warning? Was her subconscious trying to tell her something?

She deselected the "terrain" option this time, then she squinted.

The Ottawa National Forest—the border for it was in a dark green with a yellow dashed border. And the location Evan McMichael had written was outside the yellow dashed line—not by much, but enough. That part of the forest wasn't on federally protected land.

Did someone own the land where McMichael had made the discovery?

Had McMichael gotten killed for trespassing? Bernadette pushed herself back into a sitting position and ran her hand through her tangled hair, pulling gently when her fingers got caught.

Deeds and land records were public, weren't they?

She stood, holding her phone, and her bladder began screaming for relief.

Bernadette opened the bedroom door and nearly wet herself—Kep, in an undershirt and boxers, was standing five feet from the bedroom door.

"You screamed," he said.

"Like five minutes ago," she said. "Hang on." Bernadette hurried past Kep to the bathroom, firmly shutting the door, turning on the modesty fan, setting her phone on the sink counter, and sitting on the toilet just in time.

She thought about the dream she'd had again. Her subconscious was obviously trying to tell her the location of McMichael's discovery was important. And so close to the border of the national forest.

She grabbed her phone and stared at the screen. Might be easy enough to find who owned the land where Evan McMichael had discovered the Keweenaw coalhawks.

After a web search, she landed on the Michigan PuLaRec site—short for *public land records*, she assumed. After scrolling down to Porcupine County, she found an interactive map.

The county map didn't have a way to find the longitude and latitude, so she had to jump back and forth between the map application and the PuLaRec interactive map.

"Is everything all right?" Kep asked from outside the bathroom door.

"Fine," Bernadette called back, a note of distraction in her voice. "I had a nightmare, and it gave me an idea."

"Dr. Judith Pierson has some fascinating research into the power of the subconscious mind," Kep said. "Studies suggest our brain waves—"

"Quiet a second," Bernadette said. She found the hiking trail on the interactive map. And there was the stream—and there was the border of the Ottawa National Forest.

She tapped on the area between the hiking trail and the stream, then chose *Search Records* from the pop-up menu.

Mr. and Mrs. Jasper & Gertrude Fortescue.

Chapter Twenty

Bernadette finished up and washed her hands, her head buzzing. She opened the door, and Kep—thankfully—had taken several steps back, a respectful distance from the door.

"Are you quite certain of the stability of your emotional state?"

"It was just a nightmare," Bernadette replied. "This whole situation will probably buy my therapist a new BMW in two or three years, but yeah. I'm okay."

Kep didn't move, then pointed to the phone in Bernadette's hand. "Did you discover something useful?"

Bernadette nodded. "Yes. Our favorite couple, the Fortescues, own the land where Evan McMichael found the kettles of the Keweenaw coalhawks."

Kep tilted his head. "While interesting on its own, land ownership doesn't imply a motive."

"Isn't threatening McMichael enough?"

"*The fool doth think he is wise, but the wise man knows himself to be a fool.*"

"You calling me a fool?"

"I merely urge caution with our theories." Kep pushed his glasses back up on his nose. "I am unsure, however, that Jasper Fortescue's letter about bird binding is sufficient motive for murder."

"I think the land gives the Fortescues another motive."

"How so?"

"The Fortescues are obviously well-off—a house on lots of land, another property? And I bet they've got a Lexus."

"DMV records will tell us soon enough." He stroked his beard. "However, beyond the threatening letter, I don't see an enhancement for the motive. A healthy bank account is no crime, especially in the United States."

"I'm getting there," Bernadette said. "Trudy's working two jobs as a pharmacist. Why? Unless they need the money?"

"Perhaps she derives pleasure from her work." Kep pushed up his glasses on his nose. "Some people do, you know."

"People who work *one* job. She's working for both the hospital *and* for the pharmacy in the general store in the middle of nowhere. We'd have to get Lesley to dig around in their finances, but I bet they owe a lot of money." Bernadette put her hands on her hips. "So they own a bunch of land near their house—Old Victoria Township—and if they needed to sell the property to pay off some debts, then McMichael finding these supposedly extinct coalhawks would, at the very least, delay the sale by months, maybe even years."

Kep stroked his beard. "You therefore suggest that by getting rid of Mr. McMichael and removing all evidence of the Keweenaw coalhawk discovery, the Fortescues could sell their property and pay off their debts."

"Makes sense to me, but let's get Lesley to do some work for us to get some evidence." Bernadette's stomach rumbled.

"Perhaps we can meet the lieutenant for breakfast."

Bernadette nodded. "Nightmares burn a lot of calories."

❧

Bernadette kept her head down as Kep, a baseball cap pulled low over his face, held the door for her. She walked into Kerttu's Kafé; her boss was nowhere to be seen. A large man in a long-sleeve plaid shirt—even though it was already sweltering at nine in the morning—pushed past her, followed by two tall, muscular men in T-shirts with Rockland Lumber logos on the back.

There was a partition near the back of the restaurant. She and Kep made a beeline for it and found Maura in a secluded booth behind it. They both sat down.

Bernadette scooted into the booth. "I see why you chose this place."

"That, and it's an hour's drive from Lost Dish." Maura's voice was even-keeled and friendly. She picked up one of the three menus next to the upside-down coffee mugs in the middle of the table. "Since I know you're both okay, I'm famished."

The server appeared with a coffee pot as the three of them each grabbed a mug. They ordered quickly, Bernadette and Maura both ordering a Loggers Omelette, and Kep getting a bowl of oatmeal.

After the server walked away, Maura pulled out her laptop from her bag under the table and opened the lid. "Lesley's been busy," she said, tapping on the trackpad. "Jasper and Trudy have four joint accounts, and each of them has their own checking accounts. Three items of note in their finances."

Bernadette leaned forward, the steam of their coffee rising between them.

"First: debt. Jasper's son from a previous marriage—big medical bill."

Bernadette turned her eyes down. Jasper had been so unpleasant to deal with, she'd hoped his financial woes had been self-inflicted.

"Second," Maura continued, tapping on the screen, "a five-thousand-dollar cash deposit made four days ago to Trudy's checking account."

"Under the ten-thousand-dollar reporting limit," Bernadette said.

"Finally," Maura continued, "a six-figure check from Windfall 29 deposited in Jasper's bank account."

Bernadette's eyes widened. "From Windfall 29?"

"Correct."

"Was it for the sale of land?"

"Lesley hasn't found that information yet. She's only seen the PuLaRec site listing the Fortescues as the owner."

"That's the property where I think McMichael found the Keweenaw coalhawks."

Maura nodded. "It's been less than twenty-four hours—Lesley's good, but she's not a miracle worker. Give her some more time."

"So, the money is in Jasper's accounts?"

"He paid off the medical debt," Maura said. "Two days after the check from Windfall 29 cleared."

Bernadette looked down at the table, tapping her fingers. "I was hoping we'd find the Fortescues had financial trouble—like the medical debt. If the Fortescues were forced to sell the land to pay off the debt, but the Keweenaw coalhawk discovery had triggered some kind of environmental monkey wrench to delay or even cancel the sale? That's a big motive to silence McMichael. People have killed for far less." Bernadette rested her chin in her palm.

"True."

"If the debt's already paid off," Bernadette continued, "and the PuLaRec site says the Fortescues still own the land—"

"Not necessarily." Maura picked up her coffee and took a sip. "When was the data last updated?"

Bernadette cocked her head. "You mean—PuLaRec might not be current?"

"Public sites only pull updated data every month. In a rural county, maybe once a quarter. Check with the public records office directly."

"Perhaps bringing both the Fortescues in for interrogation would prove worthwhile," Kep said.

The server brought their food, setting it down in front of each of them. Maura watched the server go back into the kitchen, then turned toward Bernadette again. "You know you two can't perform the interrogation."

"We know," Bernadette said hurriedly.

"I should really put you two on the next flight to D.C. We might even have to put both of you in protective custody."

Bernadette was silent for a moment.

Maura shook her head. "Every second you're in Porcupine County is putting you in danger. You're driving around in a rented pickup without your cellphones or laptops—"

"But everyone thinks we're dead now."

Maura knitted her brow, picked up a fork, and took a bite of her omelet. She glared at Bernadette as she chewed thoughtfully, then swallowed. "I shouldn't have even let you two leave the airport. Somebody wants the two of you dead."

"And they think we are."

Maura pointed her fork at Bernadette. "I know how to protect the two of you."

"By hiding us in a two-star motel in Roanoke?"

"Yes," Maura said. "The witness in the García case. The Bugottinis' daughter. They're still alive."

Bernadette closed her eyes. Maura made a good point.

"You know how this works, Bernadette. We have a protective custody system for a reason." Maura picked up a piece of rye toast and shoved the corner into her mouth, tearing it off in a bite much too inelegant for her usual demeanor. "And even if I have to drag the two of you kicking and screaming into safety, then I will."

"If I may, Lieutenant," Kep began. "As soon as we get back on a plane, or a train, or we use a credit card to rent a car or buy fuel at a station in Mackinaw City, our names are going to pop up in the system."

Maura put her fork down on her plate.

"I believe we must operate under the assumption you are being tracked as well," Kep said, reaching across the table for a packet of honey. "So far, you have not used your government-issued mobile phone to communicate with us, which is excellent. If an outsider were to look at your digital footprint, they would believe you are taking over our investigation. However, as soon as you buy a pair of Amtrak tickets to our nation's capital, the proverbial jig is up. Were our pursuers to see a purchase through any transportation provider, they would ask: who is Lieutenant Stevenson purchasing the tickets for? Why two tickets? Why the train when she arrived by airplane? And the obvious conclusion, of course: the two of us are still alive."

"But we're safe here," Bernadette interjected. "And we can finish the investigation." As if to stress her assertion, she cut a sizeable piece of omelet with the side of her fork and shoved it in her mouth with a flourish.

Kep tore open the honey packet and drizzled it on his oatmeal. "I don't think we can use the word 'safe,' but I think the risk of us being found out is greater if we are on the move. We didn't see anyone following us yesterday." He glanced at Bernadette, who nodded. "And since the explosion at the hotel, we don't think they've been tracking our movements, either."

Maura's brow knotted.

"Because there's nothing to track," Bernadette said. "Cellphones, rental car, laptop—all gone."

"No," Maura said. "You're not going rogue on this investigation."

Bernadette looked in Maura's eyes. "I see what you're saying, but local law enforcement can't even make up their minds if McMichael and Constantine's deaths are homicides. And that means—"

"You two aren't the only homicide investigators in CSAB," Maura said. "Puckett and Durango—"

Bernadette made a face, clattering her fork against her plate.

"Puckett and Durango," Maura continued, a bit more forcefully, "can fly out here as early as tomorrow morning. They'll get your notes."

"Puckett will be paying for rounds of drinks with the sheriff by tomorrow night," Bernadette clenched her jaw. "It'll be ruled a suicide. Hell, if the sheriff said aliens killed McMichael with a death ray, Puckett would sign off on it."

"You're exaggerating."

"Not by much," Bernadette said. "This investigation requires pushing back against the locals, and they don't push hard enough."

"And you push too hard," Maura replied sharply. "That's why Puckett and Durango are still agents and you're—" She stopped, gritted her teeth, and stared at the table.

"I see," Bernadette said softly.

"I'm making a call," Maura said.

"Wait—just wait." Bernadette clenched and unclenched her fists. "Okay, we're off the case. But I still don't know how Kep and I got tracked. We don't know who we can trust."

The lieutenant cocked her head. "You don't think you can trust CSAB?"

"Someone knew where you sent me, Maura." Bernadette kept her fists clenched. "Where you sent *us*. Within twenty-four hours of buying my plane ticket to Milwaukee and setting up the call with Warden Fisk at Taycheedah, I had people following me."

Maura took another bite and chewed thoughtfully, then swallowed. "The people who will be..." She trailed off. "There aren't many people who knew."

"But you put the travel request in the system, right? I mean, yeah, you and Lesley might have been the only ones who actively coordinated things with me and Kep—"

"Hang on," Maura said, "are you saying you suspected Lesley and I might have had something to do with this?"

"The thought crossed my mind," Bernadette admitted. "But you weren't trying to keep our investigation of McMichael's death under wraps—in fact, you were trying to make it appear as official as possible. So anyone at CSAB could have gotten the information. People knew you assigned me to this case, and people knew I was flying into Milwaukee, right?"

"Only a few people have access to the travel system."

"But no—then they wouldn't have assumed that Kep would be with me." Bernadette took the last bite of her omelet, then pushed her plate to the middle of the table. "I think the leak, if there was one, came from someone who heard about my trip, not someone who saw the details."

"So we'll put in the request and keep things on a need-to-know basis."

Bernadette swallowed.

"From my understanding of the situation," Kep said, picking up his coffee mug, "Bernadette believes an insider at CSAB is responsible for sharing her whereabouts with our pursuers. And, frankly, I am uneasy about contacting the central office as well."

"You're not to investigate these deaths until further notice." Maura glared at Bernadette. "Clear?"

Bernadette nodded.

"Aren't you thinking of your daughter?"

"I *am*," Bernadette said, tearing at the corner of her paper napkin. Yes, Sophie thinking her mother was dead might be horrible—but if word got to their pursuers that Bernadette was alive, Sophie could be at risk. Unless...

"You could call," Bernadette said to Maura.

Maura nodded. "I could," she said. "Let Sophie know you're okay."

"And we're sure our pursuers can't listen in on your daughter's calls? That your ex-husband's house isn't bugged?" Kep asked.

"I hardly think—" Bernadette began, but then stopped. Yes, Barlow's house being bugged was unlikely. Would she stake her life on it? Would she stake her daughter's life on it?

"I'll ask someone from CSAB to check and see if..." Maura said, then her voice trailed off.

"Who can we trust?" Bernadette said. "Who can check for listening devices? Who can see if Sophie's phone is tapped or her conversations are being recorded? Who do we know with absolute certainly won't take that information back to whoever wants us dead?"

Kep set down his mug and studied Bernadette's face for a moment. "I'm sorry," he whispered.

"Sophie's my Achilles heel," Bernadette snapped—trying and failing to keep the emotion out of her voice. "I can't go into protective custody—Sophie won't be safe. If they put C4 under my rental car, I'm sure they'll have no qualms about kidnapping Sophie to get me to come out of the woodwork."

Kep turned back to Maura. "Lieutenant, we seem to be safe, at least for the time being, at the rented cabin in Banner Crossing. Perhaps you can make some inquiries with those who *you* trust without giving away that we're still alive."

Maura hesitated. "Your friend at the FBI has been helping you on the Nakrivo case, right?"

"Right."

"You trust her?"

When Bernadette had met Joanna Quimby at the indoor shooting range just a few days ago, Joanna's bullet holes in the target were maniacally accurate. She and Joanna had gone through parts of their training together. Bernadette's recommendation from the joint task force three years before had gotten Joanna her last promotion.

"Of course," she said.

"Okay, I'll coordinate with your friend," Maura said. "Joanna, right? Quillan?"

"Quimby," Bernadette said. "So we just go back to the cabin? Twiddle our thumbs until we get further instructions from you?"

"You got it." Maura looked at Bernadette, her face softer now.

"I suppose we can do some research online," Bernadette mused aloud. "I can ask Lesley to send me—" No, that would require her PC, back at the Up North Hotel, probably destroyed.

As if reading her mind, Kep piped up. "You can borrow my laptop," he said. "Unlike the two of you, I am not used to the stress of people attempting to end my life. I could use a nap."

"We'll get something to go so the two of you can have lunch back at the cabin," Maura said. "I don't want you showing your face at a market or another restaurant in case anyone recognizes you." She turned and caught the server's attention with her hand raised.

⚜

As soon as they entered the cabin, Kep hurried toward his bedroom and shut the door. Bernadette stood staring after him, but after a moment, she walked into the kitchen, put the two Styrofoam containers into the refrigerator, then she plopped down on a kitchen chair.

She wasn't used to the day stretching out before her with nothing to do. She had no laptop, and she couldn't bug Kep to get his—he'd looked wiped out in the pickup truck on the way back to the cabin.

Maybe another round of sit-ups and push-ups. Stay in shape, anyway.

She walked into the bedroom and took off her blazer, blouse, and trousers, then walked to her suitcase and took out a pair of athletic shorts and a tee shirt.

Between her divorce, her job, and her responsibility to take Sophie to school and rehearsals and lessons, she'd had no time for relaxing at all. She couldn't remember the last time she'd sat at a table without a task in front of her, whether it was fueling herself up for a late-night work session or research for a case.

She pulled on the shorts and shirt.

And suddenly, the weight of everything she'd been through crashed on top of her shoulders. She hadn't spoken with Sophie in two days, and probably wouldn't be able to talk with her for at least a few more.

She dropped to the floor and started doing push-ups, losing count almost immediately, but she kept going.

Her mind spun. Would the FBI or CSAB put her into long-term protective custody? Would she have to hide indefinitely? Would CSAB officially state that she'd been killed in the car bomb? And that meant—

Her breath hitched.

Was Bernadette wrong about it being temporary? Would Sophie forever think her mother had been killed? Ugh—there'd be a memorial service. Sophie would have to move in with Barlow and Lisa full time. Yes, Barlow was her father, but the idea of Sophie spending full-time with her cheating ex-husband and the woman who'd broken up their family—

Bernadette took a deep breath. At least Sophie would be safe. At least she would be alive. It was so much less than ideal, and Bernadette suspected that every day for the rest of her life, she'd worry about her secret getting out, and Sophie getting kidnapped. Bernadette's problem, not Sophie's. Bernadette made a promise to herself: she would *behave* in protective custody, no matter how long it was for.

She'd have a chance at a new life, too. Protective custody would probably mean she'd never work for CSAB—or any law enforcement agency—ever again. She'd have to find another job—and she wasn't good at anything else. But she'd manage.

And getting away from D.C.—she loved her job, and D.C. was the only place for it, but somewhere, there was a generic house or apartment and a crappy job ready for her and her new identity to move into.

She almost burst into tears but swallowed hard.

Hang on a second—that was witness protection. She wasn't a witness to anything. Well, maybe the face of the person she believed was following her—

Ugh. This was pointless. Her brain was going a million miles an hour in every direction, and it wasn't helping.

She was sweating, then rolled onto her back and did crunches. Fifty, then sixty. Then she let her mind wander until her abdomen was burning with exertion.

She got up, walked back out to the kitchen. She grabbed a handful of paper towels and wiped her forehead and temples, catching her breath, feeling the sweat evaporate off her skin.

After a moment, she grabbed the remote and turned the television on.

The cabin had live TV—something she hadn't seen for a while. She and Barlow had cancelled their cable service a couple of years before, relying on streaming services for their entertainment. Bernadette stared dumbly at the screen for a moment or two. Two men in suits sat at a desk and they discussed the multimillion-dollar contract of a baseball player she'd never heard of. She aimed the remote at the screen and turned the volume down. She flipped through a dozen channels of daytime television before she came across the local news.

"—officially withdrawing the plans for an underground amusement park from consideration," the newscaster said, her smoldering gaze targeting the camera, just a hint of a coy smile on her face. "For more on this story, Rebecca Jukko is at Lost Dish City Hall."

The screen changed to a wide shot of what looked like City Hall chambers, a long desk in a half-circle at the front of the room, several older white people in business suits sitting behind it. A podium stood in front of the half-circle, and behind it, a tall man with silver hair and red cheeks stood in a navy pinstripe suit. Victor Zorba. He was speaking, but the audio was low. "Rebecca Jukko, reporting from Lost Dish" appeared in the caption at the bottom of the screen and Jukko's voice came up.

"Earlier this morning," Jukko's voice said, "Windfall 29 Director of Operations Victor Zorba withdrew the application for the company's controversial amusement park plan. Zorba cited community feedback as the main reason for the withdrawal."

Bernadette sat up straight on the sofa.

The camera switched to a different angle, this one a closer shot of Zorba at the podium. "We've also received input that our original plan will not supply the area with the jobs we were hoping for."

The screen changed again: this time, a pale-skinned woman, probably Rebecca Jukko, appeared on screen. She was in her thirties with red hair, in a dark gray blazer holding a microphone. She stood stock-still, then began speaking after a beat. "The Windfall 29 copper mine has shrunk to just ten percent of the output it had fifteen years ago. Many locals have speculated the mine would expand and reopen, despite environmental concerns. The announcement last year to convert the site to an underground amusement park put an end to many of the environmental protests. Those protests were coordinated by a group associated with former Lost Dish mayor Kim Blackwell, who chose not to seek re-election in November and is no longer on the county board of supervisors. But Blackwell was at the meeting today and is concerned about what Windfall 29's plan withdrawal means for the future."

The screen changed again, a white woman with cat's-eye glasses, a firm jaw, and long brown hair appearing on-screen with the caption *Kim Blackwell, former Lost Dish mayor* at the bottom of the frame. "The site of the Windfall 29 mine," Blackwell said, "is in close proximity to the Ottawa National Forest. While we respect the private property rights of Windfall 29, the rivers and groundwater are just now returning to non-harmful levels of copper acid. The plan had passed its environmental impact report—and the amusement park would have brought hundreds of construction, management, and retail jobs to Lost Dish. We're saddened that this project isn't moving forward."

Jukko came back on the screen. "Blackwell appeared to be in the minority at the meeting, with cheers of support coming from the gallery when Zorba announced the withdrawal of the plan."

Bernadette grimaced. There went the motive for Windfall 29. If they'd had a problem with an endangered coalhawk messing up their amusement park plans, they certainly didn't have that issue now.

Then Bernadette jumped in her seat in surprise—there was Jasper Fortescue on the screen. "The people of Porcupine County did not want an underground amusement park near Lost Dish," he said. "But with the high levels of unemployment and underemployment in the county, we need Windfall 29 to step up and be the job creators they've promised to be."

The news went to another story, and Bernadette pressed the mute button.

Jasper Fortescue—talking on camera about Windfall 29? Why?

Bernadette got up and dug the burner smartphone out of her purse, connected to the Wi-Fi in the cabin, and went to the PuLaRec site. She scrolled down.

Last updated March 31.

The last day of the previous quarter—over two months had passed since anyone had updated the site.

She tapped the screen a few times and brought up the map of the area where Evan McMichael had discovered the Keweenaw coalhawk.

The area was owned by the Fortescues—at least, according to the information on the website. She scrolled on the map to the northern border of the Fortescues' property. She tapped on the area on the other side of the border.

It was owned by Windfall 29.

Chapter Twenty-One

As Bernadette stared at the screen, showing the Windfall 29 land ownership tag, the smartphone buzzed in her hand. A 908 area code—an Upper Peninsula number.

She tapped *Answer.* "Hello?"

"It's Maura." Ah—her burner phone. "I got ahold of your friend Joanna."

"Is she working on getting Kep and me out of here?"

"She's glad you're alive."

"Oh—yes, of course, thanks."

"The explosion is all the agencies are talking about."

"Really?"

"When I left yesterday, everyone assumed you and Dr. Woodhead were killed. Agent Quimby had already heard the news."

"But you told her to keep our fake deaths under her hat, right?"

"Nothing to worry about. And the FBI started a joint task force with CSAB to investigate your, uh, murder."

"Oh." Bernadette blinked. Of course—she might have

been demoted from federal agent, but she still worked in the field, and her murder would still be a big deal.

"They've already ID'd the guy who's after you."

"Really?" Bernadette's jaw dropped open. "How?"

"Recovered the GPS unit from the side of the dumpster at the Cartwheel Suites near Oshkosh. Unique electronic signature led them to an army surplus store in Coeur d'Alene."

"Idaho?"

"Yes. Popular with preppers and right-wing extremists. The place sells off-the-grid firearms and ammunition, equipment they say is untraceable."

"Like GPS devices."

"Right."

"But these devices *are* traceable?"

Maura chuckled. "A year ago, the FBI arrested the owner on sedition charges, but concocted a story that he died in an auto accident. The new owner is undercover FBI."

"An undercover FBI agent sold this GPS device?"

"According to Joanna. The FBI has a name, a last known address, and there's an APB out. They're looking for him in eight states and at the Canadian border. Let me get his name for you." The sound of a keyboard tapping. "Darko Divjac."

"Serbian. Just like Annika—well, her real name."

"Divjac was based in Orlando until three years ago, just like Annika's family. Recently sighted in the Western states— Montana, Idaho, eastern Washington."

"Great, but if Divjac left town as soon as the car blew up—"

"The FBI thinks he's headed back to Idaho." Maura paused.

Bernadette squeezed her eyes shut. "What about Parr

Medical? Joanna knows our theory on them. They're head-quartered in Cleveland. Is the FBI looking—"

"No," Maura said. "Agent Quimby told me the FBI intel. Divjac is acting alone. Nothing to do with Parr Medical."

Bernadette stood up and stubbed her toe on the coffee table and swore loudly.

"I know," Maura said, "since he's acting alone, it's good news—"

"No, no, I just banged my big toe against—never mind. Joanna said he's acting on his own?"

"Not only that, but he's one of the prime suspects in the disappearance of Annika's father. And FBI intel thinks Marguerite may be supplying Divjac with information regarding the Kraljevski Sindikat."

"The Serbian mob? But why target me and Kep?"

"Quimby thinks you and Woodhead got too close to Annika for his comfort."

"The only thing Annika told us is that they had her sister." Bernadette blinked. "Wait—does that mean they think Marguerite is still alive?"

Maura clicked her tongue. "Just one theory. I had to drag a lot of information out of Agent Quimby."

A weight lifted from Bernadette's shoulders. "If it's one guy acting on his own, then maybe I don't have to go into hiding."

Maura was silent for a minute, then said, "Quimby recommended we wait another twenty-four hours to locate Divjac before we take steps to put you two into protective custody."

"Are they close to capturing him?"

Maura exhaled loudly. "Agent Quimby wasn't very forthcoming with the details."

"But you think it's a possibility."

Maura was quiet, but hope swelled within Bernadette.

"So Kep and I are back on this case?"

Maura hesitated, then spoke carefully. "Your participation is still on hold. We must confirm Divjac is working on his own."

Bernadette was quiet for a moment, then spoke. "I have a theory about the McMichael murder."

Maura cleared her throat. "You want to talk about this now?"

"Keeps my mind off the fact that my daughter might think I'm dead." Bernadette's voice cracked on the last word, and she took the phone away from her face, tapped *Mute*, and coughed—it might have been a sob cut short—then unmuted and put the phone back to her ear.

"Let me hear it."

"Windfall 29 just withdrew their application to convert their former copper mine into an underground amusement park."

"Into a what?"

"It was a terrible idea. Frankly, I'm surprised the proposal ever got the green light."

"What does that mean?"

"I told you our victim discovered new kettles of the Keweenaw coalhawk, right?"

"Rings a bell."

"Kep and I thought Windfall 29 might have wanted to keep that knowledge from getting out because it might mess with their plans to build their amusement park."

"Ah—and now withdrawing this proposal removes their motive."

"Right." Bernadette rubbed her chin. "But I just found out that Windfall 29 owns the property directly north of where McMichael discovered the Keweenaw coalhawk."

"Interesting. So—you think they might have purchased the land from the Fortescues?"

"If they did, but they don't want to expand their amusement park, I don't know why they'd buy the land." Bernadette paused. "And you'll never guess who was on the news talking about how the withdrawal was a good decision."

Maura paused. "One of the Fortescues?"

"Yep. Jasper."

"Why would he do that?"

Bernadette stood and paced around the small coffee table. "I don't know. He's in that ornithological society, so maybe he wants the habitat protected for birds."

"I suppose it's possible. But he owned the property where McMichael found the Keweenaw coalhawk—"

"Which, given the payment that Jasper received, might have been for the sale of the land." Bernadette paused. "How well do you know Michigan's real estate law?"

"Uh—I don't."

"Here's a theory for you. Jasper sells the land to Windfall 29. Windfall 29 decides the underground amusement park is a bad idea, so they're looking for a way out. Jasper realized that if Windfall 29 were to discover the Keweenaw coalhawk is nesting on that land, they'd look for a way out of their contract. Depending on what the law says—thirty days, sixty days—Windfall 29 might decide that Jasper breached their contract by failing to disclose the existence of the endangered species."

"Mmm." A tapping sound—Maura's pencil on a table or desk, probably. "If McMichael informed the Michigan Department of Natural Resources—or the National Park Service—the Keweenaw coalhawk was no longer extinct, you wouldn't be able to develop on the property for years. Generations, even. It could even trigger a land title issue."

"And by failing to disclose, Jasper Fortescue would have to give the money back?"

"Or," Maura mused, "no matter who bought the property—they'd be unable to develop it. That would give them motive, too," Maura mused.

"But since Windfall 29 just withdrew their application for the underground amusement park," Bernadette said, "they don't have a motive."

"So you're concentrating on the Fortescues?"

"At least until we find out who bought the land. I'd have to figure out the date of the sale and double-check with Michigan real estate law, of course, but Jasper has already spent the money."

"So he'd have a reason to want to silence McMichael."

"Absolutely."

"And you think"—Maura rustled some papers on her end—"McMichael would have let Jasper into his mobile home?"

"I don't know. Fortescue is well respected in the community. He's the head of the ornithological society. If he showed up with a bottle of expensive whiskey, an apology, and a desire to let bygones be bygones, maybe Evan would have let him in."

"Like inviting in a vampire," Maura said under her breath. "Okay," she said, a little louder, "explain the five grand deposit into Trudy's account."

"Maybe it's legit. Sale of personal merchandise, maybe."

"I saw their house. They own a lot of expensive stuff."

"Right. As Freud said, sometimes a cigar is just a cigar, right?"

"Freud never said that," Maura said distractedly. "But point taken."

"Has Lesley gotten a look at the vehicle records?"

"Yes. Only a few Lexus vehicles in Porcupine County."

The sound of Maura's keyboard clicking. "And you were right —Jasper Fortescue is a registered owner of a three-year-old ES sedan."

Bernadette thought of the four-car garage at the Fortescues' house. "Any way we can get a warrant for the garage?"

"What do you think we'll find?"

"If we get Kep's nose in there? Sulfuric acid. Whiskey. Maybe we'll even find one of McMichael's journals."

Maura grunted. "Not enough for a warrant."

Bernadette stood and paced around the room. "There must be something we can do."

"Not without concrete evidence."

Bernadette was quiet. Their trip to the university, getting Maura from the airport, her nightmare—the rental car explosion seemed like it was weeks ago, not the day before.

"But to get evidence on the McMichael death," Maura continued, "the FBI has taken over the investigation of the explosion. Not the McMichael death."

"Ah." Bernadette nodded. "So CSAB is free to pursue the McMichael death."

"With local law enforcement."

Bernadette waited a beat. "Same as before, right? So what's the next step?"

"I'd like to bring the Fortescues in," Maura said, "but I won't know the right questions to ask. Koskinen wants to blame McMichael's death on Constantine and blame Constantine's death on an overdose."

"As you said, Maura, the options are 'dirty' or 'incompetent.' Which one is the sheriff?"

Maura was quiet for a moment. "I was about to ask you to come in and conduct the interview."

"Oh." A pang of regret for turning Maura's words against

her now that she knew Maura was doing her a favor. "But I'm supposed to be dead."

"Let's see what the next twenty-four hours brings. You better hope the FBI gets Divjac."

They said their goodbyes, and Bernadette stood with the phone in her hand, thinking. A buzzing sound—quiet, and it stopped, then started again.

Bernadette grinned in spite of herself. Kep was snoring.

She sat back on the sofa and tried to find something to watch on TV.

Chapter Twenty-Two

After fifteen minutes of flipping channels, Bernadette switched the television off and went back on her phone. She was hamstrung without her laptop or the ability to talk directly to Lesley, but she had to do *something*.

She tapped her screen and the map of the region where McMichael had discovered the Keweenaw coalhawk. Squinting, she zoomed in and out. Was it possible to go visit the area? She thought at some point she might have to, but she wasn't an experienced hiker. It might require someone more familiar with the area—like Barcelona Lute. She considered this for a moment, but the logistics made her head hurt.

She went onto the Windfall 29 website to see if there was any news about real estate transactions. A brief article stating the company's operations department oversaw land management and acquisition. A short press release regarding the withdrawal of the amusement park proposal—released that afternoon—gave no information she hadn't gleaned from the television news report.

Maybe the information she was looking for was elsewhere. She brought up a search engine and typed *Windfall 29 mining* into the search tab.

After scrolling down past the sponsored weblinks for investing large sums of money—she suspected the ads were because of the *windfall* keyword—she found dozens of links to the company website and the news articles about the amusement park. She clicked on the second page. The links were mostly repeats of the latest news or financial reports from the company; she read six versions of the same article. There was a single link at the bottom of the second page of search results from Drake Mining Equipment. She clicked on it and was met with a deathly boring press release on Drake's quarterly results.

Trailing twelve-month GAAP net income positive, fiscal first-quarter billings growing by an impressive twenty-six percent year over year. A successful product launch for a new "dragline" offering, the Ag200, with orders from Imperio de Plata—a company based in Zacatecas, Mexico, as well as Silesian Mining in Poland and Windfall 29. At least that press release wasn't from Windfall 29 itself.

She tapped on the third page of search results; nothing but internal web pages on the Windfall 29 site. She followed a link to a web page explaining the historical significance of copper mining in the Lost Dish area, but her eyes glazed over after the first paragraph.

She blinked, stood, and stretched, then walked into the kitchen and opened the refrigerator. The half-gallon of milk and the quart of half-and-half stood forlornly next to the two takeout boxes from the restaurant. Bernadette wasn't sure what she was looking for—she hadn't purchased much at Saucy's Co-op a couple of nights before.

She stood with the refrigerator door open, squinting at

the weak light and the mostly empty shelves, and clicked her tongue.

Something wasn't right.

Not with the food—or lack thereof—in the fridge; there was a connection staring her in the face she hadn't made.

But then, what did she expect? Murder investigations—especially of poisoning murders—were hard enough when she and Kep had the full cooperation of the local law enforcement agencies. Even though the sheriff in Oregon had been less than forthcoming, she could still interview witnesses without her life being in danger.

This situation, though, was ridiculous. Having to chase a killer—or maybe multiple killers—while forced to stay in the shadows, and without even her laptop or regular phone, was a degree of difficulty she'd never encountered before.

The sound of a throat clearing made her lift her head. Kep stood in the kitchen's archway.

"Good afternoon."

"Hey." Bernadette forced herself to smile. "You were really sawing logs in there."

"My wife used to complain about my snoring." Kep looked down at the floor.

"I was just thinking how weird this is."

"I admit, confinement of this magnitude is not a scenario I previously considered."

Bernadette stared into the depths of the refrigerator's maw and blinked, then shut the door with a sigh. "I think I'm missing something."

"Such as?"

"The Fortescues are in this up to their eyeballs. There's a lot of smoke from the two of them, and I've been at this long enough to know there's no smoke without fire."

Kep nodded. "Focusing our investigation on the Fortescues makes sense. They have both a financial and a personal motivation to want Evan McMichael out of the way. And they had the opportunity to rid themselves of both McMichael and Gabriel Constantine."

"And we're figuring out the means."

"Correct." Kep scrunched up his face until his mustache touched the goatee below his lower lip. "I fear my presence in this investigation has been to little effect."

"It's my fault." Bernadette exhaled. "Getting us assigned to this case was pretty much window dressing so I could interview Annika Nakrivo at Taycheedah. In fact, I was supposed to go down there a few times this week."

"While that may be true," Kep said, "I always held value in my investigative skills beyond my olfactory talents."

"I'm not doing much good without my laptop—and without being able to get information from Lesley or Maura. We're both hamstrung here."

"Like the proverbial birds on a wire," Kep said.

They stood in silence for a few moments.

Bernadette broke the silence. "I hope Maura allows us to interview the Fortescues soon."

Kep chortled.

"What?"

"You seem to deprioritize your safety in order to move forward on the investigation."

Bernadette narrowed her eyes. "It's surreal. I can't just sit on my ass watching TV and letting other people be responsible for keeping me—for keeping *us*—safe."

"Yet," Kep said, "you cannot undermine those who are working to do just that."

"I KNOW!" The words exploded out of Bernadette's mouth, and she smacked the counter with her open hand. "I know, Kep! You think I don't? I'm trying *not* to think about

Sophie being targeted if they find out we're alive! Do you think I'm *not* tossing and turning every night? Do you think I'm *not* worried out of my mind?"

She was panting, her hands balled into fists.

"At least your child is still alive," Kep said.

Then he turned and exited the kitchen.

The sound of the bedroom door closing softly behind him.

It echoed in her ears. She eased herself down to the kitchen floor, the linoleum cool to the touch.

❧

The burner phone buzzed.

Bernadette didn't know how long she'd been sitting there. The quality of the light coming in through the living room window had changed.

She pulled herself to her feet; her legs tingled with pins and needles, and she almost stumbled as she walked into the living room to grab the phone.

Maura.

"Hello?" Bernadette's voice croaked as she answered.

"You okay?"

Bernadette cleared her throat. "Yes. No. I don't know."

"What's going on?"

"I miss not talking to Sophie. And sharing a cabin with Kep is..."

"Better you than me."

Bernadette was silent.

"Sorry—bad joke." Maura's tone brightened. "I've got some great news."

"Really?"

"I'm adding Agent Quimby to this call."

A click, silence, another click, then Maura's voice. "Bernadette?"

"Yes."

"Hi, Bernadette," Joanna Quimby said.

"Joanna—if I'm hearing your voice, that must mean—"

"We got him."

"Him? You mean..."

"Darko Divjac, yes. FBI picked him up at a bar outside Fargo."

"Oh, you beautiful soul. I'll buy you *two* margaritas next time we go out."

Joanna laughed. "I'm holding you to it."

Bernadette exhaled. "Fargo—North Dakota?"

"Right off the interstate that goes to Coeur d'Alene. He took off as soon as the news report hit that two CSAB investigators had been killed." A pause. "Hang on—I'm sending you his picture."

"How did we find him?"

"Remember how Lesley told you she could cross-reference all the drivers for the organized crime groups that avoided the forfeiture corridors?"

Bernadette crinkled her nose as the phone dinged. "Vaguely."

"She told me, too. And Darko Divjac was one of those drivers. We traced his movements and found him."

Bernadette's phone dinged; the photo had come in. "Hang on." Bernadette pulled the phone away from her face and tapped on the screen. The photo came up—and she almost dropped the phone.

"Joanna—this is the guy I saw in the parking lot at Taycheedah. He was wearing a Kansas State sweatshirt. I thought he might be the guy who put the GPS tracker on my rental car."

"I'm willing to bet he was."

"Acting alone?" Bernadette tried to keep both the excitement and the desperation out of her voice.

"Yes. No communication with others for the last week. Plus, if he'd been working for someone else, he'd have needed a more reliable proof of life—well, proof of death."

"How did he find out that I was going to see Annika?"

"The late Warden Marcie Fisk," Joanna said. "We don't have proof yet, but her recent financial transactions suggest she may have been taking bribes."

"From Divjac?"

"That's what we think."

Bernadette breathed out, feeling the tension flow out of her shoulders. "So we're safe?"

"Yes," Joanna said.

"Meaning," Maura cut in, "you can come to the Porcupine County Sheriff's Office and interview Jasper and Trudy Fortescue."

"I need to make a phone call," Bernadette said.

"One more thing," Maura said. "Your laptop is fine. No damage in the explosion. So I'll see you and Dr. Woodhead at the sheriff's office in an hour," Maura said. "We've got Deputy Moncrief going down to pick up the Fortescues now."

They said their goodbyes and Bernadette ended the call. She took a deep breath, then tapped in Sophie's cell phone number and hit *Call*.

Her daughter's voice on the other end, tentative. "Hello?"

"Sophie?"

"Mom?" Then Sophie started crying.

"What's wrong?"

Between sobs: "I thought you were dead."

"No—no, I'm calling you to tell you I'm okay. I couldn't—"

"How come you didn't call before?"

"It wasn't—" The words caught in her throat. *It wasn't safe,* is what Bernadette wanted to say. But could she tell Sophie? She didn't want Sophie worrying every time she went out on the road.

But then, the cat was probably out of the bag.

"Bernadette?" Barlow's voice, rough-hewn.

"Barlow, hi. I just—"

"How dare you," he said, evenly. "Sophie saw a news report online. Two federal investigators killed by a car bomb in the Upper Peninsula. She knew you'd gone there. Why didn't you call her to let you know you were okay?"

"Calm down."

"Don't tell me to calm down. I'm not yelling—I'm not even raising my voice. I should, but I'm not. So you need to explain yourself. Sophie was hysterical last night. I had to give her a pill to get her to sleep, and you know how much I hate pills. Then she woke up, and she's been catatonic today. You have a *lot* of explaining to do."

Bernadette took a deep breath. "I didn't call because—because I couldn't."

Barlow was silent for a moment. Bernadette could almost hear the gears turning in his head.

"I see," he said finally. "This is why you had me book the rental truck and the cabin for you. I should have known."

"Listen—"

"I get it. You were targeted. The agency had to make the killer think they'd succeeded. So they put out a fake news report."

Bernadette paused for a moment. "You pieced it together pretty quickly."

"I was married to you for too long," Barlow said.

The words might have been playful in another context, but his tone was cutting, and Bernadette's throat constricted.

"Can I talk to Sophie again?"

"An apology needs to be the first thing out of your mouth," Barlow said, "and—" His voice caught.

Bernadette was quiet.

"I used my credit card for the pickup rental," Barlow said, his voice cracking. "I put the cabin rental under my name because you said you needed to lay low. And when Sophie told me about the car explosion, I freaked out. I didn't know if they'd be after Sophie. Or after me."

"They caught the guy," Bernadette said lamely.

"When you get home," Barlow said, "you're getting another job."

"Or what?" Bernadette said. "You'll divorce me again?"

"For Sophie's sake." Barlow's voice quavered. "I thought when we got divorced, I'd stop worrying about your safety. Now I have to worry about Sophie's safety—and probably my safety, too."

"Well, it's nice to know you care."

"Let's be clear on this," Barlow said. His tone was still maddeningly even despite the slight cracking of his voice; he wasn't screaming or yelling at her, which part of her knew she deserved. "Your job already ended our marriage. Now I'm worried how it will affect Sophie."

"Our marriage ended because you couldn't keep it in your pants. If not for my job, you wouldn't even know who Lisa *is*."

Barlow raised his voice. "You know what? Sometimes I wish—"

Silence.

"Sometimes you wish *what*?" Bernadette said.

"Nothing."

He's not saying it because Sophie is there. Bernadette closed her eyes. He wanted to say something. Maybe something hurtful for effect. Or maybe something true, and something he hadn't said before because it *was* mean, and he'd wanted to protect her from his invective.

But she knew what he was going to say.

Not *Sometimes I wish I'd never met you.*

Instead: *Sometimes I wish that call would come.*

The call saying Bernadette *had* been killed in the line of duty. Her death would be horrible for Sophie, of course, but these situations were horrible *now*, and Sophie went through trauma again and again, every time Bernadette left for a business trip—and especially after news came through that federal investigators were in danger.

Because Bernadette had a dangerous job.

If the car bomb *had* killed Bernadette, Sophie would be devastated, hysterical, withdrawn—but she'd process the grief. Barlow and Lisa—yes, Lisa, even though she was a homewrecker—would do an admirable job parenting Sophie in Bernadette's absence. And Bernadette would become a series of photos on Sophie's phone, a character in stories Sophie would tell future boyfriends. Maybe Bernadette would be vilified or maybe she'd be the hero of the stories, but Sophie would survive. Sophie would stop worrying because Bernadette wouldn't be around to worry about.

She sank onto the sofa. "I'm sorry, Barlow."

"Don't tell me," he said, a note of gruffness in his voice. "Tell *her*."

Chapter Twenty-Three

BERNADETTE GOT OFF THE PHONE WITH SOPHIE ABOUT half an hour later. Sophie had sobbed and then she had yelled. Bernadette stopped counting how many times she said she was sorry, and just let Sophie be angry.

Sophie finally put Barlow back on.

"Thank you," Bernadette said, wiping the tears off her cheeks with the back of her hand.

"Sounded rough."

"It was."

"Uh huh."

And in his response—flat, terse, unemotional—Bernadette could tell that she'd face hell when she got home. An *uh huh* of the seeds of a custody battle. Barlow had a case to make for Sophie's well-being, too: their daughter deserved to be safe, deserved not to relive trauma every time her mother left for a work trip. Bernadette closed her eyes: the judge—always an older man, his face weathered, grizzled, experienced, and a knot of anger on his brow—bore a hole through her with his eyes as he awarded full custody to

Barlow, along with two-thirds of Bernadette's paycheck for child support.

Then an ache of indignance in her chest: why did she keep apologizing to Barlow? Sophie, yes. But Barlow wasn't her problem anymore. He'd never apologized to her for throwing their marriage away for Lisa. Co-parenting was one thing, but apologizing for her job?

She took a deep breath. Had she been apologizing to Barlow for the last fifteen years? Just for being herself?

Bernadette put her elbows on her knees and her head in her hands. The bedroom door opened.

Right—interviewing the Fortescues. She checked the clock on the phone. If they left right then, they'd be about five minutes late. Maybe Bernadette could make up time on the road.

She ran her hand over her face, then got off the sofa. Kep was standing in the threshold between the hallway and the living room, not saying anything. Bernadette turned her head toward the kitchen.

"Maura get ahold of you?"

"Yes. I'm relieved, of course."

"Right. Did she mention we're supposed to go to Lost Dish and interview the Fortescues?"

"She did."

"Okay. Let me go to the bathroom and then we can hit the road."

She walked around the sofa and pushed past Kep without looking at him. She closed the door to the bathroom behind her and splashed some water on her face, then looked at herself in the mirror. No makeup—she'd usually have some on when interviewing a suspect, but there was no time, and Bernadette didn't want to put on makeup anyway.

She went to the bathroom, washed her hands, and walked

out, again not looking at Kep. She stepped into her flats she'd discarded in front of the cabin door. Kep followed, saying nothing.

They arrived at the sheriff's office about ten minutes late. The chipper admin at the front desk called Deputy Moncrief, who almost immediately appeared through the door, and walked them back to a nondescript side room. When the deputy opened the door, Maura was sitting at the small rectangular table on one side, with Jasper and Trudy Fortescue on the other.

"Ah, they're here," Maura said. Her face registered slight annoyance.

"Sorry we're late," Bernadette said.

"No problem," Maura said. "I was just about to take Trudy for a decent cup of coffee."

"I don't know—" Trudy began.

"It's no trouble," Maura said, standing and grabbing her purse off the table. "We'll be back in ten, fifteen minutes, tops." She squeezed past Bernadette. "Look at the folder on the table," Maura breathed so only Bernadette could hear. "Fresh evidence from the M.E." She shut the door behind her, leaving Kep and Bernadette in the room with Jasper.

"So," Bernadette said as Kep took a seat at the far side of the table, "we've got a few more questions for you, Mr. Fortescue."

"I've been cooperative," Jasper said. "And you don't need to bring Trudy into this."

"Why not?"

"Because she has nothing—" Then Jasper clamped his mouth shut.

"How can you be so certain she has nothing to do with these murders?" Kep asked, leaning over the table.

"I know my wife."

"I believe you told my colleague," Kep said, "your wife wouldn't make an error on the prescriptions either."

Jasper was silent.

"Yet," Kep said, "she *did* make a mistake on the prescription."

Bernadette opened the file folder. Right on top was a memo from the medical examiner. Bernadette scanned down.

Bottle of pills labeled modafinil was empty inside locked medicine cabinet.

Deputy Mueller noted he had given two modafinil caplets to Gabriel Constantine. Deputy states the pills were bright pink and in a hexagonal shape, not a yellow oblong caplet, as modafinil is.

Hold on a second.

Bernadette took her phone out of her purse and tapped on the screen to bring up a web browser. She did an image search for—ugh. What had it been? Ax—something.

She stared at the cinderblock wall behind Jasper's head and blinked.

Axadabutin.

She typed it in, at first putting an *O* where the third *A* should have been. But there it was: a hexagonal pill.

And it was bright pink.

She clicked on the link and on the pharmaceutical company's home page, a large warning at the bottom in a bright orange bar.

Nonsteroidal anti-inflammatory drugs (NSAIDs), such as ibuprofen, have been shown to significantly increase the risk for serious gastrointestinal (GI) bleeding and fatal hemorrhaging, observed in more than 90% of patients with significant risk factors, such as Lyme disease or stimulant addiction. Other NSAIDs, such as ketoprofen, piroxicam, sulindac, diclofenac, and ketorolac, have been shown to have similar interactions with axadabutin occurring in a significantly smaller percentage of patients, though not resulting in fatal hemorrhaging. In the majority of patients, however, axadabutin has little effect on hypothrombinemic response, unless specifically combined with ibuprofen. Because the interaction between axadabutin and ibuprofen can lead to internal bleeding and fatal hemorrhaging, an alternative to ibuprofen is recommended; acetaminophen/paracetamol is the alternative of choice. If an NSAID medication is required for the patient, nonacetylated salicylates are safer because of minimal effects on platelets and gastric mucosa, though patients should be kept under close watch until tolerance has been established.

"Guess I just found the murder weapon," Bernadette murmured, pushing the M.E.'s memo in front of Kep.

"What?" Jasper asked.

Kep turned to Bernadette. "Did you say—"

"Hold on a minute," Bernadette said, and rushed out into the hall.

She looked around for a moment, then hurried out the door: *a good latte.* From the lobby, Trudy Fortescue was visible through the plate-glass windows, next to Maura. Bernadette ran out of the building and caught the two of them just as they were about to step off the curb.

Maura turned. "Bernadette? What—"

"The ibuprofen," Bernadette said, catching her breath. "Wasn't an accident."

The color drained from Trudy's face, but with visible effort she pushed a smile back onto her face. "What are you talking about? Of *course* it was an accident."

"That's only the part we can trace to you," Bernadette said, boring her eyes into Trudy.

Maura's face was equal parts interested and angry.

"If we research what pharmacy fills prescriptions for New Sunset House, what do you think will come up?"

Trudy's face scrunched in confusion. "I don't know what you're talking about."

"You're going to lie and tell me you didn't swap out the ibuprofen on purpose?"

"I—I don't—"

"It's right here in black and white." Bernadette tapped her finger on the memo. "I know axadabutin was stolen from the assisted living facility—and it wound up in the bottle of modafinil, and Deputy Mueller gave it to Gabriel Constantine. And I know you swapped out the acetaminophen for the ibuprofen."

Trudy blinked and her jaw went slack.

"A professional pharmacist would know how deadly axadabutin and ibuprofen are when they're combined."

Trudy, still with a stunned look on her face, nodded.

"Ibuprofen would have been no problem to switch out," Bernadette said. "But axadabutin is a little pricey, isn't it?"

"Over a thousand dollars a pill," Trudy whispered.

"So I get why you couldn't just accidentally mislabel the bottle or mistakenly put a few axadabutin caplets in with the modafinil."

"But—but I had nothing to do with the axadabutin." She paused. "Or the ibuprofen."

Bernadette set her jaw. "The evidence is all pointing to you right now, Trudy. My advice is to get ahead of this."

"My pharmacy doesn't service the nursing home."

Bernadette tilted her head. "You sure?"

"I know every commercial and government customer we have," Trudy said, a sprig of confidence showing through the waver in her voice. "And I know for a fact the New Sunset House isn't one of them."

Bernadette looked closely at Trudy's face. The woman was nervous. Probably because she'd been caught switching the ibuprofen.

"Five thousand dollars," Bernadette said thoughtfully. "Five thousand dollars to switch acetaminophen out and put ibuprofen in."

Trudy's eyes hardened. "You can't prove anything."

"I can prove you made a five-thousand-dollar cash deposit a few days ago."

"But you don't know where I got the money or what I got it for. For all you know, I had it stashed under the mattress for years and finally put it in the bank."

"So where did you get the money?"

"I don't think I have to tell you."

Trudy was right. Nothing would stick.

Yet.

Bernadette leaned forward. "I want you to consider this carefully, Trudy."

Trudy set her jaw.

"We may not have the evidence we need yet. Maybe we won't get it, but maybe we will. Maybe you're confident you didn't make any mistakes. But I bet there's something you're not thinking of. A security camera somewhere. A bank statement. Login records. I bet you laid a trail of breadcrumbs you didn't even know you were leaving." She put her hands together and cracked a knuckle. "We know you took money to switch those medications—"

"That's a lie," Trudy interrupted.

"—and that's a felony," Bernadette continued, "whether it's a prescription or an over-the-counter pill. And we know Gabriel Constantine died as a result. If we get to a point where we can prove it, do you think we'll cut a deal with you? Let you go with a slap on the wrist?"

Trudy's jaw was tight, but her blue eyes widened.

Bernadette took a step back and nodded to Maura. "Enjoy your fancy coffee." She spun on her heel and walked back into the sheriff's office building.

As soon as the door shut behind her, Bernadette turned; Maura and Trudy were out of sight.

There couldn't be many pharmacists in Lost Dish, and Bernadette would bet money Trudy was friends with whichever pharmacist *did* take care of New Sunset House. Proving it would be another matter, but—

Hang on.

Who had paid Trudy for switching the medications in the first place?

She walked through the archway past the front desk and walked into an empty conference room. She picked up a phone on a side table, dialed 9 for an outside line, then called Lesley.

It rang three times before Lesley picked up.

"CSAB, Lesley speaking."

"Hey, you."

"Bernadette! Wow—crazy week. Uh—that doesn't even begin to cover it, does it?"

"No, but—"

Lesley interrupted. "I was just about to call you. I pulled a bunch of phone records the day of—well, the day your rental car blew up."

"You found something?"

"Five calls in total between the sheriff's office in Lost Dish, the Fortescues' cell phones, and an unregistered mobile number—probably a burner—with a 908 area code." The sound of a keyboard tap. "12:31 P.M., sheriff's office to Jasper Fortescue's house. The call lasted for six minutes. Then at 12:38 P.M., from the house to that unregistered mobile number, lasting one minute."

"Could be a voicemail."

"Or someone not wanting to talk," Lesley said. "At 12:40 P.M., the Fortescues called the sheriff's office again."

Bernadette rubbed her chin. "Okay, the sheriff's office might call the Fortescues if the sheriff—or one of the deputies—suspected them of one of the murders. But why would the Fortescues call back?"

"We don't have recordings of the conversation," Lesley said, "but having done this in the past, I can tell you these kinds of communications usually fall into the panic category." The sound of a keyboard clicking. "The sheriff calls the Fortescues to ask if they had anything to do with the car exploding, then the Fortescues call the burner phone's owner to see if *that* person had anything to do with the bomb. Then when they don't answer, they call the sheriff back, so they look like they have nothing to hide."

"Not really admissible in court," Bernadette mumbled. "Hang on—you said *five* calls. I count three."

"Right. Because just after one P.M., the burner phone calls the sheriff's office."

Bernadette frowned. "Is this more innocent than it seems? Maybe the burner phone is a lawyer, not a conspirator?"

Lesley paused for a moment. "A lawyer with a burner phone?"

"Or it could be a conspirator calling to speak to the sheriff's office to establish an alibi."

The sound of the keyboard clicking again. "Maura told me you were supposed to interview the Fortescues today."

"Yeah, I'll absolutely ask about those calls." Bernadette ran her free hand through her hair. "And speaking of the Fortescues, I'm onto something here. The Gabriel Constantine murder was because of a medication switch. Constantine was supposed to take modafinil and acetaminophen, but instead, he took axadabutin and ibuprofen."

Lesley let out a low whistle.

"I think I know who swapped in the ibuprofen, but that pharmacist wasn't the one in charge of the assisted living facility where—"

Bernadette blinked. Maybe she was barking up the wrong tree.

"Bernadette?" Lesley asked.

"Hold on for a second." Bernadette paced in a tight circle, smashing the receiver next to her ear. "Someone stole the axadabutin. I figured the pharmacist might have had something to do with it, but now I think maybe it was an employee."

"You got a name of the facility?"

"New Sunset House. It's on River Street."

"Hang on a second." The sound of a keyboard clacking. "A lot of these facilities need to register their employees with the state. I can access the system pretty fast."

Pretty fast turned out to be four or five minutes of Lesley mumbling to herself and Bernadette pacing in a small circle that tangled the phone cord. She spent a good thirty seconds dangling the receiver by the cord and getting it untangled.

Finally, Lesley said, "Okay—I'm in."

"Names?"

Lesley started listing the employees. Bernadette didn't recognize any of them—although there was a *Penelope Eskola.*

Probably a sister, daughter, or in-law of Ed Eskola, the man they'd rented the pickup from. She listened for any names she'd come across in the investigation, but none of the other names sounded familiar.

"Anything?" Lesley asked.

"No. Was that the end of the employee list?"

"As of last week, yes. But you can't tell a lot by just the name. There would be a spouse who hasn't changed their last name, or a significant other, or, I don't know, a second cousin who has a different last name. Or even a best friend—the kind who'd help you bury a body, you know?"

"Yes." Although Bernadette didn't have any of *those* friends. Not anymore, anyway.

"Tell you what. I'll keep digging into these names. A small town like Lost Dish, someone is bound to have a connection to your investigation."

"See if any of the patients have relatives—" Bernadette blinked. "Like Bonnie Farmington. Her mother is a resident there. Can you see if her mother is on axadabutin?"

"Medical privacy laws," Lesley said. "But I'll see what I can do."

They said their goodbyes and Bernadette went back into the interview room.

When she opened the door, Kep and Jasper Fortescue were on opposite sides of the table. Kep was relaxed, leaning back slightly in his chair. Jasper looked tense; he was clenching and unclenching his fist under the table, bouncing his leg up and down nervously.

"Sorry," Bernadette said, taking the seat next to Kep and smiling as pleasantly as she could at Jasper. She turned to Kep. "Where are you with the questioning?"

"Oh, we waited for you," Kep said. He grinned through his salt-and-pepper beard and Jasper bounced his leg faster.

Not bad, Kep. Bernadette took a deep breath, straightened her blazer, then looked up at Jasper. "Yesterday, you received a call from the sheriff's office."

Jasper said nothing.

"The call lasted for several minutes, and then you made another call—this one to an unregistered mobile phone. Then you called the sheriff's office back." Bernadette sat straight in her seat, trying to make herself as tall as possible. "Can you tell me what those calls were about?"

Jasper clasped his hands together and looked down at the table. Bernadette could see the gears in his head turning furiously. After a moment—not too long, but long enough to make Bernadette think Jasper had concocted a story—he spoke.

"I need you to promise you won't tell Trudy."

Bernadette pursed her lips. "No. This is a murder investigation—"

"Deputy Moncrief called me."

"Carla Moncrief?"

"Yes."

"To talk about the threatening letter you sent to Evan McMichael?"

"What? No, I—" Then a dawning realization came over his face—then quickly disappeared. "Sorry, I'm so used to denying I did it. Yes, to talk about the letter."

Bernadette could have kicked herself. She'd led him into a story that probably made a lot more sense than the lie he was planning to tell—but this story wasn't true either. She looked at Kep, whose forehead was creased.

"Are you sure that's the story you're going with, Mr. Fortescue?" Bernadette said.

"I'm sure," Jasper said. Then added quickly, "It's the truth."

"What did Deputy Moncrief say?"

"Just stuff about the threatening letter. She knew I had written it and said I needed to come clean if I had more to say about it." Jasper tightened his shoulders. "But I don't."

"Then who did you call?"

"Oh." Jasper's gears were turning in his head again. "She and I got cut off, then I dialed the wrong number."

"The wrong number?" Bernadette wished she'd had Lesley get information about the calls Jasper had made—she could have seen if the numbers were at all similar.

"Sure. I got voicemail, realized my mistake, then called the sheriff's office back."

Bernadette was disgusted; she'd mishandled this. She'd given Jasper a way out, and she couldn't catch him in his obvious lies.

But there was still a flicker of hope.

"Let's talk about what Deputy Moncrief discussed with you," Bernadette said. "Your relationship with Evan McMichael."

Jasper looked like he was forcing his face to relax and doing a poor job of it. "Like I told her, not much to tell."

"Yet you were on the phone for six minutes—and you called her back."

"I suppose."

"Must have been *something* to say about what went on between you and Evan." She leaned forward slightly. "He wasn't part of the Old Victoria Ornithological Society, was he?"

"No."

"Especially after you sent him threatening letters."

"Those were—well, obviously I wish I hadn't sent them with that tone," Jasper said. "I intended to be a bit, well, *metaphorical* with those."

Kep cleared his throat. "Perhaps you can explain how a threat of physical harm is metaphorical."

"It seemed to be the only language he understood—no." Jasper looked down at the table. "He didn't respond to my requests—my original *nice* requests. So I'm afraid I went a bit overboard."

"So you and he were on friendlier terms than those communiques would have us believe?" Kep asked.

"Sure."

"Friendly enough to visit each other's houses?"

Jasper's throat strained and Bernadette could see the tendons in his neck. He smiled. "I'm afraid not. Maybe he and I could have settled our disagreement like gentlemen, but I'm afraid our animosity was such that while we were civil to each other in public, neither of us would have accepted an invitation to the other's home."

"What about—" Bernadette began, then stopped. She searched Jasper's face and looked in his eyes. He was shaking his leg under the table, only slightly, but enough. Jasper was a man on the edge—and with good reason: Bernadette trusted nothing that came out of his mouth. He was one uncomfortable question away from asking for his lawyer. And if that happened, Kep and Bernadette would get no more questions answered tonight.

Bernadette might have dragged Trudy across the line as well. Once Trudy got back to the sheriff's office, Bernadette couldn't imagine a scenario where Trudy walked into the room and didn't demand Jasper stop talking. So Bernadette changed the subject.

"You own some property down near Banner Crossing."

"Between Banner Crossing and Old Victoria. But you're using the wrong verb tense."

"Excuse me?"

"I *owned* it. Well, Trudy and I did. We sold it about three weeks ago."

She'd suspected as much. "The sale's final?"

"Escrow closed, so yes."

"Who purchased it?"

Jasper narrowed his eyes. "I don't think I have to tell you that."

"Land use records are public, Jasper. How about you save me the time?"

He sighed. "PLC Enterprises."

She stopped. "PLC Enterprises? Who are they?"

Jasper shrugged. "A company whose check cleared."

Bernadette closed her eyes and tapped her fingers on the desk. "They were interested in the property?"

"Correct."

"When did you list your property?"

"In this market?" Jasper chuckled. "I didn't."

"So you're saying PLC Enterprises approached *you*?"

"Their property manager did, yes."

"But if you weren't planning to put it on the market, why sell?"

"They offered to pay the assessed price from two years ago, plus fifteen percent."

Bernadette narrowed her eyes. "Why would they do that?"

Jasper shrugged again. "Don't look a gift horse in the mouth, right?"

"So PLC Enterprises paid a premium for the property." She turned to Kep. "How does Michigan real estate law work, Kep? They can back out of the deal, can't they? Thirty days, right?"

"If you mean to clarify whether PLC Enterprises can sever the purchase agreement," Kep said, "I believe it would require proof the seller misrepresented the property."

"You mean, if PLC Enterprises discovered, for example"—Bernadette glanced at Jasper, who clenched his jaw again—"an endangered species on the property the seller knew about—"

"Hey, hey," Jasper said, leaning forward, "no one said anything about backing out of the deal."

Bernadette glanced at Kep, who tilted his head and looked at her out of the corner of his eye. Neither one of them knew Michigan real estate law well enough.

"So PLC Enterprises didn't contact you about voiding the real estate sale."

"No."

Bernadette caught Kep's eye motion toward the door, and the two of them rose from their seats and walked outside the room into the hallway.

They walked down the short corridor to the water cooler, where Bernadette grabbed a paper cup and filled it.

"This is the least prepared for an interrogation I've ever been." Bernadette downed the cup of water and refilled it.

"The circumstances are unfortunate, yes."

"I can tell this guy has been lying through his teeth ever since he sat down."

"That's possible—but haven't we established a motive? We possess the threatening letter from Mr. Fortescue to Mr. McMichael, so I don't believe the U.S. attorney will ask for much more."

"You're right; maybe it's enough."

"And yet," Kep mused, "our theorized motive leaves me less than satisfied."

"Jasper's threatening letter might only be the tip of the iceberg," Bernadette said. "If PLC Enterprises found out the land they just purchased was the new habitat of a species that had just come off the *extinct* list?" She and Barlow had been through messy escrow details a decade before: title insurance, walkthroughs, signatures for indemnity. A discovery like McMichael's might throw a huge wrench into the process. She drank another cup of water, this time more slowly.

"Perhaps PLC Enterprises has deep enough pockets to drown Mr. Fortescue in lawyer fees even if Michigan real estate law is not on their side." Kep ran a hand over his beard.

"So if Evan McMichael had gone public with his discovery of the Keweenaw coalhawk…"

"Then Mr. Fortescue might have envisioned a nightmare scenario with the land sale. And if he'd already spent the money, he may have panicked."

Bernadette nodded and crumpled the paper cup in her hand. "If he thought he'd be forced into a reversal of the sale, what else might he have thought?"

"The land could not be sold or developed," Kep ventured.

"Right—it might have bricked the entire piece of property. Maybe the state or federal government would use eminent domain to protect the coalhawks—like Barcelona Lute said."

"Giving Jasper a tiny fraction of the money PLC Enterprises had purchased the property for."

Bernadette tossed the crumpled cup in the trash can next to the water cooler. "I know our evidence is a little thin to back up that motive, but it serves to explain why Jasper sent the threatening letter." She pulled out her phone and texted.

"Whom are you contacting?"

"I'm asking Maura and Lesley to find out about PLC Enterprises." She tapped *Send* and a whooshing sound came from the phone's speaker.

Kep was quiet for a moment.

"What is it?"

"Lead me through your theoretical timeline."

"Okay." Bernadette stared at the beige vinyl tiles on the floor and absentmindedly drew a figure-eight with her foot. "Jasper doesn't want Evan running his mouth off about the Keweenaw coalhawk, so he invites himself over to Evan's home with a bottle of nice whiskey and a shtick about letting bygones be bygones."

"Where did he get the sulfuric acid?"

"We can check his financials. He could have purchased some at a local hardware store—or even had some at his large piece of property."

"And why target Mr. Constantine?" Kep asked.

"Any number of reasons, but here's what makes the most sense to me: Jasper paid Constantine to kill Evan. Constantine shot up Evan's trailer but didn't kill him, and Constantine became a liability."

"Are you suggesting that Constantine attempted to blackmail Mr. Fortescue?"

"Possibly. But even if he didn't, Constantine might start talking in jail to save his skin."

"I see." Kep held out his hand, palm up. "And how is Jasper's spouse involved?"

"I think Jasper asked Trudy for help. So she figured out Constantine is on an anti-addiction medication, gets an idea to get rid of Constantine. She purposely makes a common error in switching the over-the-counter painkillers, then uses her pharmacy connections to get access to the assisted-living facility to steal the axadabutin."

"Axadabutin," Kep repeated. "Is that the bright pink hexagonal pill Dr. Goadbury identified in her memorandum?"

"Yes. Unique shape and color combo."

Kep pinched his lips together. "Why choose that particular medication?"

Bernadette blinked. "Opportunity, I guess."

"Axadabutin and ibuprofen are well-founded as a deadly combination," Kep said, pacing a few feet down the corridor, then turning back. "But there are other medications just as deadly when combined with ibuprofen, and certainly much cheaper and easier to obtain."

"Maybe she thought she could hide the theft of the axadabutin."

Kep tilted his head unenthusiastically. "It's possible. A toxicology screen would need to be targeted specifically to axadabutin." He raised his chin. "To that point, we have not conclusively proven the cause of death was axadabutin. We only know the deputy stated he gave Mr. Constantine two bright pink hexagonal pills."

"But those pills *have* to be axadabutin—and we know the other pills were ibuprofen. That's pretty close to conclusive." Bernadette paused. "But why would the deputy lie? And about something with such a unique color and shape?"

"It's possible—" Kep began.

"What?"

"I was about to say it's possible Deputy Mueller was involved in the murders. However, if he were, he would point us *away* from the pills—or away from a unique pill shape and color, at any rate."

"Do you think Jasper was telling the truth about getting the call from Deputy Moncrief? He wasn't telling the truth about anything else."

Kep was silent and ran his hand through his hair. "No. I have little confidence he spoke to Deputy Moncrief. We can certainly ask her."

"Where does this all leave us? Jasper was lying, Trudy was lying. Are the Fortescues our lead suspects?"

"I think, as you say, they are involved with everything

going on. But I have lingering doubts pestering my thoughts about either of them as ringleader."

Bernadette's phone dinged. A message from Maura.

> PLC—Lesley is researching

Kep stopped pacing for a moment. "Your working theory: Mrs. Fortescue used her pharmaceutical connections to gain access to the assisted living facility and steal the axadabutin."

"Right."

"Perhaps we should look more closely at those people who we are certain had access to the facility."

Just then, Bernadette's phone pinged. It was a text from Lesley.

> Quick business lookup: PLC Enterprises
> owned by Jakub Csurbinsky

Csurbinsky. The name rang a bell. Had she seen it before? Her phone dinged in her hand again.

> Also Bonnie Farmington just filed a wrongful
> death lawsuit against the county in the death
> of Gabriel Constantine

Bonnie Farmington.

The lost bail money.

A lightning strike in Bernadette's head. "I went to New Sunset House because I was following Bonnie Farmington. She was there when the axadabutin went missing."

Chapter Twenty-Four

Kep raised his eyebrows. "Have we overlooked Ms. Farmington?"

"We didn't at first." Bernadette folded her arms. "She posted bail for her brother, and like you said a couple days ago, it's awfully suspicious that she didn't disclose that to us."

"And yet we failed to make the connection with the axadabutin."

"We had a lot going on."

"We are professionals. *Our very eyes are sometimes, like our judgments, blind.*"

Bernadette frowned. "May seem obvious in hindsight, but we don't have a motive, do we? Why would Bonnie Farmington want to kill McMichael?"

"Perhaps we've been so distracted by the novelty of the Keweenaw coalhawk, we've neglected to look at a more common motive: family ties."

"Family ties? Like Gabriel Constantine?"

"Precisely."

"Gabriel is the one who shot up the trailer."

"Yes. And getting rid of McMichael would rid the world

of the only person who would be able to provide evidence in a criminal case against him—or perhaps that's what Ms. Farmington thought."

"Then why kill Constantine?"

"Ms. Farmington may be an otherwise savvy business-woman, but perhaps she wasn't prepared for the loss of her bail money."

"And his death would mean her bail money would get returned."

Kep bit his lip. "I'll have to check Michigan state law, but I believe so."

Bernadette held up her phone. "Bonnie Farmington just sued the county for wrongful death." She tilted her head. "That's one way to get your bail money back."

Kep gave a low whistle. "And she perhaps is not aware the county will classify his death as a murder. Does she realize she is now a suspect?"

"Have we been chasing the wrong people this whole time?"

"The Fortescues are still compelling suspects." Kep stroked his beard. "I admit, though, that we haven't cast the net wide enough."

They walked down the hall, away from the interview room, to the sheriff's office. Kep knocked on the open door.

Sheriff Koskinen looked up from the paperwork on his desk. "What is it?"

"Lieutenant Stevenson has taken Trudy Fortescue to get coffee," Kep said.

"Where's Jasper?"

"Still in the interview room," Bernadette said. "But after talking with both of them, we need to talk with another suspect."

Koskinen blinked. "Aren't the Fortescues your prime suspects?"

"We believe—" Bernadette glanced at Kep.

"We believe Trudy is involved," Kep said. "However, she may no longer be the prime suspect. We believe she was working with someone else."

"Any proof?" Koskinen asked quickly.

"When Trudy returns, she might be ready to tell us who asked her to switch the medication."

"The ibuprofen?"

"Correct," Kep said. "We believe Constantine died from the fatal combination of axadabutin and ibuprofen."

Koskinen was silent.

"The New Sunset House had a theft of axadabutin earlier in the week," Bernadette said. "And someone was able to get to Constantine's prescription bottle of modafinil and replace the pills. That deadly combination killed Gabriel Constantine."

"What we *think* killed Gabriel Constantine," Kep corrected.

"So, who's this other suspect?" Koskinen asked.

"Perhaps someone with the last name of Constantine is not only housed at the facility, but was the victim of the theft," Kep said. "We believe that person to be related to Bonnie Farmington."

Koskinen glanced at Bernadette. "Must be exhausting to work with this guy. Never wants to say anything outside the lines."

Bernadette shrugged. "He's not so bad."

"Do you want me to keep Jasper Fortescue in the interview room?"

"How long can you hold him?" Bernadette asked.

"We have a while," Koskinen said. "Questions?"

"See if *he* knows who paid his wife to switch the ibuprofen," Bernadette said. "And keep him away from Trudy when she comes back."

◈

Kep and Bernadette walked out into the hazy sunshine of the late morning. "St. Matthew's Pub?"

"I am unconvinced that should be our first order of business." Kep pointed down the street. "The New Sunset House is several blocks away. Visiting hours go until noon, unless I am mistaken."

"Right. She's usually there at this time of day."

"And if Ms. Farmington is with her mother, we can request video footage from the front desk."

"Do we have a date and time?"

"We can ask when the medication went missing."
Bernadette nodded.

They walked in silence to the assisted living facility. How was Bernadette going to make this up to Sophie? What job could she do outside of CSAB? Maybe she'd have to transition to a desk job. She'd have more time for Sophie. And a social life.

Then another pang of guilt made her draw in a breath.
Lamar.

She hadn't talked to Lamar since all this went down. She hadn't had her phone, either, so she didn't know if he'd been trying to reach her.

Bernadette hadn't even *thought* about Lamar once since Taycheedah. Her stomach dropped and her mouth went dry.

Kep turned to her and blinked. "Everything okay?"

"I didn't call Lamar to tell him I was okay."

"Ah." Kep kept walking. "First Sophie, then Lamar."

Bernadette shook her head, not in denial, but to clear her head. "What's wrong with me, Kep?"

Kep paused. "Despite my initial frustration that your brain does not operate the same way as mine, and at the risk of sounding maudlin, very little is wrong with you."

Bernadette scoffed. "I mean, like, mentally. My marriage fell apart. I'm alienating my daughter. And Lamar is a good man and a nice guy—and he's funny and kind. What's wrong with me?"

"Ah." Kep slowed his pace. "I hesitate to play the part of armchair psychologist."

"I'm asking seriously. Not a rhetorical question."

"You are, as they say, married to your job. Yours is not an unusual case for those who have chosen a career in law enforcement."

"So my mother was right? I drove Barlow away?"

Kep's tone was sharp. "I said nothing of the sort." He paused and chose his words carefully. "When family relations are strained, many people focus on their jobs because they feel they have more control over the outcome of their work than their personal lives."

"And I'm doing that."

"I believe Maslow's hierarchy of needs can be instructive here as well."

Bernadette tried very hard not to roll her eyes, and mostly succeeded.

"You've experienced a gap in your safety needs in the last few days, so your attention to your family and to Lamar— your higher needs of love and belonging—we deprioritized. Your motivation was focused on removing yourself from danger. Maslow originally posited that individuals must satisfy lower-level deficit needs before—"

"I took psychology, Kep. Maslow walked that back."

"He walked back his all-or-nothing statements." Kep looked at Bernadette's face, not unkindly. "Your life was in danger. Allow yourself some grace for prioritizing your safety over your desire to stay in contact with Lamar." He nodded and his head bowed forward again. "You'll call him when you solve the case."

"I'm safe now. I've been safe ever since Joanna told me they caught Darko Divjac. So why haven't I called him yet?"

Kep chuckled. "I am certainly not one to lecture others on interpersonal relationships. However, I do not believe things are as clear-cut as you say. Your assigned cases are wrapped up in your safety needs and your sense of self. There is no switch that is disengaged when Joanna told you that our pursuer was in custody."

Bernadette was silent.

"I'm confident Lamar will understand. He's a law enforcement officer, after all."

"Yeah." But Lamar would understand all too well. He wasn't a priority for her. She ran her hands through her hair as they arrived at New Sunset's parking lot. "All right. Game face on."

Bernadette scanned the lot. There was no sign of Bonnie's orange Kia Soul.

Kep frowned. "I was certain this would be the right time of day for Bonnie Farmington."

They entered the front office of the main building. The woman behind the front desk—the same one whose clipboard Bernadette had knocked over the day before—frowned.

"Us again," Bernadette said, making her voice chipper.

"Are you back with a warrant?"

Bernadette stole a quick glance at Kep as the gears in her

head spun. "We're from the Controlled Substance Analysis Bureau."

The nurse's frown deepened.

"There was an incident of theft of axadabutin earlier this week, wasn't there?"

"I—I'm not allowed to discuss patients."

"We have evidence the stolen axadabutin was used in the commission of a murder," Bernadette said, stretching the truth, but confident the M.E.'s memo would give her cover. "Given the drug's status and given the incident report in which it went missing, we have probable cause to search the premises."

"You can't do that—"

Kep held up his hand. "We simply want to review your security recordings."

The nurse pressed her lips together. "We've turned it over to the sheriff's office already. There's nothing in the footage."

"What do you mean, nothing in the footage?" Bernadette asked.

"When Mr. Csurbinsky's pills were sto—" The nurse stopped, then stood from her stool. "Hold on a moment. I need to ask my supervisor if this is authorized."

"Hang on," Bernadette said. "*Jacob* Csurbinsky? Csurbinsky with a C?"

The nurse frowned. "It's *Jakub*." She pronounced the J like a Y, and the A like a schwa, not like a long A.

Csurbinsky? But—weren't the pills stolen from Constantine? Bernadette could have sworn—

"Yes," Kep said, "we're happy to discuss this with your supervisor."

"I will not get fired over this," the nurse said frostily, then walked through a door behind the desk, shutting it behind her.

Bernadette exhaled, the frustration coursing through her body, and took a few steps around the empty waiting room. She stopped in front of the cartoon map she had seen the day before and Kep stood next to her.

"Something seems to be bothering you," he said.

"I saw the form on the clipboard yesterday," Bernadette said, still staring at the map, "The patient's last name began with a C. But it was *Csurbinsky,* not *Constantine.*"

"So Mr. Csurbinsky had his pills stolen?"

"And he's the owner of PLC Enterprises—the company that bought the land from Jasper Fortescue." Bernadette curled her upper lip. "Obviously a shell company. So who actually owns it? Bonnie Farmington? And did she take the pills?"

"Perhaps Mr. Csurbinsky breakfasts with Ms. Farmington's mother every morning and places his pillbox on the table while they eat."

"Could be."

The nurse came back in. "My supervisor confirmed we sent the recordings to the sheriff's office."

Kep stepped beside Bernadette and spoke in a low voice. "Do you have any inkling why Sheriff Koskinen would fail to disclose that information?"

Bernadette frowned. "Maybe he didn't think the theft of the axadabutin was related to Constantine's death?"

Kep stroked his beard. "I suppose Sheriff Koskinen has presented himself as ignorant of basic homicide investigation protocols and expectations."

"I don't expect they get a lot of murders up here." Bernadette turned back to the nurse. "You have copies here?"

The nurse shook her head. "No. We send the hard drives."

"But you've backed up the recordings to the cloud, right?"

The nurse continued to shake her head. "Absolutely not.

Patient confidentiality. We saw too many instances of those cloud storage systems getting hacked. We're still old-school with the hard drives."

"But you looked at the footage?"

"Well—once Csurbinsky's son made the report, Koskinen came in and took the drives. We have a security officer who monitors things, but he didn't raise any red flags."

Kep turned his head toward Bernadette. "Therefore," he murmured into her ear, "no unauthorized users entering the area where the staff stored Mr. Csurbinsky's pills. A trusted visitor like Bonnie Farmington might have been able to steal them at mealtime."

"So," Bernadette said to the nurse, "how do you know the sheriff's office didn't find anything on the recordings?"

"They called and told us."

"Who?"

"Sheriff Koskinen himself."

"He called you?"

The nurse shrugged. "He called my supervisor—the phone was on speaker."

"I see." Bernadette scratched her scalp. Had she missed something? Was it right in front of her face? "Where *were* Mr. Csurbinsky's pills stored?"

The nurse set her mouth in a line. "We keep all patients' medications in a locked cabinet. We take any relevant medications out at mealtimes or bedtime—as per the doctor's or pharmacist's instructions."

"And when does Mr. Csurbinsky take the axadabutin?"

"I'm afraid I can't tell you without a court order."

Kep nodded in the nurse's direction. "We understand you're bound by confidentiality rules. I am compelled to point out axadabutin is typically taken twice a day with food."

The nurse said nothing.

"Further," Kep said, turning to Bernadette, "visitors' hours are in the morning. I expect the axadabutin Mr. Csurbinsky was scheduled to receive at breakfast went missing."

"It wasn't the staff," the nurse blurted.

"Ah," Kep said. "So between the time the staff provided Mr. Csurbinsky with his dose of axadabutin and the time he went to ingest the pills, they disappeared."

"During visiting hours," Bernadette said. "Was Bonnie Farmington here?"

The nurse opened her mouth, shut it again, looked thoughtful for a moment, then spoke. "You'll find Ms. Farmington visits her mother on most days."

After their conversation with Bonnie Farmington in the parking lot, Bernadette and Kep had also talked to Victor Zorba.

"Why was Victor Zorba visiting this facility?"

"I can't reveal that information."

"Did he want to buy this place?"

The nurse chuckled. "I'm sure the owner would jump on any offer Mr. Zorba would make. But no, Zorba is too absorbed in trying to buy the St. Matthew's Pub." She leaned forward. "And I think he's finally given Bonnie an offer she can't refuse. Which can't come soon enough—I'm sick of them negotiating in the waiting room."

Bernadette's eyes widened. "I didn't think she'd ever sell."

The nurse shrugged. "Who can say? She seemed in a hurry to get back to the pub this morning."

"Ms. Farmington has already been here and left?" Kep asked.

The nurse grimaced. "I—I didn't say that."

"No, of course not. My mistake." Kep turned to Bernadette. "Do you have further questions?"

Bernadette looked around the office. Her eyes focused on

the cartoon map's downtown. Gold Street, Silver Street, and Copper Street—each represented by a shiny metal bar with the periodic table abbreviation: *Au* for Gold Street, *Ag* for Silver Street, *Co* for Copper Street.

She closed her eyes tight. Something was right on the edge of her consciousness. Was it Copper Street? Something with the map? She tried to will it into words, but it didn't come. She opened her eyes. "I guess not." She raised her head and locked eyes with the nurse. "Thank you for your time."

The nurse nodded curtly, and Kep and Bernadette walked out into the parking lot.

Bernadette motioned toward the sheriff's office. "Now for the footage on those hard drives Koskinen took."

"It will be instructive to hear his reasoning for not informing us about the recordings."

"Yep." Bernadette quickened her pace. "And then we can go down to St. Matthew's Pub. Something made Bonnie Farmington change her mind about selling the pub to Windfall 29."

Kep raised his eyebrows as they walked. "You haven't seen the press release this morning?"

"Uh—no, I guess not." Bernadette frowned. *Press release—* she'd seen no press release about Windfall 29 except for the announcement about withdrawing the amusement park proposal.

Except for that boring Drake Mining Equipment release, but it was a few weeks old.

"A round of investment funding came in for Windfall 29."

"Good for them."

"Indeed. The press release said the new round brought in approximately seventy million dollars."

"Ah, got it." Bernadette nodded. "Zorba could provide a much better offer for the pub."

"A reasonable conclusion."

They walked another minute in silence, Bernadette trying to connect all the dots. She'd knocked the pieces of the jigsaw puzzle onto the floor, and if she could just pick them all up and put them on the table, everything would come together.

They walked into the sheriff's office, nodded to the receptionist, and walked through to Koskinen's office. He sat at his desk, bent over a set of paperwork, his head leaning heavily on one arm propped on the tabletop.

"Sheriff?" Bernadette asked, shutting the office door behind them.

He jumped slightly in his seat at the sound of the door closing, then sat up straight. His cheek was red from his hand. "Agent Becker—Dr. Woodhead. I just wanted to say— well, I'm glad you two are all right."

"Yep. Thanks for your concern."

Koskinen gave Bernadette an uneasy smile. "With that Serbian mafia guy after you, I guess that's why you two were so squirrelly."

"Squirrelly?"

"Well—yeah. We couldn't ever find you. You didn't answer your phones. I don't know—I guess 'squirrelly' isn't the right word, yeah? But I understand. I don't know how I'd react if I had some hired killer for the Serbian mafia on my tail. I'd stage my own death, too."

"Oh." Bernadette managed a weak smile. "Thank you."

Koskinen cleared his throat. "Have you found everything you need?"

Bernadette cocked her head. "Uh—no. We'd like to see the security footage from three days ago from the New Sunset House."

Koskinen blinked, opened his mouth, then shut it again.

"I—I'm not sure why you need to see that. It's not—it's not relevant to the death of Evan McMichael."

"However," Kep said, "we believe the security footage *is* likely to be relevant to the death of Gabriel Constantine."

Koskinen licked his lips and nodded. "I don't really see how—but there's nothing to see."

"Nothing to see?" Bernadette repeated.

"Damaged hard drives," Koskinen said. "They wouldn't mount to our system, and it looks like we can't repair them, either."

Bernadette crossed her arms. "That footage might show who stole two axadabutin pills at New Sunset. Those pills might be the murder weapon."

Koskinen blinked rapidly, then shrugged. "I don't know what to tell you. The drives aren't usable."

"Where are they now?"

"Uh—I shipped them to the state recovery facility in Lansing."

"In Lansing?"

"They've said there's a three-month wait," Koskinen said. "And they're in transit now. I shipped them ground, so I don't think they've arrived yet."

Bernadette clenched and unclenched her fists. This could have blown the entire case wide open, and Koskinen had— well, Bernadette wasn't sure. "Why in the world wouldn't you tell us about this footage?" An edge of anger creeped into her voice.

The options were 'dirty' or 'incompetent,' as Maura had said.

"Why *would* I tell you about the footage?" Koskinen snapped. "We deal with theft of oxy and Norco from hospitals and nursing homes all the time. Nothing's relevant to any homicide in Lost Dish. Why would this be any different?"

"Didn't you read the memo from the M.E.?" Bernadette's voice rose. "Didn't you know *why* we interviewed Trudy Fortescue?"

"But—but," Koskinen said, "we checked with the pharmacy. Trudy's pharmacy doesn't fill the medications at the nursing home."

She raised herself to her full height. "Which is why we need to find out who stole the axadabutin!" Bernadette's voice rose, and she took a deep breath before continuing with a calmer tone. "Axadabutin and ibuprofen is a deadly combination. We believe we know how the ibuprofen got swapped in for the acetaminophen. We *don't* know how the axadabutin got into Constantine's medication bottle."

"Well, if you'd told me—"

"If you had put two and two together—"

"—I'd have overnighted the hard drives," Koskinen said. "And don't treat me like some backwoods hick. I don't deal with this kind of thing. We haven't had a homicide in Porcupine County in three years."

Bernadette glared at Koskinen. Her pulse was racing—but he was right. Koskinen wouldn't have the experience or the knowledge to know how to deal with homicide procedure. He probably had said there was nothing on the recordings because he had no idea what he was looking for.

And Bernadette had certainly made her share of errors in her investigations over the last eighteen months—she hadn't been unfairly demoted to a glorified babysitter for Kep. Her shoulders drooped. "Okay." She took a deep breath. "You're right. If you haven't lived and breathed homicide procedure, maybe you don't make the connection."

"I mean," Koskinen said, "it's not like they won't get it in a few days. It'll just delay things."

Bernadette nodded slowly. "So, what do we do in the

meantime?"

Kep ran his hand over his beard. "With the lack of evidence showing the identity of the medication thief—"

Bernadette paced around Koskinen's office. "Wait—Bonnie Farmington doesn't *know* we don't have the footage."

Koskinen got to his feet uneasily. "Are you saying—are you saying you think Bonnie Farmington's the killer?"

"We believe she was at New Sunset House during the theft of the axadabutin," Bernadette replied.

Koskinen opened his mouth. "But why—" Then he clamped it shut again.

"What is it?"

"Nothing."

Kep stepped forward. "Were you going to ask why Bonnie Farmington wanted to kill her own brother? Finances may have been a motive. After the police identified Mr. Constantine as a person of interest in the death of Evan McMichael, they revoked his bail. Ms. Farmington could have lost the bar. However, if Mr. Constantine died in custody before being formally charged, Ms. Farmington would have likely been able to get reimbursement for bail."

"After a couple of months," Koskinen agreed. "Porcupine County has a process for bail reimbursement, but yeah, you're right." He folded his arms. "Still, killing your own flesh and blood?"

"And maybe having to wait a couple of months is why Bonnie Farmington is willing to sell the bar now," Bernadette said.

"Shall we begin the drive to Banner Crossing?" Kep asked.

"Let's do it," Bernadette said, turning toward the door.

"Will you need some manpower there for the arrest?"

Bernadette paused with her hand on the door handle, then opened the door. "Sure couldn't hurt. Thanks, Sheriff."

Chapter Twenty-Five

THE YOUNG MALE BARTENDER WAS MOPPING THE FLOOR, HIS back to the front door, when Kep and Bernadette entered St. Matthew's Pub. He turned, and surprise showed on his face.

Bernadette took her badge out. "It's us again," she said.

The bartender forced a smile onto his face. "Oh—how can I help you?"

"We need to speak to Bonnie Farmington."

The bartender was quiet.

"We know she's here," Kep added. "Her Mars Orange Kia Soul is outside."

"She's in a meeting," the bartender said.

"No doubt with Victor Zorba," Bernadette said.

The bartender looked down at his mop.

"His Lexus is outside, too," she said. "From the look of things, you're about to get a new boss."

"She told me not to disturb them."

"I'm sure," Bernadette said, striding across the floor and stepping through the doorway behind the bar. "This way to her office, right?"

"I don't—"

With Kep on her heels, Bernadette turned left down the corridor—which led to a storage closet. She turned around, stepping around Kep. A door marked *Office* in worn white letters on a black plastic nameplate. Two voices, a man and a woman, muted by the door and the echo of the bar.

She knocked loudly.

The woman's loud voice from behind the door. "Not now, Dave!"

"Ms. Farmington, it's Bernadette Becker from CSAB."

Silence.

"We need to ask you some questions."

"This isn't a good time."

"I'm afraid it can't wait." Bernadette turned the door handle, and it swung open.

The office was small, dominated by a metal desk with an ancient PC on it. Bonnie Farmington was behind the desk and looked up at Bernadette, staring daggers into her. Victor Zorba, his back to the door, sat across the desk from Farmington.

Bernadette craned her neck to look over Zorba's shoulder. On the desk, two sets of papers. Two pens, one on Bonnie Farmington's side, one on Victor Zorba's side.

"Making the sale official?" Bernadette asked.

"It's time," Bonnie said. "Victor's giving me a good price. And my circumstances—well, let's just say it's time to sell."

"You're happy with the offer, though, aren't you, Bonnie?" Zorba said, scooting back slightly.

She smiled. "I wouldn't be breaking out the good tequila for you if I wasn't."

Bernadette took a step to her right and the bottle behind Zorba came into view. The distinctive diamond-shaped bottle of *Traición de Ideales*. That was the same tequila the bar had offered on special a couple of days before. The label was light blue, with the word *Plata* in stylized lettering.

She furrowed her brow. *Plata*—her brain was trying to connect the dots again.

Bernadette closed her eyes.

"So," Bonnie said, "what made you burst into my office in the middle of a business transaction?"

Bernadette opened her eyes. "Your mother is a resident at New Sunset House."

Bonnie folded her arms. "What's it to you?"

"Theft of axadabutin."

A slight movement to her left—Zorba. Had he suddenly stiffened in his seat?

"Theft of what?" Bonnie said.

"Another patient, Mr. Csurbinsky, had his—"

Bernadette tilted her head and glanced at Zorba's shoes. Still the brown dress shoes, not the burgundy-and-black cowboy boots he'd worn before.

Then clear as a bell: the similarity between *Csurbinsky* and *Zorba*.

A flash in her mind: PLC Enterprises—Porcupine Lake Cabins. One of the diversified businesses Windfall 29 had made after the decline of the copper mine.

And one more: the downtown cartoon map on the wall of the waiting room of New Sunset House.

Gold Street, Silver Street, and Copper Street.

Ag for Silver Street.

Bernadette shifted her weight, turning slightly toward Victor Zorba. "Your father is at New Sunset House too, isn't he, Mr. Zorba?"

Zorba turned and looked at Bernadette, then narrowed his eyes. "I don't see how that's any of your business."

"Csurbinsky—your father's name, right? Used to be yours, too?"

Zorba shrugged. "I needed a more Anglicized name when I got into a customer-facing role."

"Sure," Bernadette said. "But you admit—Csurbinsky is your father."

"Sure."

"Because someone stole his axadabutin a few days ago," Bernadette replied.

"Don't I know it," Zorba said. "I had to take the morning to file the report."

"But you didn't know your breakfast visit with your father was on the security footage."

Zorba's neck tendons sprang to attention—and then relaxed. "If you say so." He cocked his head. "I'm sorry—are you accusing me of stealing my father's medication?"

Bernadette stepped to the side of the room where she could see Zorba's face, with Bonnie Farmington out of the corner of her eye. "I came across a press release the other day, Mr. Zorba. I didn't think much of it then, but now I find the news curious."

Zorba was staring at the contract on the desk, trying not to make eye contact.

"The press release was from Drake Mining Equipment," she continued. "A new product announcement. If I remember correctly, the press release promoted a dragline called the Ag200."

Zorba nodded. "I think that's correct."

"*Ag* being the element symbol for silver."

Zorba grinned. "I learned that in high school chemistry."

"The press release," said Bernadette, raising her voice slightly, "Talked about early customer wins. Orders from Windfall 29 and another company called Imperio de Plata from Mexico. It means *Silver Empire* in English." She nodded at the bottle of tequila on the desk. "Just like the *plata* on the tequila."

Kep took a step into the room.

"When Dr. Woodhead and I arrived in town, you were at our hotel. In fact, you wanted your workers to be housed at the hotel because of a new piece of equipment arriving." Bernadette leaned casually against the wall. "The new Drake Mining Ag200 dragline."

"No surprise in that." Zorba's breathing sped up a tick. "We're a mining company, after all."

"You were a *copper* mining company," Bernadette said. "And Windfall 29—well, your subsidiary PLC Enterprises— just paid a premium for the Fortescues' land." She nodded at the paperwork on the desk between Farmington and Zorba. "And you're about to overpay significantly for St. Matthew's Pub—and the land it's on." She tilted her head. "But the Ag200 dragline won't help you mine *copper*, now, will it?"

Bonnie stood up, her shoulders tense. "You found *silver?*"

"Now, look, Bonnie—" Zorba began.

"You—Windfall 29—ordered silver mining equipment," Bernadette said. "You bought the land from the Fortescues, and you paid a premium for it in this soft market because you found silver. Not because of any kind of amusement park."

Bonnie pointed at Zorba. "You said you'd keep the bar open. You said it was a cash cow."

"It *is* a cash cow," Zorba said. "Look—yes, we found silver on the southern edge of our property. And yes, the vein goes through the Fortescues' land, and we believe it goes all the way into Ottawa National Forest. And yes, we overpaid. We're a business. This is all just business."

"But then," Bernadette said, "Evan McMichael found the Keweenaw coalhawks."

Zorba slightly winced, then regained his composure. "There are many birds of prey around the Ottawa National Forest. I don't know about Evan finding any special hawks."

Zorba had said *Evan*. Familiarity. Bernadette could barely suppress a grin. "You know Keweenaw coalhawks were thought to be extinct, and you knew McMichael found them," Bernadette said, though she was riding the frayed ends of her knowledge. "How did you catch wind of it? Through Jasper Fortescue? Or maybe Bonnie mentioned the new discovery Evan was excited about?"

"I still don't know what you're talking about." He shook his head. "Really, I appreciate your tenacity in solving this murder, but your story about these hawks just doesn't—"

"At any rate," Bernadette continued, "you had Jasper Fortescue threaten to sue Evan McMichael and send him threatening letters, and when that didn't work, you showed up at his trailer with a bottle of top-shelf American whiskey in your hand and a bottle of sulfuric acid in your pocket." She pushed slightly off the wall, glaring at Zorba. "The big shot in Porcupine County breaks out a bottle of two-hundred-dollar whiskey, you invite him in and get two glasses, right? McMichael probably didn't even notice when you spiked his drink."

"Silver mines use laboratory-quality sulfuric acid in the refining process," Kep said. "If you ordered silver mining equipment, you almost assuredly ordered a mass quantity of sulfuric acid."

"Not much is required to kill a man," Bernadette added. "No one would miss a quarter of an ounce from the order if it went missing."

Bonnie's face went white. "Wait—you poisoned Evan?"

"Of course not!" A bead of sweat ran down Zorba's temple. "I said I don't know what they're talking about."

"Really?" Kep smoothed down his beard. "Witnesses place your Lexus in the trailer park the night someone ransacked McMichael's home."

Bonnie's hand shot across the top of the table, and she pulled the contract toward herself.

"You know why I was there," Zorba sneered. He turned to Farmington. "And you don't need to worry about the contract. My Lexus was only at the trailer park because I was dropping off my drunk friend from the bar."

Bonnie's voice from that morning: *Did you finally change out of those ugly cowboy boots?*

"If we were to get a warrant to search your house," Bernadette said carefully, "would we find glass shards in the soles of your cowboy boots?"

Zorba hesitated. "What do my boots have to do with anything? I just dropped Alvin off. I'm a Good Samaritan. You should thank me, not accuse me."

"Alvin Davies," Bernadette said quietly. "He was your target. You knew where he lived, knew he drank at St. Matthew's, and got him drunk just so you'd have a reason to be at the trailer park—and we wouldn't be able to prove *you* were the one who ransacked the trailer." She cocked her head. "What do you think we'll find when we comb through your browser history? Or your financials? I'll bet you all the silver on this property that you searched for his job history, his address, his—"

"I was running a background check," Zorba said. "He might be an exemplary employee."

"You might have destroyed evidence that you were at McMichael's the night of his murder," Bernadette continued. "Leaving that economics book on top of the pile was a nice touch to throw us off the scent."

"Off the scent of what?" But a touch of a smile at the corner of Zorba's mouth.

"Evan's birdwatching journals with the location of the eleven kettles of Keweenaw coalhawks."

Zorba blinked. "I—I'm sure I don't know what you're talking about."

"Five birdwatching journals," Bernadette continued. "What you *don't* know is that Evan had a companion when he went birdwatching."

His eyes didn't move, staring at Bernadette.

"She kept a journal, too. And we know where those coalhawks are."

Zorba's jaw dropped, but he quickly recovered. "I suppose you've created some sort of story about these birds." He stood. "But I'm not following. Because I had nothing to do with whatever you think I did."

"The birdwatching journals where they chronicled the location of the Keweenaw coalhawks. On the property you just bought from Jasper Fortescue." She looked at Kep. "You think the EPA will let Windfall 29 mine silver on the land where they discovered a species of coalhawk they thought was extinct?"

"Unlikely," Kep said.

Bonnie glanced from Zorba to Kep to Bernadette. "Wait —how does my brother figure into this?"

"My theory? A third party paid your brother to kill McMichael—but shooting up his trailer didn't do the trick."

"I subscribe to the same theory," said Kep. "I now believe Mr. Zorba was that third party."

Bernadette nodded.

Bonnie set her jaw. "So *that's* what Gabe was talking about."

"What?"

Bonnie frowned. "He said he only did 'it' because he needed the money."

"Only did what? Shot up McMichael's trailer?"

"He wouldn't tell me what 'it' was." Bonnie crossed her arms. "I wondered where the big envelope of cash under the mattress came from."

"Perhaps Mr. Zorba's fingerprints are on the envelope," Kep said.

"Maybe," Bernadette said. "Or even some of the cash."

"So, wait." Bonnie leaned forward, her hands on the back of her chair. A crease had formed in the middle of her forehead as she turned to Zorba. "Not only did you kill Evan, but you killed Gabe to cover it up?"

"No, of course not—"

"Why would you do that? You've got everything!"

"I imagine he's got a lot riding on getting silver out of the ground," Bernadette said. "A big payday—probably a percentage of the profits. And if he fails? Maybe his job is on the line."

She glanced at Zorba's face—his ears were reddening. She was at least partly right.

A tendon in Bonnie's neck pulled taut. "How did you kill Gabe?"

Bernadette held up a finger. "Trudy Fortescue's second job is at the pharmacy on that vacation rental property Windfall 29 owns. Zorba paid her five thousand dollars to switch an order of acetaminophen and replace it with ibuprofen."

Zorba's brow furrowed.

"Not Trudy Fortescue," Kep said. "The sheriff. He switched out both medications—the axadabutin and the ibuprofen."

A slight curl of Zorba's upper lip. Kep was right.

Something about Zorba put Bernadette on edge. She

pressed her hand to the side of her purse. Her badge and her handcuffs were in there, and so was her Sig Sauer nine-millimeter.

"It is quite fatal when you combine ibuprofen with axadabutin." Kep pointed a finger at Zorba. "The footage we recovered from New Sunset House shows you clearly taking your father's medication."

"No, it can't be," Zorba said.

"Why not?" Bernadette said, raising her eyebrows.

"Because you paid Sheriff Koskinen to destroy the hard drives, and you paid him to switch the medications." Kep took a step closer to Zorba. "I have yet to figure out what you promised him, but I am confident that our forensic accountants will."

Bernadette sucked in a breath. Of course—she should have suspected something was up when Deputy Mueller said Constantine was doing well with his withdrawal, while Koskinen said Constantine didn't even know what day it was. She could have smacked herself.

Then Zorba blinked, and his eyes darted over Kep's shoulder.

Too late, Bernadette caught movement out of the corner of her eye—

—and Koskinen stepped into the office and brought the butt of his revolver down on the back of Kep's head.

Chapter Twenty-Six

❦

VICTOR ZORBA WAS OUT THE DOOR LIKE A GAZELLE, pushing past Koskinen—who suddenly noticed Bernadette.

Koskinen swung the revolver around, but he didn't have it by the grip. The gun slipped through his fingers. He looked down as Bernadette pulled her Sig Sauer out—just as Kep's fist caught the sheriff under the chin.

Koskinen's head snapped back, and he crumpled to the ground as Kep, looking like he'd never moved faster in his life, grabbed the gun off the floor. The sheriff's eyes were unfocused as he blinked.

"Got him?"

"I do," Kep said, rubbing the back of his head with his free hand.

"He might—"

"*I'll fight, till from my bones my flesh be hacked.*" Kep held the revolver shakily on Koskinen.

"Not the time for a stupid Macbeth quote," Bernadette said under her breath, and shot out the office door.

The front door swung closed, the sunlight squeezing its

way through the disappearing gap, and Bernadette sprinted across the floor of the pub.

Shouts from the bartender, but she couldn't hear him as she pulled her keys out of her purse, the small bag banging next to her ribs, and ran out the front door.

The engine of the Lexus started, and the car peeled out of the parking space.

Bernadette raced to the tiny creamsicle pickup truck, opening the door and sliding inside. Bernadette started the engine and was in first gear just as the Lexus sped out of the parking lot, and she spun the small pickup around and tore after the black Lexus.

She fumbled in her purse with her right hand as she held onto the steering wheel with her left and grabbed her phone. The road was a straightaway, and she glanced down at the screen, tapping on the phone app.

Miraculously, the screen came up on *Recent Calls,* and she pushed on Maura's number as the Lexus turned onto the state highway toward Lost Dish.

"Stevenson."

"The sheriff is dirty," Bernadette yelled. "Kep's got him in the back office of St. Matthew's Pub, but he'll need backup."

"Bernadette?"

"Did you get that? Kep needs help!"

"Where are you?"

"Victor Zorba killed them. He killed them both."

"What?"

"I'm chasing Zorba's Lexus north toward Lost Dish on U.S. 45—I don't know if the sheriff's deputies will help, but—"

"Victor Zorba's the killer?" Maura said.

"Are you going to get us backup?"

"I'll get Kep help," Maura said. "And I'll get you backup—even if I have to drive out there myself."

"Thanks." Bernadette tapped wildly on her phone screen and hoped she'd ended the call. She put the phone in the pickup's center console as the Lexus sped up ahead of her. "At least I don't have to worry about Darko Divjac trying to kill me," she mumbled out loud. "It's just me and Victor."

Bernadette stamped on the accelerator, but the pickup's engine whined and the speedometer inched up slowly. She looked up from the dash as the Lexus crested the hill in front of her. Zorba was putting distance between himself and Bernadette. The pickup's engine groaned as it tried to keep its speed on the incline, and when she got to the top of the hill, the highway in front of her was empty.

She swore loudly and braked hard. Grinding from the wheels—but in front of her, tire skid marks, heading into the trees on the left.

"This was the Fortescues' property," Bernadette murmured as she spun the steering wheel hard to the left, following the tire tracks in between the trees.

An unmarked gravel road appeared just past the shoulder of the state highway, the tracks freshly made in the pebbles and dirt. She squinted—were those brake lights? This was right—Victor Zorba thought he could get away by turning into Windfall 29's new property.

The pickup's underpowered engine continued to whine. The little truck wasn't all-wheel drive, and the back end of the pickup wavered from side to side. The gravel road dipped down, and the pickup bounced so hard Bernadette lifted off the seat for a moment. She gripped the steering wheel hard, slammed back down on the seat, and gritted her teeth.

"Come back here, Victor," she whispered. She dropped

the automatic transmission into a lower gear and the engine squealed. Not such a good idea.

She turned the steering wheel as the back of the small pickup threatened to fishtail, but she got it under control.

The gravel road narrowed between a red oak and a big-tooth aspen, and she worried she would hit the aspen with her side mirror.

No clunk—a good sign.

Headlights in her rear-view mirror. She glanced up for a moment—a big, black SUV. Looked like a GMC or a Chevy. The kind CSAB drove—or the FBI.

"Didn't think the calvary would make it out here this quick," Bernadette said out loud, her voice swallowed by the engine noise as she slowed to take a gentle curve on the gravel road.

And the brake lights ahead of her, maybe five hundred feet through the trees, flashed—then stayed on.

Was that a crunch?

The brake lights weren't moving—Zorba had run into something.

"End of the road, Zorba," Bernadette said, tapping the brakes. The last thing she needed was for the black SUV to rear-end her out here.

She stopped the pickup about a hundred feet from Zorba's Lexus—and indeed, a fallen tree lay across the gravel road.

Bernadette's heart was beating fast. She pulled the hand-cuffs out of her purse. She touched the pistol in her holster out of habit, then took a deep breath and opened the door. The SUV was still a few hundred yards behind her, but it would get here any moment.

The Lexus was about half a foot from the fallen tree—it

hadn't crashed. If Bernadette wasn't careful, Zorba could spin around and mow her down with his car.

She looked at the driver's side of the car; the window was down slightly. He was in there, watching, listening, waiting.

Bernadette stepped out of the pickup. "Victor Zorba," she called, her voice stronger and more confident than she felt, "you are under arrest for the murders of Evan McMichael and Gabriel Constantine."

No movement in the Lexus.

Bernadette looked around. She squinted as she stared at the other side of the fallen tree. A hiking trail. Was it the same one McMichael had mentioned in his birdwatching journal? She looked around—she wasn't great at translating topographical maps to the real world, but if this wasn't where McMichael had found the nests of Keweenaw coalhawks, it was similar.

Had Zorba come to kill the coalhawks? Did he think he could still get away with everything?

"You have the right to remain silent," Bernadette said loudly. "Anything you say can and will be used against you in a court of law." She recited the rest of the Miranda warning.

The SUV's engine got louder, and Bernadette turned to look.

U.S. Government plates—yep, it was someone from one of the agencies, coming to save the day. As much as Bernadette had been envious of Maura's promotion, she had to admit Maura was the picture of efficiency when Bernadette needed her.

Bernadette squinted at the driver. She couldn't see clearly because of the dappled sunlight reflecting off the windshield, but the driver was probably a blonde woman.

Bernadette turned back to the Lexus. "You understand your rights, Victor?"

No response.

"Victor, I need you to tell me you understand your rights. I'm not playing games."

Still nothing.

"I'm giving you to the count of three to come out with your hands up."

The driver's side door opened, and Victor's two hands immediately appeared, open, nothing in them.

"I'm unarmed!" he called.

"Nice and slow," Bernadette shouted. She stepped forward, still holding the nine-millimeter in front of her.

"I'll cooperate," Zorba said. His hands shook. He slid out of the seat and slowly raised himself up from the car to a standing position.

Bernadette stepped forward, foot by foot, stepping around an enormous tree stump—about five feet across. She held the handcuffs in front of her.

"We're going to do this by the book, Victor," she said, loud enough for him to hear. "No funny stuff. We're in the middle of the woods, and I won't stand for any bullshit. You understand me?"

"I'm sorry," Zorba said, and his throat caught. "No other choice. I convinced management to invest in finding the silver in the first place. They would have ruined me."

"Yeah?" Bernadette said. "It was about money?"

"You don't understand—those stupid coalhawks wrecked everything. We wouldn't have been able to mine *any* silver. I would have lost my job. My dad would have gotten kicked out of New Sunset House. And where would he have gone? He has nothing."

"Did you pay Gabe Constantine to shoot up his mobile home?"

"I—I thought maybe it would just scare him. Thought it

might make him move away. Evan wasn't supposed to be home—but Gabe was so high, he didn't know what he'd done."

"I'm not sure I believe you."

"It's the truth."

The sound of the SUV door opening, someone getting out, shoes crunching on the gravel. Bernadette, still holding the gun on Zorba, glanced back—

"Joanna!"

"Hey, Bernadette," Joanna Quimby said, walking slowly toward them.

"When I asked Maura to send backup, I didn't think it'd be you. And I didn't think anyone could get here so quick."

"Guess it was lucky I was on my way."

"Sure was. I thought you were in D.C."

"After I got the call from Lieutenant Stevenson, I was on a plane out here," Joanna said. The "here" wavered slightly—was she afraid? She'd never known Joanna to be afraid before. Plus, Bernadette had the situation well under control.

"I didn't think the FBI would send you out on this assignment." Bernadette cocked her head. "You okay, Joanna?"

"Sure," Joanna said. The corners of her mouth were turned down, and her pace was measured, smooth.

"I'm fine, too," Bernadette said. "Sorry for scaring you. I didn't realize everyone would think I was dead." She scoffed. "Believe me, I've already gotten an earful from Barlow and Sophie."

"Don't worry about it," Joanna said.

"I don't know. Everyone has gone out of their way for this whole situation. I didn't mean to get you involved."

Joanna walked toward the Lexus, a gun in her hand. "Well, I'm here now."

"You helping with the arrest?"

"I'm helping as much as I can."

Bernadette paused—an unnecessarily cryptic answer. "Do you have handcuffs?"

Joanna stopped in her tracks and turned toward Bernadette. "Maybe it's a better idea to take yours."

Bernadette lowered her gun, took a few steps toward Joanna, and held out her cuffs. "There's no room in the pickup to take Zorba into custody. Good thing you showed up in your SUV."

Another scratch in Bernadette's brain.

"He says he's unarmed," Bernadette said.

"So he says," Joanna said. And her voice *definitely* wavered this time.

Bernadette looked at the gun in Quimby's hand.

Odd. It wasn't a new Glock 19—the kind she'd used at the firing range. It wasn't even Joanna's old Smith & Wesson .40. It was a snub-nosed Rossi—looked like a .38 from here.

Deputy Moncrief's voice in her head: *A lot of unlicensed gun sales here—they filter down to Chicago. We confiscated over thirty Rossi .38s last year. The FBI confiscated over two hundred.*

Why was Joanna carrying a Rossi .38? The most confiscated type of revolver last year by the FBI in Chicago?

And then the sunlight filtered through the trees and glinted off Joanna's handcuffs on her belt.

Why did Joanna need to use Bernadette's handcuffs?

Then it all fell into place.

Bernadette almost threw up.

"Joanna?" Bernadette asked, her voice shaky.

When Joanna was a few feet away from Zorba, she turned around to face Bernadette.

"I'm sorry," she said.

Joanna raised the Rossi .38.

Joanna had been the one to tell Maura—and Bernadette too —that the FBI had captured Darko Divjac. Had she been telling the truth? Was she working with Divjac? Was he even a real person?

Bernadette had suspected Maura or Lesley or the CSAB travel coordinator of setting her and Kep up, since they knew Bernadette was going to Taycheedah to meet Annika.

But Joanna knew, too. She'd known Bernadette had been working on the Annika Nakrivo case. Maura had told Joanna that she'd assigned Bernadette to the McMichael case, so Joanna had known Bernadette was flying into Milwaukee. And, of course, Joanna knew Bernadette was Dr. Woodhead's case analyst. Joanna would have naturally assumed the two of them had been traveling together.

Joanna must be working for Parr Medical. That's why she hadn't broken the encryption of the Marguerite Kerovic files yet.

Or rather, why she sent a batch of *fake* files to CSAB on an SD card that looked just like Marguerite's card. Because the real files would tell Bernadette too much.

The burner phone. Maura and Bernadette had been talking on their burner phones, then Maura connected Joanna to discuss Darko Divjac's capture. So Joanna had her number after that, and must have tracked her phone—that's why she got here so fast.

And Joanna held a Rossi .38—Bernadette was sure the gun had been from an unlicensed sale. Not her usual gun, but just as deadly, and most importantly, untraceable.

Why hadn't Joanna killed Bernadette as soon as she got out of the SUV?

Oh—so she could stand next to Victor Zorba, shoot

Bernadette, then plant the unlicensed revolver on Zorba. Probably after she killed Zorba, too. The forensics would tell the story of a shootout gone wrong.

Then Joanna could call it in: both the murder suspect and the CSAB case analyst had been killed in an exchange of gunfire.

It was brilliant.

And Bernadette had a split second to move.

❧

She dove behind the tree stump as the bullet from the Rossi kicked off the gravel behind her.

"Don't make this harder than it has to be, Bernadette," Joanna called. "You're my friend. I don't want you to suffer."

Bernadette wanted to shout out, swear at Joanna, anything to let out the anger roiling inside her. Joanna was the reason she was almost killed when the rental car exploded. Joanna was the reason Sophie almost had to grow up without a mother. Joanna was the reason Barlow was so pissed off at her.

But the stump wasn't effective cover. How could she get a shot off without making herself a target?

Bang.

Another shot skittered in the gravel next to the tree stump.

"You're not making it out alive, Becker!" Joanna yelled. One more shot—

—And the bullet whizzed by her right foot. She pulled her leg back.

"You might kill me, but I'm not giving you an easy cover story," Bernadette yelled back, rearranging herself behind the stump. Something stuck in her lower back. She reached behind her shoulder blade—it was a chunk of dead wood. She tossed it in the air as hard as she could.

BANG.

The piece of wood exploded above her, and she buried her face in her arms as the splinters fell around her.

She counted the shots. One, two, three, four.

The Rossi was a revolver; it couldn't hold nearly as many bullets as the magazine in Bernadette's Sig Sauer.

Did Joanna have another gun?

Maybe, but once she was out of ammunition in the Rossi, she'd have to switch to her service Glock. It would complicate things if forensics found an FBI agent's gun had killed Bernadette and not a random stolen Rossi .38.

Bernadette had an idea.

"We trusted each other, Joanna!" Bernadette shouted.

"I'm sorry, I truly am," Joanna said.

"You've got two bullets left, Joanna," she called. "Better make 'em count."

"I didn't mean for any of this to happen," Joanna called. "Why couldn't you just let Annika rot in prison?"

"And not go looking for her sister?"

"You keep wanting to *help* people," Joanna said. "Even criminals and murderers—"

Bernadette reached behind herself, sticking the barrel of her nine-millimeter slightly over the top of the stump, and fired into the air—then pulled her arm right back and ducked.

Another shot from Joanna. This one hit the top of the stump.

"There's no way out, Bernadette," Joanna called. "I don't have a choice. You don't know what they'll do to me if I fail."

"I guess," Bernadette said, standing up and facing Joanna, "I'll have to see for myself."

Joanna pulled the Rossi's trigger.

Click.

Her eyes went wide—and she reached behind her back.

Her FBI-issued pistol.

Bernadette fired the nine-millimeter.

Bullseye.

Joanna Quimby's body collapsed.

Her pulse racing, Bernadette sprinted around the stump and ran to Joanna's body, lying on the ground next to the Lexus. Bernadette knelt next to her.

A chest wound—Bernadette had gotten Joanna almost dead center.

Joanna looked up at Bernadette. Her lips formed a word, but no sound came out.

Five.

"Right," Bernadette said. "The Rossi .38 only holds five bullets, not six. You're smart enough to know that, Joanna."

A tear welled up in Joanna's right eye, then she shuddered with one last exhale and lay still.

Bernadette put her fingers on Joanna's throat.

No pulse.

She looked forlornly into Joanna's sightless eyes, then raised her head toward the open driver's side door of the Lexus. Victor Zorba was sitting on the forest floor, head between his elbows, shivering.

"You're still under arrest, Victor." Bernadette pulled the handcuffs out of Joanna's belt, stood, and walked over to Zorba.

"She would have killed me," he said, staring at Joanna's dead body.

"Probably, yes."

"I'm so sorry," Zorba babbled. "For everything."

"Tell it to the judge," she said, pulling Zorba to his feet. A large wet patch had formed on the front of his trousers. "Hands behind your back."

She handcuffed Zorba, thought for a moment, then marched Zorba toward the SUV. Joanna's vehicle was a better option for prisoner transport than the U-Move-It pickup.

Bernadette stopped next to Joanna's body and looked down; her chest caught, and she took a deep breath. "Damn it, Joanna, we were supposed to get margaritas next week."

Chapter Twenty-Seven

A knock on Bernadette's bedroom door.

Sitting on the bed in her T-shirt and sweatpants, she held her finger over the phone screen, debating whether to call Lamar Chesapeake. And if she did, what to say. She clicked the side button, and the phone went to sleep. "It's open."

The door opened and Kep stuck his head in. "You're awake."

"I had a hard time sleeping. Figured I'd get a workout in."

"We don't have to leave for the airport for a couple of hours."

Bernadette picked up her phone and looked at the clock on the screen. "Nope."

"I don't mean to intrude, but do you have anything to do before we leave?"

"Just shower and change. I'm almost all packed. And I already called Sophie this morning."

Kep hesitated. "Can I inquire if everything with your daughter has smoothed over?"

"You can inquire, but no, it hasn't."

Kep was quiet. Maybe he was deciding whether to ask about Lamar, too.

"Did you want something?" Bernadette asked.

"Yes. I thought we could go to the coordinates listed in Barcelona Lute's journal." Kep paused. "I have never seen an animal previously thought to be extinct."

Bernadette grabbed the creamsicle pickup's key fob off her nightstand. Anything for a distraction. "Let's go."

They walked in silence to the pickup, the morning already growing hot and humid. After fifteen minutes of a wordless drive, Kep grunted and pointed to the left. It wasn't the same gravel road where Bernadette had pursued Victor Zorba.

She slowed the tiny pickup to five miles per hour and rolled down her window, taking in the scents of the trees and the surrounding forest. Kep stared intently at his phone, murmuring "left" or "right" every few minutes, until finally he said, "We're here."

Bernadette brought the pickup to a stop and killed the engine. They got out and shut the pickup doors as softly as they could. A breeze: not too strong, but enough to push Bernadette's hair into her face. She dug in her purse and grabbed a hair tie, putting her hair into a low ponytail. Kep started up a trail leading through the woods to the left, and Bernadette followed.

They walked in silence, Bernadette alone with her thoughts. Should she call Sophie before her flight? There were more apologies in her future, and undoing the damage she had caused would take a lot of time and effort.

The woods thinned for a moment, and Kep turned at a fork in the trail that led uphill. His breathing got heavier as they crested a ridge, then the trail narrowed as it went down through the trees.

A tree came into sight on the right, about twenty yards

ahead. Bernadette's eyes widened, and she pointed. "That's the tree from the journal," she whispered.

Kep nodded.

The branch system of the largetooth aspen was exactly like both Evan McMichael and Barcelona Lute had drawn it. Bernadette squinted—could she see the next two-thirds of the way up?

"I'm afraid the juveniles will have left the nest by now," Kep said.

"And Keweenaw coalhawks are nocturnal."

"However," Kep said softly, "they often roost close to the trunk in dense evergreens." He pointed to a pine next to the aspen.

"I wish I had binoculars."

"I fear we are too far away and the foliage too dense to get a sighting."

Then, as the breeze gently moved the branches, Bernadette saw the bird: dark feathers, lightening to a reddish-brown on its chest, blue tips on its wings and crests. Then the breeze stilled, the branch hiding the Keweenaw coalhawk again.

"Did you get that?" she whispered.

Kep gave a slight nod.

They stood for a moment, willing the branches to move again, to catch another glimpse of the coalhawk long thought lost. The minutes ticked by.

"It's still there," Bernadette whispered. "We just can't see it."

Kep nodded, took a step back, then walked on the trail back the way they came.

❧

Bernadette and Maura had a layover at Chicago O'Hare. With two hours before their flight to Washington National, they stopped at a Tex-Mex restaurant when they got off the interterminal train and sat at an empty table. Bernadette caught the eye of a server, who nodded.

Maura took out her phone, tapped and swiped, then read the screen, scrolling every so often. Bernadette scanned the menu, then looked up at Maura. Her boss was looking at her expectantly.

"What?"

"I just got an update from Lesley. The forensic accountants and the CSI teams have removed everything of interest from Joanna Quimby's house and office."

Bernadette looked back down at the menu. Her stomach clenched, but she knew she had to eat.

"I thought that might give you some measure of relief."

Bernadette nodded but didn't look up as the writing on the menu went out of focus. "Speaking of relief, I can't tell you how grateful I am that you kept the shootout between me and Joanna out of the news."

Maura set her menu down as the server approached.

"Can I get you ladies anything to drink?"

"Two margaritas," Maura said. "Rocks, salt rim."

Bernadette's face fell. *Oh, you beautiful soul. I'll buy you two margaritas next time we go out.*

"Top shelf for two dollars more?"

"Sure." Maura caught Bernadette's face. "My treat."

Bernadette swallowed and nodded.

The server smiled. "Do you know what you want?"

Bernadette didn't, but the first item under *Sandwiches & Wraps* came into focus. "I'll get the chicken club."

"Fiesta salad," Maura said.

The server nodded and walked off.

"I wish I could take credit for keeping it out of the news," Maura said. "The FBI wants to keep this under wraps."

"Joanna was working for Parr Medical." Bernadette picked up a fork, examined it, then placed it back on the table.

"If there's evidence, I'm sure the forensic accountants will find it."

What did Parr Medical have on Joanna that would cause her to betray Bernadette—not to mention her FBI career? She'd thought they were close—not as close as Bernadette and Maura had been before Maura's promotion, but close. What would the forensic investigators find? "And what about the files on the SD card from Marguerite Kerovic?"

"Lesley now has the *real* folder," Maura said. "And she thinks she'll have it decrypted by the time we land at National." She cocked her head. "Have you spoken to Sophie today?"

Bernadette started to speak, then a tightening in her chest—she didn't want to cry at an airport restaurant.

Maura reached across the table and put a hand on top of Bernadette's. "I'm sorry."

Bernadette lifted her head and stared straight ahead, her eyes locking on a picture of a jukebox hanging on the opposite wall. She took measured breaths and willed the tears not to fall.

What was she even doing with her career? Her last three assignments had been more dangerous than when she was an agent. Except for Wichita.

Declan's sightless eyes, staring up at nothing.

Bernadette swallowed hard. "Do you think Parr Medical's done targeting me? After what happened with Darko Devjac and Joanna?"

Maura hesitated and let go of Bernadette's hand.

"What?"

"I had another update, this one from Joanna's case

manager. The man following you wasn't Darko Devjac. The FBI didn't pick up anyone outside Fargo."

Bernadette blinked. "But I saw his photo."

"The photo Joanna sent you? Not Darko Divjac."

"But it *was* the person who was following me."

"We're searching the databases right now. Someone might recognize him. But it's not Divjac—he's been in jail in Florida for money laundering for over a year." Maura sat back in her chair. "We think when Lesley gave the FBI the name of Darko Divjac, Joanna made up the rest. And since you recognized the man in the photo, we believe Joanna was working with him."

"So—I'm still in danger."

"I'm certain you're not," Maura said. "Parr Medical targeted you and Dr. Woodhead to keep information from getting out—at least, that's the theory that makes the most sense. Since the FBI and CSAB are going through Joanna's life with a fine-toothed comb, killing you will no longer solve any of Parr Medical's problems. The authorities know about the hit they put on you and Dr. Woodhead. Proving it's another story." She smiled gently. "But the FBI is confident you have nothing to worry about."

The server appeared and set down two large margarita glasses. Maura grabbed hers and lifted it. "I have a toast."

Bernadette picked up her glass. "What are we drinking to?"

"To you," Maura said.

Bernadette blinked. "To me?"

"The local police were ready to call it a suicide, or—the other option—arrest the wrong person for murder. You uncovered the murder. You found the killer of Gabriel Constantine, too. And you uncovered a bribery plot. It's not just Victor Zorba—the CEO of Windfall 29 is going to jail, too, and so is Sheriff Koskinen."

Bernadette stared at her full margarita.

"You can't catch every bad cop."

Bernadette closed her eyes and breathed in deeply. "Yeah, I know."

Maura clinked Bernadette's glass. "But you caught this one."

Bernadette nodded—barely perceptible, but she nodded. She took a sip.

Oh. It was cold and delicious. She took a second sip—larger this time. Then she raised her glass again.

"And to Kep."

Maura's eyebrows raised.

"He recognized the sulfuric acid. He recognized the type of whiskey. He was the one who found the evidence that McMichael's death wasn't a suicide."

"To Dr. Woodhead."

They drank.

Maura set the margarita down. "And, you'll be happy to know, I approved your vacation time. You need the break."

Bernadette cocked her head.

"Two weeks from now, right? You're going back to Milwaukee?"

Oh, of course. Summerfest. Bernadette's face fell.

Maura frowned. "Uh oh. Don't tell me you and Lamar are having problems."

Bernadette pressed her lips together.

Maura winced. "It seems I can't say anything right today."

"He's great," Bernadette said. "He's kind. He makes me laugh. He's interesting."

"And handsome," Maura added.

"And handsome. But—I didn't call him. Not when I

thought I was safe, not when I solved the case." She tapped her fingers on the side of the margarita glass. "I didn't even call him when I arrived in Lost Dish for the first time."

"You mean when you'd just discovered you were being followed? Give yourself a break, Bernadette."

"I guess." Bernadette sighed. "Maybe I'm not ready for a relationship yet. He suggested I bring out Sophie for Summerfest. And I kind of freaked out."

"Hasn't it only been a few months?"

Bernadette hesitated. "Yes."

"What did he say when you talked to him?"

"Talked to him when?"

Maura's eyes widened. "You mean you *still* haven't talked to him?"

Bernadette shrugged.

"Wait—are you saying it's over?"

"I don't know what I'm saying." But as soon as the words were out of her mouth, Bernadette knew. It *was* over.

Maura was quiet for a moment. "Is the invitation still open for me to come to Sophie's softball game on Saturday?"

Bernadette nodded. "Of course."

The server rushed out of the kitchen, plates in hand, and set them in front of Bernadette and Maura.

"Looks delicious," Bernadette said, though the last thing she wanted to do was eat.

Maura, who only had a carry-on, said her goodbyes to Bernadette in front of the still and silent baggage carousel at Washington National. The LED sign above the carousel read *Coastal Airlines 8282 from Chicago O'Hare,* and about seventy people had gathered around, getting increasingly impatient.

How many times had she stood at this exact baggage carousel waiting for her silver hard case with her nine-millimeter in it?

For a moment, she didn't care that she'd be walking away from a pension—or leaving CSAB might still keep her in the crosshairs of Parr Medical. She'd be home every night, she'd be there for Sophie, she'd start building a life without Barlow.

Her phone rang.

She pulled it out of her purse, looked at the screen, then tapped *Answer*.

"Hey, Lesley."

"Ah—I wasn't sure you'd landed yet."

"Touched down about twenty minutes ago. Waiting for my luggage. I take it you broke the encryption on the file?"

"Funny how when the file is, you know, a *real* file, things get a little easier."

"What did you find?"

Lesley paused.

"What is it?"

"It's a list of names. Some of them with other identifying information, some with notes—what kind of food they like, or regular schedules they keep."

"Have you looked into the names?"

"Yes." Lesley cleared her throat. "All of them are dead."

"All of them?"

"Yes. Some of them were accidents, some were suicides, some are solved homicides, some are unsolved homicides. All kinds of different ways, too. Electrocution, car accidents, hiking accidents. One guy got buried alive in an avalanche when he went off the ski run trails."

"What are you thinking?"

"Probably the same thing you are. That Annika Nakrivo—

sorry, Anja Kerovic—wasn't the only assassin in the Kerovic family."

"Marguerite too?"

"Yep. I think this is Marguerite's hit list. Some of these happened when Anja was clearly in another part of the country. Or even the world."

A moment of silence. "Lesley—is there more?"

"I'm looking at the dates of these deaths. The first few? They would have been when Marguerite was only fourteen years old."

Bernadette rubbed her forehead. "I've seen some footage from the wars in the Balkans. Child soldiers. It's—well, shocking, but not terribly surprising."

Lesley gave a nervous laugh. "I worry I'm going to wake up one day and be as jaded as you."

"Talk to me after you have to shoot someone you've trusted for five years."

Lesley clicked her tongue, but said nothing.

"I'm sorry," Bernadette said. "It's still a little raw. No—it's *very* raw. I won't be much fun to be around the next few days. Or weeks." She'd take that vacation time anyway, even if she wasn't going to Summerfest. She pulled a pack of gum out of her purse; the baggage was taking forever to arrive. "How many names are on this list, anyway?"

"Seventeen."

"Seventeen," Bernadette repeated. "A lot of murders for one person."

"It's over a six-year period. So about three a year."

"Still a lot."

"There's one other thing," Lesley said.

"Which is?"

"One of these names," Lesley said, "was an investigative journalist."

Bernadette's heart sank. "Oh no."

"Jack Woodhead. You know who he was?"

A loud buzz from the baggage claim speaker, then the conveyor belt clicked to life.

"I do," Bernadette said. "Five years ago, Kep's son was murdered. Kep was a suspect, but after they ruled him out, they had no other leads."

Lesley was quiet for a moment. "Well, Jack Woodhead is on the list. Unsolved murder."

Bernadette was quiet. Five minutes ago, she was contemplating her exit strategy from CSAB.

But Kep deserved to know.

And his son deserved justice.

Cast of Characters

- **Dr. Kep Woodhead**: A forensic toxicologist in his early fifties, Dr. Woodhead is both an expert in poisons and a "supersmeller"—he can detect and specify scents far beyond the olfactory range of most humans. His brusque manner rubs many people the wrong way, including...
- **Bernadette Becker**: A recently demoted case analyst who has been assigned to manage Dr. Woodhead on relevant cases. Becker is Woodhead's fifth "handler" in the last two years. Freshly separated from her husband of nearly fifteen years, Becker is trying to get back on her feet both personally and professionally.
- **Lieutenant Maura Stevenson**: Becker's immediate supervisor runs the CSAB Homicide Unit and joins Woodhead and Becker on

important cases, greasing the wheels with local law enforcement agencies, cutting through red tape, and getting the needed resources.

- **Lesley Gill:** The technical analyst working for the CSAB Homicide Unit.

FRIENDS & FAMILY

- **Officer Lamar Chesapeake:** A Milwaukee police officer, he and Bernadette have been in a long-distance relationship for a few months.
- **Joanna Quimby:** A friend of Bernadette's who works at the Federal Bureau of Investigation.
- **Barlow Finnegan**: Bernadette's estranged husband—soon to be ex, when the details of the divorce get ironed out.
- **Sophie Finnegan**: Bernadette's twelve-year-old daughter.

THE CASE

- **Evan McMichael**: Found dead in his trailer home, the retiree had only lived in Banner Crossing for three years.
- **Laura Donaghy:** Evan's sister, who is taking care of his affairs after his death.
- **Gabriel Constantine:** A methamphetamine addict and low-level dealer, Evan's neighbor has been in and out of jail for a variety of petty crimes.
- **Deputy Carla Moncrief:** The officer who found Evan's body.

- **Darcy Moncrief:** The front desk clerk at the hotel where Kep and Bernadette check in, and Carla Moncrief's college-age daughter.
- **Deputy Jens Mueller:** A sheriff's deputy assigned to the county jail.
- **Sheriff Aatos Koskinen:** The sheriff of Porcupine County and Carla Moncrief's boss.
- **Dr. Imogen Goadbury:** The Porcupine County medical examiner.
- **Victor Zorba**: The vice president of construction for the local copper mining company.
- **Bonnie Farmington:** A bartender in Banner Crossing's only watering hole.
- **Barcelona Lute:** A graduate student in ornithology at UUP, she and Evan would often communicate about birds.
- **Trudy Fortescue:** A pharmacist who fills the prescriptions of local organizations and government entities.
- **Jasper Fortescue:** Trudy's husband and the president of the Old Victoria Ornithological Society.
- **Ed Eskola:** The owner of the local U-Move-It and a rumored methamphetamine dealer.
- **Emma & Travis Mortensen:** Neighbors of Evan who have their own legal challenges.
- **Alvin Davies:** Another neighbor of Evan's, he is recently divorced and trying to get out of Banner Crossing.
- **Warden Marcie Fisk**: The warden at Taycheedah Women's Correctional Facility where Annika Nakrivo is serving out her sentence.

- **Annika Nakrivo, aka Anja Kerovic**: Caught between a rock and a hard place, Nakrivo has said her sister is in trouble—and Bernadette may be her only hope.

More by Paul Austin Ardoin

The Woodhead & Becker Mysteries

Book One: The Winterstone Murder

Book Two: The Bridegroom Murder

Book Three: The Trailer Park Murder

The Fenway Stevenson Mysteries

Book One: The Reluctant Coroner

Book Two: The Incumbent Coroner

Book Three: The Candidate Coroner

Book Four: The Upstaged Coroner

Book Five: The Courtroom Coroner

Novella: The Christmas Coroner

Book Six: The Watchful Coroner

Book Seven: The Accused Coroner

Novella: The Clandestine Coroner

Book Eight: The Offside Coroner

Book Nine: The Warehouse Coroner

Collections

Books 1–3 of The Fenway Stevenson Mysteries

Books 4-6 of The Fenway Stevenson Mysteries

Dez Roubideaux

Bad Weather

Non-fiction

From Zero to Four Figures:

Making $1,000 a Month Self-Publishing Fiction

Sign up for *The Coroner's Report,*

Paul Austin Ardoin's fortnightly newsletter:

http://www.paulaustinardoin.com

I hope you enjoyed reading this book as much as I enjoyed writing it. If you did, I'd sincerely appreciate a review on your favorite book retailer's website, Goodreads, and BookBub. Reviews are crucial for any author, and even just a line or two can make a huge difference.

Acknowledgments

Pamela Evans brought this story to me through a mutual writer friend a little over a year ago. The story is based on her brother's mysterious—and as-yet unsolved—death, and Pamela wanted someone to fictionalize the story and bring his life to light. Thank you, Pamela, for your generosity with your brother's story, and for your patience as my cross-country move delayed my writing. I can only hope I've served your brother's memory well. And I apologize that Samantha, your brother's beloved Bichon Frise, didn't make it into the final version of the novel. I had big plans for her, too!

Many thanks to my editor Max Christian Hansen, proofreader Melissa Crandall, and cover designer Ziad Ezzat of Feral Creative. Special thanks to the Wordforge Novelists group in Sacramento, whose comments and guidance are, as always, invaluable. I also appreciate the Just Write Milwaukee and Shut Up and Write Milwaukee groups, who have welcomed me and given me encouragement, support, and community in my adopted city.

Thanks to my early readers, including Dana Luco, Michelle Damiani, Beverly Ange, Josh Atkinson, Dr. Christina Bellinger, Monique Koll, Devin McCrate, Nicole Prewitt, Gavin Ralph, and Laura Regan. Your eagle eyes, your hawklike senses, and your areas of expertise helped immeasurably and made this book much better.

I'd also like to thank Jamie Sanfelippo, who keeps my newsletter, social media, and other marketing activities sailing smoothly.

To my wife, my children, and my mother: I'm deeply grateful for your continued encouragement and support.

www.ingramcontent.com/pod-product-compliance
Lightning Source LLC
Chambersburg PA
CBHW060730190726
48285CB00001B/147